PRAISE FOR MAL PEET

Winner of the Carnegie Medal

Winner of the *Guardian*
Children's Fiction Prize

Winner of the Branford Boase Award

"Peet's ability to tackle outsize themes with minutely tooled devices may be his most impressive gift."
—*The New York Times Book Review*

"Mal Peet writes with an exquisite but unobtrusive touch." —*The Wall Street Journal*

for *Exposure*

"Much as I love almost every kind and form of book for children, there are certain genres that leave me cold. One of these is books about football. I have a theory . . . that people who love reading hate team sports. . . . At least, that's what I thought until I read Mal Peet. . . . You don't have to care about football (though Peet's descriptions of what it feels like almost converted me) because he makes you care so much about his characters."
—*The Times* (London)

for *The Penalty*

"If you want to know just how much bolder and more accomplished current 'children's' fiction is than 'adult' fiction, I suggest you read . . . this glorious, cartwheeling, magical, frightening story."
—*The Guardian* (U.K.)

Exposure

Exposure

MAL PEET

CANDLEWICK PRESS

Copyright © 2009 by Mal Peet

First U.S. paperback edition 2011

The Library of Congress has cataloged the hardcover edition as follows:

Peet, Mal.
Exposure / by Mal Peet. — 1st ed.
p.   cm.
Summary: Paul Faustino, South America's best soccer journalist, reports on the series of events that hurl Otello from the heights of being a beloved and successful soccer star, happily married to the pop singer Desmerelda, into a downward spiral, in this novel loosely based on Shakespeare's play, Othello.
ISBN 978-0-7636-3941-9 (hardcover)
[1. Soccer—Fiction. 2. Fame—Fiction. 3. Scandals—Fiction.
4. Journalists—Fiction. 5. South America—Fiction.]   I. Title.
PZ7.P3564Exp 2009
[Fic]—dc22   2009007762

ISBN 978-0-7636-5291-3 (paperback)

10 11 12 13 14 15 LBM 10 9 8 7 6 5 4 3 2 1

Printed in Melrose Park, IL, U.S.A.

This book was typeset in Horley Old Style.

Candlewick Press
99 Dover Street
Somerville, Massachusetts 02144

visit us at www.candlewick.com

For Lol, Carlo, and Tomski,
with love

CAST OF MAIN CHARACTERS

OTELLO *a soccer player, the national captain*

DESMERELDA *a celebrity*

DIEGO MENDOSA *a villain, Otello's agent*

NESTOR BRABANTA *a senator, and Desmerelda's father*

EMILIA *Diego's companion*

MICHAEL CASS *Otello's bodyguard*

ARIEL GOLDMANN *directors of Rialto, a soccer team*
THE DUKE

HERNÁN GALLEGO *a politician*

JACO RODERIGO *soccer players*
LUIS MONTANO

RAMÓN TRESOR *manager of Rialto*

PAUL FAUSTINO *journalists*
NOLA LEVY

BUSH *orphaned street children*
BIANCA
FELICIA

FIDEL AND NINA RAMIREZ *owners of La Prensa, a bar*

CAPTAIN HILARIO NEMISO *a police officer*

Act One

1.1

THE BOY WITH all the dreadlocks had two lines of business: cars and the patio trade. He had been working his turf — the sidewalk along the front of *La Nación*'s building — for a few months now. Longer than most of his predecessors. The car thing was the usual, but he did it with politeness, even delicacy, and these were not qualities his victims would expect from one of his kind. So he surprised them, and it paid off. He had a plastic bucket without a handle, a squeegee, and, tucked into the waist-band of his cutoffs, three large rags: a dirty one, a less dirty one, and a clean one.

The routine goes something like this:

A car pulls into a space. The boy does not go to it immediately, because he knows that if drivers see him before getting out, they will have crucial seconds to harden their hearts. He waits until the driver has locked the doors, then appears magically. And smiles.

"Good day, señor. You like me to wash your windshield?"

Sometimes — quite often, actually — the driver will hesitate, maybe shrug, dig a small coin out of his pocket. The victims who do this are the ones who look at him.

"Thank you, señor. I'll watch your car for you, too. All part of the service."

More often, the response to the boy's offer is either nonexistent or obscenely dismissive. But his smile does not waver.

"Okay, señor. No problem. But maybe you like me to keep an eye on the car for you?"

The driver looks at him, hard. Jabs a thumb up toward the heavily built uniformed man patrolling the patio. "That guy up there's watching my car. And he's watching you, too."

The smile achieves an even greater brilliance. "You mean the doorman? My friend Rubén? Yeah, Rubén's cool. He's sound. Just not so quick on his feet as he used to be, you know?"

The boy's technique gets him about four results out of ten, and he calculates that this works out at an average of twenty-two centavos a hit. He is surprisingly good at arithmetic, considering the fact that the only way he could ever have been in school was through a window after dark.

Some days he gets his ass kicked, and this was one of those days. The car was a black Porsche 911. (The boy knew the makes and models of cars, even though he couldn't read them.) The driver was a white guy with his hair shaved close to his skull so it looked like the shadow of a bat or something. The boy had known right away that it was a no-hope hit, but went for it anyway because it was his solid rule that you do not choose; you go for everything. The man had ignored him, getting a briefcase out of the car. Checking his cell, then putting it away in the inside pocket of his suit jacket.

"Okay, señor. No problem. But maybe you like me to keep an eye on the car for you?"

The man with shadow hair sighed, drumming his fingers on the Porsche's gleaming roof. Then he turned with surprising swiftness and kicked the boy. Who had somehow been expecting it and had flinched. The kick caught him high on the right buttock just below the hip. He found himself sitting on the sidewalk, his leg numb and useless. The man loomed over him, his eyes hot with anger that seemed inappropriate to the situation.

"Listen," he said. "I'm sick and tired of wherever I go there's some street rat hustling me, and I don't need it, okay? Now, lemme make this plain to you, kid. I come back to this car and anything — *anything* — has happened to it, I'll find you and pulp your stupid hairy head. Is there any part of that you don't understand?"

"No, señor."

"Good. Now get the hell away from my Porsche."

The boy scooted himself backward across the sidewalk, soaking the seat of his shorts in the water that had slopped from his bucket. When he was sure the man had gone, he lifted his face and gazed up at the concrete and glass perspective of the office building narrowing into the late afternoon sky. He felt dizzy, maybe because he was hungry.

Seven floors above the street, Paul Faustino was checking the text of an article that would appear on the front page of the next day's edition of *La Nación*.

EXCLUSIVE: OTELLO WILL SIGN FOR RIALTO

by Paul Faustino

The gossip mills and rumor factories can shut down. I can now reveal that Otello, the man who led this country to victory in this year's Copa América, will be a Rialto player within the week. The terms of the transfer were agreed between Rialto and Espirito Santo yesterday after Spain's Real Madrid withdrew from the contest for the striker. The deal is unlikely to be on a cash-only basis — Espirito has stolidly refused to lower its evaluation of Otello from fifty million — but details will not be disclosed prior to a formal announcement at a press conference scheduled for Thursday. My information is, however, that Rialto's popular young forward, Luis Montano, will move to Espirito to offset the fee, thus adding to the controversy that will inevitably attend this affair. We can expect a bitter reaction, not only from Espirito fans but also from many in the North who will see Otello's move south to the capital as an act of betrayal.

Faustino leaned back in his chair and massaged his lower lip with his thumb and forefinger. This was a big, big story. It would warm the cockles of his editor's heart — if she possessed such an organ. It would earn him a nice juicy bonus, too. He could not quite believe his luck, actually, so there was an uneasy edge to his glee.

Talk of Otello leaving Espirito had begun well before the Copa América. And in recent days the hum of rumor and speculation had swollen into the voice of a vast beehive. The tabloids and sports channels had been obsessed with it. Lacking any real information, they'd put out opinionated babble. Chaff. Faustino had been a journalist long enough to know that very often there is, in fact, smoke without fire. But he too had been pretty sure that Otello would make a move. He had to; Espirito was not a good enough club for him. They'd had another lousy season, ending up fourth from the bottom of the league, despite Otello's twenty-three goals. Which meant that once again they wouldn't be playing in the Copa Libertadores. Which in turn meant that Otello, the national captain, would go yet another season without playing an international club game. Ridiculous, obviously.

Faustino was not a gambling man, but he'd have put money on Otello joining one of the big European clubs: Manchester United, say, or Barcelona. But a move south, to Rialto? No way. Of all clubs, not Rialto.

And then, this morning, the call from Otello's agent, Diego Mendosa, a man Faustino hardly knew.

Still scrawling notes, Faustino had said, "Why me, Señor Mendosa?"

"Pardon?"

"I was wondering why you chose to break the news to me, exclusively."

"Because you are widely respected, Paul. All these rumors have caused my client a great deal of stress, as you can imagine. Only someone with your reputation can lay them to rest."

"Yeah?"

"Yes. Also, perhaps I would like to give the finger to certain other newspapers that have pissed me off."

Faustino had laughed at that. "Yeah. Well, that's honest."

Afterward he'd wondered about that. In Faustino's vocabulary, *honest* and *agent* were not words that normally went around holding hands.

He went back to his article.

> Born in the North, and famously proud of his African heritage, Otello has done much to silence (in stadiums, at least) the racist jeers directed at black northerners. His charity work, which includes food banks and soccer academies in the slums, has given him a status, a respect, way beyond the usual scope of soccer stars. All of this, along with his much-proclaimed loyalty to the North — he has played for only two clubs in his career, both of them north of the Río de Oro — means that his transfer will have a seismic effect.

Faustino wondered if the word *seismic* was a bit over the top and decided that it wasn't. He'd been at countless Rialto games and seen their supporters jeeringly wave fifty-dollar bills at the visiting fans, especially when the game was against a team from the North. Heard the call-and-response jokes.

"What do you call a Northerner with a roof over his head?"

"A burglar!"

Then there was the fact that the owners and directors of Rialto were hate figures in the North. Members of the New Conservative government, like Vice President Lazar and that evil little sod Hernán Gallego. Multimillionaires like what's-his-name, the supermarket guy, Goldmann. And Nestor Brabanta, of course. And this was the club that the North's great hero had decided to join. My God, he was in for a rough time.

Seismic, then. Nice word, anyway.

Faustino skimmed the rest of his piece. He'd soft-pedaled on the political/social/racial issues. Mendosa had asked him to, and you don't bite the hand that feeds you. First rule of journalism.

> I for one am glad that he has faced reality and joined a club that will put him center stage, where he belongs. Let us welcome him to our city and pray that the inevitable storms in the North soon abate.

"You can be a sanctimonious jerk sometimes," Faustino told himself, and deleted the last sentence. He was dying for a smoke.

La Nación

To: Vittorio Maragall, Editorial
From: Paul Faustino

Hola, Vito —

Attached is copy for tomorrow's Otello piece. It's up to you, but I suggest we go with a crop of the photo we used on the front page July 25, Otello holding up the cup with all that red and yellow glitter stuff in the background.

I'll be at La Poma until about 9. If you get away in time, maybe I'll grant you the honor of buying me a drink.

P

1.2

FAUSTINO WAVED A salute to Marta at the reception desk and clacked across the marble-paved lobby. Approaching the doors, he slowed to a more cautious pace. *Doors* was not, in fact, an appropriate word for the vast, complex, and untrustworthy arrangement of clear glass that baffled him at least four times a day. Beyond it, in plain sight, was the outside world, yet he knew from painful experience that reaching it was not a straightforward matter. There were central revolving doors, twice the height of any normal person (presumably because one never knew when a giant or a man on stilts might be expected), but Faustino absolutely refused to use them. For one thing, the evil genius who'd designed them had incorporated a variable speed mechanism, which meant that you never knew whether to adopt a mincing shuffle or run like hell. Usually you had to do both, but because of the cunning randomizing device, you never knew when to switch from one to the other, so even at ten in the morning you looked like a stumbling drunk on a treadmill. For another thing, Faustino was borderline claustrophobic and feared the doors coming to a complete halt and trapping him inside.

Off to the right and left there were conventional doors with enormous brass handles. However, you never knew whether or not these would respond to their inbuilt sensors and open automatically. If they didn't, you could pull on them and sometimes they would open. At other times, you had to push. Just to make sure that nobody got complacent, only one functioned at any particular moment. There was no way of knowing which. You could enter through the right-hand door in the morning and find that the left-hand one was the only way out in the afternoon. A few months earlier, Faustino had entered the building, checked his mail, and tried to leave by the same door fifteen minutes later. He had suffered what the paramedic had described as a "mild concussion." Not to mention a hemorrhage of dignity.

So Faustino had developed an exit strategy. He would come to a halt a few paces from the glass wall and search his pockets for his car keys and cigarettes. Eventually he'd be spotted by Rubén, who would come to his rescue. On this particular evening, the doorman hauled the right-hand door open from the outside while Faustino stood fumbling in his jacket facing the left-hand one.

Gratefully liberated, Faustino walked out onto the wide, raised patio that fronted the building. From it, flights of steps led down to the sidewalk. On it, there was a short avenue of ornamental trees imprisoned in brutish concrete troughs, and in the shade of these trees were two rows of stainless-steel benches. It was part of Rubén's job to shoo off any weary passerby who might have the impertinence to seek rest there. Clearly no one who *walked* along the Avenida San Cristóbal could have any legitimate reason to visit the offices of the country's leading newspaper.

Rather than go directly to his car, Faustino sat and lit a cigarette. This was because two very attractive secretaries from the accounting department were sitting on the bench opposite. Also, he had recently — and very reluctantly — traded in his beloved Jaguar for a top-of-the-line Toyota Celica and was making an effort not to impregnate the new upholstery with tobacco smoke. He was distracted by a call from the street.

"'Ola, Maestro! Wha's happenin'?"

A wild head and wide smile showed above the level of the patio.

Faustino returned the smile. It was impossible not to. It was a smile that would melt an icicle from a hundred yards. He figured it must have taken a good deal of practice to perfect it, since sunny dispositions weren't exactly natural among street kids.

Faustino had never been one of the boy's car victims because, as the paper's senior sportswriter, he had a reserved (and bitterly envied) space in *La Nación*'s underground garage, which sprouted CCTV cameras the way forest trees grow bromeliads. No, they'd met because of the errands side of the kid's business. A couple of months back, Faustino had been coming down the steps from the patio, fishing a cigarette pack out of his pocket. The pack had been empty, and Faustino had crushed it in his hand and loudly uttered a curse. As if in response, the kid had appeared right in front of him, like a genie, just as the streetlights came on.

"What kind d'you smoke, Maestro?"

"What?"

"What kind of cigarettes d'you smoke?"

Faustino had squinted at him. The boy wasn't carrying a bag.

"Why? Are you selling?"

The smile. "No, no, Maestro. But your car's down there, and the kiosk's up there." Pointing up toward the traffic lights on the *avenida*. "I'll fetch 'em for you."

After a moment or two Faustino had said, "What's all this 'Maestro' stuff?"

The smile had faltered, then died. "Sorry, señor. I thought that was your name. That's what the others call you."

"What others?"

A shrug. "I dunno."

There had been a sort of standoff.

Then Faustino had said, "Yeah, well. D'you know what *ironic* means?"

"No, señor."

"Okay. Never mind. If I give you five dollars to get me two packs of Presidente filters, will you come back with them?"

14

The smile had returned like lights after a power outage. "Sure."

"Any reason I should believe you?"

The boy had gestured toward the street. "I got a reputation to keep up."

Faustino had been charmed by that, even though he considered himself immune to charm. And the kid had come back with the cigarettes in less than five minutes and handed over the change.

"Keep it."

"Many thanks, señor."

"So what's your name?"

"Bush."

"Bush? That because you were found under one? Or because your mother's a big fan of former American presidents who own oil wells?"

"Nah." The boy had waggled his head while pointing at it with the forefingers of both hands. The crazy mane of dreadlocks bounced and flew. "It's 'cause I look like one. I was born with a whole bunch of hair and it jus' kept on goin'."

Faustino had studied the kid while fumbling with the damn cellophane wrapping on the cigarettes. The Rasta hair, the longish Spanish face, the wide Indian cheekbones, the African coloring, the narrow nose from God knows where — Arabia, maybe — the good teeth. Some flecks of green in the eyes. Not tall; skinny but well muscled. The genes that had produced him had tumbled through the centuries like balls in the lotto machine and come up with a winning number. He was a good-looking boy. But someone else had walked off with the money and all the luck.

"How old are you, Bush?"

Another shrug. "Seventeen?"

Well, yeah. Any street kid who could get away with it would say that. Because the dreaded Child Protection Order didn't apply to anyone over sixteen. He might have been fourteen, fifteen — who knows?

But for whatever reason, Faustino thereafter bought his Presidentes via the kid. Add the change together, and over a week it came to about a dollar twenty. Enough for two chicken chili fajitas if you got them from one of the places down by the bus station.

The way Bush combined his two businesses impressed Faustino. The kid had eyes in the back of his head. Come the lunch break, he'd be cleaning the gunk and insects off a windshield while somehow monitoring the *Nación* staff who came out onto the patio for a bit of sun or a smoke or to say stuff they couldn't get away with in the terrible open-plan Big Brother offices they worked in. And if Maya from advertising just couldn't hack her low-fat diet for one more minute, somehow Bush would know it and catch her eye, and in no time at all he'd have covered the four blocks to and from the deli and be delivering her a toasted ham and cheese. Fantastic, baby. Keep the change. Twenty centavos. When the cold-drinks machine in the lobby broke down, which was at least once a month, he would be on a roll. Ten centavos per Coke, average, on a crate of twelve.

Faustino also admired the way Bush respected Rubén, the way he allowed the doorman to maintain his authority. When Rubén was watching the trees and the steps on the right-hand side of the patio, Bush would do business from behind the trees on the left. And when Rubén was strolling down the left-hand side of the patio, Bush would do business from behind the trees on the right. This spared kindly Rubén the embarrassment of evicting a street kid from the sacred patio, upon which the street kid should not have been allowed to trespass in the first place. It also meant that Bush's customers appreciated Rubén's way of doing things, and that was good for Rubén. Because after all, doormen, like street kids, were not exactly irreplaceable.

So now Faustino was not displeased to be interrupted in his contemplation of secretaries' legs by Bush's wide white grin.

"Hey, Bush. How're you doing? Good day? Bad day?"

The kid rocked his right hand horizontally. "So-so. You know a big shave-head guy drives a Porsche, a black one?"

"Nope, can't say I do. Why?"

"He kicked my ass an' spilled half a my water. I thought if you knew him, you might do him a bad turn."

"I'll look out for him."

"Thank you, Maestro. Anything you'd like from the kiosk?"

From the way he said it, you'd think the kiosk was a limitless trove of rare delights.

"I'm fine right now," Faustino said. He stood and stubbed out the cigarette in one of the concrete troughs, checked his watch. Because the *Nación* building was perched on one of the city's five hills, it had more than its fair share of sky, and already, at the horizon, where the petrified forest of highrises dissolved into vagueness, that sky had taken on a peculiar tan color. In less than half an hour the traffic, already thickening, would be a crawling, honking nightmare. Time to go. He descended to the sidewalk and Bush kept pace with him as he walked to the parking garage entrance.

"So, is Otello gonna sign for Rialto, or what?"

Faustino tapped the side of his nose. "You'll have to wait till tomorrow's paper comes out."

Bush rubbed his chin thoughtfully. "Hmm. Remind me, Maestro, how much a copy cost?"

"Forty-five."

The boy shook his head and let out his breath to express sad incredulity. Faustino grinned and found a fifty in his pocket. He flipped it into the air. Bush twirled and caught it behind his back. When he raised his hand, the coin had vanished. Faustino slapped his palm against the boy's.

"Ciao, Bush. Watch your step."

"And you, Maestro. See ya."

Faustino was still smiling as he went down the gloomily lit ramp. There was no way the kid could read, but what the hell.

1.3

THE PLACE BUSH slept in but didn't call home was only two miles (and a world away) from the offices of *La Nación*, but on this particular evening it took him well over an hour to reach it. Getting through the business district was never much of a problem. You hardly ever saw cops on foot there, and the gangs didn't come that far west, as a rule. Things got trickier farther downtown. His shortest route was past the bus station, but he avoided it like the plague. It was a Mecca for crackheads, hustlers, and whores, and therefore a honeypot for cops. Plus, at least once every couple of weeks the feared Child Protection Force — otherwise known as the *Rataneros,* Ratcatchers — swept through it. There was an election looming, and the government would want to boast that they'd cleaned up the streets. So Bush gave the bus station a wide berth. He had several routes that made longish detours around it, and he used a different one every trip. The bucket and the squeegee marked him as someone who might be carrying cash, someone worth looking out for. In the past couple of months, he'd been mugged three times, despite his caution. Each time, he'd handed over the few centavos he kept in his pocket, and his attackers had failed to find the rest of the meager takings hidden in his waistband. But on the second occasion he'd been given a beating just for the pleasure of it, and it had left him with a painful bubbling inside his right ear that had lasted a week.

Now, on a narrow street between the vast blank side wall of the Church of All Saints and the back of a row of small shops, he heard from behind him a faint squeal of brakes, followed by the harsh popping of a motor. Turning, he saw a scooter with two guys on it, hustlers, both wearing *bandido* bandannas. For two long seconds he watched them watching him. Then the scooter snarled toward him, and he began to run, his head frantically mapping possible escape routes. He would be okay if he could get to the Carrer Jesús and across the one-way traffic. But that was too far to outrun a scooter. It was already within twenty yards of him. Just ahead, he saw a cat, alarmed by the commotion, leap from an overflowing trash can. Bush grabbed the rim of the can with his free hand and swung it into the middle of the street. The echoing snarl of the scooter paused, revved again. A yelled obscenity. More revving.

He ran on. The street made a turn beyond the end of the church wall, and there Bush found deliverance: a red-and-yellow barrier, a wheelbarrow, a couple of bags of cement, a wooden pallet. Two men relaying paving stones, another one supervising. All three looked up as Bush hurtled into view, and yelled curses at him when he vaulted the barrier and slapped a single footprint into their patch of wet cement. Their cries turned into a violent altercation when the scooter screeched sideways into the barrier, but by then Bush was gone.

On the far side of Jesús, where the flower sellers were already accosting early-evening strollers, Bush found a quiet space on the sidewalk and sat down on his upended bucket. Traffic noise surged and ebbed. Nearby, a street musician with one leg played mournful tangos on the accordion, leaning on a crutch.

Bush's breathing steadied eventually. He was desperately thirsty, as well as hungry. It had not been a good day, but his late bonus, Maestro's fifty centavos, would get him an ice-cold *zumo*. There was a place just down the street that did guava ones thick enough to be both food and drink. But he was worried about time, which was to say, he was worried about Bianca and Felicia. Well, about Bianca, anyway. In the end he bought the *zumo* and drank it too quickly, so that it made his throat ache and filled his chest with cold pebbles as it went down.

His flight had taken him off course, and now he would have to zigzag westward through the maze of little cafés and workshops of the artisan quarter. That was okay, because it was still busy at this time. And once he was on the other side, he'd hit the Avenida Buendía, and from there, if he jogged, he'd be home in fifteen minutes or so.

He hadn't thought about the cops.

He emerged from an alley onto Buendía, walked thirty yards, and there they were. A cruiser and a big van blocking off half the street. Ratcatchers and ordinary cops working in pairs. They already had two older kids wearing baseball caps spread against a wall and were feeling them over. A smashed-looking girl — she couldn't have been more than twelve — was being dragged toward the back of the van, her thin legs giving way every time she tried to kick the cop that had her by the hair and one wrist. An old woman with a foxy little dog under her arm was yelling abuse at the police; a man leaned in the doorway of a barbershop with his hands in his pockets, laughing at her. Bush took in all this in less than two seconds, then a sort of *uh-oh* feeling made him turn. Sure enough, the sidewalk was cut off in the opposite direction too; a cop saw him and pointed him out to his colleague.

"Hey, you, Rasta kid! Don't you damn well move! Yeah, you!"

He couldn't go back the way he'd come; they were already nearer the alley than he was. He put his bucket down, dropped his shoulders, and raised his open hands in a gesture of unconditional surrender. The cops' approach slowed to a saunter. The older one grinned.

Bush grabbed the bucket and was across the sidewalk in two long strides. It was separated from the four lanes of almost solid traffic by a high curb not much wider than his foot. He ran along it toward the police van, leaning inward slightly, away from the suction of the vehicles that roared past only inches from him. The cops behind him were yelling at the ones ahead, but Bush figured that they'd be muffled by the blare of the traffic. He teetered past the front of the van and *shit!*—there was another cop, turning toward him, mouth open, arm going up. Nothing to do but raise his own arm, too skinny to be much use as a battering ram, but, praise be to God, it struck the cop's shoulder and spun him away, and Bush was past and still running along the low parapet. A huge truck shoved air at him that felt solid as a wall, and he lost his balance. For a moment that was like a scream, he nearly fell the wrong way, knowing that he would die if he did so. But his body did a trick that had nothing to do with him, and he toppled away from the traffic and went down. He felt the palm of his free hand tear, then he was rolling over. He was back on his feet and running again before he felt the hot tickle of blood on his leg.

There was a subway station up ahead of him, and if he could reach it, he had a chance of disappearing among the rush-hour bodies. He looked back, expecting to see violently angry men in dark-blue uniforms close behind him. Instead, he saw ordinary people carrying shopping bags and briefcases and talking into cell phones. Some of these people glanced at him with condescending interest. He slowed, and immediately felt the pain in his leg. At the entrance to the subway, he took shelter beyond the stall of a newspaper seller and squatted, dragging in breath. His mouth tasted like dirty coins.

He checked himself over, starting with his money. It was all still there. A little under two dollars. His hand was scraped raw from the base of the thumb to the base of the little finger, and it burned. He picked little bits of grit out of the wound with the longest nail on his left hand. It would have been nice to pour cold water on it. In fact, imagining it was almost as good as doing it. The leg was okay. The blood was already drying. It looked like a shiny brown spiderweb.

The light had switched from natural to electric. The day had gone. He had to get home. It was extremely important that he was not late, because of the girls. He was about five subway stops from the Triangle. If he could beg an unexpired day ticket, he could still be home in quarter of an hour. Actually, in his head, he did not use the word *home*. He used the word *there*.

He went down the steps and picked a spot where he would only gently interrupt the flow of travelers. He used his sad smile.

"Finished with your ticket, señora? Señor? Finished with your ticket, señora?"

1.4

DESPITE ITS NAME, the Triangle was a roughly rectangular section of the old part of the city, narrower at one end than the other. Its eastern and northern limits were formed by a section of the Avenida Buendía, the channel of ceaseless traffic that ran from the Centro out to the northern suburbs. Bush had no idea where it ended, if it ended at all. He had never been north of the Carrer Circular, which crossed Buendía in a jumble of traffic lights and tortuous overpasses. The Triangle's other long flank was more vague; there, its undisciplined maze of streets washed up against new office buildings and high-rise apartments. The southern side of the Triangle was an interzone of struggling trees and threadbare grass that marked the beginning of the university campus.

The Triangle was a district in limbo. It was almost a slum, but not quite. It was scheduled for redevelopment, but not yet. It was old, but not in a way that attracted gringo tourists. The twisted streets had names, but there were no signs that announced them, because only the locals used them. On a street known as Trinidad, there was a bar called La Prensa. The Press. Many years ago it had been one. Books and leaflets, fliers and posters, local newsletters, and — believe it or not — church magazines had been printed there. And also, for a brief intoxicated month or two, thirty years ago, revolutionary pamphlets that preached freedom and democracy, sometimes illustrated by pictures of angry and attractive young women clearly not wearing brassieres. One of the printing presses, an ancient litho machine with fancy cast-iron legs, was a feature of the bar.

Next to La Prensa was a building that would look like an old colonial house if you drove past it in the dark. In fact, only the facade, punctuated by empty windows and adorned by opportunistic plants, remained. If, as Bush and the girls did every day, you went through the gap where its front door had been, you would discover that this wall was propped up by huge timbers grown gray with age.

Behind it, at the back of a cat-haunted yard that had once been a garden, was a lean-to, a ramshackle tumbledown shed with splitting wooden walls, a small window with white paper pasted on the cracked glass, and a rusty tin roof. It had once been a store for the press. Great spools of paper half the height of a man had been kept in there; so had the wooden pallets that tubs of ink had been brought in on. And failures: blurred or unsold books, bad test runs, uncollected christening cards, election posters with the wrong name under the photograph, advertising brochures with the wrong phone number, pamphlets with a section printed upside down. When Fidel and Nina Ramirez had bought the press and turned it into a bar, they'd cleared out most of this stuff and burned it in the yard. At the time, they'd probably imagined they would use the shed for something or other. Not as a home for feral kids, of course. There hadn't been so many of those in the neighborhood back then.

The fourth side of the yard was the wall of a building that had been many things but for about a year now had been a place where women worked sewing machines. They made cheap clothes with expensive labels sewn into them. The business, which had no name, was owned by a man of Turkish origin called Señor Oguz. Señor Oguz had been antsy about the kids in the shed, about them using the tap in the yard, and about the boy with all the hair filching rags from his wastebins. The Child Protection Order made it a criminal act to provide street kids with shelter or food or anything else (including rags, probably) on the grounds that it "encouraged homelessness and destitution." But Fidel had spoken to Señor Oguz over a free cold beer and chilled him out. During the same conversation, he had also mentioned, helpfully, that Señor Oguz was misspelling the word DIESEL on his phony labels.

Felicia sat in the shed while the last of the daylight leeched away. She was not afraid of the dark. All the same, she would have liked the companionship of a candle flame. There were still several stumps in the plastic bag stashed in the corner, but she was unwilling to light one until Bush got back. The bed she shared with Bianca was a wooden pallet covered with blankets, and she sat on it cross-legged, fighting to control her anxiety. This was always the worst part of the day, waiting for Bush. She used fragments of pop songs and her small repertoire of good memories to ward off bad imaginings of what might have happened to him. And Bianca.

Sometimes she fantasized about a life without Bianca in it. These dream stories were not wrapped in a twinkling mist of happiness. They were not like Bianca's ridiculous fantasies of celebrity. They were modest. One of her favorites was that she and Bush would take over the bar from Fidel and Nina and, like them, grow old but stay in love. Another was that she and Bush would live in a house. The house moved from place to place, although she had no idea what other places there might be. But it always had real furniture like in the shop windows. And a bedroom and a bed with white sheets. In which she would lie with Bush. Alone with Bush. Sometimes there would be open windows and pale drifting curtains and sometimes the sound of the sea, which was a blue sound. But all these fantasies needed a prologue, a prologue in which Bianca disappeared. She could not — would not — allow herself to picture how this might happen. Because Bush loved his sister, and therefore she, Felicia, had to love her too.

Bianca. Mother of God, where *was* she?

Felicia was, she believed, fourteen years old. And that was a very bad age to be. It made her a victim twice over. It forced choices upon her: choices that involved the way she looked and what she wore. Choices that she could not make for herself.

If the Ratcatchers caught her, it was unlikely that she could pass for over sixteen. She had no papers, of course, and she was slightly built. They would take her, and although she did not believe all the stories about what happened next, she did not want to be taken.

But she was becoming a woman. Her breasts were undeniable, and boys — and men with wolf eyes — had started to look at her. She didn't want to be forced into an alleyway and —

Felicia should not have let herself fall asleep in the afternoon and allowed Bianca to slip away. If she was not back before Bush, he would go searching for her. He would go away into the night.

For the last six months, Felicia had worn a pair of loose Bermuda shorts that Nina had given her. They were much too big; she fastened them around her waist with a length of string. But they made her legs look thinner and less shapely, which was good. She had two T-shirts that she wore in rotation: one on, the other washed under the tap in the yard and dried on the roof of the shed. Both had gotten smaller. She walked slightly stooped with her arms crossed over her chest, so that maybe the boys and the wolf men would not notice her. Trying to look like a child. Praying that she would not turn a corner into the arms of the Ratcatchers and have to become older. To have to stare the bastards in the eye and stick her chest out and say, "Yeah, I'm nearly seventeen, and these are the only clothes I got, so what?"

Bianca was crazy. Bianca was younger, at least a year younger, but thought she could pass for sixteen because she was beautiful. Which she was. Wild hair like her brother's, but full of light. Blue, sometimes. The same big eyes that could melt you and make you foolish. She asked for nothing: she stole. Denied it, of course. Bush told her time after time, "Beg, scrounge, but never steal. They'll get you if you steal." And then Bianca had come back with a white bra and a pair of panties. Told Bush she'd found them on a piece of cardboard the shape of a body without arms and legs thrown into a yard behind a shop on Santa Josefina. And he'd believed her. So now she went out with them on, the bra hoicking her chest up, a lacy strap showing beneath the one black T-shirt she owned. Practically *asking* to be taken among the trash cans in some dirty dark alley and—

Where *are* you, Bianca? Come back to the shed alive and let's light a candle. Fidel has left food for us.

Bush was leaving the subway at San Antonio, the stop for the Triangle. He'd stood inconspicuously by the single door at the end of the car, hiding the bucket behind his legs. He came out from underground, unchallenged, into a bustling street separated from the sky by scrawls of neon.

On Trinidad he did what he always did: walked past the wrecked house, past the bar, and leaned against a wall until the street seemed safe. Then he went swiftly through the dark hole of the old doorway and picked his way across the yard. There was no light showing through the rickety walls of the shed, and he did not know whether that was a good or a bad thing.

"Bianca? Felicia?"

The door was dragged back on its lopsided hinges just before he reached it.

"Bush?"

"Yeah, it's me. It's cool."

He was close to her in the almost dark, and she wanted more than anything to take hold of him and for him to say her name again.

He said, "Where's Bianca?"

"Hey, Bush. You okay? How was it today?"

"Kinda rough. Where's Bianca?"

"I dunno."

"Aw, man. What you mean, you dunno? Shit, Felicia."

"I fell asleep. When I woke up, she was gone. I'm real sorry, Bush. I thought she was asleep an' all."

She felt him move past her, then heard him rustling in the bag. The flash of a lighter. His face came back toward her, up-lit by the stub of candle in his hand.

Hurriedly she said, "You hungry? Fidel left us food. Rice 'n' beans with some sausage in it. I been keepin' it. I haven't had any of it."

"How long you think she been gone?"

Felicia shrugged, and instantly regretted it. Bush's eyes narrowed into slits of reflected flame.

"Can't've been more'n two hours, Bush. I woke up 'bout an hour back, an' I wasn' asleep that long."

He hung his head. His face was hidden from her by the draggled mop of his hair.

She said, "You look real tired, man. C'mon, have some food. Sit. Hey, I got most a big Pepsi I found at the bus stop. Wan' some?"

"I'm gonna have to go look for her. Jesus, Felicia. I don' need this, you know?"

She knew. And she could no longer stand so close to him with the distance between them feeling so huge. She went and sat on the bed.

He said, "What you do today? You go for breakfast down at the Sisters of Mercy?"

"Yeah. We got soup an' bread an'—"

"Felicia, I don' give a shit what you *ate*. You see anyone down there? Like that Hernandez Brothers gang?"

"They was there, yeah."

"Bianca talk to them?"

"Maybe."

"Maybe?"

This was the conversation she feared and hated, that was like a bad dream you shook off and then it came back. The one they had all the time instead of the one she wanted them to have, about being in a white bed with the sea breathing

32

in the windows. This one was like having nails hammered into you.

"Yeah. I dunno. A little bit, not for long. They always hit on her, man, you know? An' she goes for it. What you expect me to do? She goes to *them,* Bush, an' that's the truth. I go to get her away, an' I get all kinds of shit from them *an'* her. You know what I'm sayin'?"

And she knew that yes, he did know what she was saying. She knew also that he didn't want to hear it, and that hearing it from her diminished the chances of him ever loving her. She wanted to confess to him the terrible visions that swelled in her when she was alone. Bianca bringing that gang back, them looming into their sanctuary when Bush was not there and when Fidel and Nina were busy. Shutting the door. Drinking, smoking. The terrible sick Hernandez boy. Giggling, then rape. Later giving birth in mess and pain and desperate ignorance.

"Any of them touch her?" Bush asked.

"Not 'specially." She could not look at him.

He came closer and set the candle down on the floor. "Okay. I'll just go an' check some places."

"You wan' me to come with you?"

"No."

"Bush? Have somethin to eat firs'. She'll most likely be back any minute, anyway."

"I'm okay. You wanna eat, go ahead. Fidel leave any bread with that?"

She shook her head. "No, not today."

"All right."

Then he was gone. Before she could ask him about the blood on his leg. Without him asking her about her day. Not that there was any need to ask. He knew what her day had been like. It had been like all the others.

1.5

O KAY," OTELLO SAYS, "it's a nice car. I'm impressed. Now, would you mind slowing down? Like to the speed of sound, or something?"

Diego Mendosa smiles, his face a dim red in the dashboard lights.

"What's the matter, Capitano? Don't you trust me?"

Capitano. Diego has taken to calling him that. Otello has gotten used to it.

"I trust you. Problem is, we don't have the road to ourselves. And I've got no reason to trust anyone else on it not to do something stupid."

"True," Diego says, and eases the Maserati to a mere thirty over the speed limit.

The city thins out; now and again there are dark spaces along the highway where there might be trees.

Otello relaxes a little. "So tell me about this Nestor Brabanta."

"*Senator* Nestor Brabanta," Diego corrects him. "He likes to be addressed as *Senator*. Power behind the throne at Rialto, even though he's officially just another member of the board of directors. He was never there when we were negotiating, but every now and again someone would go out to make a call, and I'm pretty damn sure it was him they were calling. Like, Real Madrid was closing it, then the Duke, da Venecia, went out to use his phone, and suddenly *zap!* No more Real. That was Brabanta; I'd bet my life on it. And seeing as how you really, *really* didn't want to go to Spain, especially after the riots and so forth in Espirito, that makes him one of the good guys, as far as I'm concerned. No, it makes him *the* good guy. I think da Venecia was all set to go with Real. So we *like* Senator Brabanta. Okay?"

Diego gestures with his head toward a housing project, lit dull amber by the streetlights, its roofs supporting a skeletal jungle of antennas and satellite dishes. "If you were to ask the people over there who Nestor Brabanta was, they wouldn't say, 'Yeah, the politician, the guy who owns two of the five biggest businesses in the state.' They'd say, 'Brabanta? Anything to do with Desmerelda Brabanta?'"

"Will she be there this evening?"

Diego flashes a grin at him. "*Down*, tiger. Nope, she won't. She's in the States. Visiting her mother."

He looks into the mirrors, shifts down, makes a cut across

two lanes, and takes an unmarked exit off the highway. At the lights at the bottom of the ramp he says, "I don't like to blow my own horn, as you know, but I think I did okay the first time I met Nestor. This was back in May. We talked for a while, then we took a coffee break, and he said, 'Señor Mendosa, you are a very unusual person.' 'Am I?' I said. 'Yes,' he said. 'We have been together for more than an hour, and you have not once mentioned my daughter.' And I said, you know, all innocence, 'Your daughter, señor?' And he said, 'Yes. Please don't pretend you don't know that Desmerelda Brabanta is my daughter. It is extremely rare for me to have a conversation with a young man who doesn't have a keen interest in her.' So I looked him in the eye and said, 'With all due respect, señor, I would not care if you were the father of an alligator or all the stars of heaven. I wear my heart on my sleeve. I do business. Glamour isn't something I concern myself with. If it so happens that you introduce me to your famous daughter, I will of course be honored. But that has nothing to do with what we are discussing here today. I can assure you that neither my client nor myself is interested in associating with celebrity. Otello has no need to, and I have no desire to.'"

"You cheeky SOB, Diego. What did he say to that?"

"He laughed and patted me on the shoulder. That's when I knew we'd get what we wanted. And we did, Capitano, did we not?"

"I guess we did," Otello says.

◆ ◆ ◆

When they arrive at Brabanta's suburban hacienda, Otello at last realizes that, even off the field, he is playing in another league.

In the North, he lived for the past two years in a walled and gated estate of just four houses, one of the others occupied by Espirito's keeper and his wife. A cheerfully casual guard at the entry, a fountain — usually dry — at the center, parking for ten cars. Safe from trouble, but not far from the people or the stadium.

This is a different kind of thing altogether. The remote-controlled gates to the drive are almost hidden by trees of a variety Otello has not seen before. The guards — two of them — are neither cheerful nor casual, and wear fat little machine guns over their shoulders. They know who the arrivals are but check them over anyway, as well as the car, talking all the while into phones plugged into their ears. The drive curves around a lawn bigger than most practice fields.

A beautiful dark-skinned maid opens the vast glass door to the house and shows them into the presence of Señor Brabanta. He leads them down a corridor lined with paintings and into a conservatory full of the heady night scent of jasmine. When they are seated, the beautiful maid brings in a tray of tea, soft drinks, and cakes. She takes a good look at Otello, but it isn't the kind of look he is used to. There is something like a warning in it.

When she has gone, Brabanta says, without preamble, "That free kick you scored on. The one in the semifinal.

When it was lined up, you had a discussion with Santillana. I'd very much like to know what you said to each other. Some of my friends think that Santillana wanted to play it indirect. Emilio Pearson had slipped around the right of the Mexican defensive wall. It looked to most of us like you were going for a set piece, something you had all practiced. The Mexicans thought so, too. Their eyes were all over the place. Their line was pulled out of shape."

Otello, nonplussed, shifts in his seat. He'd been thinking that a beer would be nice.

Diego says, "I had no idea you were such a close observer of the game, Senator."

Brabanta smiles. "Ah. Perhaps you thought I was one of those politicians who gets involved in soccer to persuade the voters that he has the common touch. Or so that he can be photographed with famous players. I regret to say that many of my associates share that view of me. Actually, I am a fan, a serious one."

He turns his attention back to Otello.

"I will confess something to you. One of the reasons I was so eager to sign you is that I wanted to do what I am doing now. To talk soccer with you. To get it from the horse's mouth, so to speak. I hope you will indulge me in this from time to time."

Diego clears his throat as though he is about to say something, but Brabanta cuts him off. "So, was that free kick meant to be something you had rehearsed? And did you ignore Santillana and go for the shot?"

"Uh, no. What Santillana said to me was, 'I still think those cleats of yours look like a pair of ladies' slippers.' I had a bit of trouble keeping a straight face, but we were always going for the shot."

Brabanta lets out a gleeful exclamation and clicks his fingers. "I knew it! Excellent! That's ten dollars Ariel Goldmann owes me."

It is not possible, of course, to talk meaningfully about playing soccer. To use words to convey what it is like trying to overcome the sullen outrage you feel when you have been persistently fouled off the ball throughout an entire game. Or the fierce moment of elation when you know that you will score. Or what it takes to find running within yourself when you have no running left. That is not the sort of thing sports reporters want to hear, anyway. Maybe not what their audiences want to hear, either. They are comfortable with clichés, banalities, sound bites — phrases that stumble and go sprawling in sight of the goal. The kind of half-sentences that Otello, like most of his colleagues, utters. After all, it would be disturbing to the proper order of things, it would be *too much*, if the physically gifted could also talk.

Nestor Brabanta, however, is not content with the usual platitudes. He has extraordinary recall. Either that, or he has closely studied recordings of the Copa América games in advance of this visit. Otello's responses to his questions frequently seem to disappoint him.

"Yes, but *why* did you do that?"

And: "Yes, but was it *your* decision to bring Ramón up into the attack?"

And: "Did you realize that at the time . . . ?"

And so on.

It is very uncomfortable for Otello. Apart from anything else, there are no satisfactory answers to such questions. How can a player, even an articulate one, explain to a layman the complex relationship between thought and instinct? Between practice and improvisation? Between what you know you can do and what the immense voice of the crowd tells you it wants? How is it possible to explain to one of life's winners what losing feels like?

But Otello slowly comes to realize that there is a correct way to answer Brabanta's questions, which is to give the man the opportunity, the reason, to say, "Ah, yes. I thought so." Rich men and barroom soccer bores have this in common: they need to be right, to have superior opinions.

All the same, there is something about Brabanta's manner that is . . . disturbing. The man is in charge, they are talking in his space, he is on the board, he is rich — the fifty million had very likely come out of one of his bank accounts, painlessly — and he is an aristocrat. A southern white aristo. But it's like talking to a geek. The man sits there wearing clothes that cost twice the average annual national wage. At least. In a house that probably has a staff of thirty people, minimum. And yet it's a bit like talking to, yes, some eager, geeky kid in the academy who's studied game videos and wants answers to questions about offside incidents that you can't even remember. That same thirsty hero worship. It is . . . inappropriate.

Otello leans back in the rattan chair, sips the iced guava juice. It would be nice if his agent would take the initiative, change the subject, get him off the hook. But Diego shows no sign of doing so. In fact, he seems to have eased his chair farther away from the lamplight. From beyond the open doors comes the summery chirp of a cell phone, then a murmured conversation that fades into the distance. Men out there in the darkness. Insincerely, Brabanta asks permission to light a cheroot, and Otello gives it with a small gesture of his hand. This is a mistake, and if Otello had spotted the hard glitter in the other man's eye, he might have realized it.

"Preseason training begins in two weeks, if I remember rightly?"

"Correct, señor."

"May I speak frankly, Otello? On the understanding that nothing I say goes beyond this room?"

Otello shrugs. "Sure."

"Good." Brabanta studies the drift of his smoke as if it contains the words he needs. "You will get some shit."

"Señor?"

"There was a faction on the Rialto board that was against signing you. It was not about money. I made sure of that. No, it was more a, well, *cultural* matter. Or, to be more accurate, there were members of the board who were concerned about the, shall we say, social cohesion of the team. Understand?"

Otello's face makes it plain that he does not.

"Very well, then. I will be blunt. There were those who thought that selling Luis Montano as part of the deal was a bad idea. He was having a dry spell, had not scored in his last eight matches. But he was popular with the squad."

Otello says, "Yeah. Luis is a really nice kid. And a good player. He will be great one day. They will love him up in Espirito."

"He is very bitter about the way he has been treated."

"I'm sorry to hear it."

"And he is not black," Brabanta says.

"What? Pardon, señor?"

"The Rialto squad, first and second teams, contains only four black players. *Contained,* I should say. We sold a white player to offset the cost of a fifth. There are people, players included, who are less than happy about that."

Otello is too taken aback to say anything. He glances at Diego's shadowed face, which is expressionless.

Brabanta says, "How do you feel about Roderigo being club captain, when you are *his* captain on the national side?"

"Ah, I have absolutely no problem with that. I get along very well with Jaco. I don't—"

The senator lifts a hand, almost apologetically. "Please. We agreed to be candid with each other. So I would be failing in my duty if I did not inform you of certain . . .

undercurrents at Rialto. I asked you about Roderigo because he is a close friend of Montano's. And because there has always been a, let us say, *jocular* tension between our white players and their black colleagues. On the field, these matters are of no consequence. Off the field . . . well, you know. But what I want you to understand is this: I believe absolutely that individual ability transcends race. You are a great player. Your color is irrelevant. I — sorry, *we* — have never spent so much money on a player. I think that speaks for itself."

Brabanta shows his teeth in what is more or less a smile. He leans forward and puts his hand on Otello's forearm — the first and last time he will touch his purchase. "Personally," he says, "I have no time for racism. A primitive emotion. But, as I said, you will experience some hostility. From the team, from some sections of the crowd. Perhaps even from our esteemed manager, who was not altogether convinced that we should spend our entire transfer budget on you. But I am absolutely sure that you will rise above such matters. That you will settle in. Find your place."

Because his thoughts are tumbling like leaves in the wind, Otello says, "Thank you, señor. You have given me much to think about."

Brabanta stubs his cheroot into the ashtray and glances at his watch. "Don't bother with thinking. Just score us goals. That will straighten everything out. Now, then, have you and Diego received your invitations to the reception in your honor? There are so many people anxious to meet you."

◆ ◆ ◆

The lovely dark-skinned girl escorts them out. At the front door, she looks up at his face as though she is about to speak. Ask for his autograph or something. But she doesn't.

On the way back to the city, Diego says, "Can you believe that two multimillionaires like him and Goldmann make chickenshit ten-dollar bets?"

1.6

I T DID NOT take Bush long to find his sister. She was in the second place he looked.

He walked fast, because in the dark speed was safer than caution. The *Rataneros* didn't usually operate after nightfall. Their prey knew the territory better than they did, and many carried knives. But there were other dangers, so Bush walked fast, ignoring greetings from the shadows and skirting small gatherings of people in the pools of light from street lamps.

Five hundred yards north of La Prensa, there was a building that long ago had been a cinema. Someone once told him it had been the first cinema in the city, and that when it opened, the movies they showed were black-and-white and soundless. Sometimes the screen would be just words, and then a man in a white suit would stand in front of it and read them out in a loud voice. Bush had liked that story.

The mystery of reading intrigued him. He would have liked to have been that man in the white suit, speaking in a bold voice the words that others couldn't read. But good jobs like that had gone.

The cinema was a shell now; it was used as a flea market. The space where there had been plush seats was occupied by stalls selling things that had been sold many times before. And one or two sold fruit that wasn't too fresh, or fried rissoles and coffee. Sometimes bits of plaster-work—a moldy rosebud, a cherub's wing tip—would fall from the once-ornate ceiling onto the plastic awnings below.

Even though it was late, there was still activity in the market, shadowy business conducted in the light of gas or kerosene lamps. The place never really closed, since for many of the traders, their stalls were also their homes; they slept on mats beneath the counters.

Bush went past the entrance and turned into the alleyway that ran the length of the building. This was a reasonably good place for kids to hang out. It had a roof that was more or less intact, a boon on very hot or wet days. It was strewn with flattened cartons and ripped sacks that you could sit or sleep on. The scavenging was not the best, but there was usually something that could be shared. Now and again there might be a job or an errand worth a few centavos. And the market's customers, being poor themselves, were generous. Most important, it was not too difficult a place to flee from. At the back of the market, the alleyway ended in a low wall, easily shinnied over, and beyond that was a maze of narrow ways and small houses with interconnecting yards. Once over the wall, you had a good chance of shaking off the Ratcatchers or other predators.

The alley was busy tonight. Temporary encampments had been built: two upturned wooden pallets with a ragged tarpaulin for a roof, a chained-up handcart walled around with cardboard. Small territories had been established: a square yard or two of blanket or matting; sheets of cardboard in the lee of the big wheeled rubbish bins.

Some kids felt safest clustered where faint light spilled from the side doors of the building. Others, for whatever reason, sought the deeper shadows. Bush picked his way through the dark melee from which random details emerged: pairs of knees and feet made pale by dust, a small child's face suddenly illuminated by the flare of a cigarette lighter, two little girls trying to feed pellets of bread to a thin kitten.

Toward the far end of the alley, the night's entertainment was in full swing. A tall skinny kid was doing freestyle with a peeling and under-inflated ball. A boy who looked the same age as Bush was crouched over a battered boom box that emitted reggae-flavored techno at a cautious volume. He was nursing a joint that wreathed smoke around his head. Three other boys, already high on something, performed an unstable dance that resembled slow-motion martial arts. They had an audience, and Bianca was a member of it. She was with a bunch of similar-aged girls hunkered down on the steps of a boarded-up doorway. They were holding each other, wrapped around each other, in a way that made Bush's heart feel solitary. Their hair, their smiles, their talk, their bare legs. He stopped in a patch of unoccupied darkness and watched them. Also checking out the boys who were watching them. There were none that gave him special concern, just younger kids testing their bravado by calling out the dirty taunts that pass for flirting at that age. He approached the doorway. One of the girls, seeing him, nudged Bianca. Another hid something she was smoking behind her back.

Bianca looked up at Bush and smiled. As always, her beauty filled him with dread.

"Hi, Bush," she said. "I'm late, aren't I? I'm sorry, man. We were . . . you know."

The smoking girl giggled. Another pouted up at him resentfully. Bush hardly noticed them.

"You ready to go?"

"Sure," she said, and stood up. There was nothing in either her voice or her manner to suggest that she knew she had troubled him.

On the street, watchful as they walked, he said, "What's in the bag?"

It was a plastic shopping bag with PRADA printed on it.

"Oh, yeah," she said, "I forgot. Found a pair of flip-flops maybe your size. Look like nearly new. Wanna check them out?"

49

"Where'd you find them?"

She shrugged. "They was like lyin' outside some place."

"You stole them."

"No, man. I watch them for like ten minutes an' no one come near them. An' I thought, Poor little homeless flip-flops, you'd be happier on Bush's feet 'stead of lyin' there, so I pick them up. Got two oranges in there as well, look mostly all right. An' a magazine."

After a while he said, "You shouldna gone out without Felicia. Shouldna snuck out on her. I told you about a hundred times."

She put her arm through his and leaned in on him and said, "Bro, it's not like I snuck, you know? I tried to wake her up 'cause I was lonely and everythin'. Man, you should try bein' with Felicia every day, know what I mean?"

"She's supposed to look after you," he said. "An' you're supposed to look after her."

She smiled up at him. "Felicia? Wha's to look after?"

Back in the shed, they ate the food that Fidel had left them, using the three spoons he had given them. They each took a spoonful of the rice and beans at the same time and didn't take another until they were all ready. It was a careful ritual that, Bush felt, kept the unruliness of the world at bay, briefly. Only one of Bianca's two oranges was edible. They ate sitting cross-legged on the dirt floor around the uncertain light of a candle. Bush told them about his day, about the cars he had cleaned and about the man who had kicked his ass and about the man he liked who was called Maestro. He did not say anything about the *Rataneros* or his flight along the Avenida Buendía.

There was not much noise from the bar tonight, but at one point they heard the door slam and approaching footsteps. Bush blew out the candle, and they waited in the darkness until the man had finished emptying his bladder against the shed wall and gone back to the bar. The smell of urine was strong for a while, but they were used to it.

When the candle had been relit, Bianca fetched the magazine from her bag and carefully tore out a picture of Desmerelda Brabanta and added it to the collection of similar pictures that adorned the wall above her corner of the bed. Then she knelt and studied it. She swayed her body, clicked her fingers softly, and sang in a tuneless whisper:

"'Take me up, take me up higher, baby.

Take me 'way from ever'thin

That ever brought me down.'"

Felicia sighed and lowered her head onto her folded arms.

"Thing is," Bianca said, "what makes her so cool is, she ain' nothin' special, know what I mean? Like she's not super-beautiful. Not got so great a voice, compared with some. But she made it."

Without lifting her head, Felicia said, "Yeah, 'cause she's a rich bitch got a mega-rich daddy made it all happen for her, girl. Jesus."

Like the way they ate, this was a ritual. Bush wearily resigned himself to it. He knew what Bianca would say next.

"Shit, Felicia, what is your problem? Why you always say that? Desmerelda might just the same have come from nowhere, you know? If she had, like, the dream, or, or, what is it?"

"Ambition," Bush said flatly.

"Right. That's what you gotta have. Plus the looks to start with. Which some of us has got." Bianca turned to Bush and pulled her hair back from her face. "Tell me the truth, bro. Is she that much prettier than me? She got lighter skin, but not much. I figure I got my hair done up like she got it, I'd look a bit like her. What d'you think?"

She took her right hand from her hair and put the tip of one finger in her mouth. She narrowed her eyes, as if contemplating something wonderfully wicked. She looked, Bush thought, without knowing the words, vulnerable and fragile and innocent. Also lewd, pornographic. He imagined other people — boys, men — looking at her like this; he imagined her, for a shocking millisecond, naked. He wanted to hold her, make her small, make her tiny, and fold her safely away inside himself somewhere. He also wanted to slap her.

He managed a smile. "That Brabanta chick, she saw you, she'd wanna curl up and die. That's the truth."

Felicia watched his eyes, reading what was in them.

Bush waited until the girls were asleep, which was difficult because he was very tired and dreams were offering themselves to him. Then he went to the corner of the shed that was behind the angle of the door when it opened and lifted up a piece of broken concrete. Under it was a square tin can that had once contained cooking oil. He had buried it there two years earlier. It contained all the money that he'd earned and hadn't needed to spend. He knew precisely how much was there and tried not to acknowledge how little it was. He added his day's takings to the stash and pulled out the other thing that he kept in the can: a small sheaf of paper rolled into a cylinder. He took it to the mat he slept on and sat cross-legged. He unrolled it and held it so that the light from the last of the candle fell on it.

In 1984 a nearsighted university professor named Emmanuel Fuentes was badly injured when he was struck by a car that he thought was stationary but wasn't. He spent his convalescence writing a textbook on marine biology, his private passion. The book found a publisher and was printed at the press on Trinidad, in the Triangle. In those days, color printing was done by running the same pages through the presses four times, once for each of the four colors of ink. Things often went wrong. If the pages weren't lined up exactly, the yellow or the blue might shift out of register. This is what happened to part of Professor Fuentes's book, and a whole run of spoiled pages was chucked into the shed at the back of the press. Many years later, Fidel and Nina added them to the bonfire during their clear-out. They hadn't liked burning books, or even parts of books, but what could they do?

A number of pages from the book on marine biology

had escaped Fidel and Nina's attention, and these were what Bush was looking at by the light of his candle. They were from Professor Fuentes's chapter on the regrowth of limbs by crabs and starfish. The words meant nothing to Bush, of course, but he was fascinated by the illustrations. Their off-register colors made them look sort of three-dimensional. In his favorite sequence, a crab slowly sprouted a new leg to replace one that had been lost or maybe bitten off. The new leg began as a bud that looked like soft glass, then became a slender tendril as frail as a plant's. In the next two pictures it developed segments and a tender, tiny claw. Finally the new leg was complete: smaller than the others still, but strong and serviceable. Bush had never seen the sea, and he had no particular feelings about crabs. Nor could he have found the words to explain why he was so interested in the badly printed pictures. Why he found them reassuring, why it was his nightly ritual to examine them.

Bianca stirred in her sleep and muttered something. He went to the girls' bed and kissed her, leaning over Felicia. He had no way of knowing that Felicia was wide awake behind her closed eyelids and that she was clasping her hands together, fighting the desire to reach up and caress his unhappy face.

1.7

THE LIMOUSINES SWOOSH to a halt on the gravel, pearled with black raindrops. Big men with big umbrellas greet them, open their doors, sneak peeks down cleavages, expertly assess the price of suits and shoes. Up the curvaceous staircase—careful on those high heels—and then the guests are soaked in the brilliance and warmth of Nestor Brabanta's house.

The lighting is perfect; it picks out the pearls and diamanté on the gowns without attracting attention to any slight imperfections of the skin. (The summer has been hot and long, tough on those obliged to conduct their business on yachts or at beach houses out on the islands.) Women kiss the air beside each other's ears; men, slightly less mindful of makeup, kiss the cheeks of friends and enemies alike.

Champagne? Yes, why not? And one or two of those little seafood kabobs. Mmm, gorgeous. Who's here? Is that Martha Goldmann? Yes. My God, what is that she's talking to, with the dress cut so deep at the back that you can see half the derrière? Laughing, now. Must be someone. A soap actress or something, or someone's daughter.

There are two sets of doors that open onto the drawing room. Do a sort of slalom: kiss kiss, swerve, hello, swerve, smile, hello, kiss kiss, swerve; and there is Nestor. Over against the fireplace. He looks so solemn, so serious, so cool, that you almost forget it's entirely absurd to *have* a fireplace. It's filled with flame-colored orchids. Remember to tell him you find that witty. Now, where's the fifty-million guest of honor?

Over there. That has to be him. Holding court at the far end of the room. Lord, he's black, though. Blacker than most of the staff. Good-looking, one has to admit. And already feeling very much at home, to judge by the body language. And it would be his body that does the talking, naturally. . . .

Otello is not, in fact, feeling comfortable. It seems to him that despite Brabanta's promise, there are not many people who want to meet him. To look at him, yes; to touch him, yes; to put a hand briefly on his shoulder, his back, his upper arm. Rather like gamblers at a racetrack, reaching out to touch the horse they have bet on when it is led into the paddock. One of Nestor Brabanta's famous horses. He feels that these people would like to strip him down to his underwear so as to assess his physical condition more carefully. To check on their investment.

Their movements have a pattern. There is also a script. The older men approach him directly, with a brusque heartiness. They put their cigars into their mouths and shake his hand and take their cigars out of their mouths again.

RICH OLDER MAN: Vincente da Souza. Amoco Steel. An honor to meet you, Otello.

OTELLO: Thank you, señor.

RICH OLDER MAN [*glancing around the room conspiratorially*]: You know, for a while I thought we might not get you. I said to the board, "What's the matter with you people? Here's the greatest striker in the whole damn world, and you're quibbling over a couple of million? Goddamn," I said, "let's go out and get this guy!" And of course they saw sense. Great times ahead, Otello! *Great* times ahead. This is my wife, Theresa.

OTELLO: Señora. [*They shake hands awkwardly because she offers only the tips of her fingers.*]

RICH OLDER MAN: Theresa is more of a tennis person than a soccer person. What can you do, eh? [*He looks off to the side.*] Hey, Pedro! Come over here and shake the hand of a genuine hero for once in your life. Pedro, this is the great Otello. Otello, Pedro dos Passos, vice president, Astral. [RICH OLDER MAN *and* THERESA *exit stage right.*]

The younger ones are less direct. They circle him like elegant animals pretending to hunt; they do not need to hunt. They watch him out of the corners of their eyes. The girls are amazing; the boys have gringo names.

"Hi, Otello? *Excellent.* You were great in the final. We all watched it. We should have been playing polo, you know, but we canceled. We got some serious grief for that, let me tell you. I'm Ricky Zamora; this is Estrella. So, uh, I guess all this must be pretty weird for you. Champagne? Estrella, grab the man some of that champagne. No? Ah, right. You're in training. That's cool."

(Training has nothing to do with it. In truth, Otello could murder a drink, something a good deal stronger than champagne. But he is fairly sure that it wouldn't do for a fifty-million-dollar purchase to be seen knocking back rum.)

They are skilled at party behavior, these people. They know how to drift away when they have lost interest and make it look as though it's you that's moved, not them. They talk about him when they are not quite out of earshot. The boys say something; the girls either giggle or toss their beautiful heads dismissively.

Otello begins to wonder if there will be any other black guests. It bothers him that the question has even occurred to him; he is not used to thinking this way. Brabanta's words have unsettled him. He watches the doors to see if any other Rialto players have been invited. It seems not. Not even Jaco Roderigo. Otello is puzzled by this. And worried, too.

He would like to have a word with his agent about it, but Diego is working, as always. He is over there with Brabanta, shaking hands with the people who come to pay homage to their host. Diego does not assert himself. He waits patiently to be introduced and then proffers his hand. He accompanies the handshake with a little lowering of the head: a bow, yet not a bow. It's like saying, "I'm going through the motions of respect, señor, but don't make the mistake of thinking that I don't matter." Diego never interrupts but has the weird skill of taking control of conversations. These fat cats come to talk to Brabanta and soon find themselves delighted to be talking to Señor Mendosa instead. As do their wives or girlfriends or whatever they are. Watching from across the room, Otello is reassured; he is fortunate to have someone so skillful on his side. He will leave Diego to press the flesh, work the room. To be an honest pimp, that most ancient of trades.

Otello realizes that for the moment no one is approaching or stalking him, so he takes the opportunity to get some air. The French doors onto the garden are just behind him, and wide open.

The rain has stopped, and because light pollution does not affect this exclusive district, the sky swarms with stars. Gazing up at them, Otello feels at home for an instant, even though the constellations are not quite in their usual places. He is standing on a terrace surrounded by a stone balustrade. Ahead of him the shrubbery is strewn with tiny electric lights that mimic the sky. Steps go down to a lawn, where someone is talking. It's a monologue, so whoever it is, he's talking into a phone.

"Yeah. No. No, of course I'm not. Fruit juice. Carmen, listen . . . Yeah, okay, but if you wanted that sort of information, you should have wangled an invite for that airhead, what's-her-name, does the gossip column. Okay, *society* column, pardon me. Yep, he's here. No, with his wife. Yep, he's here too. I don't know, Carmen, I'm a *sports*writer. Yeah, yeah. Okay, I'll ask. Well, he looks like a fish out of water, the poor bastard. And I know how he feels. No, of course I won't. Trust me. Well, hey, thanks a bunch."

"Hi, Paul."

Faustino jumps like a startled deer. Turning, he sees a black man in a pale linen suit. The guy is standing on the bottom step down from the patio, and that, along with the height advantage he has anyway, makes him look like a giant. Which, in Faustino's eyes, he is.

"Otello?"

"Yeah. Otherwise known as 'poor bastard' and 'fish out of water.'"

"Hey, I'm sorry. I—"

Otello lets out a reassuring laugh. "S'okay, Paul. You're wrong about me being poor and my parents not being married, but the fish out of water thing was about right. How you doing?"

He comes down the last step and puts out his hand. Faustino, who is trying to manage a large gin and tonic and a cigarette as well as his cell phone, is forced to do some clumsy juggling before he can take it.

"I was talking to my boss," he says, as if that were the right sort of answer.

"She's not here?"

"Lord, no. The editor of the country's leading independent newspaper seen schmoozing with members of the government? That wouldn't do at all. So I'm supposed to be her eyes and ears tonight. Check out who's patting whose political ass. Who's slipping off to a back room for a chat with someone he's not supposed to talk to, that kind of thing. Also, and most importantly, who Desmerelda Brabanta is with and what she's wearing."

"Right," Otello says. "She's expected, is she?"

"She's already here, apparently, although no one's seen her yet. But at least you're not the only big attraction tonight, my friend."

"Thank God for that."

"Amen."

A slightly awkward pause.

Then Otello says, "Listen, Paul, uh, thanks for the good things you've written about me recently."

"Not at all. I owed you. Diego Mendosa gives me the exclusive; I'm nice to you in the paper. It's called professional integrity. Otherwise known as 'You scratch my back, I scratch yours.'"

Otello smiles. "Yeah, if you say so. But it makes a change from all the manure the northern papers are dumping on me."

"I'm surprised you bother to read them."

Otello shrugs. "Diego tells me I shouldn't, but you know . . . You see the picture last week of my Rialto shirt with the number twenty-three and JUDAS on the back?"

"Yeah. Very witty, I thought. Listen, uh … I'm not trying to sneak another interview here, but do you mind my asking if all this stuff is getting to you? I mean, you must have been expecting it, but does it depress you? You've been keeping a pretty low profile since that brawl they called a press conference."

"I'm fine," Otello says. "I come from a long line of people used to putting up with a lot worse. I'm not talking to the media because I'll do my answering on the field. Meanwhile, I'm just resting up and settling in."

Faustino nods, recognizing the touch of steel in the other man's voice. He flicks his cigarette away into the darkness of Nestor Brabanta's garden. "I guess we should return to the cream of society," he says. "I've got some spying to do."

Just as they reach the doors, the sound inside the room dips slightly, then increases, like trees surprised by a gust of wind.

"Aha," Faustino murmurs, "I think La Brabanta may have made her entrance."

Peering into the throng, Otello catches only a glimpse of her as she makes her way through admirers toward her father. He sees white and gold.

◆　◆　◆

Nestor Brabanta takes both his daughter's hands in his own while she kisses him. There is a light scattering of sentimental applause from the onlookers. The expression on Brabanta's face is one of such simple adoration that he looks, for a second, foolish.

Desmerelda kisses a few of the guests closest by, then her father says, "Darling, I don't think you've met Diego Mendosa, Otello's agent."

"Hi."

"Delighted to meet you, señorita."

They shake hands. His fingers are long and slender, but strong. She has met a great many agents, and he doesn't look like one. He looks like someone who should *have* an agent. He resembles that American actor, Phoenix somebody, is it? He has a smile that doesn't seem to expect one in return. And calm, serious eyes.

Brabanta says, mock-sadly, "I am rather afraid that Diego might be immune to your charms, Desmerelda."

She thinks, *Oh, is he gay?*

"Diego is not impressed by celebrity. He once told me that it would make no difference to him if I were the father of an alligator."

She pouts ironically. "Are you in the habit of doing business with the fathers of alligators, Señor Mendosa?"

"Of course. But your father is being slightly mischievous, I think. I suspect he was a little disappointed that I didn't talk about you when we first met. And no one could blame him for that. I thought you were extremely

63

good in that Channel Nine interview two nights ago, by the way."

She is, he thinks, even more beautiful in the flesh than on TV. Smaller, of course, but then everybody is. Presumably the hair — all carefully tumbled swirls the color of honey — and the light skin are inherited from her American mother. The eyes are extraordinary, mesmeric; he doubts that there is a word in any language for their color. She's wearing a white broderie jacket and trousers cut like jeans but made of black silk. Not a scrap of jewelry, which in the present company is almost as shocking as nudity.

"Thank you," she says. "I'm afraid I snapped at the guy once or twice."

"I think we could maybe drop the alligator references now, señorita," Diego says, straight-faced.

She laughs. It's an honest and unrehearsed laugh, the kind you might hear on the street in a rough part of town. Then she glances at her father; it seems she expects him to disapprove. Which is interesting, and Diego makes a mental note of it. But Nestor Brabanta's attention has been claimed by a plump woman in an unsuitable turquoise dress, so Desmerelda says, "And where is your client, our guest of honor?"

"Over by the garden doors," Diego tells her, not needing to look. "I think he may have been having a quiet word with Paul Faustino, of *La Nación*. Do you know him?"

She shakes her head.

"Please. Come. I'll introduce you to them both."

◆ ◆ ◆

Faustino sees their approach. "Here we go," he murmurs.

Diego performs the introductions. There is the kind of small talk you would expect. After a while Faustino gets the feeling that he is unwanted, so he slips out of their orbit and sets off on an eavesdropping tour of the room.

Desmerelda, like her father, is interested in soccer and well informed. She asks Otello serious questions about his exploits on the field. About the social implications of his move to the South. She is serious, not flirtatious or frivolous.

Otello is hesitant and awkward when he responds to her. Although he is angry with himself for doing so, he speaks the glib understatements that soccer players are supposed to speak.

This is because the poor fool has fallen in love. Cupid has got him, not with the usual sniper's arrow but with a cruise missile, a smart weapon locked on to the victim's soul, where it explodes. There is collateral damage far from the point of impact. To the eyes, which want to focus on Desmerelda's but skitter all over the place; to the hands, which wander into his pockets and then out again and clasp each other behind his back; to his knees, which have gone slack. Also, of course, to the tongue. If he'd incurred this amount of damage on the field, he'd have been stretchered off. He half wishes he could be. He needs treatment. So he is almost relieved, as well as dismayed, when her father comes to retrieve her.

Smiling with his mouth but not his eyes, Brabanta says,

"Desmerelda, my darling, you must not monopolize our star guest. Besides, I'd like you to come into the dining room and inspect the buffet before I ask the guests to go through. You have a much better eye for detail than I do."

"Of course, Papa. Excuse me, Otello. Duty calls."

He doesn't know what to say, so he ducks his head in a miniature bow. And gazes after her as she threads her way through the room with her father's protective arm across her back. When at last he looks away, he meets Diego's solemn gaze.

"What?"

"She's no slouch," Diego says. "But then neither are you, Capitano."

After the wandering balancing act of eating light food from heavy plates, Otello finds himself penned in at the end of a sofa by an earnest young man who wants to explain the government's policy toward the social problems in the North. He believes in Free Market Forces and Wealth Creation, which he pronounces with capital letters. Because the young man clearly knows very little about the North and Otello doesn't know the first thing about economics, the conversation is going nowhere. In addition, Otello is feverishly pre-occupied with Desmerelda Brabanta. So he is unable to say anything and sits there nodding like a bull bothered by flies. Then he feels something settle along his back and hears a voice from above and behind him.

"Antonio, for the love of God, stop being so boring."

Otello turns his head. She has perched on the arm of the sofa. The thing that is in soft contact with his back is her thigh.

"Antonio," she says, "is one of my father's disciples. One day he will be minister of economic affairs. Won't you, Antonio? But unfortunately he knows nothing about the important things in life, such as music or soccer."

She stands and then comes around to face them both. "Shove off, Antonio. I need to get this guy's opinion of Rialto's chances in the Copa Libertadores."

Antonio gets to his feet, wearing a smile that is meant to look good-natured, and sidles off.

Otello and Desmerelda are left islanded on the sofa.

He says, "We will lose to River Plata of Argentina in the semifinal."

"Ah. So you are clairvoyant, as well as everything else?"

"No. But Rialto — we — are the fourth, maybe third, best club in South America. So we deserve to reach the semis. But who knows?"

"Yeah, who knows. Let's hope you get more than you deserve."

Otello senses that she means something else by this, although he cannot, or dares not, work out what it is. But he manages to hold her gaze, which is good. In the end she is the one who looks away, taking a sip from her glass.

"You seem a bit edgy," she says. "Is it because you're worried I'm going to ask if you like my music?"

Since the acrimonious breakup of Kaleidoscope, Desmerelda has made two solo albums of lightweight pop and disinfected hip-hop that no self-respecting person over the age of sixteen would be caught dead listening to. And which millions of pubescent girls listen to constantly. Knowing that sooner or later he would be bound to meet her, Otello had downloaded a few tracks onto his iPod and played them when he was alone. The only thing he can think to say about them is that they are perfect, for what they are. Which is true but not what he needs to say to her. But he is saved from saying anything, because once again Nestor Brabanta comes to his unwelcome rescue.

The senator materializes behind the sofa and stoops to murmur in Desmerelda's ear. She nods seriously, her face expressionless. But when she turns to Otello, she flares her eyes at him and silently mouths a curse.

"You'll have to excuse me. Seems there's been a bit of a catfight among the staff. One of the girls is in tears. Papa wants me to go and restore order. Apparently I'm good at that sort of thing."

She reaches across him to put her glass down on a low table. He inhales her scent as deeply as he can.

"Desmerelda," Brabanta says testily.

Otello turns and looks up at him. The senator doesn't meet his eye; he stands with his hand out toward his daughter. She takes it and he leads her away.

When she returns, Otello has gone. And so has her drink. She looks around the room, trying not to make it obvious.

The crowd has thinned a bit, but nevertheless she cannot see him. Then Diego Mendosa catches her eye and with a tiny gesture of his head points her toward the terrace.

There are several people out there, smoking, talking loudly, laughing, but Otello is alone at the far end. He has his back to her and is gazing at the stars. Her wineglass, now full again, is standing on the balustrade next to his hand.

"It's crap," she says when she is close to him.

He turns. "What is?"

"My music. But it's very high-quality crap. That's what you were going to say, isn't it? Or were you going to lie to me?" She picks the glass up and leans her back against the balustrade.

"Uh, I was going to lie to you."

"Well, don't. You don't have to. I haven't got any illusions about what I do. Any of it."

She drinks. He can think of nothing to say. These Brabantas disturb and baffle him.

"So tell me," she says now, "what are your plans? What do soccer superstars do between seasons? Apart from win the Copa América, of course."

"Well, training starts in a week, so I'm going to grab a vacation. Five days of doing nothing, just chilling out."

"Sounds good. And where are you doing all this nothing?"

He glances away from her, and she reads the confusion in his face.

"Oh, right. Top-secret location. Yeah, I suppose it would be. You don't have to tell me. You *shouldn't* tell me. It's a well-known fact that I'm a notorious gossip."

"We're going to the Bay Islands. Cypress, to be exact."

Well, she thinks, *he trusts me, then.* She also thinks, *We?* The word is huge in her head, but she pushes it aside. For the moment.

What she says is, "Cypress? Oh, fantastic. It's beautiful. Really. We shot the beach scenes for the 'Take Me Up' video there. You ever see that? Go on, you can lie if you like."

"Sure I saw it. The one with all the planes in it?"

"No. That was a different one. You're terrible at this, aren't you?"

"Looks like it."

"It does. I bet you'll be staying at the Blue Horizon. Yeah? That's a great place. It's where I stayed when we were filming. You'll love it. I can just imagine you there."

She *is* imagining him there.

Otello, however, is not paying attention. She turns her head and sees Diego Mendosa standing in the doorway giving Otello a look which means *Time to come back in here and say good-bye to Important People, Guest of Honor.* She realizes that she and Otello are now alone on the terrace.

"I think you need to go," she says.

"Yeah, I guess so."

The fact that they have made no further arrangements with each other looms between them.

He says, "Look, I—"

"No, let's not do the cell-phone-number stuff. It won't be necessary."

Why not? he thinks. *Why the hell not?*

"It's been great talking to you," he manages to say, and holds out his hand.

She ignores the hand and stands on tiptoe to kiss him on both cheeks. Then she kisses him full on the mouth. It is so wonderful that it seems to last about a year, a year in which the rest of the world goes missing.

When the clocks go back to normal and the world returns, she says, "Who is 'we'?"

She knows the question is so crude that she might as well have stripped her clothes off and stood naked in front of him.

"What?"

"You said, '*We're* going to Cypress.' I was wondering who 'we' is."

"Ah, right. 'We' is me and Diego and Michael."

"Michael?"

"Michael Cass. He's, well, he's my . . . minder."

"Minder? As in bodyguard?"

"I guess. He's good at throwing paparazzi into the sea."

She nods approvingly. "That is a good skill to have."

Later, Desmerelda stands with her father at the front of the house while their guests wait for their cars to be brought around. As Brabanta is bidding farewell to a clutch of politicians, Diego comes down the steps and touches her lightly on the arm. She turns, and he thanks her for the hospitality. Instead of shaking the hand she offers him, he lifts it to his mouth and kisses it.

"There is no one," he murmurs.

"Excuse me?"

"Otello has no girlfriend, no secret wife, no mistress, no boyfriend."

For a moment or two, caught off-guard, she can only stare at him. Then she gathers herself. "Ah. That's a shame, don't you think?"

His smile is no more than a flicker. "Not necessarily," he says.

Diego eases his apartment door shut and slips off his shoes before padding along to the bedroom. His consideration is unneeded, as it turns out; Emilia is awake, waiting for him. He is glad. He is a little excited and needs to talk. The curtains are not closed, and beyond the glass the night seems upside down. The sky is a blank, its darkness tinged with dirty orange like a stained concrete floor. Below it, the constellation of city lights glitters and shifts.

"Yes," Diego says, gazing out. "I'd say that it went very well, Emilia. Very well indeed."

He unknots his bow tie and tosses it on the floor. He undoes the top button of his white shirt and turns to her.

He takes his jacket off and holds it in front of him by its shoulders.

"Otello is the bull, you see? And I play him like a matador."

He shakes the jacket, rippling it.

"The big black bull is very powerful, of course. But very stupid and dreadfully nearsighted. He sees only the cape, and when he charges it, I execute an elegant *valenca*."

He holds the jacket out from the left side of his body, then sweeps it backward, twirling on tiptoe, his back straight.

"The bull's horns pass within inches but do not touch me. The stink of him is strong in my nostrils. He lumbers past, baffled by the disappearance of his enemy. He turns back, grunting and drooling. Now I go down on one knee, as if in submission, holding the cape out with one hand, so. He charges again and . . ."

Diego, in a slow elegant gesture like a stage courtier's, wafts the jacket behind him.

"He misses me again. And so we do this dance of death and he never really sees who his partner is. It would be sad if it weren't so beautiful. And tonight, Emilia, no less a person than Desmerelda Brabanta handed me the cape."

He reads a question in her eyes.

"No, I'm not drunk, my love. Absolutely not. I sipped one glass of champagne all evening. I was, after all, on duty. Keeping a sharp eye on my client's interests. Especially his new one."

1.8

MICHAEL CASS TRUDGES across the swept white sand of the private beach to where Otello lies on a lounger. Cass is wearing a wide-brimmed straw hat, sunglasses, and a nine-millimeter automatic pistol in a shoulder holster, incongruous under the unbuttoned Hawaiian shirt. Otello looks up when his bodyguard's big shadow falls across him.

"Your tan's coming along nicely," Cass says, and to please him, Otello chuckles. Cass, whose grandparents were German or maybe Swiss, is blond and liberally coated with sunblock, despite which his fuzzy knees are blushed like peaches.

"What's hap'nin'?"

"Nothing much," Cass says. He perches on the lounger alongside Otello's and squints at the horizon. "I was just talking to the old guy does the gardens, you know? He says there's a storm brewing."

The sky is cloudless, a vast blue umbrella with the sun burning a hole in its center.

"No way," Otello says.

"That's what I said. And he says, 'See that little old island over there? When the water runs kinda milky behind it, there's a storm coming. Any boats out when that happens, they come back real quick.'"

Otello lifts his head. The nameless island is a greenish-gray stain at the foot of the sky. On their first day at the Blue Horizon, he'd asked the hotel manager about it, wondering if it was possible to go out there. The manager had looked at him a little strangely and said, "Why?" And yes, there is now a faint stream of whiteness beyond it, like low-lying smoke.

"What's Diego up to?"

Cass shrugs. "I dunno. He's out on his balcony, doing stuff on his laptop."

"Working," Otello says.

"Or cruising porn sites."

"Hey."

"Only kidding."

Now Otello turns onto his side, supporting himself on his elbow. He studies Michael's profile. "Listen, are you guys okay? I know Diego was against you coming down South with me, but I thought that was all sorted out. You don't still have issues, do you?"

Cass puts his forearms on his knees and stares at the sand between his feet. "Nah, not really. We're cool."

"Good. 'Cause I need him. Honest agents aren't that easy to come by, you know? You don't have to like him, Michael, but you do have to work with him."

"No problem," Michael says, keeping his eyes down. "He's okay."

"Yeah. He's okay. Like, the hustling he did, getting this together. Keeping the lid on where we were going. Persuading the hotel to be 'closed for refurbishment.' Arranging the security."

"Yep. Guess so."

"Which means," Otello says, "you've got it nice and easy, right? Three days in this tropical paradise so far and no reporters disguised as waiters, no guys hanging out of trees with cameras, none of that stuff. Remember that time back home when we went out to Santa Louisa, how on the first morning we got to the beach and there were, what, five boats full of photographers, and you had to borrow an outboard and have, like, a small naval battle to get rid of them?"

Michael Cass smiles at the memory. "Yeah, I kind of enjoyed that."

After a while he says, "Listen, I'm going back up there to sit in the shade. You want me to fetch you anything while I'm on my feet?"

An hour later, the thatch on the sun shelters begins to rustle and softly hiss. Otello sits up and sees that the horizon now looks slightly pixillated, like an over-enlarged photograph.

A couple of guys from the hotel appear and begin gathering up the loungers.

"Big wind comin', Señor Otello," one of them says. "Maybe you wanna go up on the terrace. Soon the sand gonna whip, take the skin off you."

By the time Otello has been up to his suite, showered and dressed, and gone down to the bar, Cypress Island has undergone a change. The sea is moving fast and lumpish past the swirling beach, and the palms are swinging their ragged heads. The sun flickers behind veils of racing cloud.

Sitting just inside the half-closed doors of the terrace, Otello and Michael Cass turn their heads when Diego speaks from behind them.

"I logged on to the coast guard website. Checked out the weather pattern. This is the edge of a hurricane on its way to beat the Caribbean up. It looks like a damn great tadpole on the map, and this is just the tickle of its tail."

"Fairly decent sort of a tickle," Cass observes as a plastic beer crate tumbles through a flower bed.

"Yep," Diego says. "At a guess, I'd say that tonight's beach barbecue is a nonstarter." He leans forward, a hand on the back of each chair. "How about a game of cards? Black Maria, say a dollar a point? Okay, okay. Fifty cents a point. Jeez, you tight-fisted northerners. Beer?"

Otello is almost fifty dollars up, Michael about twenty, and Diego is therefore well down. It interests Otello that someone so cautious about everything else is inclined to bet unwisely on a hand of cards. It is reassuring, in a way.

The lamps have come on, and Michael is dealing when Diego says, "My God, did you ever see a sunset that color?"

Beyond the glass the sky is a livid green behind sallow streamers of cloud. It is so unlikely, it might be painted scenery for the last act of a melodrama. Front of stage, the beach is dissolving into sand devils, miniature whirlwinds that set off in pursuit of the gray running sea.

A waiter enters. "Happens this time of year," he says. "She'll blow over real quick. Two, three hours, maybe. Tomorrow you won't believe it happened. All will be calm again." He smiles. "It refreshes the sea."

A minute or two later, the card players are again distracted when their waiter and the barman and the assistant manager go to the windows and argumentatively share a pair of binoculars. Otello gets up and wanders over to them.

"What's the excitement?"

"A boat," the assistant manager says. "Not the ferry. The ferry don't put out in this weather. Got to be some crazy *americano*. They don't think anything got the right to stop them doing what they wanna do."

The barman has the binoculars now. "There she is," he says. "Wow, look at her buck. Jus' north of the island. Man, I bet they losin' their lunch."

"Mind if I look?" Otello asks, and the barman passes him

the binoculars. Otello fiddles with the focus and finds the boat, a ghostly wedge that comes and goes between walls of water. A launch of some sort. The sort that rich people sit on to drink cocktails.

"Where's it heading?"

The assistant manager says, "Well, if it's got any sense, it'll come here and wait out the weather." Struck by a thought, he looks at Otello. "You expecting someone, señor?"

"No."

"Good. Like I thought, some dumb gringo. What time would you like dinner?"

The star, the agent, and the bodyguard are at a table in the softly lit restaurant when a subdued clamor occurs in the lobby. Cass, who is facing that way, looks up and freezes with a forkful of steak en route to his open mouth.

Desmerelda Brabanta stands in the doorway. Her hands are deep in the pockets of a yellow waterproof jacket that is far too big for her and conceals whatever other clothes she is wearing, if any. Her long legs are bare and wet, and the canvas sneakers on her feet are soaked a dark shade of blue. Her saturated hair is golden serpents; her eyes are brighter than anything else in the room. She looks like something timeless that the sea has treasured while waiting for the human who deserves her. At her back, several members of the hotel staff cluster, smiling and uncertain like film extras who have not been told what to do.

Otello and Cass get to their feet. Diego lays his knife and fork neatly parallel on his plate and remains sitting. He has seen Desmerelda, but now his eyes are fixed upon the remains of the crayfish he was eating, almost as though they might reveal the reason for this spectacular intrusion. But he is smiling.

Desmerelda is the one who breaks the silence.

"Lord," she says, speaking exclusively to Otello, "that was a rough ride. I need to get out of these wet clothes. Do you think you might have something that would fit me?"

1.9

SHORTLY BEFORE ELEVEN o'clock, the phone on Nestor Brabanta's bedside table rings. He has already taken his sleeping tablets, but because calls that come through to his private number at this time of night are unusual, he answers it.

The voice in his ear is coarse and slightly muffled; he thinks he detects a northern accent. At first he assumes it is a long-distance call on a poor connection.

VOICE: Are your doors locked?

BRABANTA: I beg your pardon?

VOICE: You are being robbed, Senator.

BRABANTA: Who is this?

VOICE: Someone who keeps a closer eye on your belongings than you do, Senator. As I say, you are being robbed as we speak. Your heart is being broken, and you do not know it.

BRABANTA: Who the hell is this? How did you get
    this number? What are you talking about?
VOICE: One of your horses has been stolen, Senator.
    Your most valuable horse. Your beautiful golden
    filly. And right now she is with a big black brute
    of a stallion.
BRABANTA: You are a lunatic. I'm hanging up now.
VOICE: Do you know where your daughter is, Señor
    Brabanta?
    [BRABANTA *sits up and swings his legs over the side
    of the bed. His drug-induced sleepiness is dispelled
    by something that feels like a shower of ice. He has
    sometimes imagined, dreaded, a call like this. The
    kidnap call.*]
BRABANTA: Who is this? What do you want?

The line has gone dead.

Brabanta presses the last-call redial buttons, but, as he
expected, a robotic voice tells him that the caller withheld
his number. He dials Desmerelda's apartment and gets the
answering machine, as usual. He waits, dry-mouthed and
impatient, for the beep.

"Darling? Are you there? Pick up the phone. Desmerelda, please pick up the phone. Okay, listen, darling — call
me back the instant you hear this. I'm going to try your
cell."

He cannot remember the number and curses himself.

82

He goes to where his dressing gown is draped over a chair and finds his own phone in the pocket. He scrolls down the list of names and when DES appears on the display, stabs CALL.

"Hi. I can't take your call at the moment, but—"

Brabanta swears and cuts her message off. Five seconds later, he tries again and waits.

"Desmerelda. It's Papa. Call me back now. Right now. I don't care what time it is. This is serious."

He drops the phone onto the bed and clasps his hands together because they are shaking. It occurs to him that he is one of the best-connected men in the city, and he can't think whom he can talk to. After a while he takes up the phone again and calls Desmerelda's so-called personal assistant. He listens to the ringtone for what seems an eternity, and then she answers.

"Hello?"

"Ramona, this is Nestor Brabanta."

"Señor. Hello. Just a second, I . . ."

There is a little patch of silence; she has put her hand over the mouthpiece. Then he hears her clear her throat.

"Señor, how can I—"

"Ramona, do you know where my daughter is?"

"Um . . . no, I'm afraid I don't."

"Why not? Dammit, girl, aren't you supposed to know? Isn't that what you're paid for?"

"Well, I . . . Señor, is there a problem?"

Brabanta's bedside phone rings.

He says to Ramona, "I'll call you back."

BRABANTA: Desmerelda?

VOICE: I wouldn't bother waiting up if I were you, Senator. I don't think she'll be calling you back tonight. I imagine that Daddy is the last thing on her mind right now.

BRABANTA: Listen, whoever you are. If you do anything . . . if any harm comes to my daughter, I'll find you and kill you. I promise you that. [*A pause. He hears what might be wind or surf, or perhaps just electronic slush.*] How much do you want?

VOICE: Oh, no. No, no, Senator. Money can't get back what you've lost. You think you can put a price on your reputation? Your honor? Your family name?

BRABANTA: What the hell are you talking about? Listen, if this is a hoax or —

VOICE: I just want to put you in the picture.

BRABANTA: What picture?

VOICE: *King Kong.*

BRABANTA: What?

VOICE: *King Kong.* The movie. You've seen it? Of course you have. And I know the bit you remember best. It's where that dirty great gorilla picks up the half-naked blonde in his paw. Right?

BRABANTA: What is this crap? Tell me where my daughter is, damn you!

VOICE: I just did. But you're not listening. I'm wasting my time. Good night, Senator.

BRABANTA: Wait! Okay. Please. I'm listening.

VOICE: That's better. Where was I? Oh, yes. The
pale vulnerable girl in that big black fist. What
did you think, Senator, when you saw that? What
do men like you and I think when we see that?

BRABANTA: I don't know.

VOICE: Yes, you do. We imagine our wives in that
situation. Or our daughters. Wriggling and squeal-
ing. Hmm? Don't we?

BRABANTA [*hoarsely*]: Who are you?

VOICE: Mind you, that King Kong is a real superstar.
I read somewhere that he cost a cool fifty million.
And right now your daughter must be thinking
he was worth every cent. Probably thinks it's the
best present her daddy ever bought her.
[*Click and hum.*]

Brabanta sits holding the phone. After a while it starts
to feel slimy, probably because his hand is sweaty. He
drops it. Something like a knuckly claw is closing around
his heart, and for a terrible moment he loses control of his
breathing. He tells himself that there is no damn way he's
going to have a coronary until this thing is sorted out, so he
puts on his dressing gown and makes his way downstairs
to his study, clutching the banister all the way. He goes to
his desk and looks up Diego Mendosa's number. He calls

85

it, waits for the answering message to end, and says, "This is Nestor. Senator Brabanta. I need to know where Otello is. Call me."

Diego is standing in the deep shadow of the palms that mark the boundary of the hotel's private beach. The trees are calmer now; their thick leaves rub together as quietly as fingers. He waits for his phone to bleep and then checks the number that has just tried to call him. Smiling, he picks up his shoes and walks back along the sand, just out of reach of the luminous, turbulent surf.

Desmerelda gets up to use the bathroom. Returning, she realizes that the storm has passed. The curtains move in time with the sea's slow breathing. She goes to the window. All is darkness apart from a tattered net of stars and the dim lacework where the waves break onto the beach. She catches a brief scent of something rank — seaweed, perhaps — and turns away.

Otello is sleeping, facedown, on the bed. She feels that same little stoppage of breath that took hold of her the first time she saw him. *Black* is a useless word for him. Even in this scarcely lit room, his skin gathers light and transforms it. His cheekbone is shaped by a faint line of indigo. The lamplight on the muscles of his back is both gold and green. The paleness of the upturned palm of his left hand is like a mistake; otherwise his beauty is simply ridiculous. It makes her shudder slightly, and she wraps her arms around herself.

She is used to getting what she wants, but this is different. She is not in control of this.

Fear is part — a large part — of the thrill of it. As if she has stepped through a door to find the sky at a new angle and the colors of familiar things different. As if she no longer knows the name of anything. For the first time in her life she wishes she weren't famous. But she is. They are. Privacy, let alone secrecy, will not be an option. So.

She picks up the sheet from the floor and drapes it around herself like a cape, then kneels on the bed. The movement brings Otello up through the surface of his sleep. He rolls onto his back and opens his eyes, and as he does so, Desmerelda leans down to him, lifting then releasing the sheet so that it billows, then falls, enclosing them completely. Her face hovers just above his; her eyes have tiny flickers of light in their depths.

"Hey," he says.

"Hey, you."

He runs his hand up the outside of her arm.

"Listen," she says. "There's something I want you to do."

"Mmm. And what might that be, Señorita Brabanta?"

"I want you to marry me," she says.

Act Two

2.1

UMBERTO DA VENECIA (popularly known as the Duke)
is very glad that the private committee room is well
soundproofed, because Nestor Brabanta shows no sign
of calming down. He won't sit down, either; he comes
back to the table only to bang his fist on it. As chairman of
the Rialto board of directors, the Duke has presided over
some pretty fiery meetings; he deserves his reputation for
soothing diplomacy. But he is beginning to think that the
only thing he can do is call the city zoo and get them to
send someone over with a tranquilizer gun and the kind of
dart that floors a rhino. The other two men present, Ariel
Goldmann and Pedro dos Passos, sit staring at their
clasped hands like seasick ferry passengers. The mild-
mannered Goldmann, apparently appalled by Brabanta's
language, has a face like vanilla pudding. Even so, it is he
who tries to interrupt.

"Nestor. Nestor, *please*. Drugs? Witchcraft? This is craziness."

"You think so? What, you think it's a *myth*, that stuff? Listen, I've been up North. I've *seen* what those damned Africans are into. I've seen normal people turned into animals, Ariel. So don't shake your head like that! Not unless you've got a better explanation."

"Look, Otello is a black man from the North, yes, but he's not, you know, he's not into that. He's, well, charming and—"

The Duke thinks, *Oh, God, Ariel.*

And sure enough Brabanta flares like oil lobbed onto a fire.

"Ah! *Charming.* You want to think about that word, Ariel? You want to ask yourself exactly what kind of *charms* persuade a girl who has everything, *everything*, to marry this, this *nigger*, two weeks after meeting him? You ever wonder why black magic is called *black* magic?"

Pedro dos Passos coughs lightly. "Actually—" he begins, but gets no further because Brabanta comes to the table and puts both hands on it and leans across it; his eyes are hot and moist, and his voice is congested. The Duke wonders if the man might be on the verge of a seizure.

"My daughter is a *star*. That's not sentimentality; it's a *fact*. She's worth millions in her own right. You all know that. And she's my only child. So she has men hitting on her all the time, okay? Nice men. White men. Rich men. Men from the best families. Maybe she sleeps with some of them—I don't know. I don't ask. But marriage is an issue we talk about, me and her. Because I understand the pressure she's under. And you know what she always says? She says she doesn't believe in marriage. Which, yes, has something to do with me and her mother. I accept that. I do accept that. Then all of a sudden she's married to a black she hardly even *knows*? And you think this is *natural*? You think something as, as . . . *gross* as that can be explained in normal terms?"

At last he sinks into a chair. He lowers his head onto his hand and surreptitiously wipes an eye with a finger. The Duke has never before seen a senator shed a tear, so he waits a couple of seconds.

"Nestor, you called this meeting. So I assume there is something you want us to do."

Without looking up, Brabanta says, "For a start, I want this so-called marriage annulled."

The Duke, who is, among other things, Brabanta's legal adviser, sighs. "As you asked me to, I've looked into that. I'm afraid that, despite its hastiness, the, er, ceremony was perfectly legitimate. Unless, of course, Desmerelda was acting under duress. Or indeed drugged or brainwashed or some such thing."

"She was! She *must* have been!"

"Unfortunately there is no proof of that. Of course, if *she* were to testify that she was . . . But that seems extremely unlikely."

Brabanta thrusts his fists forward and sits up straight.

"In that case, I want us to sell the black son of a bitch."

Goldmann and dos Passos react as though both their heads have been tugged by the same length of string. Goldmann opens his mouth, but the Duke lifts a hand to silence him.

"Nestor, my old friend, you know you cannot ask for that. Imagine—"

"No, *you* imagine. Imagine what it would be like if you had to watch that bastard play for your club, knowing that after the game he was going to go home and clamber into bed with *your* daughter. Eh? Could you do that? Could you bear that?"

The Duke, whose two daughters are plump, plain, and inoffensively married, pretends to give Brabanta's question serious consideration. "I understand your pain, Nestor. Your outrage. We all do."

Dos Passos and Goldmann nod, solemnly and synchronized.

"But let's be realistic. We could never persuade the board to sell Otello. Apart from anything else, there would be huge legal and financial problems. And think of the fallout. Think of the effect upon the club. Think about the ridicule in the media. Rialto is bigger than any one of us. It is bigger than *all* of us. Those are not my words. You yourself said that, three months ago, in this very room."

Brabanta turns his head toward the Duke. He has the look of a fatally wounded bull preparing for a last lunge at the matador.

"Then I'll resign from the board. I'll dump my shares on the market."

The Duke sits back in his chair. He takes his spectacles off and lays them on the table. He gazes at them for a moment or two. Eventually he says, "Yes, you could do that. To spread the pain around. But in the end, who would be hurt the most? I can tell you who would *not* be hurt, and that's Otello. He's got a contract tighter than a squid's rectum. You yourself made sure of that."

Half an hour later, Ariel Goldmann and Nestor Brabanta descend together in the elevator.

Goldmann feels he should put his arm around the other man's shoulders but somehow cannot bring himself to do so.

"Nestor, please. Try to allow this rage, this bitterness, to pass. Give it some time. The Duke is right—it's hurting you more than anyone else. And, you know, the victim who smiles takes something back from the thief."

"Christ, Ariel." Brabanta spits the words. "I can't stand it when you come on like a goddamn hippie rabbi."

Goldmann flinches visibly.

The elevator doors open onto the VIP parking garage, underground. Brabanta doesn't get out. Instead, he presses his hand on the button that holds the doors apart. Leans on it, looking sick. "Sorry, Ariel. I shouldn't have . . ."

Goldmann at last manages to lay his hand on his colleague's arm. "It's okay. Forget it."

Brabanta lifts his head. "Tell me this, though," he says. "How would you feel if one day *your* little princess presented you with a piccaninny as your first grandchild?"

2.2

I'T'S RIALTO'S THIRD home game of the season. Faustino, in his seat at the front of the press section, looks up and over to his right, scanning the faces in the directors' box. Only five minutes before the teams will emerge from the tunnel, and still no sign of Nestor Brabanta. It looks as if once again the senator will not be watching his son-in-law play. Interesting. Maybe there *is* something in the rumors. . . . *She* is there, though, leaning across the vacant seat next to hers to listen to what the Duke is saying. The PA system is blasting out one of her so-called songs that manages to be both frantic and bland at the same time. The San Lorenzo supporters—and a good many home supporters, too—are doing their best to drown it out.

Faustino adjusts the items on the ledge in front of him: his notebook, the game program, the press briefings. His comment column will not appear until Monday; around him, the hacks who have to file reports for the evening editions fiddle with cell phones plugged into their laptops. Because Faustino does not have these gadgets, the hacks feel slightly superior to him. For the very same reason, Faustino feels superior to them.

The man to his left, Mateo Campos of *El Sol,* leans nearer. "Whatcha think, Faustino? Is Dezi's piece of ass gonna start doing the business on the field as well as off?"

Dear God, Faustino thinks, *the man actually speaks the way he writes.*

In Faustino's considered opinion, *El Sol* is the most putrid of sores on the diseased body of the South American press. A filthy rag you might use only to clean up after a dog with a bowel complaint. Campos is its head sportswriter. According to his byline, he is *The Man Who Speaks Your Mind.* In his darker moments, Faustino fears this might be true.

"I presume you mean, do I think Otello will play well? The answer is yes. But I don't suppose anything that actually happens on the field will have any influence on what *you* choose to write."

Campos makes a blubbery hiss with his lips, meant to express contempt. Faustino notices that it leaves little prismatic spangles of spit on the screen of Campos's laptop.

The fact is that, in his first five games for Rialto, Otello has scored only once—a deflected volley from a poor defensive clearance. Nor did he score in a bad-tempered friendly international against Colombia. After his first game for his new club, the general view of his performance was summed up in the headline in *El Correo*: OTELLO FAILS TO IMPRESS. Faustino could not argue with that. But his own view was that Rialto would have to learn how to play with Otello, rather than the other way around. In his column, Faustino had argued that Otello was simply quicker at reading the game than his teammates, and once they had learned how to give their new striker the kind of service he needed, Rialto might well be unbeatable. And, so far, his fellow commentators had tended to agree with him. Faustino had been gratified when the highly respected Milton Acuña, appearing on *Sportsview,* had said that Rialto "needed to raise their game to Otello's standard."

But then *El Sol* had broken ranks. The smutty rag had been obsessed, predictably, with the "sensational" marriage of Desmerelda Brabanta and Otello. As had all the "celebrity" trash mags. The snatched photos of the couple, the "interviews" with their "close friends," the "astrological analyses" of their compatibility, the snide innuendos about her father's supposed "shock" and "fury": all these — and worse — were no more than you'd expect. The subtext of these stories was, of course, that the *americana* daughter of a political millionaire had bedded and married a dumb black soccer player and thus turned the world on its head and doesn't it make you sick?

After a month the distinction between *El Sol*'s so-called news pages and the sports pages had become blurred.

You didn't have to be an expert in linguistics to spot the real meaning of the words. Mateo Campos kicked off with the headline DIM OUTLOOK FOR RIALTO? followed by ANOTHER DARK AFTERNOON FOR RIALTO and OTELLO: FIFTY MILLION POURED INTO A BLACK HOLE? The previous Sunday, *El Sol*'s lurid weekend supplement had a piece (by Campos) dominated by a grainy paparazzi shot of a topless Desmerelda taken on a beach two years back. The caption read: IS THIS WHY OTELLO CAN'T KEEP HIS EYE ON THE BALL? (Grudgingly, Faustino has to admire the use of the protective question mark in these headlines. And if he were honest with himself—which he is, sometimes—he would have to admit that his own thoughts have occasionally strayed into the same dingy and juicy territory. He had, after all, been there at the very moment when the famous couple met. He had seen the hero's knees go weak and the tiny sunrises in her eyes. He had even been tempted to write it up: a surefire—but tasteful—eyewitness piece called something like WHEN DEZI MET OTELLO. But no, no. Paul Faustino has his principles. And he doesn't need the money.)

So far, the other papers—even the down-market ones— have refused to follow *El Sol*'s lead. They have not turned on Otello like dogs in a pack. Not yet. They don't dare to, because although Otello's honeymoon with Desmerelda has ended, his honeymoon with the fans is still full of hope and passion. But theirs is a love that feeds on goals, and they are getting hungry. Faustino is surprised by how anxious he is for those goals to come. And how fearful he is that they won't. He fidgets in his seat, moving as far from Mateo Campos as he can. Then the teams come onto the field.

The roar swells like a delayed bomb, and his own chest fills in response. These are the good moments when he feels as clean as a child, bathed in what he loves. Red and yellow and blue and white waves of rising bodies, clouds of glitter litter, competing blares of horns, drumming that summons up lost tribal faiths. Red and blue flares. The animal smell of something ridiculously important. For Faustino, there is nothing quite like this. Nothing that brings him closer to joy. As always, he wants to laugh.

Otello is last in the line of Rialto players to emerge, and the home crowd delays its climactic roar until he appears. And as before, Faustino thinks that this is a mistake on Otello's part. Or maybe self-indulgence.

It's a lousy game. As halftime approaches, the frustrated Rialto supporters maintain a ferocious chorus of whistles and jeers. Then, in the forty-third minute, Otello scores. It is a goal he manufactures single-handedly and out of nothing. He robs an over-casual San Lorenzo midfielder of the ball and evades another en route to the goal. At the eighteen-yard line, he seems to be blocked off and is forced along the edge of the box, tracked by two defenders, who cut him off from the goal. He seems to be going nowhere and has no support. The shot is therefore completely unexpected. Otello hits it on the run with the outside of his right foot; the San Lorenzo keeper, unsighted by his own players, can only turn his head to watch the ball strike the inside of his post and bulge the back of the net.

There is a silence as long as the beat of a slow heart, and then the stadium erupts. Faustino knows this because he looks across at Mateo Campos, who is typing the words *The stadium erupted when* . . .

He taps Campos on the shoulder. "If I were you," he says, "I would call that 'doing the business.'"

Campos scowls, concentrating on his tiny keyboard.

"Actually," Faustino says, "if I really were you, I'd probably say that 'Dezi's darky got lucky with an opportunistic shot.' Want to know how to spell *opportunistic*?"

In the second half, Otello, again without support, wins three corners. Rialto's second goal comes from the last of these. Roderigo's kick is poor — short and too close to the near post — but Otello comes to it and wins the ball. Hustled and jostled, with his back to the goal, he somehow slides a diagonal pass to Enrique, who scores with a joyous first shot.

This assist and the earlier goal are the only telling contributions that Otello makes to the game. By the end of it, Faustino reckons, the striker must have covered six miles, harrying, going back to collect or tackle, running into space, switching from left field to right and back again. Yet the good touches he gets on the ball probably number less than a dozen. As Otello leaves the field, he turns and applauds the Rialto supporters, who howl his name appreciatively. There is, Faustino thinks, something ironic in the player's gesture; his face, slick with sweat, wears an expression that suggests stubbornness, not triumph.

When the press box has thinned out, Faustino moves to the end of his row and sits below a NO SMOKING sign. He lights a cigarette and watches the crowd eddy and swirl toward the exits.

There are, he reflects, many subtle ways in which players can make a colleague look inept. There is the perfectly accurate but slightly under-hit or over-hit pass. There are the driven passes that are at groin height when they arrive. You can try to ensure that you play the ball to the victim's weaker side, which is especially effective when he is a striker with his back to the goal and a defender is breathing down his neck. Springing the offside trap against your own man is also very good. Otello is exceedingly skilled at timing his muscular runs past or through the defensive back line. Sometimes he likes to disconcert defenses by deliberately wandering offside, only to step back into an onside position a second before the through pass is played, then turning and accelerating onto the ball.

Everyone knows these things about him, of course. Teams who like to play a flat back four—such as San Lorenzo, this afternoon—watch him with hawkish nervousness. As do assistant referees; their little flags quiver eagerly whenever he looks poised to break. And so the Rialto players use this against him. All it takes is a slight, almost imperceptible, hesitation—as if, for example, you might be correcting

103

your balance—before the through ball is played. Just enough time, a split second, for Otello to move a pace, half a pace, offside. And up goes the flag, and the referee's whistle is just one of ten thousand derisive noises. It happened no fewer than eleven times during the San Lorenzo game, prompting Mateo Campos to turn, smirking, to Faustino. "Whaddya say, Maestro? Still reckon he's got—what was it you said?—'exquisite timing'? Or maybe he keeps that for Dezi Brabanta now, eh?"

At the time, Faustino hadn't graced the idiot with a reply. But now he was wondering whether he should. In print. Forcefully express the view that Otello was not playing against eleven men, but against twenty-one—ten of whom were wearing the same colors as himself. That would stir things up, get a lot of attention. Win Faustino some brownie points with Carmen d'Andrade. Would it do Otello any good, though? Probably not. More likely to make things worse.

Faustino stubbed his cigarette out and got to his feet. He'd hold fire for now. Rialto would have to get over themselves sooner rather than later and start playing *with* Otello rather than *against* him. There was simply too much at stake for them not to.

2.3

PAUL FAUSTINO MAY believe that Otello's colleagues are sabotaging his game, but Ramón Tresor, the Rialto coach, *knows* it.

Late evening. The staff and players' parking lot at the Rialto stadium. A dozen or so vehicles are still there, sweating raindrops. They gleam in the light from the high lamps that illuminate the fenced-in compound.

RODERIGO emerges from the unmarked door through which players and officials enter and exit the stadium. He is wearing a light-blue linen shirt beneath an expensive leather jacket and is smiling at the text message displayed on his phone. He walks toward his car—one of his cars—a bronze Lexus coupe. As he passes a big four-wheel drive, its window slides down to reveal the face of TRESOR.

RODERIGO: Boss?

TRESOR: Get in the car.

RODERIGO: What?

TRESOR: Get in the car. You and me are gonna have a private chat.

RODERIGO [*holding his phone up as if it has the power to ward off evil forces*]: Um, yeah, but . . . Does it have to be now? Like, I've—

TRESOR: Yeah, it does have to be now. Get in the damn car.

[RODERIGO *gets into the car. He and* TRESOR *look at the rivulets on the windshield, not at each other.*]

TRESOR: Actually, I shouldn't have gotten you into the car. I should've made you go down on your knees in the rain and beg like a dog for your job.

RODERIGO: What? What the hell is this?

TRESOR: Don't "what" me. You know *exactly* what this is. What in the name of Christ did you think you were doing out there today?

RODERIGO: Er, winning? Like, two—nothing? Against the division favorites?

[*Now* TRESOR *does look at his captain, and his eyes are like fire inside black ice.* RODERIGO *tries not to flinch, but he does.*]

TRESOR: And who did the business for us? Who stole the first goal and made the second? The one player out there today who worked his ass off while the rest of his team behaved like moody schoolgirls. Wanna tell me who that was?

[RODERIGO *doesn't answer. Instead he leans back in the four-by-four's big seat and stretches his legs out.*]

RODERIGO: Oh, right. I get it. Someone upstairs had a word with you, Ramón. That right? What is it, a change of policy? How's that work? Brabanta come to terms with Otello sleeping with his daughter all of a sudden? Vice President Lazar realize having a black superstar on his team gets him a fat slice of the liberal vote? Like, "Hey, we're not right wing or racist; look how we spent fifty million on a black socialist from the North."

TRESOR: What *is* all this crap? I'm running a soccer team. Politics's got nothing to do with it.

RODERIGO: Really. Listen, I know you're from Spain, Ramón, but Jesus. Wise up. Soccer *is* politics in this country, man.

[TRESOR *puts his hands on the padded steering wheel and braces his arms as though he has brought the machine to an emergency halt on a wet mountain road. He lets out his breath.*]

TRESOR: All right. But it's time to stop. You've made your protest. Okay. But today, *today*, the way you sold Otello short was just *embarrassing*, man. And he won us the game. So, enough. It stops right now. We're six games in, and that's enough.

RODERIGO [*after a longish pause*]: Fifty million, less, could've got us Saja and maybe Pozner. Best two defenders in the country. Both itching for a transfer. And we'd still've had Montano. You know, it pisses us all off, the way these things are done.

TRESOR: Oh, c'mon, get over it, Jaco, for Chrissake. You've got maybe the best striker in South America playing in front of you. Any team in the world would give their eyeteeth for him. And you're not giving him anything because you're sulking about Luis Montano. Who is a great kid. I liked him. But for God's sake, there's no comparison.

RODERIGO: You're dead right there, boss. Absolutely right. There's no comparison. Luis was one of us. Comes up from the youth academy, signs for Rialto at the age of thirteen or something, his whole damn neighborhood turns out to watch him play for the Juniors. He's out there selling programs when he's not picked, comes to every practice on offer, makes his first team appearance age seventeen, scores in his first cup game. Name straight on the team sheet for two seasons, and then, hey! Sold up the river to the Deep North. In part exchange. How the hell d'you think he feels about that, man?

TRESOR: Christ, Jaco, listen to yourself. I'm running a soccer team, not some kinda charity. No one's indispensable. Not even you.

RODERIGO: And what the hell is that supposed to mean?

TRESOR: I'll tell you exactly what that's supposed to mean. When we signed Otello, we put the best striker in the business together with the best provider in the business. That being you. The combination that won the Copa América, right? And is it working? No, it damn well isn't. Because you're making sure it's not. And you think you're being so smart, don't you? Huh? Making it look like Otello is a pace behind the game, all of that. And yeah, certain lunkheads like that Campos guy are buying it, putting it in their papers and so forth. But you're gonna have to wake up, Jaco, because sooner or later certain people, people who matter, are gonna start asking how come Roderigo's game has gone off, that he can't distribute the ball like he used to. How come Otello has to steal goals out of nothing, not getting any service from you? Right?

And when that starts to happen, I might just park your sorry ass on the bench. Or maybe even leave you at home, watching the game on TV.

RODERIGO: Oh, yeah?

TRESOR: Yeah.

RODERIGO: You can't drop me, and you know it.

TRESOR: I don't know any such damn thing. Like I said, no one's indispensable. And my job's on the line every game we play. So you and the other guys stop this game right now, okay? If you don't, I might just have to go to the board and say, "Jaco Roderigo's not doing the business. Let's sell the son of a bitch and buy someone who can." Someone like Beckham, who can play the ball. And he knows at least seven words of Spanish. Those being, "Here's the ball. Go score a goal."

RODERIGO: Screw you, Ramón.

TRESOR: Jaco, you ever say that to me again, your career is finished.

RODERIGO: I'm getting out of the car now.

TRESOR: Okay. Go ahead. I'm kinda tired myself. But before you go, one last thing. I won't be at the training ground on Tuesday. And what you're gonna do is have a quiet word with the other guys and tell them it's over, right? That you play with Otello or you don't play at all. I think it would be nicer coming from you rather than me, don't you?

◆ ◆ ◆

Two weeks later, Paul Faustino writes:

One–nothing against Porto may not seem a re-
sounding victory, but yesterday Rialto at last
looked like a coherent team. Much of the credit for
this must go to Jaco Roderigo, who seems to have
shaken off his post-cup indolence and woken up
to the possibilities presented to his side by having
Otello leading the attack.

The move that led to the goal was without
doubt one of the most elegant I have ever seen.
It began, inauspiciously, with a forced back pass
to the Rialto keeper, Gabriel. Instead of hoofing
the ball clear, Gabriel, with two attackers bearing
down on him, played a calm pass out to Airto.
The back, finding space yawning in front of him,
made twenty-five yards before laying the ball off
to Roderigo. Two weeks ago, the Rialto captain
would have held the ball or played a square pass,
but on this occasion he turned beautifully away
from one challenge, beat off another, and then fed
the ball out to Enrique, who had run wide to the
right.

Otello, making an expertly timed run (as
always) seemed surprised that Roderigo had
moved up to support him, and when Enrique's
cross came in, Otello took it superbly on his
chest, dummied his marker, and rolled the ball
to his captain. Roderigo, twenty yards out, had
every right to make a shot, and the Porto defense
expected it. As they rushed to close him down,
Roderigo lifted the ball with the outside of his
left foot — his weaker foot, as we all know — into
the only vacant spot inside the Porto penalty area.
Given that Otello has hardly received a decent
pass from Roderigo this season, it seems unlikely

that he could have been expecting such a ball, yet he moved onto it with extraordinary speed.

Most strikers would have gone for a full-blooded volley to the near post. That is certainly what the Porto keeper expected, and so he was left helpless when Otello's almost gentle side-footed shot curved past him into the bottom left corner of the net. Nonpartisan lovers of the game will want to see this incisive attack as a promise of things to come and hope that Rialto has at last recognized the enormous potential that their new signing has brought to the club.

There are certain things that Faustino chooses not to mention. Such as, when Otello turned away after scoring the goal, the first of his teammates to embrace him was the only other black Rialto player, Airto. Such as, there was a significant hesitation before Roderigo and others joined in the congratulations, and Roderigo's way of doing so was to ruffle Otello's hair briefly in the way that old ladies touch the heads of small children. Nor does Faustino record the fact that immediately after the goal, he looked up at the directors' box (from which Nestor Brabanta was again conspicuously absent) and saw, as he expected, Desmerelda doing her arms-high celebration samba to the obvious pleasure of the men surrounding her. But two rows below Desmerelda, Diego Mendosa sat with his arms folded, his face like a grim idol carved from stone. And that *was* interesting.

2.4

A W, DIEGO, C'MON, man. This is not what I *do*—you know that."

"I know it's what you have so far *refused* to do, Capitano, which is not quite the same thing."

Otello goes to the big window of the penthouse and gazes down at the boats that are packed densely into the marina. He wishes Desmerelda were home.

"Yeah, well, maybe the things we don't do are more important than the things we do."

Diego, seated on the sofa, seems to consider this. "That's deeply philosophical," he says eventually. "And as your friend, I wouldn't mind passing the afternoon debating it. But as your agent, I need to concern myself with money. Elegante has agreed to a fee of six hundred thousand. Which is far more than they had in mind before I took them to lunch."

Down at the quayside a couple of skinny boys are lugging a basket from one pontoon to the next. A security guard is watching them from just inside the gate of the compound. Otello cannot see what it is that the kids are trying to sell, but he knows they will have scant luck. On weekdays the place is a graveyard, the sleek white yachts and cruisers aligned like magnificent sepulchers.

"And it's for a woman's razor, right?"

"Elegante does grooming products. It's a huge market, and they have a big chunk of it."

"A razor."

"Yeah, okay, a razor. But we might well be looking at other stuff. A long-term brand relationship, you know?"

"So what would I have to do?"

Diego gets a folder out of his briefcase, although he doesn't need to. "Okay. Two days filming, max. Stills for posters and so forth to be done at the same time. By a very good agency; I've checked them out. Dates to suit you, so long as they're in the next two months. And if — you have the final say in this, of course — we go on to do other things with them, we negotiate from scratch. Which means, naturally, a bigger fee."

Otello lets out his breath slowly and turns away from the view. "I dunno, Diego. It's not like I need the money." He raises his hand, because his agent is about to speak. "Okay, okay, I know what you're going to say. You're going to say, as usual, that I've got maybe five, six more years playing at this level. That after I quit I'll have, God willing, fifty years

114

left to me, and if I don't want to end up as an old bum on the street, we need to—what's your expression?—'broaden my career base.' "

Diego's smile is rueful. "I didn't realize I'd become such a bore. I apologize. But yes, I do see it as part of my job to get you maximum exposure. Because, let's be honest, the fate of most ex-players is obscurity. And a lot of them end up broke or a joke. Am I wrong?"

"No. I guess not."

"No. But in fact I wasn't going to say that. I was going to point out that half of this fee would finance your drop-in center for homeless kids up in Espirito for at least a year. And because it's a legit charity, that makes a nice reduction on your taxes. And I'm assuming that not paying taxes to your father-in-law's nasty government is something that would appeal to you. Am I right?"

The TV commercial is an instant, scandalous, enormous success. It is condemned by no fewer than nine bishops; it is banned by BVTV, the Catholic channel, and it outrages the Committee for Public Decency. In response to public demand, Elegante puts it on their website so that it can be downloaded onto iPods and cell phones. You'd think no one had ever seen a black man shaving a white woman's body before. Elegante's sales—not only of the Ladyshave Silk, but of the company's entire range—increase by forty percent. But it's the poster—*that* poster—that lingers in the popular consciousness. The morning it appears on the

115

huge electronic billboard in the Plaza de la Independencia, drivers are so utterly transfixed by it that they fail to notice that the traffic lights are sometimes green, and as a result half of downtown is gridlocked within twenty minutes. One of the inconvenienced travelers is Nestor Brabanta. He sits fuming in the back of his chauffeur-driven limousine for almost three quarters of an hour. When the car eventually reaches Independencia, he looks up at the billboard, and the blood drains from his face.

Although the woman on the poster has her head turned away from the viewer, her light skin, the soft cataract of honey-and-tobacco-colored curls, and the tiny hummingbird tattoo on her exposed shoulder all suggest very strongly that she is Desmerelda Brabanta. (She is not, of course. She is a model, the hair is a wig, and the tattoo will be easily erased by a dab of Elegante cleanser.) Her right arm and hand cover her breasts. Her left arm is raised and bent so that the forearm rests on her golden head; the hand is clenched into a fist. Thus the viewer's eyes are drawn to her exposed armpit, the armpit that Otello (standing slightly behind her, leaning down and forward) is, with rapt attention, de-stubbling with a turquoise plastic razor. Both he and the model are wearing only sarongs. *Sarongs!* Hers is black; his is white.

On the seventh floor of *La Nación,* Paul Faustino is struggling with the hot drinks machine when Edgar Lima arrives and helps him with the buttons. Lima is the photo editor for the weekend color supplement. He looks about seventeen years old, has his hair in a gelled tsunami, and in the top of his right ear wears a clip fashioned from an antique silver coffee spoon. Naturally they begin to talk about the burning issues of the day.

"It's absolutely *brilliant*," Edgar says. "One of those images that are instantly iconic."

"Yeah?"

"God, yes. I spend my days praying that one of our guys will come up with something like that."

"What, a soccer player shaving a woman's armpit? I don't want milk with that, by the way."

"Okay, there you go. Actually, it's not really about shaving armpits. Well, it is, but hey, Paul, c'mon. Deconstruct it a bit, and what do you get?"

"You tell me. I know you're dying to."

"All right. It's wonderfully complicated, but the first thing is, of course, it's about Otello and La Brabanta."

"It's not her, though. Is it?"

"I very much doubt it. But we want to believe that it *is,* right? We want to believe that we're seeing an intimate moment—albeit a slightly grotesque intimate moment—from the private life of the country's most celebrated couple. Like they've just got out of the shower or something, and she says, 'Darling, would you mind shaving my armpits?'"

Lima sips his tea. "No, it's more than that. What we secretly want to believe is that she says, 'Darling, would you please shave my armpits because you know how much it

117

turns me on.' That's why she's hiding her face. She doesn't want us to see how turned on she is. Which signals to the viewer that she is very turned on indeed. That's why she's holding herself the way she is, right? And the intent expression on Otello's face tells us that he knows it. The armpit itself is a metaphor, of course."

Faustino considers this for a moment or two. "You are a very unwholesome person, Eddie. I've always thought that."

"No, I am a very ordinary person. I see what everybody else sees. That's why I have my job."

"No, you have your job because you have a university degree in stuff that most people don't understand, and because somehow you charmed the pants off our man-eating boss at your interview."

"That is also true."

"I'm glad you know it. Please continue."

"Okay. So. As well as the sex thing, there's the violence thing. Or maybe 'violation' is a better word. You know, the way he *looms* over her. He looks twice the size she is. The photographer obviously got him to pump that arm up, because the muscles stand out like knots in a ship's cable. Like he's doing something that requires a lot of effort. And what he's doing is taking a razor to this defenseless, submissive white chick."

"Aw, c'mon, Eddie. It's a stupid little green plastic thingy."

"Maybe. But it's a razor nonetheless, a thing with a blade. One false move, and there's bloodshed. At the same

118

time, he's doing this slightly icky task for her. So you get this dangerous twist on the master-servant relationship. Or mistress-servant relationship, I should say."

Faustino harrumphs skeptically, but Edgar Lima is not deterred.

"All that is pretty obvious. You might even say *crudely* obvious. But what makes the image really interesting, its stroke of genius, is that Otello is wearing a skirt."

"No, no. It's a *sarong*. Perfectly conventional beach-wear."

"Well, yes. Some guys wear them at the beach. But at *home*? What kind of guy wears a sarong around the house? But the point is, Paul, right, that in the poster *she* is wear-ing one, which is like saying quite plainly that this is girls' wear. Thus, by extension, that Otello likes wearing the same clothes as his wife. And enjoys joining in with the kind of thing that women normally do in the privacy of their bathrooms. It's brilliant. It's got it all: race, latent violence, sexual ambiguity. It's very erotic and rather disturbing at the same time."

Faustino shakes his head, marveling. "So let's see if I've got this right," he says. "This ad for a woman's razor is ac-tually telling us that the country's number-one soccer hero is a brutal, blade-wielding, transvestite rapist. That it?"

Edgar Lima grins. "Or that our leading black sports star is a gentle, wife-loving man who is perfectly confident in his sexual identity. You pays your money and you takes your choice. You see what you want to see. Anyway, gotta go.

I have to Photoshop the vice president's wife to make her look less like the witch she is. See you around, Maestro."

Faustino muses, finishing his coffee. Despite Lima's colorful analysis, his own view remains unchanged — which is that someone has persuaded Otello to make himself look like an idiot.

He is halfway back to his office before it occurs to him to wonder why anyone would want to do that. And, for that matter, *who*.

Desmerelda presses the remote, and the TV says something like *zonk* and goes off. She sinks into the sofa and stretches her arm along the backrest. She's wearing a loose, long-sleeved silk shirt. No armpits on display.

"And you didn't notice that she looks like me?" Her tone is neutral.

Otello has been standing at the picture window, looking out into the night, while his wife has been watching him shave a girl's legs.

"She doesn't. She doesn't look anything like you. The guy at the studio introduces us; she's got short dark hair, dark eyes, you know? She's maybe half Japanese or something. Even when she comes out of the makeup room with the wig on, she doesn't look like you. I mean, if you could see her face, you wouldn't think —"

"I kind of imagine that even if we could see her face, it wouldn't be the main thing we'd be looking at."

"Yeah, well . . ."

"And the tattoo? You didn't see that and think, *Whoa, what's this?*"

"Well . . . I guess it'll sound weird, but I don't remember her having the tattoo. I dunno, maybe the lights and everything, so much going on . . . I didn't notice it."

"Hmm. I guess they could've added it on, postproduction."

"They can do that, can they?"

Desmerelda huffs a little laugh. "Oh, yeah. You'd be amazed at what they can do. You've got a lot to learn."

He turns to face her. "I'm sorry."

She regards him somberly for a moment, then pats the seat beside her. "Come here. Sit down."

He does as he is told.

She says, "Right, Señor Elegante, I think it's honesty time, don't you?"

He nods. "Okay."

"Look at me."

He looks at her. Her face is very serious.

"I had doubts about this thing from the word go, remember?"

He sighs. "Yeah. I should've listened to you."

"So listen to me now. That ad is seriously the coolest, sexiest thing I've ever seen on TV. You look fabulous. The camera loves you, man, and so do I. When I was watching it, I wasn't thinking, *Take your hands off my husband, you bitch.* I was thinking, *My God, look at that guy. And he's mine. I can hardly believe it, but he is.* I'm so proud of you."

And, at last, she smiles.

Later, in bed, she says, "Diego was right. You should do more modeling, stuff like that."

"What? Diego said I should do *modeling?*"

"Yeah. Well, not *fashion* modeling, maybe. But, you know, magazine work, advertising, things like that. Why not? Other players do. Come to think of it, why *not* fashion modeling? You look great in clothes, as well as out of them. And it'd be a change from all those wasted-looking rent boys you usually see in the magazines. You should think about it. I know lots of people who'd love to use you."

"When did Diego say this?"

"Oh, I dunno." She yawns, nuzzles her face on his shoulder. "A couple of weeks back. We had lunch."

"Did you? You didn't mention it."

"Didn't I? Mmm . . . turn the light off, honey. I'm really sleepy now."

The following Wednesday evening, Rialto wins a closely fought cup tie against SV Catalunya. Immediately after the game, Otello does a brief and breathless television interview in the cramped space off the players' tunnel, then heads for the locker room. As he opens the door, the hubbub fades slightly. Over at the entrance to the showers, against a backdrop of steam, Gabriel, Airto, Bernardo, and Enrique are standing in a line, wearing white towels around their waists, shaving one another's armpits. When they and the rest of the squad see Otello's face, they crack up. After the shortest hesitation that he can manage, Otello joins in the laughter.

B USH EASED THE shed door open, lifting it against the hinges so that it wouldn't squeal. The girls weren't awake, and because it wasn't a Sisters of Mercy breakfast day, he didn't want to disturb them. The longer they stayed like they were, folded against each other in their sleep, the better. He smelled the threat of rain in the air, which was bad news for the windshield business but maybe good news for the errands. You had to look on the bright side, even if you ended up drowned like an unwanted puppy.

He slipped out and softly hefted the door shut, and when he turned around, he saw Nina and Fidel. They were sitting on the sorry-looking bench by the back door to the bar. Nina had a pile of potatoes on a sheet of newspaper and was peeling them. She had a bowl of water between her feet, and the peeled potatoes—big yellow ones—were in it. Fidel sat beside her as if he just felt like coming out to admire the patch of gray sky that swung above the yard like a dirty hammock God had just climbed out of.

Bush thought, *Uh-oh*. Because Nina and Fidel didn't sit in the yard peeling potatoes on a regular basis. Not at this time of day, anyway.

"Yo, Bush," Fidel said, smiling.

Nina let a long shaving of potato skin fall onto the newspaper and lifted her face. It was still fine, Nina's face. Some old Spanish aristocrat blood had gone into the making of it. That was what Fidel liked to say, adding, "She's a class traitor, man. Like all hardcore revolutionaries." Now she had on that distant, tender expression she wore when she was troubled.

Fidel used his foot to hook an upturned plastic beer crate closer to the bench. "Spare us a minute," he said. "Park your ass."

Bush went over to them and sat. "Some problem, Fidel? Nina?"

"Well, maybe not," Fidel said.

"And maybe yes," Nina said.

"You wan' us to leave?" Bush asked, because it was the obvious question, and he was always expecting to have to ask it.

"Hey, man, whoa," Fidel said. "Nothin' like that. It's just Nina and me, we thought we should have a talk with you. On account of what's going on, you know?"

Bush looked at their faces in turn. "Like what?"

Nina wiped the potato peeler on the hem of her skirt and said, "Are the girls still asleep, Bush?"

"I think so, yeah."

"I, we . . . we're worried about them. And you."

"We're always careful, Nina, honest to God. No one knows we're here, on my life."

"I know that," she said. "You're cool, Bush. You do okay. But the thing is, you're not here all the time. No, listen, don't bristle up. We know you have to do what you do. But . . ."

"What're the girls doin' that I don' know about? They havin' boys back here or somethin'?"

Nina almost smiled. "No. Nothing like that. Which is amazing. At their age, with a place to go, I'd've—"

Fidel gave her a mock-shocked look, and she touched his plump arm. Which gave Bush that solitary feeling again. He waited.

Fidel said, "You must've noticed how there's a lot more police on the streets these past weeks, huh? And Ratcatchers?"

Oh, yes, Bush had noticed that all right. Recently the early morning journey to work had become difficult, and the journey back . . . He'd had to find ever more elaborate routes, check every alleyway before turning into it, watch every unmarked van that passed by or stood parked. Many of the vacant lots and archways below bridges, gathering places for kids, were semi-deserted now. He felt nervous, exposed, slinking through the city.

"Yeah. Somethin' to do with the election, is what I hear."

"Right. Those sonsabitch so-called New Conservatives."

126

Fidel spoke the phrase with a sneer that caused his heavy mustache to spread its wings. "They want to say, 'Hey, look how our Safer Streets Campaign and our Child Protection Order and so on have cleaned the city up, so vote us in again.' Forgetting to mention it's their damned economic policies is what forced kids to hustle and pull tricks on the street in the first place."

Bush looked down at his feet. He didn't know anything about politics. He didn't *think* it was the government that had kicked in the door of a shack eight years ago and shot his mother's boyfriend and then his mother when she started screaming. It might have been. He'd only seen their feet because he was on his blanket, which was under his mother's bed, with his hand over Bianca's mouth.

He said, "Yeah, well. Things'll prob'ly settle down when it's all over."

Nina said quietly, "Fidel, I think you should tell Bush about what Donato told you last night."

Fidel resettled his mustache with his thumb and forefinger. "Okay. Yeah." His eyes were uneasy, though. "Donato's a friend of ours from the student days, comes in the bar now and again. Works for the city, in the department of waste management. He likes to say, 'All the crap in the city comes across my desk, and a heap of it stays there.' Anyway, he was in last night, and he told us something he wasn't supposed to. It seems . . ."

Fidel's voice trailed off, then he inhaled lengthily through his nose and looked directly at Bush. "You must've wondered, of course you have, about what happens to the kids they take off the street."

Bush shrugged. "Yeah, well. I dunno. I guess they get sent off to one of them screws, but I ain't never talked to somebody who's been to one."

Fidel laughed, a mirthless bark. "Screws. *Screws!* Man, I'd like to meet the bureaucrat who decided to call those places State Centers for Rehabilitation, Education, and Work. He must've had a sense of humor. I'd like to meet him and shake him by the throat."

"Fidel," Nina said.

"Okay, okay, sugar. I'll get back to Donato in a second. But this is important, right? And it's like no one wants to talk about it. There was some state programming on the TV three nights back. You know, an ad for the government. And it had a bit of film in it of one of these screw places. That's what it said it was, anyway. Didn't say *where* it was, mind you. Showed a bunch of happy-looking kids doing farm work and sports and learning computers, stuff like that. And it just didn't look right, did it, Nina? Way too good to be true. It was like one of those old propaganda movies from Stalin's Russia, but in color."

Bush had no idea what Fidel was talking about. He shifted on the uncomfortable crate and said, "Yeah, well, you know, me 'n' the girls don' aim to get took. Like I say, we're always careful. You don' need to worry. Now, uh, I better get going . . ."

"Wait," Nina said. "Please."

"Yeah," Fidel said, "'cause this is the bit. Last night Donato comes in, and we get talking politics, as usual. Then he says he wants a quiet word and we go off into a corner. I figure maybe he's broke, gonna ask for credit or something, but no. What it is, he's got a story he needs to get off his chest. Seems that a couple of days earlier, one of his guys comes into his office, late in the day. This is a guy drives one of those big garbage dumpers, you know? He looks real shook up, won't say anything to Donato until the two of them are alone in the office. And what he tells Donato, eventually, is this.

"He'd been on the early shift and taken his truck out to this big landfill site where they bury all the crap, yeah? This is out east somewhere, way past Santa Monica. He gets there just after daybreak. He backs his truck up to where there's always a guy who directs him where to make the drop. It's like a ramp down into this great big dip, okay? But the guy isn't there, so the driver gets out, thinking, *What's going on?* And he sees the people who work at the landfill all looking down into the dip, and there's a man, the foreman, with a knife in his hand. He's right where yesterday's stuff was dropped—this, like, avalanche of garbage, yeah? And there's seventeen big black plastic bags in a straight row half covered with other rubbish. For some reason the foreman had thought this didn't look right. Maybe they weren't there the night before or something. So he'd gone down and cut one of the bags open. There was a girl inside it. He'd cut another one open, and there was a girl inside that one, too.

He felt some of the other bags, and it seemed to him there were probably bodies inside all of them. Donato's guy, the driver, said it was weird, the scene. It's a scummy place, you know, with paper and crap hanging off the wire fence. And all these people standing there silent like they were in church.

"After a while the foreman gets up and walks out of the dip and goes to the cabin, where there's a phone, and calls the police. Takes the best part of an hour for the cops to get there. Meanwhile, the landfill people have gone down and opened the other bags and there's a girl, a kid, in every one, man. Every damn one."

Without taking his eyes off Bush's face, Fidel reached over and took hold of Nina's hand. Nina gripped it, looking down at the skinned yellow potatoes in the water in the bowl between her feet.

"And when the cops do get there, it's not just the usual blueflies. As well as the uniforms, there's a car of plain clothes. And the main man calls all the people there together and tells them this is a major crime scene and not to say anything to anybody about it in case it jeopardizes the investigation. Makes them sign a piece of paper that just about sentences them to death if they do say anything. Then the bodies are loaded into a police truck and taken away."

Nina looked past Fidel at Bush but couldn't see him. He had reduced himself somehow. Had lowered his head and folded his arms across his body, become just a curtain of dreadlocks above a pair of dusty knees. The only part of him that was moving was his left foot, which was jiggling, fast, against the sole of its blue flip-flop.

"So," Fidel continued, "the driver eventually gets to make his drop in some other part of the site and heads off. On the way back into town, he gets this powerful need for a coffee and a cigarette, so he pulls into a place where the Santa Monica road crosses the interstate highway. There's another waste department truck in the lot, and when he gets into the café, he spots the driver, on account of they all wear these yellow vest things, you know? So he goes and sits with this other guy, and they get talking. And guess what? This other driver'd had the same thing, on another site, the previous week. Twelve bodies. All young girls. And the same routine: the cops come, make everybody take a vow of silence, more or less at gunpoint, and take the bodies away."

On the far side of the yard, a high window in Señor Oguz's factory opened, and female talk flew out of it like angry birdsong.

"This other driver told Donato's guy that all the girls had been killed the same way. Shot in the head. And that they'd been . . . that things had been done to them. Before. You know what I'm sayin'?"

A mournful sound came from Bush, which Fidel took to mean *yes*.

"Then," Fidel said, "Donato says to me, 'I know you got girls living out in that shed. Are they okay?'"

Bush stood up. "This's bullshit, man. Jus' bullshit.

Stories like that, they go around all the time. I hear it all the time. Like, you never wonder who put them stories out? *Jesus!* How come I never hear someone say a thing like that happen to his sister or somethin'? Huh? How come?"

Fidel shrugged and shook his head slowly. He suspected the kid didn't spend much time talking to other people on the street, but he didn't say it.

Bush stood there, turning his angry face this way and that as though he was looking for a good direction to run in but couldn't find it. So when Nina spoke, her voice was calm and cautious.

"You may be right, Bush. But we've known Donato for thirty years. He's not a fool. I don't think he'd have told Fidel about this if he didn't believe it was true."

Bush jabbed his fists into his pockets. "So what you sayin' here, Nina? It's not like I can keep the girls with me all the time, you know? Have 'em hangin' around my turf. We'd get moved on jus' like that. Or you think I can make 'em stay in the shed all day? How can I do that?"

"Well," Fidel said, hesitantly, "maybe you could keep with them for a while. Like you say, things will probably settle down after the election."

"Man, how can I do that either? I got a nice thing goin' uptown, you know? I got an understandin' with the door guy. I don' get no hassle. An' you know how it works—I don' show up there a while, someone else'll move in. Then what do I do? Start over someplace else? You know how hard that can be?"

"Yeah. I do know."

"Bush," Nina said, "I need to say this, and I don't want you to fire up on me, all right? What we're worried about is Bianca."

"Bianca's all right. Bianca's cool, okay?"

Nina took her glasses off and pinched the skin over the bridge of her nose between her fingers. "Man, Bianca is *not* cool. That's one thing she is not. She's a really sweet kid, but she's sort of *disconnected*. It's like she's not in the same world as the rest of us."

Bush took his hands out of his pockets and wrapped his arms across his chest. "She's okay," he said, scowling at the ground.

Nina sighed. "I was down at the market yesterday. Bianca and Felicia were there, just hanging out along with a bunch of other kids; some I knew, some I didn't. But the thing is, Bush, Bianca *stands out*. No one looks at her just once—you know what I'm saying? She's very beautiful. And when that's not a blessing, it's a curse. She doesn't understand that, Bush. I think you do, though."

He said nothing, didn't lift his face.

"I watched her. And I can't tell if she knows what she's doing, the effect she has on other people, and likes it. Or doesn't know, or care. Either way, it's . . . not good. It's dangerous. Down the market she's okay, I guess. Lots of people around, plenty of them know her. But in other places, well . . ."

Nina waited, but still Bush refused to speak.

"I think . . . I think if she dressed different. Showed less of herself. I mean, look at Felicia. She's a good-looking girl, but in those old things she wears, no one's going to pick her out, take any special notice. You hear what I'm saying, Bush?"

"Yeah."

For several seconds the only sound in the yard was the stumbling whir of Señor Oguz's machines as they stitched fakes.

Then Fidel said quietly, "And it's not just what Donato told me. For a while now, there've been these rumors. About kids getting disappeared. Okay, okay. I know what you're gonna say. Usually I don't pay much attention to that kind of crap either. But now I'm starting to think . . . Well, I'm not so sure anymore."

Bush knew these rumors. A week or so ago, working *La Nación*'s patio at lunchtime, he'd overheard some people talking about the same thing. One of them, Maestro's friend, the woman with the gray hair, had gotten angry. There had been tears in her eyes, too.

He sat back down on the beer crate and hunched over, his forearms on his knees, his long hands dangling. "It sucks, man," he said.

"What does?"

From behind his dreads, Bush said, "Life."

"Yeah," Fidel said. "It does, sometimes."

It started to rain. Fat, slow drops at first that made dark patches on the ground the shape of starfish.

2.6

DIEGO ARRIVES AT the marina penthouse for his weekly breakfast conference with Otello. He ignores the fruit and cereal but accepts coffee.

"How's Dezi? Enjoying Florida?"

"She's fine. I spoke to her just now. She was lying on a float in the middle of her mother's swimming pool."

"Really?"

"Yeah. Seems like since her old man stopped talking to her, she and her mom get on like a house on fire."

"Fancy that," Diego says, fiddling with the combination lock on his briefcase. "Now, I've been drawing up a schedule, which is kind of complicated because it depends slightly on whether or not Rialto qualifies for the next round of the cup. I've worked on the assumption that you will, which seems reasonable, now that those moody boys you play with appear to have sorted their heads out. So I've organized possible dates for the next Elegante things around that, okay? Then there are the personal appearances we talked about, and a couple of magazine pieces that I think are cool. Quality things. Oh, and Paul Faustino has requested an interview. I think we could toss him another bone, don't you, seeing as how he's kept pretty onside as far as we are concerned?"

"Yeah. Paul's all right."

"I agree," Diego says. "A little bit up on himself, but sound, I think." He lays three stapled sheets of paper on the table. "Anyway, it's all in here, so I'd be grateful if you'd find time to look through it. When is Dezi back?"

"Day after tomorrow."

"Okay, so maybe you could go through it with her then. Any problems, call me. Right, next."

He produces from the case two thickish, identical documents, spiral-bound into gray plastic covers. Otello regards them bleakly.

"Your six-monthly financial statement," Diego says. "Read and rejoice."

"Oh, God."

"You really ought to check through these, you know, Capitano. Someone might be ripping you off."

"What, and you think I'd find out by reading this? Show me a column of figures and I'm brain-dead inside a minute. You know that."

Diego shakes his head sadly. "Yeah. But the information in this is also on the computer disk inside the back cover. Here, see? You could run it through that U-Account program I put on your computer. It'll flag any suspect—"

But Otello has lowered his head onto his folded arms and begun to snore loudly.

"All right, all right," Diego says. "Point taken. But you could at least cast an eye over the summary on the last three pages. Seven-digit figures have a certain charm, I find. And you need to sign one copy to hand over to the tax people."

Otello lifts his head and holds out a hand. "Okay. Gimme a pen."

Sighing, Diego takes his French fountain pen from his inside pocket. "Last page. First of the two dotted lines."

Otello signs his name, then Diego writes his, neatly, under the words *Witnessed by.*

"Thank you," he says. "I have now successfully embezzled you of half a million dollars."

"Yeah, yeah," Otello says, grinning. "What's next?"

"We're meeting Shakespeare at one thirty. I've told Michael to pick you up at twelve forty-five."

Otello pushes away from the table and stands up. "Good. Plenty of time, then. C'mon. There's something I want to show you."

In the underground garage, Otello takes a key fob from his pocket and presses it. Twenty paces away something black and gleaming, the size of an elephant, blinks its bright eyes.

"Dear God," Diego cries, halting. "What is *that?*"

"A Hummer. Deluxe version of the U.S. Army Humvee. A beast, isn't it?"

It is, too. Taller than a man, it protrudes a good five feet out of its parking slot. Wheels as big as a truck's, chrome hubcaps, smoked-glass windows. It looks like it has eaten two other cars for breakfast and is sizing up a third.

"Took delivery of it yesterday afternoon," Otello says. "Haven't had a go in it yet. I can't wait to see Michael's face when he sees it. Come on, climb in."

Climb is the appropriate word. Diego puts his foot on the gleaming step rail and hauls himself up into an ivory-white leather passenger seat larger than most armchairs. The smell inside is wonderful: the clean and confident aroma of money purged of guilt. Behind him there are two more rows of voluptuous car furniture. The knob on the end of the gear shift is a miniature chrome soccer ball.

Otello settles himself behind the wheel. "Six-and-a-half-liter engine," he says. "This thing could pull the wall off a building, then drive over the rubble. Best GPS on the planet, DVD for the rear passengers, twelve-speaker Bose stereo, beer cooler. Practical, too. Bulletproof body panels, shatterproof glass, more security systems than I can get my head around. The manual is fatter than the Bible. So, where to, *amigo?*"

"Anywhere you like," Diego says. "But go slowly. This is the first car I've had vertigo in."

◆ ◆ ◆

Otello drives northeast for a while on quiet suburban roads. Diego responds appreciatively to Otello's comments on the car. Then they turn left onto the Transversal into the city.

He wants to be seen in this, Diego thinks. *No, not seen, of course. He wants people to look and wonder.*

Surprising him, Otello says, "Shakespeare is a weird name. What are they, American?"

Diego asks, "Did you read that prospectus I sent you?"

"Prospectus? Oh, yeah. I skimmed it."

Sure you did, Diego thinks. *My fool.* He says, "They have branches in New York and Los Angeles, but they're based here. And they are the best PR company there is, believe me."

"Yeah, that's what Dezi told me. According to her, they've been trying to sign her for over a year."

"Indeed they have," Diego says. "They're big fans of hers."

"That's nice. But what Dezi thinks is that Shakespeare wants the two of us as a package deal. They get me, they'll be more likely to get her. Make a killing. Is she right?"

"As a matter of fact, yes."

Otello leans back from the wheel, unable to resist smiling. "Diego, your honesty always amazes me. How come it doesn't make your life impossible?"

"Simple. I am only honest with you."

"Ha! So you lie to everyone else?"

"I represent you, Capitano. Which means, basically, that I tell other people what they want to hear."

139

Over to the right, Diego sees, between the office spires, the brown baroque tower of the Catedral San Marco. At the next junction he asks Otello to take the turn. As they wait, the rain stops, and slanting sunlight strikes the windshield.

They pass the cathedral, then Diego says, "You want to pull in here? There's something I'd like to show you."

Otello glances at him. "Where, the cemetery?"

"Yeah."

Otello brings the Hummer to a stop in the semicircular lot at the foot of the thirty-foot-high statue of Christ. Beyond the Redeemer's outstretched arms, tombs radiate into the distance. Before any questions can be asked, Diego opens the door and gets out and walks away. Otello locks the car and follows him.

The graves, memorials, and mausoleums closest to Christ are ornate and well kept. Diego walks briskly past them. When Otello catches up with him, Diego slows and says, "I come here quite often."

"Yeah? Why?"

"It's the only big open space in the city. I read somewhere that it contains thirty percent of the city's trees. I rather like trees. Their roots have the same spread as their branches. They have the same amount of life under the ground as they have above it. Did you know that?"

"Nope."

"Trees flourish here, of course. Rich soil for their roots."

"*Ach*, Diego, please."

Diego grins. "Sorry."

The trees drip on them as they pass. After a while Diego says, "This way" and turns down a narrow avenue. In this suburb of the necropolis, the graves are packed together, mean, and neglected. Undergrowth has repossessed many of them. The path is broken asphalt with weeds swarming through its cracks. The rain has given the air an acrid flavor.

"Here," Diego says. "I found him by accident a few weeks ago."

It's a low slab of stone huddled among others, leaning slightly backward. Otello steps around to where he might read the name, but the lettering has been blurred by time and weather. The inside surface of the glass over the photograph has been made opaque by a coating of mold.

"'Esdras Caballo,'" Diego recites expressionlessly. "'1944–92.' Underneath it says: 'A great player and a great man.' That's all."

Otello looks up. "*The* Esdras Caballo?"

"Yep. *The* Esdras Caballo. Died in a boardinghouse out in Estramura. They didn't find him for a week."

"That's terrible," Otello says, stooping over the grave. "He was amazing. When we were kids, we all wanted to be like him."

"You will be, one day. At the top of his game, Caballo earned a thousand dollars a week. Unheard-of at the time. In today's money, that's more or less what you earn a minute. But that's no guarantee you won't end up in a miserable hole in the ground like this, forgotten."

"Hey, Diego, c'mon, man. Lighten up. What's brought this on?"

"Sorry. I didn't mean to sound morbid. But, well, it has to do with what you yourself talked about a while back. About only having a certain amount of time left at the highest level. Then what? Dezi too. Pop music is a fickle business."

"I know. That's why Dezi doesn't take it too seriously."

"Okay, but look—right now you two are the hottest item in the country, agreed? You're not just two famous individuals who happen to be married; as a couple, you're something else, something unique. If you don't mind my saying so, my friend, your stars now burn more brightly than they did before you met."

Otello shrugs uncomfortably. "Yeah, well . . ."

"Which is why Shakespeare thinks—and I agree with them—that career-wise it's time to make a quantum leap. To move into a whole new dimension."

"What's that mean?"

"In the crudest possible terms, making more money. Lots more money."

"I've got lots of money, Diego."

"Yes. But not enough."

"No?"

"No. Fame comes at a very high price, Capitano. And you have not been paid it."

Otello frowns. He is quite out of his depth now.

Diego perches his backside on Esdras Caballo's headstone and folds his arms. Surveying the tilted slabs and damaged angels, he says, "Listen, Capitano. To those who don't have it, fame is enormously desirable. It's like food to the hungry, sex to the lonely, cash to the poor. And they have no idea what it costs. You live in a multimillion-dollar penthouse. But the building is surrounded by a steel fence topped with razor wire and is patrolled by men with dogs. Your lobby is protected by armed guards twenty-four hours a day. There are security cameras in the corridors and the elevator. It's extremely risky for you to go anywhere public without a bodyguard. Your every move, both on and off the soccer field, is recorded, analyzed, published. You have no privacy. If you and Dezi want to go shopping, it has to be after hours in shops that stay open just for you. If you want to go out for a meal, it has to be in a private room with men stationed at the door. Paparazzi stalk you, follow your car on their whining little motorbikes like a cloud of mosquitoes.

"If there is no story, the tabloids and magazines print lies, rumors, gossip. A snatched snapshot of Dezi looking less than radiant, and suddenly your marriage is on the brink of collapse. Or she has an eating disorder. A photo of you with another woman who just happens to be in the frame, and you're having an affair. Trip on the sidewalk, and you are an alcoholic. You sneak vacations in secret locations, yet thousands of sweaty men in thousands of dirty little rooms are soon leering over a picture of your wife in her bikini. And this shit becomes part of your life whether you like it or not. It invades your bedroom; it enters your bloodstream."

Diego looks at his client now, meets his puzzled gaze. "Fame involves the sacrifice of almost everything that ordinary people take for granted. It leaves you with practically nothing that you can call uniquely your own. Your own body — its changes, its aging, its damage — will become the subject of street humor. Your accountant, your dentist, your doorman, will be offered bribes. Your friends will become sources of information. Your casual remarks will be recorded by directional microphones; the tiniest moment of indiscretion or ill humor will be translated into vast headlines. Fame guts you like a fish and lays you on the slab in the marketplace to be sniffed and prodded by the grubby populace. I happen to think that no amount of money can adequately compensate the very famous for that. To be merely rich is nothing like enough."

Diego glances at his watch and straightens. "Time is catching up with us, Capitano. We'd better clamber back into that battle tank of yours."

They have to run the last fifty yards; the rain has resumed, heavier than before.

Rubén was wearing a see-through plastic raincoat over his uniform and was sporting a big green golf umbrella. He hauled open the glass door when Faustino came scuttling across the patio, but Faustino, instead of going inside, took shelter under the umbrella and looked back toward the avenue.

"You seen the kid today?"

Rubén stuck his bottom lip out and shook his head. "Nope. The weather, I guess."

"Hmm. I doubt it. It's never stopped him before."

Rubén shrugged. "Yeah, well. These kids come and go, you know."

The spectral traffic hissed behind its veils of rain.

"I guess they do," Faustino said, and went inside.

From the window of the bar's kitchen, Nina saw Bush return to the shed. He splodged across the yard, holding something in a plastic bag over his head as if he hoped, absurdly, that it could keep him dry. She warmed milk in a pan, whisked into it a big spoonful of powdered chocolate and a pinch of chili, and poured the mix into a jug. She cut the last of the banana cornbread into three chunks and balanced them on top of the jug, then, with Fidel's raincoat draped over her head and shoulders, carried the breakfast over to the shed.

"People? C'mon, open up! You need gills to live out here!"

It was Felicia who dragged the door open and welcomed Nina in. Apart from the breakfast, the smile was the only good thing in the room. Bush, wearing just his shorts, stood scowling. Rivulets of rainwater ran from his hair down his narrow body. Over on the girls' pallet, Bianca had her hands

145

on her hips, portraying rage like a bad actress in a soap opera. Even in the pallid light from the papered-over window, Nina could see the glint of her wet and angry eyes.

She turned to Nina. "Bush says I gotta wear this crap from now on. He's gone down the market an' spent money on it. I mean, *why*? What've I *done*?"

The oversize sweatshirt was made of some cheap synthetic material. It had once been red, perhaps, but had sickened into a nasty pink. On its front there was the faded image of a gringo rock star who had gone out of fashion several years ago. The knee-length shorts looked like the underpants of a tragic old man. Protruding from these garments, Bianca's limbs looked thin, not slender, and frail.

She pinched the sides of the sweatshirt and stretched it out. It was at least three times the width of her body; tight across her torso, it gave lewd prominence to her breasts.

"Man," she said in the voice of a dying heroine, "who's gonna look at me like this?"

Felicia sighed theatrically. "That's kinda the *point*, girl."

Nina saw that it would not work. The ugly clothes served only to draw attention to the child's beauty, the same way a desolate patch of ground attracts the eye to the single flower that blooms there. About the only thing that would do, she thought, was one of those black sack things with a slit for the eyes, like you saw Arab women wearing on the TV news. Maybe not even that. She set the bread and the jug down on the old suitcase that served as a table.

"Eat," she said, and smiled up at Bianca. "You got room for some extra belly inside that outfit."

Bianca collapsed into a cross-legged sulk, her hands cupping her face. On the way out, Nina rested her fingers briefly on Bush's shoulder. He nodded but did not meet her eyes.

2.7

THE DIEGO-SHAKESPEARE strategy—nothing less than promoting Otello and Desmerelda as modern symbols of married love—works like a dream. They become, as Shakespeare promised they would, iconic. No celebrity magazine dreams of going to press without at least one picture of them, usually on the cover. The gossip columns, even those in the trashiest rags, coo rather than spit. They do not—would not—attempt to prick the gorgeous bubble of love that surrounds the couple. Because the public adores this bubble, its slightly garish prismatic colors, its reassuring fragility. (Paul Faustino, in a comment piece for *La Nación*, uses the word *uxorious* to describe Otello. It's a word he has always liked but has never found the occasion to use.) The new Elegante ads are erotic, but they manage to convey legitimate and domestic sexiness rather than the dangerous, perverse variety. In response to Shakespeare's gentle urging, Otello and Desmerelda wear expensive but slightly vulgar clothes when they make public appearances; the common touch is very important. They must be out of reach, but only just. They must dictate fashion, but that fashion—or something like it—must be affordable. (Señor Oguz's sweatshop doubles its shifts.)

Marriage becomes increasingly fashionable among the poorer classes, which greatly pleases the clergy. (Although they remain a little touchy about the Elegante thing.) The couple poses with the archbishop at the opening of a new Catholic orphanage to which Otello has made a significant financial contribution. Desmerelda grants interviews to teen magazines in which she celebrates the joys of wedlock. (Bianca retrieves these from trash cans and scans them avidly by the light of candle stubs in the shed behind La Prensa, wishing she could read.)

Toward the end of the year, the happy couple purchases a second home, a villa in an exclusive and heavily protected estate on the coast. There is a bidding war between three magazines—*Célebre, Celebridad,* and *Centella*—to decide who will have exclusive first access to this love nest. *Celebridad* wins. (And it looks like it might bankrupt the magazine, but then the sales and advertising revenues are incredible.) A certain kind of furniture is installed, then removed when the photo shoot is completed. The actual housewarming features a charity auction; Otello and Desmerelda preside over it from high-backed gilded chairs. They each have little auctioneer's hammers, which they bang on little

149

lecterns to signal a successful bid. It is a black-tie event, so all the male celebrities—even the radical ones—have a strange uniformity. Only Otello is wearing white, a silk tuxedo that sets off the sculptural handsomeness of his face. The bids are reckless, ridiculous. The film star Antonio da Rama pays eighty thousand for a signed pair of Otello's cleats (white, never worn). Lisboa Ritz, who is famous for being rich and rich for being famous, parts hysterically with two hundred and ten thousand of her hardly earned dollars for the gold-sprayed divan upon which Desmerelda reclined for the cover of her *Cleopatra* album. Cielo, the satellite TV channel, pays two million dollars for the right to film the proceedings. Broadcast on Christmas Eve, the show wins the TV ratings war hands down.

With dwindling patience, Diego waits for the backlash to begin, for the rot to set in. For the public to sicken of this unvaried diet of love and sweetness and fidelity. For the poor to realize how stupid it is to idolize the rich. For a dissenting note to enter the adulatory articles, the naive news coverage, the inane babble of radio DJs. For the appearance of a single photograph showing Otello and Desmerelda looking dejected, disheveled, discordant, even slightly grumpy.

None of this happens. An article in *El Guardián* had sneered at the "grotesque vulgarity" of the housewarming event, and this had cheered Diego briefly, but he knows that *El Guardián* is read only by intellectuals, left-wing politicians, and other persons of no importance or influence.

Much as he would like to, he cannot see its snide little article as the first shoots of the spiteful spring he is waiting for. It is as if those human qualities that Diego believes in most deeply — envy, cynicism, resentment — have taken a vacation. It is as if this nation, famed for pulling down statues and spraying graffiti on heroic murals, is stoned on worship. It is deeply frustrating.

Diego had expected, quite reasonably, that Otello's inflated celebrity would rekindle the hostility of his fellow athletes. But there is no sign of this, either. Perhaps this is because the bastard is playing so well. He is scoring in almost every game, and Rialto is already six points ahead at the top of the table. Blissful marriage has not softened him. In fact, his performance in the last game before the Christmas break is remarkable for its hunger and aggression; he scores twice, reducing the opposing defense to a panicky shambles.

In his weaker moments, Diego contemplates poisoning, unfortunate accidents on staircases, punctured brake pipes on cars.

And he had assumed that continuous exposure would illuminate the cracks, the fissures, in that preposterous marriage. In the couple's presence he eagerly seeks such signs. He is very good at reading body language. He is abnormally alert to those little glances, those tiny moments of inattention, the hundreds of ways that posture can display or disguise friction. Yet he has detected nothing. Nothing at all.

So Diego broods. He sits in the chair in his bedroom, staring at the distant restless neon of the city. Emilia watches him with her lovely eyes, waiting for him to come to her, to speak. She is neither hurt nor impatient; she understands that his silence is a way of sharing his unhappiness. When he does come to her, he caresses her and says things about her beauty. That is all, but that is enough. Later, in the darkness, she waits for his eyes to close, then closes her own.

Then, early in the new year, three men in two vehicles attempt to kidnap Desmerelda Brabanta. Whether or not she is their specific target is unclear; perhaps they are opportunists willing to ambush any large Mercedes-Benz with mirror windows. The only man who might clarify the situation dies of a gunshot wound before the police can interview him. All that can be said with certainty is that Desmerelda's bodyguards do not exactly cover themselves with glory.

She is returning from the studios of Miracle, the company making the video for her new single. She is not happy, because for most of the day she has had to hold dance poses in front of blue screens wearing a black body stocking coated with a web of tiny lights that, in theory, technicians will later computerize into a Desmerelda-shaped constellation of stars moving through the universe. It has been very boring. She has had heated discussions with Miracle as to why a body double couldn't've done the work. The caterers were late with the lunch. Ramona, her PA, has been off with a migraine — again — so Desmerelda is now having to work through a backlog of phone messages and texts as long as the Old Testament.

The route into the city takes her car along a sweep of the highway that skirts a mix of housing projects and haphazard slums. Her driver, who has made this trip nine times in the past four days, fails to notice that he has overtaken the same rusty white Toyota sedan three times. Nor does he clock the brown Ford van that has been reappearing in his rearview mirror for some distance. Worse still, because a spot of domestic disharmony made him late for work that morning, he has not filled the Merc's tank. So when the red warning light comes on, he has to make a decision. Which is less embarrassing: running out of fuel before they get back to the marina or making an unscheduled stop at the scruffy rest stop up ahead? He goes for the second option.

There are two licensed guns in the car, both Colt automatic pistols. One is in a clip mounted under the steering column, the other in the shoulder holster under Enrico's jacket. Enrico, according to the rules, should be in the back with Desmerelda, but because he is sensitive to bad vibes, he is sitting in the front passenger seat, having figured that this evening La Brabanta would rather be left alone.

When the driver signals to pull off the road, Enrico murmurs, "What you doin', man?"

"Gotta get gas."

"Aw, for Chrissake. You're kidding."

"Sorry, man."

Enrico sighs and pulls out his phone.

Indicating the turn is another mistake. The white Toyota, now just ahead, sees and slows down. When the Mercedes pulls into the rest stop, the Toyota—without signaling—whips in behind it and parks, engine running, in a space unlit by the canopy lights. A guy wearing greasy overalls and a red baseball cap gets out of the front passenger seat. The brown van follows the Mercedes in and pulls up at the other side of the pumps. The driver climbs out and yawns with his hand across his face while checking for CCTV cameras. Then he goes to the back of the van and opens the doors, as if he's fetching a fuel can. Or maybe he's got a dog in there that has to take a leak.

"What's happening?" Desmerelda wants to know, not looking up from her phone, which for some stupid reason has frozen up.

"Sorry, señora," Enrico says. "We had to stop for gas. Can I get you a soft drink or anything?"

"Uh, I dunno. Maybe a juice, if they've got organic."

The driver says, "So, er, you gonna get the gas, or what?"

Enrico has the door open and is trying to reach the office of A1 Security on his phone. "What?"

"Are you gonna get the gas, or am I?"

"Hang on, there's no signal here. . . . Damn! Er, what? Is this a self-service place?"

"I dunno. No, here's a guy."

154

The man in the overalls comes up to the Mercedes, smiling. He leans down to the car and looks past Enrico to speak to the driver. If he recognizes the passenger in the back, he gives no sign of it.

"Can I help you, señor?"

"Yeah, fill her up."

Enrico figures that he has to get out from under the canopy to get a signal, so he walks away, scowling at his phone.

The man in the overalls goes to the rear of the car and then comes back. "Excuse me, señor, but your fuel cap is locked. You wanna unlock it for me?"

"Yeah, sure, sorry," the driver says, and presses the switch. When he turns his head back, there's the deep black eye of a handgun staring straight at him.

"Okay, my friend," the now unsmiling face behind the gun says, "unlock the doors. In case you think we're not serious, look over your right shoulder."

The driver does so, cautiously, and sees that the man studying the prices on the neighboring pump is holding a big sawed-off shotgun down beside his leg. It is the kind of gun that will blow a major hole in a reinforced window.

Desmerelda finally looks up from her phone and says, "Oh, my God."

The way the rest stop is built, there's only one window in the coffee shop that commands a view of the fuel pumps. (They can be overseen from the window in the gas station pay booth, of course, but the underpaid kid in there is stressed out, dealing with the lights going on and off on his register and the people getting their PIN numbers wrong and such, so he never looks out.) And it so happens that the two people sitting at that coffee-shop window are armed police officers. They do not look like police officers. The woman, Sergeant Olympia Res, is wearing torn jeans and a jacket that might have been made from the skins of rats. Her hair is made of the tails not used in the tailoring of the jacket. Her colleague, Officer Alessandro Scuzo, shades parked on top of his head, looks like a pessimistic pimp.

They are here because the unlit overnight parking lot behind this particular rest stop on the Circular has been identified as a place where trucks bringing in raw cocaine from the coast pause to transfer the stuff to smaller vehicles. The police officers are awaiting a container truck that is possibly carrying more than the furniture that appears on its customs declaration. They are edgy because they've been sitting there for over an hour, drinking bad coffee and smoking, and they think that maybe they've been made by members of the staff who possibly have something to do with the setup.

It's Scuzo who murmurs, "Hey, check that out. The black Merc. Looks like an ongoing to me."

"Yep," Sergeant Res says. *"Damn."* She jabs her cigarette into the ashtray. "Okay, let's go. Call the cavalry while we walk to the door."

◆　◆　◆

Outside, the two officers walk briskly toward the Mercedes. The overalled man has one arm hooked around Desmerelda's throat and is dragging her toward the rear doors of the brown Ford van. His free arm is behind her back. When he sees Res and Scuzo approaching, he pulls Desmerelda in front of him, but she stumbles and goes down onto her hands and knees. His arm comes up, but before he can level the gun, Olympia Res shoots him square in the chest and he slams against the side of the van and slides onto the concrete without a sound. The man on the far side of the Merc shapes up and lets off something like a cannon, but all it does is blow the top off a pump. Res and Scuzo hit the ground, expecting a major gasoline explosion, but that doesn't happen. When they look up, the van is accelerating out of the station.

Scuzo gets up onto one knee with both hands on his gun, pure textbook, and fires three shots at the vehicle's tires. They all miss. A white Toyota revs ferociously and heads off after the van, tires screaming. Scuzo thinks about spending a couple of rounds on that as well, but by then his sergeant is bending over the girl on the ground and she's in his line of fire. So he stands up and lets his breath out. Then something makes him turn around, and he sees a guy wearing a brown leather jacket holding the blue glow of a cell phone in one hand and a big automatic in the other.

"Don't shoot!" the man yells, but Scuzo is so wired that he can't help himself. His first shot misses, but the second makes a sizable hole in Enrico's thigh. A little while later, the moaning starts to blend with the incoming sirens.

A week passes, during which time Nestor Brabanta pulls strings. He doesn't need to tug very hard. His daughter's name, his name, does not feature in any of the brief stories about a "failed holdup" that appear in the newspapers. He ensures that Enrico and the driver no longer have a future in the security business, regretting bitterly that it is far less easy to dispose of an unwanted son-in-law.

2.8

DIEGO ARRIVES AT the marina penthouse just before eight thirty.

"How is she?"

Otello turns away from the complicated chrome coffee machine and folds his arms. "Fine. Back at work."

"You're kidding me."

"Nope. She was pretty freaked out for a couple of days, then she gets up early, takes a shower, brings me coffee in bed, and says, 'Well, we've only got the studio for another week, I've got thirty people hanging around not knowing what to do, so I'm going back to work.'"

"I'm impressed," Diego says. "She's a great girl."

"She's amazing. Really strong."

There's something slightly challenging, as well as ridiculous, in the way Otello says this. So Diego nods his head like a man receiving wisdom. The coffee machine emits a high-pitched gargle, and Otello busies himself with cups.

"So who's with her?"

"For now, Michael. But I'm thinking about making that a permanent arrangement. That's what I wanted to talk to you about."

"You're thinking of switching Michael to Dezi?"

"Yeah. D'you have a problem with that?"

There is nothing in Diego's manner to suggest that the night-black interior of his head is suddenly lit up brighter than an autopsy. He sips coffee, considering the possibilities. At last he says, "Well, the obvious question is, if Michael watches Dezi, who watches you?"

"When we're out together, Michael is with us anyway, right? And when I'm with Rialto, well, the club security is pretty sound."

"Yeah, but . . ."

"I mean, Diego, think about what went down at that gas station, okay? You think if Michael had been in the car, any of that would've happened? No way, man."

"Yeah, maybe. Okay, you're right. Let's do it."

"You don't sound too happy about it. What's the problem?"

"No. It's fine. I think you're right. Honestly."

"No," Otello says, quietly insistent. "What's the problem?"

Diego puts his cup down carefully. "Okay, then, two things. First, I think he's too fond of her."

Otello blinks. "What?"

"Well, he doesn't exactly try to hide the fact that he adores her, does he?"

"Yeah, but hey . . . What are you saying here?"

Diego drinks more coffee before replying. "I'm saying that despite him being built like a tank, Dezi could twist Michael around her little finger. And that's not the ideal bodyguard-client relationship. Look, you say that what happened last week wouldn't have happened if he'd been in the car. But think about it: Dezi puts her hand on his and says, 'Michael, sweetheart, can we pull into this place just ahead and pick up some coffee?' Or they're somewhere else and she says, 'Michael, let's make a little detour and watch the sun set over the river.' You think he'd say no to her? D'you think Michael could say no to *anything* Desmerelda wants?"

Otello is staring as though a second nose has sprouted from Diego's face.

"It's about discipline, Capitano. Or *self*-discipline, I should say. That's what security is all about."

Otello shakes his head very slightly, like a man coming out of a trance. "Uh . . . okay. I take your point. But I think you underestimate Michael. You always have. He's tough up here"—Otello taps the side of his head—"as well as everywhere else. I don't think there'll be a problem with his self-discipline."

Diego nods. "Okay. You know him better than I do."

"Yeah, I do. What's the second thing? You said there were two things."

Diego hesitates. He shrugs and sticks his lower lip out. If you didn't know him well, you'd think he was slightly embarrassed.

"What?" Otello says, and there's a rough edge to his voice now.

"I'm just being straight with you here, Capitano."

"So, what?"

"Okay. The booze."

Otello sits back in the chair and goes slack like a supporter whose team has just, predictably, conceded a goal.

Diego holds his hands up in an apologetic gesture. "I know, I know," he says.

"Michael hasn't touched a drink for three years," Otello says flatly. "And I know that for a fact."

"He still goes to Alcoholics Anonymous."

"Yeah, he does. But that's like, you know . . ."

"For the support. The discipline. Of course."

Otello says nothing for several heavy seconds, so Diego does his manual apology again. "Okay, fine. End of subject. I'm done. If you're happy to put Michael on Dezi, that's fine with me. I'm sure she'll be very pleased with the arrangement."

On the way back to his car, Diego smiles. It's like walking on eggshells, talking to Otello about drinking. Diego likes the way the shells crunch beneath his feet.

2.9

OTELLO LOUNGES ON the bed watching Desmerelda put on her makeup. It is a ritual that fascinates him, absorbs him; he finds himself making the same slightly comical faces that she makes, applying the eyeshadow, the lipstick. On occasion she has caught him at it in the mirror, and rewarded him with that dirtily artless laugh of hers, which delights him. The intimacy of such moments is softly shocking; he thinks, *We are married. Married.*

It is the first time in three days that they have been in the penthouse together. On Sunday he arrived back from an away game two hours after she had flown down to the delta for a photo shoot. And tonight they are guests of honor at a party for the U.S. executives of Desmerelda's record company. Soon he will have to put on his gray silk suit. Desmerelda likes him in gray.

If he were honest with himself, he would perhaps admit that he does not want to go. More than that, he might admit that just lately he has started to feel, well, a sort of resentment. Impatience, perhaps. That his life, their marriage, is managed by Diego and Shakespeare and people whom he barely knows. Stitched into a glittering patchwork of events at which, usually, he feels like an exhibit. He has started, before games, to find it more difficult to get clean, to focus. To concentrate on the spaces that need to be made, the routes to the goal, to find the deep disregard for pain. (And avoiding injury has become more important; it would inconvenience too many people.)

Of course, he cannot confess any of this. He cannot tell her that he would like to come home from work to his wife. He cannot admit to the idiotic simplicity of his needs. She'd told him from the outset that they could never be ordinary. On that astonishing night at the hotel on Cypress, she looked down at him and said, very seriously, "We can never be members of the public." She'd said it with capitals: Members of the Public. And then, smiling, "But hey, who wants to be?"

At another level entirely, none of this matters. Because he, and he alone, is married to Desmerelda Brabanta. And he is the only man on the planet watching her as she puts on her makeup dressed in a couple of scraps of white lace.

He says, "How's it going with Michael?"

She leans closer to the mirror, checking the symmetry of her eyes. "Michael? Michael's great. Really solid."

"Yeah? So you're happy with the arrangement?"

"Baby," she says, "if he's good enough for you, he's

got to be good enough for me." She studies her eyelashes. "Lord, he's strict, though, isn't he? It's like everywhere I am, someone comes in the door, he's on them, taking their names, checking them over and everything. And if there's any change to the schedule, he's like a new world war might break out."

"That's good. It's what we pay him for."

She tilts her head in another direction. "He's cute, too. The plane back, it was one of those little ones, you know? Thirty seats or something, and Michael had to sit next to me, which is not what he likes to do. He prefers to sit two rows back on the opposite side, on the aisle. Anyway, I was really wiped out, and pretty much as soon as we took off, I was dead to the world. Didn't wake up until the plane was coming in. And I realize that I've been asleep on his shoulder the whole time and that I've drooled on this nice white shirt he's wearing, and because I'd been chewing fruit gum to stop my ears from popping, the drool is pink. I was so embarrassed. I said, 'Michael, I'm so sorry; we'll get that cleaned.' And he said, 'No, sign your name to authenticate the drool and I'll get it framed.' Sweet, huh?"

She turns away from the mirror and does a *ta-da!* gesture. "How do I look?"

With very little difficulty, Otello smiles. "Like the most beautiful woman in the world."

She raises a perfect eyebrow. "Only *like* the most beautiful woman in the world?"

◆ ◆ ◆

They return to the penthouse a little after two in the morning. Otello goes to their bedroom, throws his jacket on the couch, and flips on the TV, which has recorded the UEFA game between Arsenal and Barcelona. Three of his international colleagues are involved.

In the bathroom, Desmerelda watches herself in the mirror carefully cleansing away the makeup. The evening has been beautiful. The dinner, the elaborate courtesy of the *americanos,* the politeness of the photographers, the smoothness of the security arrangements, Michael's funny filthy stories on the way home. But.

She turns on the taps, adds a measure of aromatherapy oil, and goes back to the bedroom. "I'm going to take a bath. You going to come and scrub my back?"

"Try and stop me," he says. His speech is blurry; he has drunk more than usual.

The oil forms shifting archipelagos on the surface of the water. Below them, mottled by their shadows, her body seems remote, unfamiliar.

Things are going wrong.

No, things are *changing.*

She is slightly shocked that the word *wrong* entered her head. It means *unhappy.*

She is not unhappy. But.

Her new single, "The Darker the Night, the Brighter the Stars," is not getting the airplay they had expected. After the launch week, press coverage had dropped away sharply.

The singles chart is completely rigged, of course, but all the same, it is disappointing that the new song by that tart Carmina Flor has beaten hers to the number-one spot. The video for "The Darker the Night" is not the most requested item on TVQ, the twenty-four-hour music channel. Tonight, discussing the proposed mini-tour of the U.S. with the *americanos*, their eyes had dimmed slightly, as though they had suddenly found the need for lightly frosted contact lenses.

She considers these things calmly. She sees them for what they are: the beginning of the end of this part of her life. Which is, therefore, the beginning of the next part. The difficulty is that she does not know what this next part will be. She does know what is bringing about this shift, this key change, sea change. To be the wild rich rock chick is one thing; to be the *married* wild rich rock chick is quite another. It does not, in fact, work. It is one word too many. That's why she won't be top of the singles chart again. Because she's not single anymore. Ha!

She stirs the hot water, breaking up the little islands of oil, sending them swirling. She sinks lower and closes her eyes. He has not come to wash her back, then slip into the bath with her. She thinks about calling to him but decides not to.

It is slightly embarrassing that she has not foreseen all this. Did not foresee it when she drove to Puerto Río and cajoled those two wide-eyed rich boys into ignoring all good sense and taking her over to Cypress on their playboy boat.

167

Did not predict it when she descended onto his beautiful body and asked him to marry her.

Or maybe she did. Yes, perhaps she did. Reliving the moment, she remembers feeling that she was standing in the doorway of a room. A dark room full of brilliant possibilities. Now it connects with another memory. On the evening of her thirteenth birthday, her father blindfolded her and guided her to the doorway of the dining room. She stood with his hand on her shoulder for several seconds, listening to a silence that could barely contain itself. Then her father had removed the blindfold and there, ranged behind the laden party table, were her family and friends, smiling, holding gifts, beneath a cloud of gold and silver balloons. But it is those moments when she was still blind that she now re-experiences: standing there, knowing that something amazing was waiting for her. Feeling a thrill that was almost fearful. Almost sexual.

Soon, very soon, she will no longer be Desmerelda Brabanta. She will no longer own, much less control, her own celebrity. She will cease to be a star because she has stopped being dangerous, outrageous. She has married; she has become safe. She has become one half, maybe less, of a fixed constellation called Otello-Dezi.

She has always known that one day something like this would happen, that the party would come to an end, the table cleared, the cake and balloons shared out among the other children. And she has told herself that she would not care. She is not, after all, needy. But in the warm soothing water, in a warm room lined with Italian marble, she allows herself a minute or two to grieve.

She will not confess her thoughts to him. It would hurt him to do so; it would be stupid. At the heart of a true marriage is a shared silence, as her divorced mother used to say.

She calls to him now, but there is no reply. When she goes through to the bedroom wrapped in a towel, she finds him asleep. He has taken off some of his clothes and rolled onto his side. She turns the TV off, then stands marveling at him, astonished all over again that he is there, that he is what has happened to her.

When she has maneuvered him between the sheets and switched off the lights, she remembers that she has forgotten to take her contraceptive pill. But because he has fitted himself to her body and she doesn't want to disturb him, she does not get out of the bed to go to the bathroom cabinet. She will take the damn thing in the morning.

But she forgets. She somehow forgets the following night, too. And the nights that follow, one after another.

Act Three

3.1

PAUL FAUSTINO BLUFFED his way out through the fiendish glass doors by concealing himself inside a small knot of other employees, and to celebrate this small triumph, he lit a cigarette, hunching his shoulders over the flame. A chilly evening wind eddied around the patio; the ornamental trees dipped and shook their heads. A plastic bag wallowed through the air like a jellyfish. Something attached itself to his ankle: a flier for the New Conservative Party, bearing the slogan A CLEANER TOMORROW. Faustino flipped it off, although, usefully, it reminded him that *his* cleaner hadn't shown up yesterday. He went down the steps to get into the lee of the wind and saw Bush slooshing his wash bucket into the gutter.

The kid had been out of sorts lately. Nothing that Faustino could put his finger on, but something like a shadow had settled over the boy. He hadn't been quite the same since he'd disappeared for three days a while back. The smile and the eagerness were still there, but somehow less authentic than they used to be. And now, when he looked up and saw Faustino, his greeting was flat.

"Maestro."

"How're you doing, Bush?"

"Pretty good."

"Yeah?"

"Yeah. Kinda cold today, though."

"Well, maybe you should be wearing more than just that T-shirt, you know? Don't you have something else you could put on?"

"It wasn' so cold when I come out this morning."

It was an answer of sorts. But Faustino felt stranded. Bush held on to his bucket, shuffling his feet a bit, glancing right and left.

"Hey, c'mon, Bush. What's up?"

The boy shrugged.

"And don't just do that shruggy thing."

"Well, you know, Maestro. Woman problems."

Faustino laughed. He couldn't help himself. "What, all your girls fighting over you?"

"Not exackly."

Faustino could not tell from the boy's body language whether he was anxious to go or had something he wanted to talk about. Possibly both, or neither. With an awkward jocularity, he said, "So, d'you have a girlfriend, Bush? I bet you do."

"Nah. A sister an', uh, like another girl with us. Tha's trouble enough."

Faustino had wondered, of course, about the boy's life. Whether he was alone, where he slept at night, what he did with his paltry earnings. He knew that street kids often formed themselves into small clans, established territories, protected each other, operated a harsh kind of communism whereby they shared whatever they could steal or scavenge. Memories of his own childhood—a suburban childhood that had been solitary and frequently anxious, but ordered and comfortable—could not help him to imagine such a way of life. And, in truth, he shied away from imagining it, just as he avoided actually seeing it. He knew that he was not strong enough to cope with his helplessness in the face of it.

For some reason he did not think that Bush was a member of a clan. The boy seemed too . . . *independent,* was that the word? Or was it *unprotected*? But the mention of a sister and another girl was a glimpse into his life. A kind of offering.

"So, uh, you look after them, do you? Your sister and the other girl?"

"Kind of. Mostly they look after each other."

"Right." Not knowing what to say next, Faustino dropped his cigarette butt and ground it under his foot.

"Time to go," Bush observed. "Things to meet, people to do."

Faustino smiled. "Yeah. You could say that."

Bush's skin looked grayish and puckered. Faustino realized that the boy's restlessness, his fidgeting, was a way of concealing the fact that he was shivering. He reached into his inside jacket pocket and took out his wallet. He found a twenty, folded it lengthwise, and held it out. Bush looked at it but didn't move.

"Take it. Buy yourself a sweatshirt or a hoodie or something, okay? Something warm."

Bush pulled his gaze from the bank note and glanced toward the avenue. A woman walking to her car grimaced and turned her face away.

"Bush?"

"You wan' me to get in your car with you?"

"What?"

The boy looked back at Faustino but did not meet his eyes. "For the twenny. You wan' me to come to your car with you?"

It took perhaps three seconds for Faustino to understand the question; then his hurt was so deep, so shocking, that before he could think of anything to say, he had already hit the boy. The slap made a wet sound that was audible above the noise of the traffic; Faustino's hand registered the shape of teeth through the flesh of the boy's cheek.

Bush stumbled backward. He dropped the plastic bucket, made as if to retrieve it but did not; the wind tumbled it away. Then he was gone, running awkwardly, an erratic shadow in front of the oncoming headlights. The fallen twenty-dollar bill was plucked up by invisible fingers, dangled briefly above Faustino's head, and then thrown into the slipstream of the hurtling cars. The cry of pain that seemed to linger in the air was not the boy's. It was Faustino's.

DESMERELDA IS SITTING upright in bed with her phone in one hand and the TV remote in the other. Every now and again she says, "Oh, my God." Several newspapers are spread-eagled over the sheets. The headlines are pretty much the same:

OTELLO BODYGUARD ARRESTED

DEZI'S BODYGUARD IN SAVAGE ATTACK ON FORMER RIALTO STAR

OTELLO BODYGUARD AND LUIS MONTANO IN NIGHTCLUB BRAWL

OTELLO AND MONTANO: THE GLOVES COME OFF

Several of the photographs are of Desmerelda herself attending some function with Michael close to her. Or of Otello with a stern-looking Michael watching his back. Other pictures show a disheveled Michael being manhandled toward a police van by half a dozen cops. Or Luis Montano, bloody-faced, being helped into an ambulance. (It has not occurred to her, yet, to wonder why so many photographers were on hand to witness the incident.) The television is yabbering commentary at her over footage of Michael emerging from a downtown police station. He looks terrible. Stunned, like someone who has suffered a great loss. The only good thing she sees is Diego, who is trying to shield Michael from the cameras, ushering him into a car. She hears Diego's voice, blurred and broken by background noise, saying something like, "Misunderstanding . . . no . . . absolutely not. Nothing to do with that. No. No further comment." She switches channels, and her own face appears on the screen. She presses the mute button.

In the breakfast room, Otello is speaking to Diego's voicemail. For the ninth time. He slams down the phone and goes through to the bedroom. He leans against the door frame with his arms folded, gazing grimly at the screen. "Anything?"

"I just saw Diego. Seems he's bailed Michael out of police custody. I guess he's taken him home. Isn't he answering his phone?"

"Nope."

The phone rings.

"Capitano?"

"Diego. What's going on? Where are you?"

"Outside Michael's place."

"How is he?"

"Kind of rough."

"I should hope so. Look, Diego, get over here now, will you? I'll call him."

"I wouldn't bother, Capitano. I made him go to bed and told him to turn his phone off."

"Right. I guess that's sensible."

"And from the look of him, I'd be surprised if he's not already dead to the world."

"Okay. I'll leave it."

"Yeah. He won't be going anywhere. I'll see you in ten minutes."

In his suburban hacienda, Nestor Brabanta smiles and turns the TV off. His morning has improved. Earlier, while brushing his teeth, he had experienced again that little spasm of pain behind his right ear. Like a distant flicker of lightning that has gone before you can focus on it. As on previous occasions, it was followed by a slight blurring of the vision in his right eye and a touch of nausea. His doctor is of the opinion that the source of the problem — the root of it, so to speak, ha, ha — is a diseased tooth in his upper jaw. Brabanta has not done anything about it because he has a morbid fear of dentistry. Of the awful vulnerability of it, lying under the blinding lamps with your mouth open while a masked man uses steel tools on the inside of your head. But the images of Otello's hired oaf being dragged out of a nightclub have restored him completely.

He gets up out of the armchair and goes to his study. It will not be difficult to ensure that the story stays in the news. First he will call the two TV stations and the two tabloid newspapers that he has shares in. Then that slug Mateo Campos.

"Coffee?"

"God, yes. Black, please."

Diego leans his elbow on the table and massages his forehead with the heel of his hand. He is evidently tired, despite his appearance being as immaculate as ever. When Desmerelda comes into the kitchen, her hair still damp from the shower, he starts to get to his feet but she shoves him down and kisses his cheek.

"Okay," Otello says, "what the hell happened? Did Michael tell you?"

"He didn't have to tell me. I was there."

"What? *You* were at El Capricho as well?"

Diego sighs heavily. "Yes. I guess maybe this whole thing is my fault. I suppose I should have known that Michael . . . Well."

"Wait a minute. Wait a minute. Are you saying that you went there *with* Michael?"

"Yep. It was my idea." He takes a sip of coffee, needing it.

181

"The thing is, I knew that you two were having a rare night at home together. So Michael would be having the evening off. I also happened to know that it was his birthday."

"Oh, no," Desmerelda says. "He never said anything. Oh, man. We'd have come with you if we'd known."

"It's just as well you didn't, as things turned out. Anyway, I thought it would be nice to treat him to dinner."

"That's so sweet of you, Diego." She glances across at Otello and bites her lip. She recognizes the look on his face. As, to his pleasure, does Diego.

"So, I booked a table for two at El Capricho. On account of the food isn't the best in town, but they are discreet there and the security is sound. Michael turned up a bit late, not much. And it seemed to me he was in a pretty good mood."

Otello frowns. "What kind of a good mood? D'you think he'd been drinking?"

Diego shrugs. "Couldn't say. I had no reason to suppose so. Just that he was a bit more talkative than usual."

"All right. So what happened?"

"Well, we had dinner—"

"What was Michael drinking?"

"You know, those big fruit-juice cocktails they serve there. The ones that look like a rainbow in a glass."

"Is that all?"

"Yep. While I was with him, anyway."

"What d'you mean, 'while I was with him'? Where'd you go?"

"Well," Diego says, "when we'd finished eating, I went

to the men's room. And who should be in there but Luis Montano. Seems he'd come back home to visit his family and so forth. He was out on the town with various people. His actress girlfriend whose name I can never remember, and that singer, Emilio Parez. Plus a couple of Rialto players."

"What Rialto players?"

"Well, Roderigo—"

"*What?* Are you telling me that Jaco was involved as well?"

"Capitano, let me just tell it, okay? Then we can talk about the damage. We *have* to talk about the damage."

"All right."

"So, I'm in there with Luis, and I know he thinks I'm the evil genius behind his transfer up North. Which I am not, of course. But I managed to get him talking, and eventually he said, 'Listen, why don't you come and join the rest of us in the music bar?' Which I agreed to do. So, later, Michael and I went through. You know what it's like in there. You have to stand right up against someone and yell if you want to make yourself heard. And usually they don't listen, because they're watching the girls up on the dance platforms. My thinking was to give it another half-hour or so and then take Michael somewhere quiet for coffee. I was standing with Montano and his girlfriend, when suddenly there was a major uproar behind us. I turned to look, and Roderigo stumbled past us with the front of his shirt all ripped. And Michael was coming after him."

"Oh, my God," Desmerelda says quietly.

"Okay," Otello says. "So what was that about?"

"I had no idea until this morning, when I talked to Michael in the car. He claims that Roderigo said something about Dezi."

"Like what?"

"He wouldn't say. Actually, he says he can't remember. But obviously something that Michael took exception to. Very serious exception to. Because he was shoving through all the bodies to get at Roderigo again. So I got in front of him and put my arms around him, which is a bit like tackling a charging rhino, as you know. But I stayed on my feet somehow and managed to calm him down a bit. Roderigo had vanished into the crowd by this time; I didn't see him again after that. The bouncers were taking an interest by then, but I waved them away thinking that was the end of it.

"Unfortunately, it wasn't. Because Montano, the young idiot, took it into his head to have a go at Michael. Verbally, I mean. Called him a drunken gorilla, polite things like that. Michael stood this for about five seconds and then went off like Vesuvius. He punched Montano on the side of the face, and when the kid fell back against the bar, Michael hit him again and then had him down on the floor. I thought he was going to kill him. It took about ten of us to drag him off. Everyone was screaming and yelling. Then it seemed like just seconds before the police swarmed in."

Otello has his forehead resting on his hand as he stares down into his empty cup. "How is Luis? Do you know?"

"They took him to Santa Theresa. I called there this morning, talked to the duty sister."

"And?"

"Well, it could've been worse. He lost a couple of teeth, had to have five stitches in his upper lip. Severe bruising all over the place and possibly a fractured rib. Some concussion. They scanned him for a fractured skull but it was okay. He was discharged a couple of hours ago."

"Jesus."

"It'll be a while before he plays again. There is no doubt that his club will sue."

"I can't believe it," Desmerelda says. "I mean, Michael—"

Otello interrupts her. "So he was drunk?" It is barely a question.

"Who, Montano?"

Otello slams the flat of his hand down on the table so fiercely that his coffee cup leaps and clatters. Desmerelda flinches.

"No, *Michael*, for Chrissake!"

Diego does not answer immediately. Nor does he look up. It seems he cannot look Otello in the face. Eventually, reluctantly, he says, "He thinks someone spiked his drink."

"And is that likely?"

"Well," Diego says, sighing, "it's maybe possible. But we're talking about El Capricho, you know? Not some sleaze joint down in Castillo or somewhere."

"And you say he was drinking fruit juice? Did you see him drink anything else?"

"Well, no, but . . ."

"But what?"

"Nothing. The honest answer is no, I didn't see him drink anything else."

Desmerelda says, "So—" but Otello cuts her off.

"Listen, Diego. I pay Michael to protect Dezi and me. I don't pay *you* to protect *him*. So tell me, no bullshit. In your opinion, was Michael drunk?"

Diego sighs again, more unhappily than before. "I think so. Yes."

There is a longish silence. Desmerelda's gaze flicks from one man to the other, then comes to rest on her husband. She has never seen him angry. Or, rather, she has never seen him, sober or otherwise, give vent to anger. As a man who suffers sly kicks, minor assaults, verbal abuse, and professional fouls on a weekly basis, he has had to become extremely good at anger management. He has been red-carded off a soccer field only twice in his career, the last time two years ago. His calmness is one of the things she loves about him. He seems calm now, but—and this comes to her as a cold shock of recognition—he is not. She understands that this stony stillness is the form that his rage takes. His rage, or something worse. She has to summon up courage to speak to him, and that is shocking, too.

"Otello? Honey? What are you thinking?"

186

Instead of answering her, he walks over to the phone. He scrolls the memory, then thumbs the call button. He waits. Then he says, "Michael? Call me. I don't give a damn how rough you feel." He hangs the phone up but doesn't come back to the table. He leans against the wall and puts his hands in his pockets.

Desmerelda watches him warily. "What are you going to say to him?"

"I'm going to tell him that he's fired. It's what he'll be expecting."

She clasps her hands together and stares down at them. Diego's face is expressionless, but his dark eyes are narrowed and moist with expectation. She says, "Baby, don't you think we should hear Michael's side of the story before we make a big-time decision like that? I mean, you know, this thing is so out of character. . . ."

"No, it isn't. Unfortunately, it isn't."

"Okay. You know him better than I do. But right now Michael is *my* bodyguard, okay? And he's good. It feels good having him around. And I just don't feel right about losing him without knowing exactly what went down last night, you know? I think this is something we should discuss."

Diego interrupts the proceedings by getting to his feet. "Dezi's right. You two have issues over this thing that are none of my business. And I've got some crisis management to do. Let's talk later."

◆ ◆ ◆

In the elevator down from the penthouse, Diego looks up at the security camera and winks. A small self-indulgence.

Desmerelda goes to make more coffee, but, as usual, the complexities of the machine frustrate her, and she slaps it angrily.

Otello goes over. "I'll do it."

She turns and laces her fingers together behind his neck, looking up into his still-impassive face.

"Don't," he says. "Don't plead Michael's case. Please."

"But—"

"But nothing." He pulls her hands away. "Look. Michael Cass and I go back a long way. I know what drink does to him. It's like there's this other person inside him, an ugly, violent person, that takes over. He's been in rehab twice. And we made a deal. He works for me for as long as he likes if he can stay sober. If he can't, that's it. Because he's basically an alcoholic. If he's started drinking again, he won't just think, *Okay, that's it. I had a night of it. Now I'll stop.* Because he won't be able to. And what that means is, instead of him watching us, we'll be watching him. Think about it, Dezi. Like this awards thing we're supposed to be at on Tuesday. There'll be as much free booze there as anyone could want. Imagine if we take Michael and he kicks off, in front of the TV cameras and everything. Nightmare."

Desmerelda has to concede that this would not be a good thing. She takes an orange from the fruit bowl and sits at the table to peel it, concentrating on getting all the white pith away from the flesh. In the bedroom, her phone rings. She waits until it gives up.

"Don't you think," she says carefully, "it's kind of strange that all the papers had pictures of Michael and Montano and everybody coming out of El Capricho? Like, the people call the police because there's this big fight, they get there pretty fast, yeah, but as soon as they come out with Michael, there's all these photographers? Isn't that slightly weird?"

"I guess somebody tipped them off."

"Yeah, but how come they got there so quick? It doesn't make sense."

Otello shrugs. "I dunno. Maybe they didn't. Maybe the paparazzi knew that Luis and his celebrity friends were going to be there, and were just hanging around for pictures. Maybe they hang around there all the time. It's that kind of place, isn't it? It's why we don't go there anymore."

He pours the coffee. "Or what's more likely, come to think of it, is that people took pictures with their cell phones and sold them to the papers. It happens all the time. Everyone with a goddamn Nokia is a paparazzo these days."

Desmerelda pulls the segments of her orange apart so that they look like the petals of a fleshy flower, or a starfish.

"Maybe," she says. "It still seems kind of funny to me, though."

It *is* funny. Marvelously funny. Diego, gunning the Maserati at the traffic lights on Independencia, laughs out loud. Really, who could have predicted that it would all work out so well? The taxi to his right has two young guys in it who are checking out his car, and his laughter. They grin back at him, lifting their thumbs in an admiring salute. He returns the gesture. The lights change, and he pumps the accelerator, cutting off the cab for the simple pleasure of it.

Soon, he knows, Dezi will start working on Otello to give Cass his job back. And Otello will start to ask himself why she cares so much. Yes. But just to make sure, he will talk to Cass. Not now, though. Later. Let things simmer awhile. Besides, Emilia will be missing him.

3.3

YAWNING, FAUSTINO SHAMBLED into his kitchen and switched on the kettle. He opened the fridge and sniffed suspiciously at the pineapple juice. It smelled slightly fermented, but he glugged some down anyway.

He had not slept well, but could not recall the dreams that had troubled his night. They had slipped away to wherever it was they spent the days lying in wait for him.

While the coffee brewed, he went to the tiny bedroom he used as a home office and fired up his aging PC. Once he had deleted the usual baffling messages about firewall updates and virus checkers, then the spam (why was it that these people assumed he was lonely, impotent, and sick?), he discovered that he had one new e-mail. From Diego Mendosa, suggesting possible dates and times for the next interview with Otello. The message was logged at 6:04 a.m. Either the man started work very early or he didn't sleep. It occurred to Faustino that he knew nothing about Mendosa's private life. Just as — he tried to avoid the thought, and the memory that went with it, but couldn't — he knew nothing about Bush's.

He consumed his usual breakfast of two cups of coffee and two cigarettes while gazing blankly at the strips of world showing through the venetian blind. Then he called his office at *La Nación*. A robotic voice informed him that the departmental secretary was not at her desk at the moment. When the bleep went, he thought about saying, "And why not, exactly?" but then decided he couldn't be bothered and hung up without leaving a message. It would hardly be a shocking novelty if El Maestro was late on duty.

Faustino drove the Celica as quickly as he dared up through the lower tiers of the multistory garage. Bad shadowy things lived at these levels, and he would not leave his car there. There were spaces on the roof, and he parked in one that was within sight of the attendant's glass booth. He walked through the tubular glass bridge that arced above the squalling traffic and onto the concourse that overlooked the vast atrium of Beckers, the biggest and best department store in the city. From his vantage point, it resembled a colony built by termites that declined to use any building materials other than crystal or chrome. Here, as always, he felt almost religious. The Muzak and the ascending voices of a thousand shoppers blended into something that could be mistaken for prayer. He rode the escalators down to the

192

menswear department, trying to look uninterested as he sank past the brazen mannequins that beckoned him into women's lingerie.

Faustino knew about clothes. His fingers could tell the difference between the genuine article and the product of some local or Asian sweatshop. He was halfway to the cashier with a nice cotton crew neck when he realized his mistake. He returned the garment to its rack and went to rummage in the discount bin for something that looked less stealable. Almost everything in there made him wince, but eventually he found a gray-and-black synthetic sports top that wasn't entirely disgusting and was probably windproof. He took it to the register. There was no point using a credit card; Faustino paid with the change in his pocket.

He headed back to the escalators, then paused to study a floor plan. Household goods, maybe. Down in the bowels of the store, where he had never ventured. He hesitated, checked his watch, then began the descent.

The plastic buckets were pastel-colored, flimsy-looking affairs with unconvincing handles. Girly things, accessories for oversize Barbie dolls. He found his way into home decorating, and there he discovered a small tower of black rubber pails. It resembled the trunk of a burned palm tree. He pulled the topmost one free. The handle was made of galvanized metal with a wooden grip. Faustino wedged the pail between his feet and yanked at it, testing the fixings. A shelf stacker paused in his work and watched him with some interest. Satisfied—or as satisfied as a non-expert in bucketry could be—Faustino bought the thing.

Rubén watched Faustino approach the glass doors. The senior sportswriter arriving at *La Nación* carrying a black rubber bucket was not an everyday event. It was possibly sinister. The doorman braced himself.

"Hi, Rubén."

"Señor Paul."

"A little less chilly today."

"Yeah," Rubén said, glancing down at the bucket. There was something in it, something in a purple shopping bag.

"You, er, seen the kid this morning?"

That question again. And the man seemed edgy. Uh-oh. "Nope. Not yet."

Faustino turned away and walked to the edge of the patio. He looked up and down the avenue. Rubén studied the trees, his face neutral. Faustino came back.

"Look, Rubén, do me a favor, huh? If you see him, give him this." Faustino held out the bucket, and after a flicker of hesitation, Rubén took it. "Tell him it's from me, okay?"

"Okay."

"And listen, say, um, say that this is to make up for the misunderstanding, all right?"

Rubén frowned at this difficult idea. "The bucket is to make up for the misunderstanding?"

"Yes. Well, no, not exactly, it's . . ."

Faustino looked distinctly shifty, which was a new thing in Rubén's experience. It made him cautious.

"No? Sorry. It's what's *in* the bucket that makes up for the misunderstanding. Is that right, Señor Paul?"

Faustino had not expected the need to explain himself. Indeed, he could not have done so. A motorcycle messenger stumbled out of the revolving doors. A skinny yellow dog came up the patio steps, looked around, and went back down.

"Look, er, forget the misunderstanding bit, okay? When you see the kid, just give him the damn thing. You don't need to say anything."

"Okay."

"Right. Let me in."

Rubén put his hand on the huge brass door handle, then paused thoughtfully. "Thing is, Señor Paul, if I don't say nothin', the kid's gonna think it's from me, maybe. So you want me to say it's from you?"

Faustino's shoulders fell. He looked at the ground, nodding as though he were suddenly afflicted by Parkinson's disease. "Yes," he said as calmly as he could manage. "Fine. Thank you."

Rubén pulled the door open, and Faustino passed through. Halfway across the lobby he said, "Jesus!" so loudly that Marta, the receptionist, dropped her lipstick.

3.4

FAUSTINO SPENT THE first hour of his working day watching the TV in his office and keeping up with the stuff from the Press Association that popped up on *La Nación's* intranet. There was nothing new; none of the leading characters were saying anything. There was footage of Otello arriving at the Rialto training ground, ignoring all questions from the press pack at the gates. Luis Montano was saying nothing because, obviously, lawyers had told him not to. Ditto Jaco Roderigo. Nothing from Desmerelda; a smooth, long-haired young man representing Shakespeare made a brief media statement to the effect that although "distressed" by the affair, the star was "continuing to fulfill her professional and other engagements." Nobody had seen her, though. As for Cass himself, he had gone underground; incredibly, no one seemed to know where he lived.

La Nación had reported the brawl and its aftermath almost reluctantly, on page three. So Faustino was surprised to get a call from the news editor, Vittorio Maragall.

"No, Vito, I do not have Otello's personal phone number. No, we're not 'great pals.' I've met him half a dozen times, is all. And in any case, I wouldn't . . . Look, Vito, what is this? We're not chasing this story, are we? It's just tabloid fodder . . . We are? Carmen thinks what? Yeah, well, she's always been a bottom feeder at heart. Okay, I'll see what I can do. Maybe a sort of 'thought piece' on how this is all so much bullsh—Yeah, well, if she doesn't like it she can stick it. Yeah, and you, Vito. Chin up."

Faustino already had two things that he was meant to be working on: an obituary of the former Deportivo San Juan and international goalkeeper Pablo Laval, and a longish piece for the weekend supplement on the latest corruption scandal seeping out of Italian soccer. He'd retrieved a manila-bound file on Laval from his famed Library of Useless Knowledge, a packed and eccentrically cataloged storeroom that opened onto his office, and he sat for a few minutes leafing through it. Then he set off on the long trek to the drinks machine. He got as far as the elevators and paused, jingling the coins in his pants pocket. He made a thoughtful popping noise with his lips, like a man who has just remembered something, then pressed the down button.

Rubén was not in sight beyond the glass doors, so Faustino went over to the right-hand side of the lobby and peered through them at an angle. There was the doorman, looking bored, close to the wall next to the far door. The bucket sat on the ground just behind his feet. Faustino scanned the patio, then returned to his office.

The marina penthouse. Just after midday. The phone rings.

OTELLO: Michael?

CASS: Yeah.

OTELLO: How are you?

CASS: You don't want to know.

OTELLO: Man, I don't know what to say to you.

CASS: Yes, you do. I say, "I'm sorry." Then you say, "You're fired." Right?

OTELLO: Michael, man, I love you. But . . .

CASS: But I'm fired.

OTELLO: I'm relieving you of your duties.

CASS [*laughs harshly; it's like a bark*]: Relieving me of my duties? Where the hell did you get that from? You don't have to talk like that to me, man. Save that crap for the press release.

OTELLO: Maybe this isn't the right time to be having this conversation. Why don't I call you in a couple of days? When you're feeling better.

CASS: Yeah. Listen. How's Dezi?

OTELLO: I'll call you, Michael. Promise. Look after yourself. You know what I'm saying?

CASS: Someone spiked my drink, man. That's the

truth. Think about that. I want you to make sure
Dezi is looked after, you hear me?
OTELLO: I'll call you.

Bush's head was messed up. He didn't think the spliff he
was smoking was going to help, but for now, what the hell.
He'd got it from Rocco, who sold tiny paper cups of coffee
and single cigarettes (and spliffs to customers he trusted
and friends who needed one) from a little pushcart
made out to look like a steam locomotive. Rocco
leased his mobile business, and bought his coffee and
cigarettes, from a man who owned a great many of these
little carts. This man was not the kind you mess with,
and so Rocco never got mugged, even though he was
always carrying cash. Bush was hiding money in the tin can
buried in the shed with a view to getting into the same line
of work. It wasn't the kind of thing you could work on the
Avenida San Cristóbal outside *La Nación*, though.

He groaned smoke, remembering. When he explored the
inside of his cheek with his tongue, it still felt kind of pulpy.

Maestro or no Maestro, he'd have to go back, or lose
the damn turf. Try and hustle another bucket from Nina
tomorrow and go back. But he didn't want to have to say
sorry to the guy. Couldn't think how to. Shouldn't *have*
to, for Chrissake. Like, who'd hit who? The man holds
out twenty dollars. What's anybody gonna think? He was
always friendly, so he could've been queer, right? The
friendly ones usually were.

None of this consoled Bush, however. Because he was just talking to himself in his head. What he felt, the thing that was hurting somewhere other than his mouth — well, that was something else entirely.

He was sitting with his back against the low wall of the dry fountain in Los Jardines, the Gardens, down at the southern end of the Triangle. A hundred years ago, Fidel had told him, these really had been gardens: fabulous ones, with parrots in the trees. The huge *palacio* to which they'd originally belonged had been pulled down to build the university whose raw-looking concrete towers loomed beyond the growling traffic over to Bush's left. Now Los Jardines was a large area of patchy grass and reddish earth, randomly broken up by footpaths, stubborn trees, and meaningless wire-mesh fences. Boys came here to sleep in the sun, in little packs with sentries, or to stage unruly, day-long games of soccer. The girls came to support, mock, gossip, hang out. There was a certain safety in the openness of the space; you could see something happening from a long way off. It would take an army of Ratcatchers to surround the place. Bianca and Felicia had become part of a cluster of girls gathered on and around a couple of benches fifty yards from where Bush sat smoking.

Felicia. There was another thing messing with his head.

Last night. He'd sat on his sleeping mat with his knees drawn up under the old knitted blanket for maybe an hour, playing the scene with El Maestro over and over in his head, trying to picture the next day, how things might go. He'd fallen asleep without noticing how, and then there'd been something moving up against him. He'd turned, thinking, *What?* And he must have said it, too, because she'd put her fingers on his mouth and gone, *"Shh."*

"Felicia? Wha—?"

"Shh. Bianca's asleep."

Felicia's eyes, just two pale circles in the darkness, very close. He'd watched them, listening to the sound of Bianca's mumbled breathing.

"What you want, girl?" he'd whispered. "Somethin' the matter?"

"I need to talk to you, Bush."

"Well, you sure picked a poor time to start. Can't it wait? I need to sleep."

"No, it can't wait. I gotta talk to you when Bianca ain' listenin'."

He'd moaned quietly.

"Bush, you just got to face up to this. I can't watch her no more."

"Aw, Felicia—"

"No. Listen to me, now. This isn' me complainin', right? This's me sharin' the cares we both got. And you've gotta take your share of it. I know, I know. I know you got other things you need to do. But she's your sister, man. I just don' have the hold over her you do."

He'd turned onto his back and shut his eyes. Somehow

he'd brought himself to say, "Okay. So what's been happenin'?"

"I dunno. Maybe nothin'. All I know is, she spends like all the time tryin' to get away from me. It's drivin' me crazy. Like, today, down the market, the old woman does the barbecue, she says, 'Felicia, you wanna do me a errand, I'll give you somethin' nice to eat.' And I gotta say no. 'Cause I know soon's I'm gone, Bianca'll scoot off, and I'll spend the rest of the day shit-scared lookin' for her."

Her eyes. Shinier than before. Tears, maybe. He didn't need this.

"So what you think she's into? She into anythin' you know about?"

Felicia had moved onto her back beside him then. Her shoulder warm against his.

"No," she'd murmured after a while. "It's just . . . like she sees the world a dif'ren' way, you know what I mean? It's like she sees the world full of . . . of, I dunno, promises. She ain't got the sense to be afraid of anythin'."

He'd wanted a hand to hold, but the only one nearby was Felicia's. Bianca had stirred, muttered something on the verge of speech. When her breathing had returned to its rhythm, Bush'd found himself looking into Felicia's eyes again.

"So what you think I should do?"

"I dunno. Talk to her, I dunno. All I know is, I'm scared."

"What of?"

"Of takin' care of her. That if somethin' happens, you'll blame me."

Tiredness had swept over him then, like a soft wave he'd wanted to go with. It was perhaps this tiredness that'd made him feel gentle toward her. "No. It's all right. I know how hard it is for you, girl. Things'll be fine. Get some sleep."

He'd touched the backs of his fingers to her face, then turned away, dismissing her. But she hadn't moved.

"What happen to you today, Bush?"

"What?"

"Side of your face is swole up."

"Yeah, well . . . Ain't nothin' to worry about. I'm okay."

Then she'd leaned over and brushed the hair away from his face and put her fingers lightly where Faustino had slapped him. At the same time, he'd felt a soft double caress come to rest against his shoulder. Her breasts. Something like electricity happened. Her thigh against the back of his. She kissed his neck.

"Jesus, Felicia," he'd said, the words thick in his throat. He'd turned over, but she'd gone before his hand could reach her. He'd heard her settle back into bed with Bianca, who'd murmured something before the darkness went still and silent. His foolish lonely body sending him needful messages he didn't want to hear.

What you doin'? he'd asked himself. *Tha's* Felicia, *man.*

Now, almost as if she knew what he was remembering, she stood and looked over at him, folding her arms across her chest, miming *I'm cold*. And yes, despite the sun, a chill wind patrolled Los Jardines. For twenty dollars he could've gotten warm tops for all three of them. Bush stubbed the joint and raised a hand to her. She smiled and turned back to the game. He looked at the sky. Flat-bellied clouds with outrageous towering crests drifted from left to right. He indulged a stoned vision of ordering them into a regular, geometric parade.

When he'd told the girls that they were all going down to Los Jardines, Bianca had sulked, saying that no one cool went there. He'd told her that yeah, it was a sorry place, but the sky was bigger there than anywhere else in the city. Felicia had been happy. Unlike Bianca, she'd understood that Bush was taking a day off. At almost all the crossings she'd linked her arm in his, pretending to be afraid of the traffic. And he hadn't shaken her off.

Yeah, his head was messed up. So it was surprising that he wasn't unhappy. When he stood up, the dope hit him, and he set off toward the girls on uncertain legs.

When Faustino left for lunch at a quarter to one, Rubén's place had been taken by a guy in a janitor's uniform. The bucket containing the sports top had disappeared from its position by the wall.

"Rubén on a break?"

"Yessir. Said he'd be ten, fifteen minutes."

"Right. He, er, give you anything to look after?"

The janitor looked anxious, as though this were a trick

question slipped into a job interview. "No, sir. Should he have?"

"Nah," Faustino said. "Don't worry about it."

When he returned at two fifteen, Faustino found Rubén engaged in an animated discussion with the driver of a van double-parked in front of the building. He loitered for a while, but it looked as though the dispute might go into extra time and maybe even a penalty shootout, so he fought his way single-handed into the lobby and headed for the elevators. On the way he glanced over at Marta, on the principle that Marta always deserved glancing at. And she was looking back at him. She had her phone cradled between her chin and her shoulder, and with her right hand she was holding aloft Faustino's bucket. Her face had a big amused question all over it. Three women who were signing the visitors' book turned to look at Faustino, then the bucket, then back at Faustino. He made a downward, put-it-away gesture with his hand and continued on his way, scowling.

He spent the rest of the afternoon half-heartedly researching the financial and political hanky-panky of a perma-tanned little Italian billionaire called Silvio Berlusconi.

3.5

Dusk. The calls of cicadas and birds returning to roost mingle with the calls of boys playing soccer in the threadbare park below Michael Cass's apartment. Beyond the ragged fringe of darkening trees, the sky has taken on the color of a bruised peach. The first bat of the evening scoots past the balcony where Michael and Diego are sitting.

"I talked to the Espirito lawyers," Diego says. "They want damages, of course. They huffed and puffed a bit, but I'm pretty sure they'll settle out of court in the end."

Michael nods but doesn't speak. He'd limped to the balcony, and now Diego notices that there are grazes on his neck and dried blood inside the folds of his ear. The police would not have been gentle with him.

"How are you feeling?"

"Damaged."

"You think you should see a doctor, get yourself checked out?"

"Nah. Besides, the main damage isn't physical."

"No, I guess not," Diego says understandingly. "Look, Michael, you and Otello have known each other for a long time. You're probably the best friend he has. Why don't you give him a day or two to cool down, then call him? My guess is that he'll take you back on."

"I don't think so. He's not the kind of guy who changes his mind. And you know what? If I was him, I wouldn't either. My reputation's gone down the drain in this town. I was unprofessional, man. I mean, what kinda bodyguard doesn't keep an eye on his own drink, never mind the client's? Huh?"

Diego nods as though the thought has not occurred to him before now. He lets half a minute go by and then says, "What puzzles me is, why would anyone spike your drink in the first place? You know, forgive me for saying so, my friend, but it's not like you're a famous face—some celebrity someone wanted to make a fool of, or take advantage of. So why you? Do you think whoever did it thought your drink belonged to someone else?"

"I've been thinking about that. And no, I don't think it was a mistake. The only thing I can figure is that it has to do with Dezi."

"Dezi?"

"Yeah. Maybe someone wants me off the case. Wants me out of the picture so that I'm replaced by people who're less careful. Or people who could be bribed, even."

Diego rubs his jaw, considering this. "Well, maybe. But—"

"Listen, Diego," Michael says, leaning closer. "Tell Otello to be very, very careful about security from now on, okay? I mean it. Especially with Dezi."

"Sure," Diego says. "I'll do that."

"But hey, listen—don't say anything to her. I don't want her getting paranoid."

"Fine. Okay."

"How is she, anyway?"

Diego sighs. "Well, she's pretty upset, as you can imagine."

"I'm sorry." Michael looks away and down. "I'm sorrier than I can say."

"I know, but that's not what I meant. She's upset that Otello fired you. She was very strongly against it."

Michael lifts his head. Something distantly related to a smile stirs the stubble on his face. "Yeah? That's nice. She's a great kid. Really great." He laughs, a short incredulous noise more like a cough. "And I never thought I'd hear myself say that about someone called Brabanta."

Diego gets up and goes to lean on the balcony rail. Below, the boys are playing on, stubbornly ignoring night-fall. Their ball is a small ghostly moon taking an erratic course through the gathering darkness.

"Michael, you know what I would do if I were you? To remedy this situation? Talk to Dezi. Privately. Explain what happened. Apologize, whatever it takes. She'll listen to you. And get her to argue your case with Otello. It might take a while, but she'll get around him. Can you imagine him denying her anything she wants?"

"Ah, man, I dunno. . . ."

Diego turns. "What's the problem?"

Cass shrugs, looking down at the space between his feet.

"Ah," Diego says. "A matter of pride, right? You and Otello really are two of a kind, aren't you? Pair of stiff-necked northern bastards."

"Hey, Señor Mendosa, you better smile when you say that to me."

"I am smiling," Diego says. And he is, of course. "Look, if you're right about what happened, we need you back with her. It's her best interests we're talking about here."

"Maybe."

"I think so. Call her. Arrange a meeting. And Michael? Don't leave it too long. She may have to mount a charm offensive."

3.6

THE MORNING TRAFFIC was even more infernal than usual, so when Faustino got to his underground parking space, he sat in the Celica listening to the faint ticking of the cooling car, trying to mimic the process. Then he clambered out and, as usual, took a rather childish delight in using the key fob to chirrup the door locks. He became aware of the sound of running water. People off the street sometimes slipped in here to take a leak — on camera — but this was louder than that.

Over in the shadows below the ramp, Bush was filling the bucket from a tap that Faustino hadn't known existed. Even in the subterranean gloom, the boy's mad head was unmistakable. It was shameful, how nervous Faustino felt. Just for a second he considered getting back into the car until Bush had gone. But there was something in the kid's posture, his intentness on his task, that told Faustino that Bush was fully aware of his presence. So he walked over, conscious of how dreadfully loud his footfalls sounded in the low, echoing space.

"Looks good on you, the top," Faustino said. "I had to guess the size. How'd I do?"

Bush let the tap run a bit longer, then shut it off and turned around. "Yeah, pretty good."

"The color okay?"

Bush shrugged. "Yeah, it's fine. Don't show up too much, you know what I mean? In the dark."

"Good," Faustino said, nodding. "That's good. The bucket suit you? It seemed, you know, well made and everything."

"It's heavy, full. But the handle is cool."

"Right."

Faustino waited, hoping that Bush would say something more. He didn't, but at least the boy's eyes met his own, and he managed something close to a smile—a brief flash of bright teeth.

"Okay," Faustino said. "Well, I guess we've both got jobs to get to."

And because neither of them was prepared to make the first move, they found themselves walking up the ramp together toward the light and the surge of the traffic.

At Desmerelda's suggestion, she and Michael Cass meet for lunch at a place called Tako, tucked away in the district popularly known as New Tokyo. Michael likes sushi. The restaurant is divided into discreet booths, and Desmerelda has ensured that theirs is visible from only one other table. At that table, one of her two bodyguards is sitting, nibbling crunchy little things that he finds slightly disgusting yet interesting. He has a phone mounted on the side of his head; it looks as though a silver cockroach is feasting on his ear. The second bodyguard is outside in the agency car. He has already called Señor Mendosa, as instructed, to tell him of their whereabouts.

"Look, Michael," Desmerelda says. "He'll come around. I know he will. This is like politics, you know? He'll have to keep his distance for a while because, well, because there's so much involved."

"Yeah. I'm bad for the image."

She wants to deny this, but can't, so she stirs her seafood with one chopstick. Eventually she says, "He's going to miss you more than you miss him."

"Dezi, let's not get all sentimental here. You and him, you've got stuff happening all the time. I'm not dumb. I know that a month, two weeks from now, there'll be so much going on that if someone says 'Michael Cass,' you'll say 'Who?'"

"Michael, that's not true. Please don't say that." She reaches over and lays her hand, briefly, on his.

Her bodyguard pops another seaweed-flavored something into his mouth.

"I want you back with me," she murmurs. "These two stooges I've got today—I mean, can you imagine? The

212

other one, the one in the car, is positively obese. I talk to them, it's like, *duh,* you know?"

Cass smiles for the first time.

"Michael, be patient a little while. We'll get you back, I promise."

An exquisite waitress comes to take their bowls away. An equally exquisite waiter sets in front of them square white plates and a complex work of food art that they hesitate to spoil.

"No disrespect," Michael says, "but he's a stubborn bastard."

Desmerelda makes a fond noise. "Well, you know what? I don't think so. Not with me, anyway. It's a matter of timing. A word or two over dinner, a little ask at exactly the right moment, you know? Keep the issue on his mind. I'm on the case, Michael. Don't worry."

Otello is doing warm-downs after training when one of the juniors, his equipment boy, brings his phone to him.

"Capitano? This a bad time?"

"Diego. No, it's fine. Something up?"

"No. Just a couple of things I thought we might talk about. I wondered if you'd like a late lunch."

"Yeah, okay. Where?"

"There's a quiet little place down in New Tokyo I've been to once or twice. Good sushi. The steak is excellent, too. Pick you up in, what, fifteen minutes?"

◆　◆　◆

The lunchtime business on *La Nación*'s patio had been poor, and Maestro had not appeared. Bush was about to give up on him, refill his bucket, and take up position at the curb again, when Faustino emerged from the building. Within five minutes he was back with Faustino's two packs of Presidentes.

Bush waited, solemn but awkward, while the man battled with the cellophane and lit up. Then he said, "Maestro, I was wonderin' if you'd do me a favor."

Faustino raised one eyebrow. "Well, I guess that depends on what kind of favor that might be."

From his pocket, Bush produced a scroll of printed pages and held it out.

"What's this?"

The boy shrugged. "Somethin' I found."

The rolled-up pages kept curling back on themselves; Faustino found them difficult to manage with the cigarette in his hand. Their margins were yellowed and the few illustrations were badly printed, their colors off-register. They appeared to be part of a chapter from a book about, of all things, crabs. He looked at Bush, flummoxed.

"I was wonderin' if you could tell me what this says here," the kid said, pointing.

"Er, okay . . . It says 'Limb regeneration in the species *Callinectes exasperatus.*'"

The boy's face was somehow blank and expectant at the same time.

"That last bit is Latin," Faustino added helpfully.

"You mean, like Mexican?"

"Ah, no. It's a language. An old language. It's the name of this particular crab."

Bush nodded, impressed. "That's one helluva name for a crab, huh?"

"Well, it's not just this . . . Yeah, I suppose it is. Why do you want to know, Bush?"

He shrugged again. "I dunno. Been buggin' me, I guess."

"Yeah, well, maybe that's why it's called *exasperatus*," Faustino said, smiling, and then felt ashamed of himself, seeing the baffled seriousness in the kid's face.

"The way I figure it," Bush said, pointing again, "is these pictures show this crab can grow back a leg. One that's been bit off, maybe."

"Yep, that's right. Crabs can do that. So can starfish and, if I remember correctly, some lizards too."

"Yeah? That's a pretty good trick, ain' it?"

"It is indeed," Faustino said. "Be kind of neat if we could do that, wouldn't it?"

"Wouldn' it, though," Bush said soberly. "And what do the words under the pictures say, Maestro?"

"Um, the first one says 'Leg bud,' then the next ones say 'First molt. Second molt. Third molt. Fourth molt.'"

"Uh-huh. What's a molt?"

"Well," Faustino said, stalling while he skimmed Professor Fuentes's enthusiastic but turgid prose. "Yeah. What happens is that when a baby crab grows, sooner or later it

215

gets too big for its shell. So it has to, er, discard . . . well, basically, it sort of climbs out of its shell. That's a molt. Then it grows another one. A bigger one. Then after a while it gets too big for that shell. So it does the molt thing again, and grows an even bigger shell. And it has to keep on doing this until it's fully grown, you know? Then it's got a shell it can keep."

And that, Faustino thought, *is a trick we can do. Have to do.* But it was probably not an idea he could share with the boy.

"So I guess what the pictures are telling us, Bush, is that it takes old *exasperatus* here four of these molts to grow that leg back. I imagine that's a pretty long time."

Bush was silent for a while studying the pictures, nodding thoughtfully. Then he looked up. "He does it, though," he said.

"Yeah," Faustino agreed, grinning. "It's amazing what you can do if you've got the—"

"Ambition, maybe?"

Faustino laughed aloud now, and in response a huge smile dispersed the solemnity in the boy's face. Then his eyes switched to the road. He took the pages from Faustino and rolled them up.

"Cars comin' in," he said. "I gotta run. Thanks, Maestro."

"Bush, tell me . . ."

But the kid was already halfway down the steps. Then he stopped, turned back. "Maestro? I'm sorry about . . . you know?"

"A simple misunderstanding," Faustino said.

"Yeah."

His hair bounced out of sight.

"Hey, señora! Wan' me to keep an eye on your car? There's people round here needs watchin', you know what I mean?"

The bodyguard with the silver insect on his ear stands up when he sees Otello and Diego. He doesn't think this is in the script. Looks like an *uh-oh* situation. . . .

He takes a couple of paces toward Desmerelda. "Señora?" She looks up from her phone. He wags his head toward the door. "Your husband, señora."

"What?"

She leans forward and peers around the side of the booth. A waiter is showing Otello and Diego to a table, but Otello walks past it, toward her. She stands up. Her face feels hot, suddenly, and that is awful.

"Baby! My God! What are you doing here? Hi, Diego. Hey, I can't believe this! Why didn't you tell me you two were going to be here? Aw, I've just paid the bill. I've got to meet Ramona in twenty minutes. If I'd known . . ."

"It was a last-minute thing," Diego says, smiling. "I didn't think to call you. I'm so sorry."

Otello glances down at the table, the two tea bowls, the two empty glasses. He says, "Was that Michael I just saw heading off down the street?"

3.7

THE AIRPORT. RIALTO is flying down to Dos Santos for the second leg of the cup tie. Half the squad, plus Tresor, have already left on the afternoon flight. You just don't put a billion dollars' worth of soccer players on one plane. Otello wanders over to a far corner of the VIP lounge where the Muzak doesn't reach and taps Diego's number on his phone. Waiting, he looks down through the dark glass to where people in luminous vests are doing mysterious things that his life probably depends on.

DIEGO: Hi. You're checked in?

OTELLO: Yeah. Anyway, like we were saying.

DIEGO: Well, I'm not sure I have any further thoughts on the subject. To be honest, it's not really any of my business. Well, it is, but essentially it's something you and Dezi have to sort out.

OTELLO: Diego, I don't need to see you to know you're doing that thing.

DIEGO: What thing?

OTELLO: That frowny thing you do when you're thinking stuff you think I don't want to know about.

DIEGO: You're spooky, Capitano. You read me like a book, and I don't know if I like it.

OTELLO: I know you saw Michael. You did, didn't you?

DIEGO: Yeah, okay. I saw him.

OTELLO: And did he look guilty to you, or what?

DIEGO: Well, I don't know. Furtive, maybe. Embarrassed . . . I'm really sorry, Capitano. I had no idea they'd be there. It's sort of my fault. I'd told Dezi it was a good place to eat, but . . . Look, he needed to apologize to Dezi in person, right? There's probably no more to it than that.

OTELLO: You're doing it again.

DIEGO: What? Christ, have you got me on camera or something?

OTELLO [*laughing a little*]: No. You're easy, is all. So tell me what you really think.

DIEGO: You mustn't rely on what I think. Seriously. I'm an agent. It's in the nature of my business to think the worst of people. It's my affliction. And it's useful to me, Capitano, but not to you. Jealousy, suspicion, paranoia, they're not useful to a player. I strongly suggest you forget all about this and concentrate on tomorrow's game.

OTELLO: It's not like she denied it, right? She admitted straight out that Michael had been there.

DIEGO: She did. Mind you, there'd've been little point in denying it.

OTELLO: And as soon as we got home, she was on it again. About giving Michael his job back.

DIEGO: And what did you say?

OTELLO: I said I'd think about it. But not yet. Listen, they've just called our flight. I've got to go. I'll talk to you tomorrow maybe.

DIEGO: You and Dezi are spending Thursday and Friday at the villa, right?

OTELLO: Yeah. Dezi's going down there ahead of me, tomorrow night.

DIEGO: She say anything to you about Michael taking her?

OTELLO: What? No, why?

DIEGO: I just wondered. Listen, Capitano, don't let this business get to you, okay? Take it out on Dos Santos tomorrow. Have a good flight. Ciao.

That night, with Emilia, Diego is playful.

The following evening, the tie between Rialto and Dos Santos ends in a goalless draw. It is a game that lacks shape and rhythm. And excitement. The result is, however, satisfactory from the Rialto point of view: they progress to the next stage, having scored twice in the first leg. Otello is substituted in the sixty-third minute.

In La Prensa the match is watched with noisy derision. Fidel is pleased. He is not, of course, a Rialto fan. He supports unfashionable and struggling Gimnasia, although the truth is that he only does so to be awkward; in reality he does not take much interest in soccer. Besides, a bad game means that his customers buy more drinks. When the bar begins to empty he goes out back for a little smoke — a thing Nina pretends not to know he still does. The sky is overcast, so featureless that it doesn't seem to be there at all. There are no lights in the windows of Oguz's sweatshop. Maybe his workers have gone on strike. A nice thought, but improbable. So the yard is in darkness, except where slanting rectangles of dingy yellow from the street lamp spill through the gaps in the old house front. He peers over at where the shed is, wondering about Bush and the two girls.

Fidel has scanned the newspapers these past weeks, looking for stories about kids who've disappeared, bodies. And found nothing. Not that he expected to find anything. The socialist paper he buys every week has become increasingly savage and hysterical now that the date of the election has been announced, but it's like it's stopped covering actual news, stopped digging the dirt, stopped looking for the source of the smell that rises to its nose. And as for the other

221

papers—well, Jesus, you'd hardly notice that the country was heading for an elected dictatorship. All you get is Otello and Dezi this, Otello and Dezi that. Celebrity as the opiate of the masses, man. Otello had seemed like a good guy, a man of the people, all the stuff he did in the North. Then he comes down here, and before you can say *knife*, he's married to the superstar daughter of that fascist pig Brabanta, and next minute they're like Mary and Joseph, Evita and Perón, King and Queen of Fairyland. Take everybody's eye off the ball while her old man and his cronies steal the country. Conspiracy? You betcha. Her daddy put her up to it, no question. Sad, though, when smart black guys get suckered like that.

He stubs the joint and puts the butt into his pocket, and is about to return inside when he hears movement and murmured speech. The kids coming back. That's Bianca, first, then Bush and the other girl, Felicia. You can tell them apart by their hair, even in the dark. He sits silently on the bench until he hears the shed door scrape shut.

Anxiety bubbles in his gut like blocked wind. As they have so many times before, the words *They can't stay here forever* appear in his head. And, as always, they lead nowhere.

Felicia lies awake with her eyes shut. She wonders if Bush wants her to go over to him. Her own need is like a delicious itch down the center of her body. She won't do it, though.

When what she wants to happen happens, it's not going to be a hurried, furtive thing in the darkness of a dirty old shed that stinks of piss. She clings, foolish girl that she is, to her vision of a white bed, of pale curtains gently billowing at open windows.

And no Bianca.

3.8

DIEGO'S GLEE IS short-lived. Within two weeks, Michael Cass is reinstalled as Desmerelda's body-guard. In fact, the three of them—Cass and the happy couple—seem tighter than ever. Almost to the extent that he, Diego, feels excluded.

He paces the bedroom. "It's incredible," he tells Emilia. "The guy is too stupid to feel jealous. Can you imagine that? Too stupid, too lamebrained, to be jealous. I mean, I led him to it like a donkey, pushed his nose into it, said, 'There it is, look.' For God's sake, I almost had *myself* believing that she was having a thing with Cass. There was motive—forgive me, sweetheart, but who wouldn't want to bang La Brabanta?—and there was opportunity. *Endless* opportunity. Any sane jury would convict. But not Saint Otello. Oh, no. He's on some other planet entirely. Planet Idiot, in the constellation Moron. Any normal, intelligent man, hearing his wife going 'Michael this' and 'Michael that,' and 'Baby, can't we please have Michael back,' any man with half a brain would think, *Ah-hum.* But no. Instead, the pair of them have a 'sensible discussion of the issues.' Ha! You don't need much imagination to know what a 'sensible discussion' between those two would consist of.

"It's my own fault. He believes anything I say. So I should've just said, 'Capitano, Cass is sleeping with your wife when you're not there.' Spelled it out, maybe written it in capital letters on a big piece of paper. But you know what? That wouldn't have worked either. Because he'd have looked at me with those big dumb eyes of his and said, 'Yeah, well, Dezi says Michael takes his job very seriously.'"

He stands looking through his own reflection at the lights of the city. "You know, it's at times like this I wish you hadn't made me give up smoking." He turns to her. "I think I'll have a drink. Just the one, don't worry."

When he returns to the bedroom, he is carrying a large measure of imported Scotch whiskey in a heavy crystal tumbler. Standing at the window once more, he takes a mouthful and shudders as its fuse burns down into him. He takes another mouthful to smother it.

"Do you remember when heroes used to be greater than us? Generals, liberators, on huge horses. Makers of history. Men who led other men through unexplored mountains, invented countries, gave names to things. Died for causes, became immortal. Now heroes are mere celebrities. Fashion designers. Soccer players. Pop singers. People you think you could be like, given the chance, the luck. Pathetic, isn't it? No, it's more than pathetic. It's insulting. It reduces all of us; it reduces *me*. And I won't stand for it. Cannot stand for it."

He drinks again. "I'm getting impatient, Emilia. And that is disturbing. I am a patient man, as you know. A lover of subtleties, of elegant stratagems. The long game. A user of poisons, not explosives. I used to think I had centuries of patience, an infinity of patience. But I find myself becoming restless. I want to bring them down *soon*. I want those towers to crumble and plunge; I want to relish the numb shock of the people in the streets. Hear them wailing, 'Why did we believe? Why didn't we listen?' Even though I know that soon afterward they'll forget they ever wanted answers to those questions. That they'll go clambering over the rubble to greet the next liar who says he can make everything right again. Tells them he can give them their dreams back."

He drains the glass.

"I'll never be out of work."

Later, in bed, he is silent for a time.

Then he looks over at her and says, "There was nothing wrong with my approach. He has become so big, so gross, that he will—must—collapse under his own weight. But

I miscalculated. When he met her, when I saw the fool go slack at the knees, I thought, *Aha, my friend, now I have you. Now you have wandered into the alligator swamp.* But together they are stronger than I thought. Yes, I underestimated them. I shall have to work a little harder."

3.9

TEN MORNINGS AFTER her missed period, Desmerelda goes to brush her teeth; but as soon as the electric toothbrush whirs inside her mouth, she turns aside and vomits into the toilet bowl. It's a neat and fairly untroublesome process, but she is glad Otello is not there to witness it. When she is sure that it's finished, she tries to continue cleaning her teeth — she really needs to now — but realizes that the familiar toothpaste tastes foul. Like rotting shrimp or something.

When she walks through to the kitchen, the answering machine on the landline is flashing and her cell is ringing. She ignores both. The kitchen is big — very big — but this morning it seems bigger than ever. It takes her a long time to get to the fridge, which is much taller than she is. She tries a sip of juice, straight from the carton. It's okay. It tastes like it ought to taste.

She goes back to bed. There's a pulse in her head where there shouldn't be one, but she calms it and starts to think. To take stock. It's like a luxury she has postponed.

The American tour is off. Well, thank God.

The book contract is on. The ghostwriter is expensive, but you can't bluff what comes out in print. He won't write quotes you can't defend. She wishes she could remember his name.

She is pregnant.

There is not going to be another single lifted from the new album. There were five from the first album. Three from the second. Now only one from the third. It's not like you need a graph.

She is definitely pregnant.

And yesterday someone had called Ramona asking if Desmerelda Brabanta would consider appearing on *Celebrity Lock-In.*

No, of course she damn well won't. Appear on something with *Celebrity* in the title, and you might as well be dead. But it's another sign. This part of it is over now, for sure.

She can feel that she is. It is only her imagination, obviously, but she can feel things gathering inside her.

She puts her hands on her belly and imagines several possible ways she will tell Otello. And how she will tell her estranged and bitter father, who doesn't answer her calls or e-mails. As soon as that thought strikes her, she swings her legs off the bed and hurries back to the bathroom.

◆ ◆ ◆

Desmerelda decides, eventually, that she will tell no one. Not for a while. You never know. Don't tempt fate.

As things turn out, the first person to know is Diego. And she doesn't need to tell him.

He calls her and invites her to lunch at the Parisino. There is something he wishes to discuss with her. She arrives ahead of him, and when Diego gets there, he is greeted by Michael Cass, who has already taken up his station in the armchair facing the doors. Diego notes that Cass is looking a good deal tidier these days. Today he is wearing a well-cut dark-blue linen suit over a pale blue shirt, and proper shoes. Maybe Dezi has taken to buying his clothes for him. Sweet.

Diego looks at his watch. "I'm not late, am I?"

"Nah. We're early. Dezi said she was starving."

"Right. Are you okay? Need a drink or anything?"

Cass lifts a bottle of water from the floor beside his chair. "Nope. I'm fine." There is perhaps something ironic in his expression.

Desmerelda looks charmingly embarrassed when she sees Diego. She is already digging in to an avocado-and-smoked-chicken appetizer.

"I know it's terrible of me. I just couldn't wait. I somehow didn't get around to breakfast."

"No problem," he says, smiling. "A girl's gotta eat."

She lifts her face to him, and he kisses her on both cheeks.

When the waiter materializes, Diego says, "I'll have the

same as *la señora*. It looks excellent. After that, I don't know. Ask me later." To Desmerelda he says, "Wine?"

"Uh-uh. I'll stick to mineral water."

When the waiter leaves them, Diego regards Desmerelda appraisingly. "You look particularly lovely today, if you don't mind my saying so."

"I think I can stand it."

"I'm glad you were free."

"I'm really glad you called. I was feeling a bit . . . well, you know. I didn't used to mind when Otello was away for internationals. Well, not a lot. Lately, though, I find that I do mind. Quite a bit."

"Can't say I blame you. Some of those girls in Rio are pretty spectacular."

She laughs. "Yeah, yeah."

He tilts his head very slightly. His face now displays kindly concern. "You are all right, you two?"

"Absolutely." She eats a sliver of chicken by way of closing the subject. "So, do you really have something to discuss with me, or did you just think your charm needed a workout?"

"No. I have an idea I'd like to run past you."

"Mmm-hmm. Okay. Go on. I can eat and listen at the same time, you know."

"Right. Well, a couple of weeks back I was negotiating a new deal on Otello's sportswear franchises. Despite all the piracy that goes on, the sums involved are pretty significant. As you probably know. Anyway, because the subject was on my mind, I guess, I started really noticing how many

231

people—kids, mainly—go around wearing Otello soccer jerseys and sweatshirts and stuff. And I started thinking that just getting a percentage of all that business wasn't the best we could do."

"This is completely fascinating, Diego."

"Bear with me. Because then I got to thinking about fashion. Kids' fashion, to be precise."

"*You* started thinking about kids' fashion? Were you running a fever or something?"

"Or just maybe experiencing a violent attack of inspiration. Look, Dezi, thousands—hundreds of thousands—of boys go around wearing Otello gear. And hundreds of thousands of girls go around wearing what you wear. Or cheap imitations of what you wear. Right? In a very real sense, the two of you dictate street fashion in this country. Why not take the logical next step?"

"Which is?"

"Produce it."

Her eyebrows lift. "What, you mean go into the clothes business?"

"Exactly. Look, I'm talking off the top of my head here, obviously. You know more about this than I could learn in a lifetime. But what I'm thinking of is sort of funky, sportswear-slash-streetwear, right? Like athletic but cool. For both boys and girls. I mean, that's the kind of thing they're wearing anyway, but it's mostly downmarket crap. This would be different. Quality stuff, but affordable. And it would be your own label. D and O, or whatever. You'd have control over it. And control is what matters."

Desmerelda rests her right cheek on her hand but says nothing.

Diego says, "Okay, maybe my, er, vision is way off. In terms of what kind of clothes, accessories, whatever. What do I know? But I did take the liberty of seeing what Shakespeare thought of the idea before discussing it with you."

"Uh-huh. And what did they say?"

He smiles. "I got the impression that they were slightly miffed that I'd thought of it before they did."

He sits back and waits. Her eyes are lowered. On her plate she traces patterns in the avocado smears with her fork.

"Dezi? Speak to me."

She looks up at last and says, "You must think I'm a very dim girl."

"What?"

"I know what this is really about. What you're up to."

Something wormy wriggles close to his heart, but he holds her gaze. "You do?"

"Yes. You've come to the conclusion that my glorious musical career is screwed."

"I have done no such thing." His surprise is genuine.

"Oh, yes, you have. And as a matter of fact, so have I. I'd have to be deaf, dumb, and blind not to. And this brilliant

233

idea of yours is about rescuing my self-esteem. Giving me something to fill the horrible post-superstar vacuum you imagine my future to be. Don't deny it. And don't look like that. I'm not upset. I'm really touched."

Diego has put on the brave but wounded smile of a man listening to his therapist.

"Also," Desmerelda says, grinning now, "it *is* a great idea, actually. Shall we have something else to eat and talk about it some more?"

Later, they order coffee. Desmerelda has one sent out to Michael.

"So," Diego asks, "shall I set up a meeting between the three of us and Shakespeare in, say, the next couple of weeks?"

"Sure."

"And do you want me to put the idea to Otello, or . . ."

"No, no. I'll do that."

"And you think he'll go for it?"

"I don't see why not. I can't imagine him being particularly hands-on, though, can you?"

Diego allows himself a chuckle. "No, not really. It'll be the promotion stuff where he comes in."

"He'll almost certainly want to build in some charity aspect to the business."

"Obviously. And that reminds me. I had an idea about presentation. Models and so forth. This is months away, of course, but when we start the advertising campaign, I think we should use real kids. Not squeaky-clean little models from some agency. Real kids, off the street. Kids with attitude. That other kids can relate to. Do you know what I mean?"

"Hey, Diego, that is very good. I like that. I like that very much."

"Thank you."

She puts her cup down. "I don't think I can drink any more of that." She checks her watch. "Well . . ."

He is looking at her in a slightly peculiar way.

"What?"

He is awkward. He lowers his voice. "Dezi, may I ask . . . I'm sorry. This is an outrageously intimate question, but I can't . . ."

"Come on, Diego, spit it out. What?"

"Dezi, are you pregnant?"

She cannot say anything. There is no need to. It's like the blood ebbs from her face and wells back up like a tide.

"I'm sorry," he says.

She stares at him, shaking her head. "How did you know?"

"The mineral water. You never used to eat avocado. You couldn't drink your coffee. And there is, I don't know, something different about your complexion. Your skin tone. I recognized it."

"Christ, Diego."

"I'm sorry. I must be sensitive to these things. Does he know?"

"No. Not yet. And don't you dare say anything about it to anyone."

"Of course I won't. Cross my heart." He takes her left hand tenderly in both of his. "Congratulations, Desmerelda. I am very, very happy for you both."

3.10

RIALTO ENDS THE season as league champions, seven points clear of their closest challengers. Otello, as the league's top scorer, is awarded the Golden Ball even though he misses three games with a knee injury and struggles to regain his form in the last five games, scoring only twice.

The club's success is soured when they lose four–three on aggregate to the Brazilian team Grêmio in the semifinal of the Copa Libertadores. The tabloids, who had over-excited themselves at the prospect of a rare double, are less than charitable. Predictably it is Mateo Campos of *El Sol* who leads the chorus. Deploying his repertoire of neo-racist terminology, he accuses Otello (yet again) of being more interested in celebrity than soccer. The refrain is taken up by, among others, the mass-circulation soccer maga-zine *Gol!*, which juxtaposes a fashion shot of Otello modeling a white suit with one of Roderigo urging his players on, looking sweaty, bruised, and defiant.

La Nación prints an end-of-season report by Paul Faustino, which takes a different and more sober view. It reminds readers that in his first season with Rialto, Otello has scored more goals in all competitions than any other player in the club's history, with the exception of the great Esdras Caballo back in 1968. That, notwithstanding the team's exit in the semifinals, Otello is the first Rialto player ever to score two hat tricks in the tournament. Faustino also dismisses, with Olympian disdain, the attempts by the tabloids to slime the man's reputation. He mentions Mateo Campos by name, describing him as "ophidian." (Faustino had smiled, keying the word, knowing that Campos would have to look it up in a dictionary, if he possessed such a thing.) He points out that it is ironic (to put it politely) that papers whose circulation is built upon juicily fostering the cult of celebrity should turn so savagely upon a man who has had celebrity thrust upon him by those very same publications. On the evening that the piece is published, Faustino appears on *Sportsview* and forcefully reiterates these views.

Faustino is invited to the celebration of Rialto's league championship, when the trophy will be formally presented to the club. The event is held in the vast ballroom of the Hotel Real. The buffet is absurd; Faustino surveys it, wondering idly if there is anything remotely edible on the planet that has been overlooked. He wonders, too, if he might be the only guest who is not a multimillionaire. Or a multi-millionaire's escort. The congregation of all this money in human form is not the only reason for the presence of a large number of big men with lumps under their jackets, wired-up ears, and restless eyes. Vice President Lazar and that vulture Hernán Gallego are here, as are several other members of the government and the Senate. Waiters and waitresses weave through the throng, holding aloft trays of glasses of champagne that seem to float like golden dreams above the heads of thirsty dreamers. Along three of the four walls, screens show silent video loops of Rialto's goals; Otello's joyous face appears repeatedly above the heads of the assembled plutocrats. The man himself appears a little later, when Ramón Tresor leads the team onto the stage.

Faustino endures two of the speeches, then carries his glass out into the Real's roof garden. The nicer parts of the world's jungles have been brought here to overlook the city. Full-grown trees nudge each other and whisper. An electrically powered stream empties itself into shallow pools where real flamingos pose on one leg among lotus flowers and shadowed golden fish. He wanders toward the edge of the garden, daring himself to cope with his vertigo. His foot slithers on the fiberglass cobblestones, where there is a slick of excrement; looking up, he finds himself meeting the amber gaze of a tethered macaw.

He reaches the chrome railing and smokes a cigarette, resisting the sickening urge to look down. Human voices chirrup behind him, then fade. He stubs out the cigarette and turns to behold Desmerelda Brabanta. She is standing a few paces away, in the dappled shade of a weeping fig tree, smiling at him. She is wearing a gravity-defying dress made of what appears to be the skin of a silver snake.

"Hi, Paul," she says.

He does a little bow, unable to help himself. "Señora."

She laughs, walks up to him, and kisses his cheeks. "Don't you 'Señora' me, Faustino. It's Dezi. We're on first-name terms."

"Are we?"

"Of course. We have a very romantic connection. You may not remember this, but I met you at the very same time I met my husband. At my father's house."

"I certainly do remember it. A historic occasion. Diego Mendosa introduced you to both of us. Unfortunately, you fell for the other guy. I have been cursing my luck ever since."

Desmerelda laughs again and leans alongside him. She reaches out sideways and perches her glass on the parapet. Her hand misjudges; the glass tips, then disappears. Appalled, Faustino pictures its lengthy downward plunge, its shattering into the head of some innocent pedestrian. But he cannot bring himself to look down to see if this has happened, if there is some tiny bloodstained disturbance in the world far below him.

Desmerelda seems completely unaware of the event. She gazes at the garden's orderly undergrowth. She is almost certainly the most attractive woman Faustino has ever stood close to. He wonders if her beauty might not be a burden to her. Whether it might obliterate whatever else she is. Or isn't. It is extremely surprising that he is alone with her. Where are her people? And she seems a bit . . . what? Tipsy? Surely not. No, something else. He has very limited experience of how pregnant women behave.

"Incredible place, this, doncha think? You see the flamingos?"

"Yes," he says. "It's strange that they stay here, isn't it? You'd think they'd fly off."

"I guess they've had their wings clipped."

"Ah. Yes, I suppose so. I hadn't thought of that. Many congratulations, by the way."

"Thank you. For what?"

"Well, the baby. And for looking, if I may say so, even lovelier than the last time we met."

Desmerelda's slow reaction to this gallantry is not what Faustino expects.

"Yes," she says seriously. "I am radiant. Blooming. Sometimes I am glowing with health. Or even serenely beautiful. It depends which magazine you read."

Faustino laughs uncertainly.

She turns her head and smiles at him. "Anyway, I'm glad we bumped into each other. I saw you on TV the other day. You were great, honestly. I always read what you write about Otello. I appreciate it. We both do."

"Thank you."

"No, really, I mean it. If there's ever anything we can do, you know?"

"Thanks. That's very sweet of you."

They lapse into companionable silence for a while. Something croaks from among the greenery.

"Okay," she says, moving her head as though to ease a stiff neck. "I'd better get back to the orgy before Michael notices I've gone and has a panic attack. Um . . . didn't I have a drink with me when I came out here?"

"I'm afraid it fell," Faustino tells her reluctantly. "Into the street."

"What? Oh, my God!"

She leans over the railing to look down. Too far over the railing, with her right foot high off the ground. Faustino cannot help himself; he bleats, terrified, and grabs her upper arm, dragging her backward. She almost tips over on her high heels.

"Sorry," Faustino says, releasing his grip. "I'm sorry. I have a thing about heights."

It's clear that he does. He looks like someone who has narrowly avoided a highway pileup.

"Hey," Desmerelda says softly.

"I'm all right. Really. Forgive me."

"It's okay." She grins at him. "High places are one of the few things that don't scare me. Snakes, leeches, spiders, sharks—I've got a long list of things that freak me out. I'm fine with heights. The trick is not to imagine yourself falling."

"It's not the falling that worries me," Faustino says. "It's the sudden stop."

She laughs. *It's a nice laugh she has,* Faustino thinks.

When she has gone, when he has stopped watching her go, he lights another cigarette with a shaky hand.

3.11

*A*N ARMORED GOVERNMENT *limousine with four motorcycle outriders is driving fast along the Circular toward the headquarters of the New Conservative Party. A yellow-and-black police helicopter hangs in the sky above the convoy like a plump hornet. In the soundproofed passenger compartment of the car sit* HERNÁN GALLEGO, *minister of internal security; and Senator* NESTOR BRABANTA.

GALLEGO: I still say it's too close to call. If the great unwashed vote in large numbers, we could fail to win the National Assembly.

BRABANTA: So what? We'll win the Senate, and that's what matters. The Assembly will contain, as usual, a ragtag collection of socialists and greens and bloody vegans and ancestor worshippers and God knows what. They'll spend all their time arguing about who gets into bed with whom to form what they stupidly call "a popular coalition" while we run the country. As we have done for the past five years.

GALLEGO [*more or less patiently*]: Of course. But that's not the point, is it? The point is that for the first time we have a real chance of winning the Senate *and* the Assembly, and governing unopposed. Get things *done*. Not have to make damned compromises. I'm sick to death of having to negotiate my department's budget with a committee of liberal half-wits from the National Assembly. Last year I had to settle for half—*half*—the special squads I needed. I had to go to people I'd promised jobs to and say "Sorry." Which is a word that sticks in my craw. [BRABANTA *does not respond. He continues to stare moodily through the window. It saddens—and deeply irritates—*GALLEGO *that his old friend and ally has become semidetached from political realities. It's all because of his daughter's preposterous marriage, of course. And now the fact that before long he's going to have a half-caste grandchild. Awful, yes, but also awkward, because sooner or later* GALLEGO *will have to raise the subject of the dreaded son-in-law. He is a little startled that* BRABANTA *provides him with his cue.*]

245

BRABANTA: What makes you think the common herd are going to vote in droves, anyway? They've never done so before.

GALLEGO: Well, the polls—

BRABANTA: Oh, come on, Hernán. The polls aren't worth a damn.

GALLEGO: I'm not so sure. They consistently predict a big turnout, and if something happens in the next three weeks . . .

BRABANTA: Such as what?

GALLEGO: Well . . . [*He clears his throat.*] Well, let's say, for example, that Otello comes out in support of the Reform Party . . .

BRABANTA: The man's an idiot. He's a soccer player. Politically, he doesn't know his ass from his elbow. Who'd listen to him?

GALLEGO: Actually quite a lot of people, according to our research department. Every time he does an interview, the left-wing press spins it into an attack on us. The president would like us to come up with a way to guarantee that he keeps his fat lips zipped.

[BRABANTA *turns away from the window at last and looks at* GALLEGO *with something like a smile on his face.*]

BRABANTA: You're thinking of having him bumped off? Do tell me that it's so.

GALLEGO [*chuckling*]: Sorry to disappoint you,

Nestor, but no. We had something more modest in mind. Discredit him. Some scandal or
other, you know? Caught with his pants around
his ankles in a brothel. Or discovered to have a
taste for underage girls. Or a newspaper happens
to find out that his charitable donations actually
end up in an offshore bank account. Such, er,
unfortunate things have happened to people
before. Often, as it happens, to people we have
found inconvenient.

[BRABANTA *considers this solemnly. Then shakes
his head.*]

BRABANTA: No. My daughter's feelings aside, it's
too risky. Too obvious. I forbid it.

[GALLEGO *shrugs and sighs.* BRABANTA *turns
back to the window. A minute passes.*]

BRABANTA: Desmerelda will make sure her nigger
keeps his trap shut. She owes me that, at least.

GALLEGO: You're talking to her?

BRABANTA: Through gritted teeth.

GALLEGO: Good. That's very good, Nestor. Make
sure she listens.

Desmerelda does listen. It has taken her several months to
restore some sort of relationship with her father, the grandfather of her unborn child. Several months of phone calls
that she has kept secret from Otello. These often terse and
difficult conversations do not amount to anything like a

reconciliation. Not yet. But the last thing she wants is for her husband to make some ham-fisted political gesture that will slam that door shut again.

Then she gets lucky. Eight days before the election, Otello pulls a thigh muscle in a preseason scrimmage. By the following Wednesday, it begins to look as though he won't be fit for Rialto's first league fixture. The club physical therapist orders a rest regime.

Desmerelda runs hesitant fingers over the damaged thigh and says, "Honey? Why don't we go down to the villa for a few days and relax? Get away from everything."

"What, now?"

"Yeah. Why not?"

His eyes are full of reasons. For one thing, he has just read an e-mail from Angelica Sansón, who does the administration for his charities in Espirito. Desmerelda had read it before Otello got back from his checkup. Like all Angelica's e-mails, this one was upbeat and supportive. But at the end of it she'd written:

> Fire me for saying this if you like, but lots of us up here are waiting for you to climb off the fence and do some little thing that might stop those evil NCP bastards from getting in for another five years. I understand your situation, but I keep looking in the papers and watching the TV hoping you

might come out and rally the goddamn troops, if you know what I mean.

A

P.S. Check out the pics in the attached file. The smiley kid with the jug ears is Ronaldo — remember him? His big sister who used to be with us disappeared last week after she helped organize a poverty demo.

Desmerelda says, "What's the problem?"

"Well, I dunno. You know. It might look kinda weird if we . . ."

"What?"

He shrugs by way of answering. He has also had e-mails, forwarded by Diego, from the wrong kind of journalists. He is thinking about them in a troubled, indecisive way. She knows this, too.

"I know you," she says. "If we stay here, you'll start getting antsy and want to do things that aren't good for you. Resting is not something you're exactly brilliant at. Unless we're at the villa. And to tell you the truth, I've been feeling a little bit rough these last few days."

"Have you? You didn't say anything."

"I didn't want to worry you. Anyway, I'm sure it's nothing serious. But I think a break would do me good. Some sea air, peace and quiet, you know?" She takes his hand and places it on her belly. "I think baby needs it too."

On Friday, three days before the election, Otello, Desmerelda, and Michael Cass fly on a privately chartered plane down to the coast. Secrecy has been maintained, and the three of them are out of the little airport and into the chauffeur-driven four-by-four in less than ten minutes.

By the following morning, however, word has spread. A small but vocal mob of reporters and photographers, plus a couple of camera crews, have set up camp outside the gates of the estate. They've got folding chairs, beach umbrellas, coolers; they're not planning to leave for a while. From the shade of the gatehouse, two estate security people, a man and a woman, regard the siege with bland hostility. Their Doberman pants in the heat, its long tongue hanging from its mouth like a limp red pennant.

In the master bedroom, where the white curtains tremble and shift in the onshore breeze, Desmerelda puts on a bikini. She looks at herself in the full-length mirror and tries not to be dismayed. Because she is happy. She is going to have a child, their child. She has become someone else because that is what she wanted. And afterward she will be beautiful again. She is beautiful now.

But she does not like the things her body is doing to her. She has for many years been continuously and acutely aware of what she looks like, of course. And her body has never dismayed or betrayed her—never, even in her anxious and motherless teens, disappointed her. It has been a graceful machine that has transported her almost effortlessly along the splendid road of her life, needing nothing more to sustain it than frequent pleasuring. Now her body is something else. At times it seems to her to have become a sinister laboratory packed with fleshy alembics and glandular tubing through which mysterious chemicals surge and bubble. This dark alchemy sometimes hurts her: her breasts burn beneath the skin; vinegary ropes fasten up her guts and bowels. At night she dreams lurid melodramas from which she wakes shocked and perspiring. Taste and smell have become perverse. Recently, rain on the hot streets gave off the aroma of pineapples.

She knows, in a scholastic sort of way, why these things are happening. She has acquired a small library of books about pregnancy and childbirth. Unfortunately the illustrations—calmly bulbous women with the sides of their wombs removed to show the curled purplish dolls tethered inside—frighten her. The helpful information fills her with anxiety about swollen ankles, varicose veins, softening gums, anemia, stretch marks. Her bathroom cabinets have become a treasury of lotions, creams, dietary supplements, vitamins. And the little creature growing inside her, doing all this to her, fills her with a fearful love more intense than anything she has ever experienced.

She changes out of the bikini and into a silvery-white one-piece. Then she wraps herself in a sarong and goes down to the pool.

◆　◆　◆

They have agreed: no incoming calls. The villa number is unlisted and known to very few, but Cass disconnects the phones anyway. Cell phones are turned off; they will devote a maximum of one hour an evening to checking messages and e-mails. They have given the part-time staff a paid vacation; they will microwave or barbecue stuff from the freezers. Otello and Desmerelda swim a little or lie plugged into their iPods. Cass immerses himself in a thick book about the American Civil War or, when he is restless, patrols the estate and the private beach wearing his big straw hat and his gun in a shoulder holster beneath a loose cotton shirt.

On Tuesday morning Otello leaves Desmerelda sleeping and goes downstairs. He is groggy from his previous night's drinking. In the kitchen he downs a tumbler of water and then discovers that the coffee jug is hot and half full. He pours himself a cup and carries it through to the room off the lounge where the TV is. Cass is hunched in a chair, glowering at the screen. The sound is down low. An excitable woman is conjuring up graphics: pie charts, maps, columns in red and blue and yellow, skittle-shaped things representing politicians slowly filling the banked seats of the National Assembly. Most of the skittles are blue, the color of the NCP.

Without looking up, Cass says, "Looks like the bastards have done it."

The picture cuts to a studio. Four men and the presenter

sit at a curved table. One of the men is Nestor Brabanta, smiling.

Cass presses the mute button on the remote and turns to look at Otello. Otello does not like the expression on Michael's face.

"What?"

"Nothing," Cass says.

Lunchtime, and Paul Faustino stopped doing more or less nothing and went down to the patio and sat next to Nola Levy on one of the steel benches. He liked Nola. Not everyone did. Officially she was the senior social affairs correspondent. Unofficially, and behind her back, she was known as La Conciencia. The Conscience of *La Nación*. Or the Pain in the Neck. She wrote the kind of stories that certain important people, and organizations such as the police and the Ministry of Internal Security, did not want published. Indeed, it had often surprised Faustino that Carmen d'Andrade did publish them, given that they almost always caused trouble. But they were good stories, with legs, and well written. Nola Levy was blacklisted by at least two government departments; there were official press conferences that she never got invited to. This didn't seem to cramp her style one bit. She had other sources of information. Not that official press conferences were about giving information. "Bullshit buffets" was what Nola called them, and Faustino rather liked the phrase. She represented the trade unions on the General Executive and helped maintain a website devoted to tracing missing persons. Children, in particular. (In fact, she financed the website, although Faustino didn't know that.) She was maybe fifty years old, wore her heavy, wiry hair in a short bob, and was unmarried, so her male colleagues—including Faustino—blithely assumed that she was a lesbian. She smoked, which was one of the reasons Faustino enjoyed her company; she argued fiercely, which was another.

He sat, saying not very much, while she lamented, predictably, the result of the election. His attention wandered.

Then she said, "And what about your friend Otello, Paul? Where was he?"

"What do you mean?"

"I mean that he comes on like a caring guy, concerned for the poor, for damaged kids, all of that. People listen to what he says, even if what he says is crass. Which it usually is. And although I hate to admit it, he could've made a difference."

"What, to the election?"

"Of course. He's got to be just about the most famous man in the country, right? He could have stood up. Declared himself. I mean, for God's sake, if he believes in the things he says he believes in, he can't be a supporter of the NCP, can he? Ah, but I forget. His daddy-in-law is that creature of darkness Nestor Brabanta. Is that why he stayed dumb, Paul? Or is it because he just *is* dumb?"

Faustino sighed heavily. He and Nola had locked horns

over Otello before. "Nola, please. The guy is a *soccer player*, okay? He's—"

Nola Levy lifted her hand in protest. "No, Paul. That won't do. Yes, he's an athlete. He's also the name on a hundred thousand shirts you see on the streets. He commands the kind of publicity that politicians would die for. He breaks wind, there's headlines. He's worth millions. To my mind, there's a certain responsibility comes with that."

"Like the responsibility for deciding who forms the government? Come on, Nola. I'll say it again: the man is a soccer player. No matter what else he does, that's what we judge him on. His job. At which, as I've said several times in print, he is a genius. It's terribly unfair, I think, to expect him to be something he can't be. To do things he can't do."

Levy lit another cigarette and through smoke said, "Or *chooses* not to do. How do you feel about that, Paul? What about the idea that the things we don't do might matter more than the things we do? You reckon that thought might have occurred to your Otello?"

"Probably not," Faustino said. Then after a sad silence he put his left arm around Nola's shoulders. She relaxed against him.

"Sorry."

"For what?" he said.

Bush bounced up the steps on the far side of the patio, carrying a greasy bag of hot sandwiches in one hand and three clinking bottles of Pepsi in the other.

Nola said, "I doubt if he knows it, but today that boy's future got a whole lot worse."

Bush made his deliveries, then looked across and caught Faustino's eye. He grinned hugely and blew on his fingertips, then shook his hand in the air. A gesture that meant *Phew! Hot babe, man.*

Despite himself, Faustino laughed.

Diego drinks black coffee while studying the newspapers. Most of them, of course, are owned by right-wing proprietors and merely celebrate the NCP victory. He discards them and concentrates on *La Nación* and *El Guardián* and the other liberal papers. To his delight, they all have comment columns that ask more or less the same question: did Otello's silence swing it for the NCP? He goes through to his office and checks the websites of the northern papers. They are blunter; brutal, even. The tabloid *El Norte* runs an editorial headed WHERE WAS OTELLO WHEN WE NEEDED HIM? The slightly more literate *Voz de San Juan* wants to know WHY WAS OUR AMBASSADOR TO THE SOUTH SO SILENT?

He carries his happiness through to the bedroom and gently parts the curtains. Emilia stirs, opens her lovely eyes. He turns and smiles at her.

He says, "I admit that my faith in the cynicism of the common people has wavered from time to time. But I have the feeling that on this occasion they'll come through. After all, they've been let down so many times before. 'Hey,' they'll say, 'maybe our hero *is* Brabanta's stooge after all. Maybe we've been had.' Because that's the way they like to think, Emilia. In simple terms. In tabloid headlines. And once they start to doubt his integrity, they'll start to doubt other things as well. Like his morality. And then, by God, I'll give them something to sink their teeth into."

He is silent for a moment or two, then rubs his hands together. "Speaking of which, I'm hungry. Are you, my love?"

Act Four

4.1

Paff! It has taken a lot of research and several torrid meetings—plus two hundred thousand dollars—to arrive at these four letters and an exclamation mark. Which must remain a closely kept secret until the day the label is launched.

The actual logo design has not yet been decided. That's what this meeting is for. Imagista has prepared several versions: in grungy capitals, like a tired stencil or rubber stamp; in crisp typefaces with the *f*s reversed or inverted; scrawled, like a signature; in speech bubbles. There are still other key decisions to be made, such as whether the word will be different colors for boys' wear and girls' wear. But today Ricardo, the head of Imagista, has the task of selling the word itself.

"It's like a sound, right? Maybe of a big fat raindrop landing on the ground. Hitting the dust. Nice image.

Refreshment, freshness, rejuvenation, all of that. See what I mean?"

They do, yes.

"But what I love, what I absolutely *love*, is that it is also like a disrespectful noise that kids might make. Are you with me? Like, Daddy says, 'What in God's name is that you're wearing?' And the kid says, *'Paff!'* Which is like, 'What do *you* know?' So it's like a swear word, but not a swear word. Just a cool thing to say."

Desmerelda and the others smile.

Isabel of Shakespeare says, straight-faced, "*Paff!* might also be construed as the sound of a fart. Was that something that had occurred to you, by any chance?"

Ricardo grins disarmingly. "I cannot deny it, señora. It is something that lurks within the word, yes."

"And which adds to its youthful, disrespectful resonance."

"Exactly, señora."

On good days, Desmerelda is thrilled and energized by the speed of the project. On other days, she feels something like panic. The panic of a dreamer who cannot keep up with the frenzied narrative of her dreaming. During the vanished months since Diego pitched the idea to her, their fashion house has become a reality. There is an office, staff, a welter of contracts, papers that need signing. A website in development. An inrush of investment. Business plans. Accountants smoking cigarettes. All of it secret.

Diego himself has been wonderful, briefing her and Otello (often separately, because they are not together anything like as often as she needs them to be) on developments. It's really rather touching. He—Diego—is so high on the idea. He so desperately wants it to work. It's because he thought of it, of course; it's his baby. All the same, it's really nice to see him smiling so often, so childishly thrilled when things go right. It's surprising. And deeply touching. She likes him more because of it. And he is there. He is with her.

At the same time, her pregnancy has made her prey to inappropriate but acute attacks of loneliness. Now that the new season has started, Otello is absent more and more of the time. He sleeps on planes, then steals into the apartment and undresses in the dark before sliding into bed and cupping his hand around her belly. Then—it seems to her—he is gone again, and she wakes to his ghost voice on the phone. And she aches, sometimes, remembering him bringing coffee to the bedroom on slow mornings. The coffee going cold while they made love. When she still liked coffee. And, for that matter, when they still made love.

But it is not simply her husband's absences that conjure these spells of loneliness or fear. It is the sudden, irrational feeling that the world has shrunk into her, that she contains it and that she alone can sustain it. This sense of being the center of the universe is not new to her, of course. But now, for the first time, it comes burdened with responsibility, and it sometimes frightens her. Very occasionally it makes her angry. Angry with him. Angry with the quietly fierce man who put the baby in her. She knows this is also irrational, but the knowledge brings no comfort.

So it is good that she has Diego. And Michael, who drives as if she were a priceless Venetian glass full to the brim with rarest wine.

The hotly contested competition for the *Paff!* contract has been won by Dario Puig and his Japanese wife, Harumi. Under their trade name, Reki, they have designed for most of the national labels and several internationals. Their studio and exhibition space is the top floor of a refurbished 1930s warehouse in the old commercial quarter. On the morning of the unveiling of the designs, most of the key players are there: Desmerelda, Ramona, and Diego; a couple of Shakespeare people; the *Paff!* project manager and two of her staff; three anxious people (the woman in a smart suit, the two men looking like pirates or something) from the fabric design company; about half a dozen Reki employees who seem to be an average age of sixteen; and Ricardo with another young man from Imagista. Oh, and Michael Cass, who stands awkwardly against the back wall next to a life-size naked mannequin painted dark purple except for her lips and hair, which are gold. They make a nice couple, although it seems that of the two, she is the more likely to strike up a conversation.

Harumi has done the drawings. They are scattered, in careful abandon, over the surface of the table. The faces are asexual, drawn — predictably — manga-style, with huge tear-glossed eyes, like dolls that weep. It is not the right look at all; Desmerelda glances across the table at Diego, who widens his own eyes ironically.

The designs are good, though. Very good. For most of them—the lightweight parkas, the sweatshirts, the hoodies, the T-shirts, the beachwear—Dario and Harumi have combined a severely limited range of colors: black, three shades of gray, cream, white. In an entirely magical way, these anonymous colors draw attention to the cut, the style, the desirability, of the clothes.

Dario explains the guiding principles behind their work; helpfully, these are written with elegant carelessness on big sheets of paper taped to the wall. These sentences, he and Harumi believe, express the "core sentiments" of teenagers that have inspired their designs.

Don't look at me. LOOK at me.
I'm nothing: special.
　　　　　　　Boredom is sexy.
Here's where I am: in hiding.
　　　　　I'm just like you: unique.
Safety is what frightens me.
Why did they name the nuclear family after a bomb?
Take care of me; leave me alone.

"There is a deep attractiveness in all forms of contradiction," Harumi adds, by way of clarification.

In addition, Dario and Harumi have completely reinvented the soccer jersey. The designs are displayed on a second table. Dario removes the dust sheet that covers it like a matador whisking his cape from a whirling bull. These images are quite unlike the stylized drawings of the leisure clothes. They are glossy Photoshopped print-outs, highlighted and arrowed with marker: works of art in themselves. The colors are outrageous, extravagant; they suggest how wonderful soccer might be if it were allowed to escape the limits of tradition and history. The only thing that connects these shirts is Otello's number: 23. In many of the designs the numerals are frames for weirdly colored prints of Otello's face. On a black shirt he smiles through the numerals in violet and green. On a magenta shirt he rejoices for a goal in yellow and indigo. On another the numbers are formed by tiny images of Otello like Andy Warhol's multiple portraits of Marilyn Monroe. The only colors missing from the display are those of Rialto.

Looking directly at Desmerelda, Harumi says, "Our idea was to liberate your husband. To subvert the idea that he belongs to his club. That he could be owned. To assert that he belongs to all of us, to kids especially. That by wearing a shirt like one of these, you are saying, 'This is *my* Otello; this is what he means to *me*.' Do you see?"

With all eyes on her Desmerelda says, "Yes, I do."

"And that is why we have done this to the fronts of the shirts also," Harumi says, indicating.

They have replaced the heraldic Rialto badge with all sorts of things: a clenched fist, a rubbery gun with its barrel in a knot, Fidel Castro smoking a cigar, the Statue of Liberty, a lollipop, a condom in a pink foil wrapper, a madonna. The name of the Rialto sponsor, the electronics and armaments company ESP, has been replaced by words like *love, touch, ecstasy, desire, money, respect*. These words are not in Spanish. They are in Arabic, English, Chinese, French.

The Reki juniors bring in refreshments. There is discussion of schedules, budgets, photographers, production costs. Diego frequently takes the lead, interrupting the artistic twittering to focus on practicalities, to set dates and deadlines.

Later, in the car on the way to Desmerelda's weekly appointment at the reassuringly expensive prenatal clinic, Cass says, "Diego's really jazzed about this thing, isn't he? Kinda surprising, don't you think?"

She is experiencing a flattening swipe of tiredness, and she is still vaguely disturbed by all those innocently sinister eyes that had gazed out at her from Harumi's drawings. She feels close to tears, which is ridiculous, so it is good that Michael has spoken.

"Yes," she says, stirring herself. "I guess all this appeals to his more creative side. I think it's sweet."

"Uh-huh," Cass says. "He took the cattle prod to those people, though, didn't he? Like it's a big rush."

"Well, Diego's thinking is that we need to do the launch before I have the baby. It makes sense. I guess I'm going to be sort of preoccupied afterward."

"Yeah. I guess so."

The phone plugged into the dashboard warbles.

"Don't answer that," Desmerelda says. "Unless it's Otello."

He squints at the display. "Nope."

"What did you make of the stuff? The clothes."

Cass shrugs his big shoulders. "Not my area. The jerseys were wacky, though. My guess is they'll sell in cartloads. There's nothing like them out there, that's for sure."

They hit the first set of lights on the Circular. Cass sets the handbrake, checks the mirrors, looks all around. He says, "So what d'you think the man himself will think of them? The shirts."

Reki has provided Desmerelda with a handsome folder packed with designs. She will show them to Otello this evening. She has no idea, actually, what he will think. And it is awful, not knowing. She feels desolate, and also resentful. He could have been there, to be persuaded. It should not be up to her to persuade him, when she is busy with their child inside her.

"He'll love them," she says.

◆ ◆ ◆

At the Rialto training complex, the team has finished watching the videos of the last two games played by their next opponents, Cruz Azul. Now they are out on the field for leisurely individual practice, or being worked on in the training rooms.

Otello is receiving balls from three members of the junior squad and driving shots at the reserve keeper, Mellor. He tries an overhead kick from an outswinging cross and blows it completely. The shot flies so wide that it narrowly misses the corner flag. He lies on his back with his arms spread, gazing at the white sky, while Mellor and the three kids crack up laughing. He does a backward roll and flips to his feet.

"Thanks, guys," he says. "I guess that's enough for me today."

Alone in the shower cubicles, he leans against the cool white tiles and lets the water run down his body. Anyone can slice a kick. He'd once seen Ronaldinho actually hit the corner flag, screwing up a shot from fifteen yards out. But it isn't that. He is losing his edge. He is still scoring, but every game now feels about ten minutes too long. He needs a rest. From everything. On the field, the squad works with him, feeds him, protects him. Off the field, some of that old coldness has returned. He does not know how to explain that he isn't what they think he is, what the media has turned him into. That he has no control over it. It hurt when Roderigo, in an interview, had described him as "like

Jesus, but better dressed." What's it going to be like when this fashion thing kicks off? Kids' wear. No, *kidzwear*. God, they'll crucify him.

He turns the water off and wraps himself in a towel. The clock on the locker-room wall tells him it is four fifteen. Dezi will be on her way to the clinic. There's another thing: the baby. The obsession.

For a shameful moment, he allows himself to feel lonely and neglected. A famous, lonely, neglected man. He dries himself and dresses quickly. With any luck he'll be home in time to have a couple of quiet drinks before she gets back.

The nurse rubs lubricant onto the snout of the ultrasound probe and takes it on a slow patrol of Desmerelda's lower belly. Desmerelda has to force herself to watch the monitor. She is ashamed that this is so, but the shifting, granular images both puzzle and disturb her.

"The head," the nurse says, pointing. "Here, see? Baby's eye."

But what Desmerelda sees might be the jerkily swirling pictures transmitted by a weather satellite: a deepening depression, an in-coiling hurricane. Something too huge, too unstable, to be inside her.

"Aha," the nurse murmurs. She is Swedish, maybe.

"What?" Desmerelda is alarmed.

The nurse keeps her eyes on the screen. "Decision time, señora, I think."

Oh, my God.

But then the nurse turns to Desmerelda and smiles. "I am pretty sure I can tell you the sex of this little rascal now. The question is, do you want to know?"

Utterly surprising herself, Desmerelda says, "It's a boy."

4.2

A T THE NORTHEAST corner of the Triangle, almost
in the shadow of the elevated section of Avenida
Buendía, there is a narrow street called Castana. It used to
lead to another street called Palmera, but Palmera disappeared when the area was improved in the 1960s. So now
Castana comes to a dead end at the brown wall of a four-story
garage. The garage is disused and scheduled for demoli-
tion; its entrances have been crudely sealed with concrete
blocks. A good many people live and sleep in there, despite
the parties—for want of a better word—that take place
on the top floor most nights. Number 9 Castana has wire
mesh over its window and a sign on the door that reads:
SWIFT FINANCIAL RECLAMATION SERVICES. Its proprietor,
Juicy Montoya, was reading a magazine called *Rich* when
the phone rang close to his elbow.

"Hey. *Hey!* Lucky. Get the phone. It might be someone."

Lucky Lampadusa was not as quick getting across the room as he might have been because his left leg, from just below the knee to down under his heel, was in a plaster cast. Also, he'd just started eating a bean fritter and he couldn't think where to put it down.

"Yeah," he said thickly. "Swiff. How can I help ya?" He listened for a moment or two, swallowing. "Yeah. He is, but he's on the other line. Okay. Hold on." He cupped his hand over the mouthpiece. "It's some guy."

"Well, Lucky, that's really informative. So it's not the goddamn kangaroo that usually calls this time of day, huh?"

"No, it's some guy."

Juicy sighed and flipped the magazine onto the desk. "Okay. Gimme. And listen—don't eat when you're on the phone. It creates a bad impression. Hello. Yeah, this is he. Aaah, yeah. I do remember. Quite some time ago, though, huh? What? Sorry, the line's bad. Yeah, that's better."

He was silent for a long time. Then he said, "Well, it's not our usual line of business. No, that's not what I'm saying. Just that . . . No, that's really fair. Plus expenses, right. Yeah, we can do it that way. No, what I meant was, how do we know what kinda kids we're looking for? I see. And this guy will be with us all the time? Okay. Wait a second."

Juicy tugged a pen from his shirt pocket and wrote a name and a phone number on the cover of *Rich*.

"And you want *me* to contact *him*, yeah? And I say, like, uh . . . Okay. No problem. All right. I'll have to check a couple of things out, you know? Talk to people. Sure we do. Absolutely. You have called the right people, without doubt. What? That was my assistant, Lucky. Okay. Thanks for calling. We appreciate your business."

Juicy dropped the phone onto its cradle. Then he commenced to rock himself back and forth on the expensive orthopedic chair that he'd reclaimed, with the aid of a baseball bat, from a clairvoyant who'd failed to see his debts building up.

Lucky, who'd propped his plastered leg back up on the narrow window ledge, watched him, eating the rest of the fritter. After a while he said, "Juicy, 'scuse me, I don' wanna do more stuff with kids. I heard you say kids. Sorry. I couldn' help hearin'."

"Who asked you?" Juicy said. He nodded toward the phone. "That was, possibly, the voice of an angel. That was maybe someone with the answer to all my problems. He spoke sums of money into my ear that no one's mentioned to me for some considerable time. He might just be the one who prevents us from suffering the ultimate embarrassment: the indignity of being repossessors who get their stuff repossessed. So shuddup and let me think."

Lucky shuddup. He listened to the rumble and honk of the highway.

Juicy did not believe for a second that this proposed roundup had anything to do with the fashion business.

274

Street kids as models? Yeah, right. And the moon's a pickled egg. This "photographer's assistant" who was tagging along to do the selecting — well, Juicy had to admit it was an original thing to call a pimp. None of this bothered him at all, of course. No, the only problem was the usual one – how to get close to the brats in the first place. Like the guy on the phone imagined you just walk up to a bunch of kids and say, "Hey, any of you wanna be fashion models?" and they say, "Sure, señor, thank you very much" and get in the car? They'd be gone quicker'n cockroaches when the light goes on, leave you standing there with a knife wound in your leg to stop you from chasing them. No, the only way was to recruit some street-level help. Cheap help.

Juicy said, "Lucky, refresh my memory here. What was the name of that gang you used to hang with? The Hermanos Brothers, something like that?"

"Hernandez. The Hernandez Brothers. Juicy —"

"Yeah. Hernandez. You reckon you know where we might find them, have a quiet conversation?"

"I dunno."

Juicy swung the chair around and regarded his assistant gravely. "You know, I sometimes ask myself if there mightn't be a better way to waste my hard-earned dollars than employing some hop-along with a bad habit of saying 'I dunno' every time I ask a simple question. You understand what I'm saying?"

"Yeah," Lucky said, sullen.

"So?"

Lucky wiped his nose with the back of his forefinger and said, "You know them sisters, give out breakfast, weekdays?"

"What sisters?"

"Them nuns. Sisters a Mercy."

"Ah, yes. Bless their souls."

"The Brothers sometimes go down there, see what's goin' on."

Juicy nodded. "Excellent, Lucky. I'm glad I managed to coax that out of you." He swiveled back around and picked up his magazine. "One of these days we might have to get up early and see if we can get you some of that godly coffee."

4.3

NONE OF THE Hernandez Brothers were brothers, and only two of them were named Hernandez: Segundo, who for perfectly good reasons was better known as Slice, and his cousin Angel, who looked like Death's apprentice. The gang had a fluctuating membership but a strict hierarchy; at just fifteen and sixteen respectively, Slice and Angel were not the oldest, but no one questioned their leadership. No one who liked having an ear on either side of his head, anyway. Their home territory was a zemo (a zone of special economic measures, in government-speak; in truth, a slum) that tumbled down a ravine just west of the Circular. (It provided a startling introduction to the capital, viewed through the vast yellow arches of McDonald's, if you happened to be driving in from the airport.) Several times a week, though, the crew would descend on the city, freeloading rides on the subway, vaulting the ticket gates with impunity, occupying a hastily vacated car. One of their favorite entertainments was to hang upside down from the handrails as the train came into a station so that waiting passengers would be presented with a nightmare vision of ragged, grinning, humanoid bats.

Like other gangs, the Hernandez Brothers from time to time lost members through what you might call natural wastage. Unlike other gangs, they did not lose members to the *Rataneros*. There were dark mutterings about why this might be. It was rumored that they had a thing going with the Ratcatchers, trading tip-offs for protection or money, or both.

On a morning that already smelled of sweat, the crew arrived at the shelter where the Sisters of Mercy set up their breakfast kitchen. They had too much dignity to get in line for the food; they boosted it off the other kids and made a big play of tossing most of it away uneaten, proclaiming their disgust at its quality.

They were hunkered down in the shade of a wall when an eleven-year-old called Chili took his cigarette from his mouth and said, "Hey, Slice. Look what the cat dragged in."

Slice switched his eyes away from the Bianca chick and her sister or whatever she was. The crew watched while Lucky Lampadusa made his awkward progress across the street, but most looked away, like he wasn't there, when he came to a halt in front of them. He was a big slab of a boy with dark patches under the arms and across the front of his yellow T-shirt. The cast on his leg was dirty, and frayed where the toes poked out.

"Slice. Angel. Guys."

"Well, look here," Slice said eventually. "Lucky Lampadusa. Don' tell me you in need of a free breakfast. You fall on hard times again?"

"Uh-uh. I'm all right."

"No, you ain't," Angel said, without opening his burned-out eyes. "Who bust ya leg for ya?"

"No one."

"Yeah? Ya do it yaself? Maybe you was in the hammock with ya sister and tried it standin' up?"

Chili coughed, having tried to smoke and laugh at the same time.

Lucky shifted his weight back onto his good leg and said, "Listen, I got a proposition for ya."

Angel opened his eyes. Lucky couldn't look at him. God, that gray shine on his skin, like the belly of a dead fish.

"*You* got a proposition for *us*," Slice said.

"Well, not me, Slice. The man I work for."

"That'd be that repo man, huh, Lucky? Wha's he call himself?"

"Name's Montoya. People call him Juicy."

Angel said, "Why d'they call him Juicy, Lucky?"

"I dunno." Lucky stood there while the crew grinned at him. Then he said, "He'll pay."

"He'll pay for what?"

"Talent-spotting," Lucky said.

279

4.4

THE SO-CALLED photographer's PA sat looking around the bar, taking in the old printing press, the posters from the June Uprising thirty years back, the framed yellowed newspaper pictures showing student revolutionaries at barricades. One of them, apparently, was of the old lady who cooked the bar's budget lunches, back when she was a looker and not afraid to show it. Juicy Montoya would bet that when he was again with his own kind, the so-called PA would describe the place as "funky." He was a white guy, which came as no surprise. What did come as a surprise, though, was that he was youngish and clean-looking, with plenty of blond hair, like a Yankee rock star or something. And nice clothes. All of which was a problem.

"Look, er, Marco. The thing is, there's no way someone like you can just walk into the areas we're going to, you know? You'd stand out like . . ." Juicy's talent for simile was not up to the challenge. "Plus, you've got that expensive camera hanging around your neck. It's like I couldn't guarantee your safety."

The camera was a Nikon digital with manual override and a telescopic lens like the mouth of a rocket launcher. For the previous two hours Juicy and Lucky had nervously guarded the guy while he took "location shots," mostly of the scuzziest places he could find. Like walls sprayed with gang tags, shop frontclosed up with steel sheeting, alleyways hung with washing like sad festival banners, the wrecked housefront next to the bar they were sitting in. Maybe this deal wasn't what Juicy'd thought it was. Maybe it was something weirder.

"I see," Marco said. "This would seem to be a serious difficulty. I suppose I could change my clothes."

Yeah, Juicy thought. *Plus maybe live on the street for six months and acquire a crack habit.* He said, "I don't think that would do it, to be honest."

"Well, Señor Montoya, we do need to find a way around this. We have less than a week before the shoot. I've got to have a gallery of kids together by the end of Thursday at the latest."

"Absolutely. Absolutely. What I think is, we take the pictures from the car."

Marco slumped like someone hit by a sniper.

"No, listen, Marco," Juicy said. "It's taken a while for my assistant and me to set this up. What you got to understand is that the kind of kids you're looking for are leery little bastards. They don't trust *anybody,* and they got good reason not to. So what Luciano and me have done is make diplomatic contact, right, with certain influential kids we know. That is our area of expertise. Local knowledge. This crew, our contacts, will assemble the kind of kids you're looking for at three points. One here in the Triangle, two down in Castillo. But the thing is, see, these have to be public places. Places where the kids can scatter if they get spooked. And they're going to be *extremely* edgy. You and me get out of the car, they're ninety-nine percent certain to think we're cops — or something worse."

"I honestly don't see why," Marco said. "They'll know what this is all about, won't they? We're going to give them cards explaining what we want them to do, where to be, what they'll get paid, and everything."

Lucky seemed to be having some trouble swallowing his Pepsi.

Juicy regarded his beer solemnly for several seconds before saying, "There probably won't be many of 'em can read."

Marco stared at him, then said, "I see."

"Hardly any, I'd say."

Marco's cheeks pinkened. "So what exactly is the point of the cards in the first place?"

Juicy had the answer to that one. "The point of the cards is, Lucky gives them to the ones you pick. So when they turn up to be collected, they got the cards, and you can be sure they're the right ones."

282

Marco thought about it. "What if they trade them or something?"

Hmm, Juicy thought. *The gringo's not quite as dumb as he looks.* He smiled and said, "To some extent, my friend, we are always in the hands of God. Now, Marco, explain to me the problem with taking the pictures from the car. How we can make it easier for you. Another drink?"

A while later, Marco said, "Is there a toilet in this place?"

"There's a *cabinetto* out back," Juicy said. "If someone's already in it, use the yard. Most people do."

Marco went out and found the *cabinetto* locked. He turned away from it and liked the back view of the house-front he had already photographed. The big old timbers holding up the crumbling facade. He could imagine a nice sequence, using both views. Ironic. He took several shots of it, and a couple of the slumping shed with the papered window at the back of the yard. And then, because his bladder couldn't wait, he urinated against it.

Felicia came back with the coffee seller's cigarettes and Bianca was gone. It almost didn't matter, she was so used to it, until she tried to get out of the market and realized she was being tracked and surrounded by half the Hernandez gang. Not the deathly one, though, or Slice.

"Hey, girl. How ya doin'?" The stoned boy with the pockmarked face.

"Hey, c'mon, sister. We ain't got nothin' against you."

283

"Not yet, anyways."

Their voices like fingers all over her. She turned back.

Three streets away a querulous bunch of kids was being marshaled by Lucky and a couple of the crew. Slice stopped a little way short of it and penned Bianca up against the wall with his arms.

"Here's the deal," he said. "See him with the plaster thing on his leg? Yeah? In a minute he gonna take you roun' the corner an' you gonna stand where he tell you. Then a guy inna car's gonna take your picture. Tha's all you gotta do, right? An' don' try an' take off or nothin'. 'Cause if you do, I'm gonna be trouble to you."

"What guy?"

"Don' matter what guy. Jus' some guy wanna take your picture. You jus' look at him nice."

"Okay."

Slice smiled, bringing his face closer to hers. "No. Look at him *real* nice, know what I mean?" The fingers of his right hand slid down her arm and onto her hip, where they pressed and urged.

"Yeah," he said. "Like that. Look at him like that."

It was weird, Marco thought, *shooting the kids mustered against the wall. Like, how come no one was walking down the street?*

"That one," he said to Lucky, who was leaning against the wing of the car. "The one in the blue T-shirt. And the boy three along, with the short dreads." He took his eye away from the viewfinder, said, "Wow," and put it back again. "Her. No, her. The one near the end with all the hair."

He held the button down, taking maybe ten, fifteen shots of her.

She could see that he was gold-haired and beautiful, and he was the first man ever to take her picture. She leaned back against the dirty wall and closed her eyes and parted her lips and lifted her hair up with both hands just like Desmerelda in her favorite photo. When she came out of it, the big boy with his leg in a cast was giving her a blue piece of card with writing on it.

"Wha's this?"

Lucky started explaining, but then Slice was back close to her.

"Don' worry 'bout it, Lucky. I'll make sure she's there."

4.5

BIANCA WAITED UNTIL Bush eased out the door, then another five minutes: an agony of waiting. For the first time in her life, it mattered hugely what time it was, and it was a bitch that she had no way of knowing.

She gentled out of the bed and was halfway out the door when Felicia, goddamn her, murmured, "Bianca?"

"S'all right. I just gotta go pee."

Then she was in the yard, no one there. She dug out the folded-up piece of card from her bra and, clutching it tight, slipped through the ruined wall and onto the street. The morning was joyous with light and promise. She began to run.

The music filling Diego's Maserati is the opening to *Oklahoma!* When his phone rings, he swears softly and kills the stereo.

"Hi, Diego."

"Dezi. Everything all right?"

"No, not really. Listen, I don't think I can make it."

"What? What's the matter? Wait, let me pull over. Stay on the phone."

He hassles his way onto the forecourt of a shopping mall two blocks down from the Plaza de la Republica.

"What's the problem?"

"I had a very bad night. Baby's doing very strange things. I feel hellish."

"Christ, Dezi. I mean, how bad is it? Do you want me to come over?"

"No. I've called Michael. He's going to take me to the clinic."

"Right."

"So look, I'm probably not going to make it to the shoot. Or maybe I could come later on, if everything is okay."

He lifts his glad eyes to the sky and takes a calculated risk. "Forget it," he says. "We'll cancel the shoot."

"No. No way, Diego. Not after all we've been through, setting it up. Look, call my cell this afternoon, yeah? Tell me how it's going."

"I'll call, of course I will. But how will I know how it's going? You're the expert in this kind of stuff, Dezi. Without you there, I dunno . . ."

"It'll be fine. They're all top people."

"Well, yes. I guess so. But I still—"

"Listen, I gotta go. Michael's just buzzed the door."

"Okay. Take care of yourself, you hear me?"

Halted at the next set of lights, Diego sees that the office buildings to his left are in deep shade, while those to his right flash gold diagonals of sunlight. The narrow sky above the glass canyon is a virginal blue. He clicks the stereo back on, and after a while begins to sing along, in a murmur at first, then letting it swell. "'Oh, what a beautiful mornin' . . . '"

Slice helped her onto the bus—well, it was like a van with seats in it—with a hand on her backside. Bianca didn't know any of the other kids who piled on, but she was too high to worry about that. It pulled away.

At the corner, she saw Angel standing there. He looked at her with his dead eyes and grinned his ratty teeth.

It's impressive, Diego has to admit. It's an old basketball court out in the suburbs, but you'd hardly know it. One end is screened with huge blown-up photographs: shuttered-up shop fronts, graffiti-sprayed walls, the windowless facade of a colonial-era house. Props, too: the wreck of an ancient Chevrolet, a skeleton in carnival costume, soccer balls, Caribbean-style steel drums. A few yards in front of all this, two camera tripods, lamps, light reflectors, aluminum stepladders. In the center of the court is a low tower of scaffolding with spotlights attached to its bars; at the top of it a girl in dungarees is talking urgently into her headset.

At the far end, a second big screen is a beach scene done

cartoon-style in graffiti spray paint. On the floor, a care-fully vandalized beach chair beneath a wickerwork parasol bathed in electric sunlight. Another collection of photo-graphic apparatus, and a group of people having animated discussions around a tall, thin man with long black hair, whom Diego recognizes as the photographer, David Bilbao. A blond young man who looks like a gringo spots Diego and breaks away from the group.

"You must be Señor Mendosa," he says, holding out his hand. "Marco, David's assistant."

"Diego," Diego says. "Hi."

Marco peers behind Diego as though someone might be concealed there. "I thought Desmerelda Brabanta would be with you."

"Er, no. I'm sorry to say that she is unwell. I think it's unlikely she will be able to join us."

The effect of this news on Marco is remarkable. It is as though someone has informed him that his entire family has died in a plane crash.

"Oh, my God," he moans from behind his long fingers. "That's all we need."

Diego is concerned. "Why? Are you having problems?"

Marco directs a haunted look over toward the beach set, then takes Diego by the arm and leads him to the front row of the spectator seats. They sit. Diego sees that on the other side of the court, close to the gap in the seating that must lead to the locker rooms, Dario Puig and Harumi are inspecting wheeled racks of clothes sheathed in plastic.

Their staff is all wearing black ninja-style outfits with REKI on the back printed in acid green.

"Well," Marco says, after taking a deep breath. "Let's just say that things thus far haven't gone *entirely* smoothly. First off, only about half the kids turned up at the collection points. And some of those weren't the ones we were expecting. They were — how can I put this politely? — little urchins. One of them managed to smuggle a knife past the security. As a result, one of the boys we want to use now has a wound in his arm. But, thank *God*, David saw it positively. The bandage we put on the kid will look nice, he thinks. We may have to touch the blood up a little, but that's fine."

"Good," Diego says. "But you've got enough kids? Don't tell me we're going to have to round up some more."

"No. There are fifteen that David likes, which is plenty. More than enough, if you ask me. The ones David didn't pick didn't take it too well. The girls were particularly dreadful. Still, we managed to get them all back on the buses with their thirty dollars in their sticky little fists. Let's hope they spend it wisely."

Diego blinks at this, but manages to keep his face straight.

"Anyway, they've gone," Marco says. "The others are down in the changing rooms. We went out and got some buckets from a twenty-four-hour fried chicken place, and that seems to be keeping them quiet. Then there are the technical problems. But I won't bore you with those."

"Thank you," Diego says appreciatively. "I like the sets, by the way. The backdrops."

Marco brightens. In fact, he blushes slightly.

Noting it, Diego says, "Your idea, by any chance?"

"Yes, actually. I'm rather pleased with the beach one; it was quite problematic. For obvious reasons, we couldn't take these . . . children on actual location, down to the coast. Can you *imagine?* And there was absolutely *no way* we were going to fake it, with a truckload of white sand and hokey plastic palm trees. So I came up with the graffiti idea. We have these lovely rough-looking kids in gorgeous shorts and bikinis and so forth, and we shoot them up against a dream, a *fantasy,* of a beach that's been sprayed on a wall in a slum. It's ironic, you see. It sort of ties in with Dario and Harumi's concept. The contradictions involved in being a teenager, all of that."

Diego nods thoughtfully; Marco waits expectantly.

"Excellent," Diego says. "Perfect, in fact. Well done."

Two hours later, and Diego has come to the conclusion that fashion shoots must be among the most tedious things ever devised. Golf is thrilling by comparison. He has removed himself to a high place in the banked seats beyond the reach of the lights and sits brooding, calculating. The business is going to last well into the evening, he now realizes. It will make things difficult for him, perhaps. During one of the intense fusses that punctuate the actual photography, he sees Marco head off toward the bathroom and intercepts him on the way back.

"Marco, excuse me. Look, I have to go and see to a couple of things. I probably won't be able to get back until late afternoon. What I was wondering is, would I be able to look at the shots you've taken by then? Señora Brabanta is expecting me to report back to her on how things have gone, and, well . . ."

Marco considers this with immense seriousness, trying not to dwell on Diego's beautifully lustrous eyes.

"Well," he says at last, "what I could do is download the digitals onto disk. We'd be doing that anyway, obviously. So you could have a little peek at them on my laptop."

"That would be great, Marco. Thank you."

"But we'd have to be *very* discreet. David would murder me twice if he found out I'd let you look at unedited stuff. He's an absolute perfectionist."

"I understand that," Diego says solemnly. He pats Marco affectionately on the upper arm as a token of his appreciation.

The thrill of it all, the strangeness of joy, is almost scary. It is as though her heart has risen to a higher place in her body; it beats at the base of her throat, so that she has to breathe in quick, light gasps. But she is not scared. She is so happy, so very happy that she has been found at last. It was surprising that in the mirror she could not see the aura made of starlight that must certainly surround her. A young man, serious as a priest and wearing white latex gloves, had teased out her hair using the long handle of a steel comb. She had been expecting makeup, the full works: eyes, lips, everything. Instead he had only brushed her cheekbones and the tip of her nose with a powder that didn't show. It was a little bit disappointing. Still, the brush was the softest thing she had ever been touched by. She'd closed her eyes, lifting her face to it.

Now she is taken to a space behind some curtains, and two kind of creepy but smiling girls all in black dress her in such beautiful new clothes, clothes no one has ever worn before, knee-length shorts, tight to her skin, but soft, soft as cream and the color of cream, and like a long hoodie in the same color but with these thin dark stripes running all down it. It is *so* cool, she feels like she can fly, and they tell her she can keep them for always (because what else can they do with them after kids like her have worn them, but that's not something she hears them say), then they take her out into the bright colored lights that look like they're shining through rain and she hopes it isn't because she's crying, and then all the people look at her and some clap—yes, they *clap*—and smile at her, and it's like something wonderful unfolds inside her and spreads and whispers, *Yes, it's you. It's you at last.*

And they take pictures, lots, not just one, saying, "That's lovely, Bianca. Just like that. But don't smile, okay? Try not to smile. Maybe think about something sad."

And that is the only hard thing, trying not to smile. To remember something sad.

◆ ◆ ◆

"This one's a honey," David Bilbao murmurs, switching cameras. "You did well finding her. How old is she? Any idea?"

Marco shrugs modestly. "None at all. Kids like these, they could be anything."

Bilbao turns away and calls over to the stands. "Harumi? Harumi, I'd like to see this girl in some other things, okay? Some of the sweatshirts, maybe. Or the soccer jerseys."

Then he says to the woman standing next to him with the clipboard, "Put her down for the swimwear, too, please."

They shoot her again late in the afternoon. On the beach chair, webbed by the shadow of the umbrella, pretending to read a magazine. Then with her hands on her hips, a volleyball between her feet. Then standing with her back to the camera, looking over her shoulder as if someone unwelcome has just walked onto her private spray-painted beach.

Marco is fretful. "She's *posing*. It doesn't seem to matter what we say to her, for God's sake."

Peering through the viewfinder, Bilbao says, "Don't worry about it. We've got some good ones when she's not ready. Besides, I think the posing is kind of charming. Precisely because she's not good at it. There's a rather touching awkwardness about it. I'm inclined to think we should use some of those."

294

"Well, okay. But isn't some of it a bit, you know . . ."

"Obvious? Lewd?"

"Yes, quite frankly."

"It's all in the eye of the beholder, Marco. All in the eye of the beholder."

Diego sits outside the light, looking down at the beautiful half-naked child drenched in light. Absolutely focused on her.

And when, later, alone in the now empty office behind the ticket booth, he copies Marco's disks onto a memory stick, he makes sure they include all the pictures of her.

From his car, he tries ringing Desmerelda again. This time she answers.

"Hi, Diego." She sounds tired.

"Dezi. I've been so worried about you. I tried to call but—"

"Yeah, I know. I had to turn my phone off."

"Are you all right?"

"I'm fine. My blood pressure went way up, and baby chose that moment to change position. It's normal, apparently. So, how was the shoot?"

"In my wildest dreams I couldn't have imagined anything more boring."

She laughs. "Well, I guess you're a virgin when it comes to this kind of thing. Did you expect it to be fun?"

"I suppose I did."

"Well, now you know. It's like work, but worse. Was it okay, though?"

"I think so," he says, leaving room for doubt. "There were problems with the kids, as we expected. But Bilbao and his people seem happy with the results."

"Have you seen any of the pictures?"

"No. They're being pretty cagey. I guess they want to edit and so forth before we all get to look at them. I imagine it might take some time."

"Yeah. Look, the people here want me to stay overnight. Just for observation."

"You mean you're still at the clinic? Dezi, are you sure everything's all right?"

"Yeah, I'm fine, like I said. But the thing is, Otello doesn't know I'm here. I didn't call him, because the game kicked off at six thirty, right? And I reckoned the last thing he'd need before going out was me giving him stress. So look, Diego, would you do me a favor? Call him, or maybe text him, after the game's over, tell him where I am, and not to worry?"

"I'll do that. Promise."

"Bless you. And tell him I'll call him first thing in the morning, before his flight leaves."

"I'll do that, Dezi."

"Thanks. Talk to you tomorrow. And thanks for everything."

He sits in the dark assessing the possibilities. Otello

and Desmerelda's penthouse will be unoccupied tonight; he knows the five-digit key code that will get him in; he knows the night security guys by name, and they won't find a visit by him at this hour odd or memorable. They'll know that Otello is not there, of course; the one at the desk will be watching the game. Will they know that Desmerelda is not at home, either? Maybe not, but maybe isn't quite good enough. The crucial thing is the CCTV. How long do they keep the tapes before they wipe them? A week? A month? He curses himself; he should have found out.

No, he decides. It's too risky. But it's all right. His luck is good. It's not even luck; the world is on his side. An opportunity will present itself.

The clock on the dashboard says it's ten minutes to eight. The game has twenty-five, maybe thirty minutes to go. The kids could come out of the basketball court any minute; they must, surely to God.

He calls Otello's cell, waits for the beep, relays Dezi's message, spicing it with a little twist of anxiety, just for his own pleasure. Then he switches his phone off and, although it's a bit risky, drives across the parking lot closer to where the dim lights illuminate the vans. He waits for another fifteen minutes before the kids are brought out. The girl gets into the second van, and when it coughs its way to the gate, he follows it.

Later, much later, he eases himself into his apartment and drinks a large glass of water from the kitchen tap. He will not go to Emilia until his nerves have settled, just in case she is awake. He holds the glass in one hand and checks his phone with the other. Amazing what hands can do. Surgery. Embroidery. Murder. He sniffs the one holding the phone. A slightly stale, musky smell — or is he imagining it?

There's a message from Otello. "Thanks for the call, Diego. I managed to get through to the clinic, and they say Dezi's fine and she'll be able to come home in the morning. I'm going to fly back tonight so I can pick her up. There's a late plane. I'm in the taxi on the way to the airport right now. You see the game, or did you have something more interesting to do?"

Diego leans against the sink, wondering whether or not to drink some whiskey. And wondering what time a private prenatal clinic might discharge a rich and famous client. Not early, for sure.

He steals into the bedroom. Emilia is asleep. He decides against the Scotch and goes along the corridor to the study and turns his computer on. He slots the little black memory stick into a USB port. When the screen fills with tiny images, he studies them intently for a considerable time. Then he begins to edit.

4.6

A T NINE O'CLOCK the following morning, Otello is coming out of the shower wearing a bathrobe and toweling his hair when the door buzzer sounds. He groans, so Michael Cass goes through to the hallway and looks at the little screen.

"It's Diego," he calls. "Looks like a goddamn florist shop on legs."

"Hi," Diego says from behind his extravagant bouquet of white and yellow blooms. He looks flustered and concerned, and there's orange pollen on his nose.

Cass grins. "I didn't know you cared."

Diego looks at him blankly for three seconds, then smiles. "You know I do, Michael. But these aren't for you. Sorry to disappoint. How is she?"

"Fine, far as we know."

"She's not back?"

Otello comes into the room, zipping up his jeans. "No," he says. "Michael and I are just about to go and get her. Nice flowers, man. Nice thought."

"Yeah, well," Diego says. "I figured you wouldn't've had the time to . . . Anyway, she's okay, is she?"

"She's great. I talked to her about fifteen minutes ago. Look, uh, we need to get going."

"Right," Diego says. "I thought Dezi might be back and settled by now. I'll be sorry to have missed her." He looks quite desolate.

So Otello says, "Look, why don't you wait here? Find something to put the flowers in, load up the coffee machine? I know Dezi will want to see you, anyway. To talk about the photo shoot and stuff. I want to hear about that, too. How long'll we be, Michael? Forty-five, fifty minutes?"

"Yeah, something like that," Cass says.

"Ah, I don't know," Diego says. "I don't want to be in the way. Besides, I've got meetings from eleven on."

"Loads of time, man. Do like I say. Stay here. We'll have a breakfast party. Dezi'll love it. Tell you what, call that good deli. The number's on the board in the kitchen. Get them to send some pastries and whatever around. They know what we like."

"Well, okay. But if Dezi needs to just, you know, rest up when she gets back, I'll make myself scarce."

"Sure. Okay, Michael. Ready?"

◆ ◆ ◆

When they've gone, Diego wanders into the bedroom and looks around. He sniffs at some of the jars and bottles on the dressing table. Then he goes into the dressing room and runs his hands through Dezi's clothes hanging in the closets. He urinates in the en suite bathroom and doesn't flush the bowl. Then he walks down to the study and sits at the computer. The screen saver is running: a slide show of stills from Desmerelda videos. He takes a pair of latex gloves from one of his jacket pockets and puts them on, then taps the space bar. Out of idle curiosity he reads the first six e-mails in the in-box, then takes the black memory stick from his inside pocket and clicks on START.

FAUSTINO HAD SPENT two days in Brazil, where work and high humidity had kept him away from his usual temptations. On his return, he'd startled Marta and his colleagues by turning up at the office before nine in the morning. He had a lot of stuff to write up, but a backlog of e-mails and numerous phone calls thwarted his efforts. By lunchtime he was irritable. It would have been sensible to work through the break, but he needed air — by which he meant a cigarette or two. He'd go and sit on the patio, get Bush to fetch him a toasted sandwich and a juice. Besides, it was a beautiful day.

And because it was a beautiful day, the patio was pretty crowded. The benches were all taken, so Faustino propped his backside on the edge of one of the plant troughs. He looked around for the familiar glimpse of the kid's dreads and smile. After a while he went over to Rubén.

"He ain't been here since the day you left, Señor Paul."

Like there was a connection between the two things.

Faustino had just returned to his desk when his phone rang again.

"Yeah."

"Paul? It's Marta."

"Hi, Marta. What's up?"

"Well. You know that kid, the one from the street, with all the hair?"

Faustino clicked the save icon on his screen. "Yes. What?"

"Paul, he's down here in reception. Says he wants to talk to you."

"He's at the desk?"

"I sent him over to the waiting area. He's got a girl with him, and a middle-aged guy."

"What did he say?"

"Just that he wanted to talk to you. Do you want me to tell him you're busy?"

"No. No, keep him there. I'll be right down."

"He shouldn't be in here, Paul."

"I know. Just make sure he stays put."

Faustino stepped out of the elevator and looked across to the waiting area, an arrangement of chairs and sofas partly screened off from the lobby by potted plants in square marble tubs. Bush was perched on one of the sofas, his forearms on his knees, his head lowered so that his face was invisible behind the tumble of dreads. The young girl sitting beside him had a longish, rather lovely, and very somber face. Her arm was against Bush's back, the fingers resting on his shoulder. The man standing with them wore a baggy cotton suit that had seen better days. As a group, they looked like a couple of kids who'd been nabbed by an undercover store detective and were waiting for the cops to arrive.

Bush raised his head when Faustino came over, but didn't stand. Nor did the girl. The guy was in his mid-fifties, maybe. Paunchy. His graying hair was pulled back into a short ponytail. A *bandido*-style mustache drooped down to the corners of his mouth. He might have been someone who'd been in a rock band in the seventies, then gone to seed.

"Señor Faustino? My name is Fidel Ramirez."

Faustino shook the man's hand, then looked down at Bush. The boy seemed terribly tired. No, worse: stricken.

"Bush? What's up? What did you want to see me about?"

"I'm sorry, Maestro. I didn' wanna bother you. It was Felicia's idea."

Faustino looked at the girl. "You're Felicia?"

She nodded.

Faustino said, "Uh, listen, shall we go outside and talk? It can get kind of busy in here."

Bush and Felicia sat on one of the steel benches, adopting exactly the same positions as before. Fidel sat on the other side of Bush. Faustino didn't feel right about forming a line of four, so, as earlier, he leaned against the nearest trough, from where he could see their faces. He lit a cigarette and offered one to Ramirez, who shook his head.

"Bianca's gone missin'," Bush said, not looking up.

"Bianca?"

"My kid sister."

"Ah. How long has she been gone?"

"She ain't been back for three nights. She took off Monday mornin'. Me an' Felicia an' Fidel been lookin' everywhere, man. Everywhere. Jesus."

He shook his head and inhaled wetly through his nose. Felicia's fingers tightened on his shoulder. Faustino would have liked to put an arm around the boy also, but thought better of it.

He said, "So, Señor Ramirez, you are a, er, relative?"

"No," Fidel said. He looked slightly uncomfortable. "I, my wife, Nina, and me, we have a bar. On Trinidad, down in the Triangle. And we, well . . ."

"He give us a place," Felicia said quietly. "When we didn' have nowhere to go."

"I see."

"Well, it's not much of a place," Fidel said hastily. "There's this shed out back, and . . . Look, Señor Faustino, the thing is, we can't go to the police about Bianca. For all sorts of reasons. You understand?"

"Yes," Faustino said. "Yes, I do."

"Yeah. And Bush says you are a good guy. That he

trusts you. And we thought maybe you could help. In some way."

Bush was jigging his legs up and down, like someone listening to music. "I'm real sorry, Maestro," he said, still not quite able to look directly at Faustino. "I jus' run out of other ideas."

"No, it's all right. I'm glad you . . . Listen, Bush, how old is Bianca?"

"Thirteen and some. Nearly fourteen. Looks older, though."

"Right. She ever done this before? Like take off for a day or two?"

"No. Felicia keeps her tight most of the time. When she can."

Faustino thought about that. "So you don't think she might've, you know, gone off with someone? Of her own accord?" He tried again. "I mean, with a boyfriend or something?"

"No way," Bush said. But Felicia's eyes flickered, and Faustino noted it.

Bush lifted his face at last, and Faustino realized why it had taken him so long to do so. The boy's eyes were wet, and he was ashamed of it.

"I got a real bad feelin' about this, Maestro. Real bad."

Faustino stubbed his cigarette out. "Right. Listen. I need to go talk to someone. Wait for me here, okay?" He looked at Fidel, who nodded. "I'll be right back."

He strode to the door that wouldn't open and swore at it. Rubén opened the other one and let him in. Faustino went over to the desk and spoke to Marta above the heads of a couple who were taking an age to fill in the visitors' book because they couldn't agree upon what their car registration was.

"Marta? Call Nola Levy for me, would you? And give me the phone if she answers."

There was only one spare seat in Nola's office, and because it wasn't obvious who should sit in it, her guests all stood. Bush recognized her as the woman he'd seen weeping out on the patio a long time ago. She made notes as they spoke. She wrote down their description of Bianca and her clothes.

"Is there anything else? Like, for example, are her ears pierced? Does she wear a bangle, or anything around her neck? Does she have any scars, or a birthmark?"

"No," Felicia said.

Fidel cleared his throat. "She is very beautiful, señora," he said unhappily. "That is her main distinguishing feature."

Nola wrote that down too. Then she said, "Paul, maybe Bush and Felicia might like a Coke or something."

Faustino looked at her. She tipped her head in the direction of the door. "I'd like a few moments with Señor Ramirez."

When they were alone, Nola said, "Please sit down,

señor. Now, I have some experience when it comes to missing children. I have to say that not many of the stories I could tell you have happy endings."

"No," Fidel said. "I would not think so."

"I would not wish to offer you any false hopes."

"No."

Nola gazed at him for a couple of seconds, then said, "You put yourself at risk, harboring these children."

Fidel shrugged. The shrug meant several things, including *Yeah, but what can you do?*

"Okay. So, I need to ask you two questions. The first is, do you have a number I can reach you at?"

Fidel gave her the number of the bar, and Nola wrote it below her notes and drew a rectangle around it.

"The second question is, what can you tell me about Bianca that you didn't want to say in front of the others?"

Later, when Fidel and the kids had gone, Faustino and Nola lingered on the patio.

"So," he said. "What do you think?"

Nola drew in a long breath and let it out as a sigh. "Well, the least worst scenario is that she's gone off with someone. From what Ramirez told me, that's quite possible. And if that's the case, she'll most likely show up when whoever it is has finished with her. Unless that person trades in girls."

"Yeah," Faustino said. "It's not terrifically good news

that she's a beauty, is it? What about Ramirez, anyway? Is he kosher, do you think? He doesn't exactly look it."

"My instinct is that he's okay. But then my track record when it comes to judging men is lousy."

Faustino was intrigued by this confession but stashed it away silently for future reference.

"I've got a contact at the Central Criminal Bureau," Nola said. "I'll call him. But if he knows who Bianca is, it'll mean she's dead." She looked at her watch. "I've got a piece to finish. If I hear anything, I'll call you."

"Please."

"Paul, I know you care about this boy. But these kids live in a world people like you and me have no access to. I'm sure you want to help, but get yourself ready for the fact that you can't."

"Yeah," Faustino said. "Don't worry. I'm pretty expert at being useless. But call me, huh?"

4.8

POLICE CAPTAIN HILARIO Nemiso's intolerance for unsolved cases was one of the things that distinguished him from his colleagues and made him unpopular. Like his striking appearance, this had a great deal to do with his father.

In the late summer of 1977, a navy patrol vessel on a routine exercise off the southern coast spotted a drifting twelve-foot fishing boat with nobody on board. This was about eight miles out from the isolated village of Salinas. When three sailors in the ship's inflatable raft went to investigate, they found that the boat's diesel engine was in good working order and that there was plenty of fuel in its tank. There were also several splashes of blood aft of the boat. When the nets were hauled in, they held a catch of a good many fish and a man's body. Back in Salinas, the body was quickly identified as that of an immigrant Japanese fisherman named Takashi. He had never learned much Spanish, and now he never would. The boat was named *Hilario*, after Takashi's son, who was eleven years old at the time. Two police officers came down from Santiago. They conducted a cursory investigation, went away again, and wrote a report that was filed and forgotten.

Takashi's wife was a handsome woman of mixed African and native blood who had many envious admirers. After the policemen had gone away, she laid her husband's body in his boat and cremated it on the beach, as was the local custom. When her son was eighteen, he made his way to Santiago and got jobs laboring on building sites and went to night school. When he was twenty-one, he joined the police. He proved to be a very good policeman and was soon recruited to the federal force and sent to the capital. There he won, first, promotion and, second, enemies. He was efficient, introspective, and apparently incorruptible. He did not seem to know where to draw the line. He did not seem to understand the difference between murders that mattered and murders that didn't. He insisted on conducting investigations beyond the point where they started to have political implications.

This brought him to the attention of Hernán Gallego, who was at that time commissioner of police. Gallego's intelligent response to the Nemiso problem was to promote him to captain and give him his own department. It was called the Special Investigations Unit and had its own budget. A tried and tested tactic: put someone who's too good at his job in charge of something, and he'll become so enmeshed in bureaucracy that he'll get nothing done.

Astonishingly, it didn't work. Nemiso somehow did all the paperwork and attended all the interminable interdepartmental meetings while continuing to dig up dirt about disappeared kids and other undesirables. So when Gallego was appointed minister of internal security, one of the first things he did was merge Nemiso's unit and its budget into the CCB, the Central Criminal Bureau, where there were people who could keep an eye on him and thwart his excessive and inconvenient zeal.

Nola Levy was one of the very few people whom Captain Nemiso respected, and she was one of the very few people who called him by his first name. They'd met when she was still a crime reporter. Her seriousness of purpose, which made her the butt of her fellow reporters' jokes, impressed him. In time he began to provide her, privately, with information — the kind of information his bosses would have preferred to keep out of the public domain. Sometimes when Nola's articles caused serious political embarrassment, there would be searches for the source of the leaks, but Nemiso did not come under suspicion. He was considered to be too much of a stickler for the rules, too much of a prig, to do anything underhanded.

Nola and the captain did not often meet face-to-face.

When they did, it was usually in a car. On rare occasions, like this one, he visited her apartment after dark.

"Only five young female homicides in the last eight days. Five *recorded* homicides, that is. Three have been positively identified. Either of the other two could be your girl, although I very much hope not."

He opened the large envelope he was carrying and passed the photographs over to Nola. The second set was of a girl who was beautiful even in death.

"It could be her," Nola said. "In fact, I have an awful feeling that it is. All that hair, like the boy's. The clothes aren't right, though."

"I think you said that no one actually saw her leave the place she lived in. She might not have been dressed the way the other girl said she was."

"Maybe. But I rather doubt that she had an extensive wardrobe."

"No. The timing fits, though. She died five nights ago. Strangulation with a thin ligature. Unusually, no sexual assault."

"Where was she found?"

"In an alleyway off the Calle Flor."

"Where's that?"

"In the Triangle."

"Ah," Nola said.

Nemiso looked at his watch. "I think we should show these pictures to the people that know Bianca," he said.

"What, now?"

"Why not? I'll drive us over there."

Nola glanced at her watch. "Okay. I'll call Ramirez and let him know we're coming."

She paused with the phone in her hand. "Hilario? I think it might be a good idea if Paul Faustino came with us."

Nemiso considered this.

"He knows the boy better than we do," Nola said. "And if . . ."

"Yes. Very well."

La Prensa was closed when Faustino, Levy, and Nemiso arrived, but there were beads of light edging the shutters. Fidel let them in, then led them to the table where Nina sat and laid his hand on hers. Faustino made the introductions. When Nemiso displayed the photographs, there was no need for him to ask the question. Nina covered the lower part of her face with her hands, stifling a cry of pain that made Faustino flinch. She closed her eyes, but this did not prevent her tears. Fidel put his arm around her shoulders and gazed at Nemiso with doleful rage in his eyes. After perhaps a minute, Nina straightened up and wiped her face with her hands. She glanced at the photographs again, then pushed them roughly across the tabletop toward Nemiso as though they were works of vicious pornography. The policeman shuffled them together with the closeup of Bianca's face uppermost.

Ramirez had told the truth, Faustino thought. *She was — had been — a very beautiful child.*

"I have to ask you formally," Nemiso said. "Is this the girl named Bianca who has been living here under your protection?"

"Yeah," Fidel said. "It is." He sounded as though he had a throat full of catarrh.

"Could you tell me her full name?"

"No."

"You don't know it?"

"No." Fidel stood suddenly. "Jesus Christ," he said fiercely. "Jesus bloody Christ. I knew, I knew . . ." He stopped himself and turned to look at the back door of the bar, working his fingers over his mustache. "Someone's going to have to tell Bush. And Felicia. Dear God." He inhaled deeply, as if preparing himself for the task.

Fear took hold of Faustino, too. He cleared his throat, needing to speak but not knowing what words to use.

"No," Nina said sharply. "Not tonight. Why wake them to . . . to this? Let them be. We'll tell them in the morning. Together."

Fidel looked a question at Nemiso, who said, "I think Señora Ramirez is right. But I'm afraid there will have to be a formal identification of Bianca's body. By the next of kin."

Fidel looked blank for a moment, then said, "What, you mean Bush? Oh, no, man. That's too much. It'd kill him."

"It has to be done, I'm afraid," Nemiso said.

"So I'll do it."

Nemiso shook his head. "No. I'm sorry."

"That's shit," Fidel said. "That's cruel, man."

"Yes. And I think, for several reasons, it would be best if we got it over with sooner rather than later. I'll arrange things for tomorrow afternoon. Say two o'clock? I assume you'll want to accompany the boy. I'll send a car to collect you."

Faustino noticed the look that passed between Fidel and Nina. Later, in Nemiso's car, he said, "I don't think it's such a great idea to send a police car tomorrow. The boy's going to be badly freaked out. I think it might be better if someone he knows picks him up."

"You're volunteering to do this, señor?"

"Yeah," Faustino said bitterly.

4.9

FAUSTINO AND THE taxi driver had some difficulty finding the place.

"I don' get much call to come down here," the driver said unhappily.

It was close to two o'clock when they pulled up at the bar, and Fidel was standing outside it, scanning the street. It seemed to take him several blank seconds to recognize Faustino when he got out of the cab. Then he managed something that approximated a smile.

"We appreciate you doing this, señor," he said. "Bush isn't too good."

"No," Faustino said.

"Okay. Well. I'll get them." He turned toward the door, then back again. "It's okay if I come along too?"

"Of course. I'd be grateful for it."

It was Nina who appeared first. She held the door open, and Felicia led Bush out by the hand. It was hard for Faustino to look at the boy. He was more like a thin old man in disguise, or a victim of some sudden wasting sickness.

"Bush?"

"Maestro," he said, almost inaudibly, and nodded. And kept nodding, like a doll with a spring for a neck.

Faustino's breath snagged at the bottom of his throat, and for an awful moment he thought he might moan, or worse. Instead he stepped briskly up to the boy and put his right arm around his shoulders.

"Come on," he said. Then added stupidly, hopefully, "You'll be okay." He held the back door of the cab open and Fidel got in, then Bush, awkwardly.

Felicia said, "I'm comin' too."

"Right," Faustino said. "Good. Thank you." He got into the front passenger seat.

The driver said, "That everybody?"

Nobody spoke. It was almost unbearable. At the lights on Buendía, the driver jockeyed the cab over into the left-hand lane and said, "You're that Paul Faustino, right?"

"No," Faustino said. He'd been wondering if Bush or Felicia had ever been in a car before. He'd been wanting to turn to look at them and been afraid to.

The driver said, "No? Well, you sure look like him. You know the guy I mean?"

◆ ◆ ◆

The police mortuary did not announce itself. Two of its three stories were underground. Its black glass doors parted automatically. Hilario Nemiso was talking into his cell phone when they opened.

It was difficult to settle upon an order of parade. Bush was the important one, but also the most unreliable. Jittery dread came off him like waves through the conditioned air. So Nemiso led the way down the stairs, with Fidel alongside him. Felicia and Bush followed, then Faustino, who didn't know if he would block the boy if he tried to flee or run with him up and away from the horror into the hot light of day.

They came down into a corridor that ended at a pair of heavy-looking doors with scratched plastic windows set into them. There was a telephone on the wall, and Nemiso spoke into it. The doors opened, and a woman came out wearing white clothes, a white paper hat, and, appallingly, white rubber boots. She stood clasping her hands in front of her like a weird and solemn usherette.

Nemiso turned to Bush and said gently, "Are you ready?"

The boy gasped, perhaps an attempt at a word, and managed no more than three paces toward the door before his legs gave way. He stumbled sideways and leaned for support on a metal wastebin strapped to the wall. The bin had the words NONCLINICAL WASTE on it. Faustino was the first to reach him. He held the boy awkwardly from behind, his hands under the kid's arms.

"Oh, man, oh shit, man. I can' do this. I jus' can' do this."
The words were snags in Bush's shallow breathing.

"Okay, okay," Faustino murmured. He looked around, dismayed that his peripheral vision was blurry and wet. There was a bench against the wall, and he led the boy to it, supporting him.

Nemiso stood with his hands behind his back and his head lowered. Felicia stepped up to him. "I'll do it," she said. "You can put me down as her sister if tha's what you gotta do."

"Okay," Nemiso said after a moment. "Thank you."

Fidel was standing close to Felicia. She reached out and took his hand. It was the first time she'd ever done that, and although Fidel was startled by it, he held on tight. Nemiso nodded to the woman in white. She held the door open and Felicia and Fidel followed Nemiso through it.

It was a big room, but most of it was closed off by gray curtains hung from rails fixed to the ceiling. The cart was gray, too. The white bundle on it looked too small to be Bianca. The white usherette went to the end of it and pulled down the sheet just as far as the chin.

It was a trick. Bianca was asleep. Apart from the grayish pallor to her skin, she looked just like she always did asleep: serious but untroubled.

Fidel groaned like someone disappointed by a joke and turned away. Felicia stared down silently for several seconds, then nodded, spilling her tears. She reached out and stroked Bianca's left temple with the backs of her fingers. It was shockingly cold.

"You fool girl," she whispered. "You fool, fool girl."

Nemiso did not lead Felicia and Fidel back to the corridor. He took them through a door and into a room lined with numbered metal lockers. On a steel-topped table there were zip-sealed clear plastic bags containing items of clothing.

"I'd like you to look at these," Nemiso said. "These are the clothes Bianca was wearing when she was found."

Felicia picked up a bag containing a reversible hoodie, cream on the inside, slate-gray and cream stripes on the outside. Even through the plastic she could feel how soft and new it was. She put it down and took up another bag: a pair of gray canvas sneakers with striped gray-and-cream laces.

She looked at Nemiso blankly. "It ain' her stuff," she said. "You got things mixed up somehow."

"No, I promise you. These are what Bianca was wearing. You don't recognize them? Do you, Señor Ramirez?"

Fidel gingerly picked up a couple of items. "No. Never seen her wearing anything like this. All this stuff looks, like, brand-new. And kinda expensive."

"Yes. As far as we can establish, it is all new. There are no stains, marks, rips. It seems likely that Bianca was the first person to wear any of it. It's also strange that there are no manufacturer's labels."

Felicia found herself crying again and fiercely wiped her eyes with her hands. "It don' make no sense," she said.

Nemiso waited until the girl had collected herself. "Felicia, I have to ask you this. Did Bianca ever steal things?"

"Like what? She ain' got nothin'. You think she got a whole buncha nice clothes stashed somewhere I don' know about? No. No way." She calmed herself a little. "Anyway, are you sayin' like she went out that day, stole all this stuff from some high-class place uptown? An' changed into it all, an' went walkin' around in it back down the Triangle? Man, tha's jus' stupid. Not even Bianca's crazy enough to do that. There's people would kill you for this kinda—"

She stopped.

Nemiso nodded. "Yes. But she wasn't robbed. And there's also this." He took from his pocket another plastic bag, smaller than the others, and put it on the table. There was money in it, green and blue bills, folded.

"A hundred dollars," he said. "It was inside Bianca's brassiere. Or, I should say, the bikini top she was wearing."

4.10

FAUSTINO WAITED FOR two days, which was the most he could manage. On the third day he left his office at lunchtime, headed for the underground garage, then thought better of it and hailed a cab. The driver shrugged when Faustino gave him the address; the shrug said, among other things, *Whatever, man*.

At the top of the Carrer Jesús, the taxi was held up in the usual traffic chaos. Faustino noticed that they were alongside a bookshop called Bibliófilo. He told the driver to pull over and wait. The shop was a labyrinth meandering over two floors, and the youth manning the counter was the kind of nerd who needs a computer to tell him what he should already know. Such as the meaning of the words *marine zoology*. So Faustino spent the better part of ten minutes finding what he was looking for.

◆　◆　◆

It was dark inside La Prensa after the glare of the street, and it took a second or two for Faustino to see Fidel wiping tables in the far corner, emptying ashtrays into a small plastic bucket. Nina came in from the kitchen, bringing bowls of pork and beans to a couple of workmen wearing luminescent vests. They were the bar's only customers. Faustino wondered how anyone could make a living out of the place.

Fidel came over and greeted him. He waved his wipe rag in an obscure gesture of apology and said regretfully, "Life goes on."

"Yeah. How is he?"

Fidel pulled his mouth down at the corners. "He won't come out. Won't speak to us. Felicia says he don't eat the food we take out to them."

"Would it be okay if I talked to him, do you think?"

"It's worth a try, I guess."

Fidel led the way out through the back door and pointed Faustino to the shed. Faustino stood in front of it and looked around the yard at the propped-up facade of the old mansion, the litter blown in from the street, the sleepily watchful trio of feral cats, the patched and streaked wall of Oguz's factory. He felt, and was, incongruous. A character who had somehow wandered onto the wrong stage set. A well-groomed man in a fresh blue shirt and pale chinos. A man carrying a big and very expensive book which he intended to give to a penniless boy who couldn't read.

And then, very quickly, before he could take evasive

action, he was overwhelmed by an emotion that he knew and dreaded. It was like an implosion, a shrinkage of the soul. He became a displaced person marooned in a world he couldn't touch or be touched by. There is a moment in Stanley Kubrick's film *2001* when an astronaut's lifeline is severed and he drifts, struggling in his space suit for a last breath, into dark and dimensionless infinity. Watching it for the first time (alone in his apartment, fortunately), Faustino had let out a yelp of terror — and recognition. Now he only groaned, quietly, and waited for the hopelessness to pass. When it did, he knocked softly on the shed door. After several seconds, he heard Felicia's voice.

"Who's that?"

"Felicia? Bush? It's me. Paul Faustino. Can I talk to you?" His voice was that of someone seeking sanctuary rather than offering consolation.

He heard a murmured conversation, and then after another long delay, the door scraped open.

"Señor Paul?"

"Felicia, hi. I . . . how are things with you? How is Bush?"

"Not too good," she said.

Then she smiled at him. It was a complex sort of smile. There was a welcome in it, and perhaps gratitude, as well as hurt. It was, Faustino thought, the kind of smile much older people use. And the girl did seem older. She seemed to have acquired something like — what? Authority, was it?

"Could I talk to him?"

She hesitated, then pulled the door wider. He stepped inside.

There was not much light, and he waited for his eyes to adjust before he dared to move his feet. The hot air contained the odor of human bodies and the autumnal smell of marijuana. There was a wooden pallet strewn with blankets against the far wall, and Bush was on it, folded up. His arms were around his knees. He was all hair and thin black limbs. Above his head was a large patch of lurid color; it took Faustino several squinty seconds to understand that he was looking at torn-out pictures of Desmerelda Brabanta.

Felicia went to sit next to Bush and laid her hand lightly on his shoulder. Faustino realized that he did not understand, could not imagine, their relationship. He had wondered about couples before, many times, but they had been adult couples. Childless men do not, as a rule, spend much time thinking about what kids feel about each other.

He felt clumsy. Clumsily he perched on the edge of the pallet, because he was unhappy standing above them.

"Bush? How you doing, kid?"

The head came up at last. The eyes were yellowish, the lower lip sticky and cracked. He looked poisoned.

"Maestro."

"Yeah."

"What you doin' here, man?"

"I was sent."

"Uh-huh."

"By the approximately two hundred people who work at *La Nación*. Who all want to know where you are and how they're going to keep the place running without you taking care of business. They're giving Rubén hell, man. Plus, I haven't got time to keep running down the street for my cigarettes. So I came to find out when we can expect you back."

The phony humor was pitiful, even to his own ears. Neither Bush nor Felicia said anything. It was intolerable, so Faustino pulled the book out of the plastic bag and placed it on the pallet close to Bush's feet.

"Also," he said, "I wanted to give you this."

It was a coffee-table book called *The Wonders Under the Sea*. It weighed about five pounds, had cost Faustino ninety-five dollars, plus tax, and contained hundreds of photographs and not much text. Some good crab pictures.

Bush gazed at it blankly. He said, "Wha's gonna happen to her?"

"Sorry?"

"My sister. Wha's gonna happen to her?"

"Right," Faustino said. "Well." He wasn't up to this at all. "I guess they'll keep her there. Until, you know, they find out who—"

"They keep her in a freezer, don' they?"

"I suppose so. Yes. Bush . . ."

"Makes me so sick, thinkin' about it," the boy said, lowering his head again, resting it on his knees. "Jus' so sick."

Faustino, lost in space, his voice gluey, said, "Come back to work, Bush. Come back to life, man."

A little later, outside in the yard with Felicia, Faustino lit a cigarette. The flame of his lighter trembled. The girl had her hands in the pockets of her grubby outsize shorts. She looked at the ground; her long black hair hid most of her face. Faustino, out of habit or possibly desperation, wondered what she might look like in other clothes. What kind of a woman she might become, given the chance.

"Fidel says he's not eating."

The girl shook her head, just once. "Not yet."

"He's smoking dope."

"Yeah, some. He'll stop, though. 'Cause it make it worse, not better."

Faustino nodded, exhaling smoke. "Right."

"Thank you for comin', Señor Paul," Felicia said.

It was almost a dismissal.

"He needs to get back to work, Felicia. I know how terrible this all is. No, I don't know. Sorry. I can only *imagine*. But life goes on, you know? He has to do stuff to take his mind off what happened. Isn't that right? I mean, you guys have a future. It's really, really important, right now, to, like, focus on that."

Crap, and he knew it.

It shriveled him when Felicia looked up at his face and back toward the shed where she lived, somehow, with her wrecked boy. And said, "The future ain't somethin' we like to think about too much, Señor Paul."

Faustino went back into the bar to say his good-byes. The two workmen had gone, and Nina and Fidel were alone.

"We're brewing coffee," Fidel said. "A cup for you?"

"Er . . . yes, why not? Thank you."

The coffee was good. They sat silently for a while, as though listening to the sluggish whoosh of the ceiling fan.

Faustino said, "I know it's early days, but I told Bush he should come back to his territory. Do you think he will?"

"He needs time to grieve," Nina said.

"Yes, of course. But grieving isn't the same thing as brooding. I just think the longer he stays in there, the worse he'll get."

He realized he shouldn't have said it. Nina and Fidel hardly needed him to tell them.

Fidel put his cup down and wiped his mustache with his fingers. "The thing you got to understand, Señor Faustino, is that they are scared. Really scared. For one thing, Felicia still thinks it was the Hernandez Brothers who killed Bianca. She thinks they might kill her too. In case, you know . . ."

Faustino shook his head. "Nemiso's people are sure it wasn't them. For what it's worth, so am I. I mean, she still had money on her. Quite a lot of money. And the way she . . . she died. If it had been a knife, a gun, maybe . . . And she hadn't been sexually assaulted. It doesn't sound like the work of a gang to me."

"That's logical," Nina said quietly. "But we're not dealing with logic here. The fact is that Felicia will be too afraid to go anywhere by herself. And Bush won't want her to. He'll fret about leaving her alone."

"There's another thing worrying them," Fidel said. He glanced, uncertain, at his wife. "That's worrying all of us. Which is, the police know where they are now."

"Yeah," Faustino said, "but Nemiso isn't a Ratcatcher. I also think he's a decent man. I can't see him as a threat."

Fidel shrugged. "Maybe not. But he's not the only one who knows."

Faustino swirled the coffee grounds in the bottom of his cup. He had foolishly logged on to a world whose default settings were uncertainty, vulnerability, and dread. It was bleak, alien. He wanted out. To say, "Thanks for the coffee" and go.

"The fact is," Fidel said, "Bush and Felicia don't feel safe here anymore. They're *not* safe here anymore. They need to move on, but they've got no place to go. It's as simple as that."

Faustino looked up. Fidel's eyes were fixed on his, and there was perhaps something challenging in his gaze.

Faustino glanced at his watch and stood up. "I have to go, I'm afraid. Thanks for the coffee."

Nina and Fidel also got to their feet. They shook hands with Faustino.

"I might drop by again, if that's all right with you."

Fidel spread his hands hospitably. "It's a public bar. Well-behaved citizens are always welcome."

Nina said, "He'll come back to you. Felicia will make sure he does."

In less than five minutes, Faustino was cursing himself for not calling for a taxi from the bar. By the time he'd worked his way far enough west to find one, his blue shirt was dark with sweat.

"Do me a favor," he said to the driver. "Turn the air-conditioning up for a minute, would you?"

"This is as up as it gets," the man said.

Reclining stickily in the backseat, Faustino closed his eyes and saw again Bush folded up below those glossy and incongruous pictures of Desmerelda Brabanta. He wondered what she would think if she knew. He recalled her standing with him, wearing that silver dress, in the roof garden of the Hotel Real. He groaned softly, remembering how he'd grabbed her, dragged her away from the railing. What was it she'd said, just before that? "If there's ever anything we can do . . ."

He opened his eyes and stared out the window, dismissing the thought.

But it returned.

Act Five

5.1

CAPTAIN HILARIO NEMISO had been distracted from the Bianca case by several more pressing matters. Since the NCP election victory, he'd been engaged, more or less continuously, in subtle but nasty battles to preserve his authority and his budget. Despite his best efforts, he'd lost two of his trusted staff to Hernán Gallego's expanded Ministry of Internal Security. Then he'd been put in charge of investigating the abduction of a nephew of a member of the Senate. (It had not gone well; the boy was dead when they got to him, as were the kidnappers. On the upside, the money had been recovered.) Bianca's murder continued to preoccupy him, however, and not only because Nola Levy persisted in inquiring about it.

Beautiful girls die all the time. They die, often, simply because they are beautiful. Or because they stop being beautiful. But they do not die unraped, wearing clothes they cannot own, in possession of an improbable amount of money, in places where they should not be.

He had insisted on a full postmortem. On the day she died, Bianca had eaten well. An analysis of her stomach contents had revealed chicken and vegetables; a high sugar content suggested the ingestion of cakes or sweets as well as soft drinks. Logic insisted that she had not paid for any of it; a hundred dollars was a round sum. Also, she had consumed much of it early in the day. The Ramirez couple gave the three kids food on a regular basis, but had not done so on the morning she disappeared. The Sisters of Mercy had immediately, and with great distress, identified Bianca from the photographs. They could not remember if she'd come to the kitchen on the morning in question; it was always something of a melee, anyway. But they never served anything as ambitious as fried chicken. Nemiso had put his already overworked sergeant and a second plainclothes officer onto the streets of the Triangle for two days. They had met, of course, with very little cooperation. The kind of kids who might have known Bianca scarpered on sight. Two people thought they might have seen her, or someone dressed like her, on the night she was killed, but both were vague and deeply unreliable.

Nemiso had, reluctantly, dismissed Ramirez as a suspect. Men can fake grief, but there could be no reasonable doubt that he had been in his bar on the night the girl died. The captain's suspicions had been aroused again when Ramirez called him to suggest they check out the fashion sweatshop in the building next door, on the grounds that the Turkish guy, Oguz, might have manufactured the clothes that Bianca had been wearing. But the cheap fakes that Oguz produced had nothing to do with anything, and Nemiso was now almost one hundred percent sure that Ramirez hadn't been trying that classic culprit's tactic of volunteering help.

All of which left him nowhere. No, actually: it left him in a perfectly familiar place in which people who didn't matter a damn, people adrift, got found dead, and what you did was fill in a form, if that, and file it under O for Oblivion.

On a day when his car was in for servicing, Paul Faustino took the subway to work. He was reading the trash in *El Correo* about the game against Uruguay when the train stopped at Independencia. He looked up from his newspaper and saw Bianca glowering at him from a poster on the station wall. She was wearing some sort of gym outfit and flexing the muscles in her slender arms. It was immensely baffling and shocking, and Faustino wondered for a moment if he were hallucinating, if he were ill. He got to his feet, but the influx of passengers prevented him from reaching the doors before they closed.

He left the train at the next stop and fought his way through to the southbound platform, intending to return to Independencia, but there was no need. She was there on the wall across the track, the second in a sequence of four kids wearing sort of posh grungy clothes in gray and cream.

Hers were the ones she'd died in. The meaningless word *Paff!* ran along the bottom of the poster, one letter for each model. A huge exclamation mark filled the fifth panel in the sequence.

He returned to the northbound platform and tried to call Nola Levy but couldn't get a signal. There was another *Paff!* poster at the next stop; Bianca wasn't on it. But she was there again, twice, in posters alongside the escalator that carried Faustino up to the street. He gazed at her as he rose past her and she sank away behind him. He always felt off balance on escalators, but now he experienced something like full-blown vertigo.

He hurried, almost ran, toward *La Nación*, then back-tracked to a news kiosk. He picked at random three glossy teen magazines and paid without bothering to wait for the change. Bianca, in a swimsuit, occupied a quarter of a double-page spread in the first one he opened.

In his office he typed the ridiculous word into a search engine and clicked on the first of the three results. He was astonished when his monitor melted into Otello and Desmerelda Brabanta standing amid a mob of shabbily dressed kids who all raised their arms and yelled, *"Paff!"* in one voice. The word then filled the screen and jittered through several lurid colors, finally becoming graffiti on a grimy wall. Then, in speeded-up footage, a hooded teen-ager added the legend REAL KOOL KLOTHES FOR KIDZ in spray paint and raised his fist in a goalscorer's gesture.

This was followed by a fast sequence of stills of rather moody-looking but very well-dressed teenagers accompanied by rap music. Bianca appeared three times. Curving around the top left of the screen the words *Check us out* appeared, written in designer scrawl, with an arrow pointing to a vertical row of tabs. The last was labeled *About Paff!* and Faustino clicked on it. He discovered that *Paff!* was a Brand-New Breakthrough Fashion Concept devised by Desmerelda Brabanta and her husband, the great Otello. There were further pictures of the radiant couple. The *Contact us* tab got Faustino an e-mail template; there was no postal address or phone number.

He picked up the phone and asked Marta to put him through to Nola Levy's office. Voicemail. He found her cell-phone number and got voice mail. Damn! Then he ran the *Paff!* website again. It *was* Bianca, surely. Even though it couldn't be. He riffled through the magazines. Multiple *Paff!* ads were in every one; the girl who had to be Bianca featured in most of them.

It made no sense at all.

He sat staring at nothing for almost a minute, then opened his desk drawer and took out the plastic box he kept business cards in. He found the one Nemiso had given him and called the number that the policeman had underlined.

At an intersection on the Avenida Buendía, there's a fifty-foot-high electronic billboard—one of those that change their image every thirty seconds or so. Bush never looks up at it. Why would he? He's never going to buy the new four-wheel-drive BMW or fly to Rio de Janeiro or see the new Spider-Man movie. Besides, looking up is a bad idea. You look forward and backward and from side to side, because those are the directions that trouble comes from. Looking up makes you vulnerable.

In fact, Bush wasn't really paying attention to anything much. He was just making his legs go, trying not to think. Carrying the big black bucket. It was good that he didn't look up, because if he had, he'd have seen a gigantic picture of his dead sister wearing a tight little crop top and looking so sassy you'd think she owned the world.

Captain Nemiso sat staring at his computer screen while holding the phone against his ear. Eventually he said, "Yes. I think so. No, I . . . Okay, Paul. I will, of course. Thank you. Good-bye."

Detective Maria Navarro knocked on the door and came in before he could tell her to.

"Sir? Um, you'll think I've lost my marbles, but on the way in I thought I saw—"

Nemiso held his hand up. "I know. Come and sit here."

Navarro did as she was told. Nemiso leaned over her and clicked on the mouse. "Now, watch this carefully while I go and find Sergeant Torres," he said.

Faustino took the elevator down to the lobby and, after the slightest hesitation, went out through the revolving doors.

At the patio's low parapet, he looked right then left. Bush trudged up from the garage lugging his bucket. Faustino watched him. There was nothing to be read in the boy's movements. Faustino felt he was observing the life of a remote and deeply submarine creature. When Bush took up his station at the curbside, Faustino, with Rubén's assistance, retreated into the building.

Otello and Desmerelda have been quarrelling. No, bickering. Having a conversation from which love has absented itself.

The famously physical Uruguayan defense had beaten him up for an hour and a half. He'd been deliberately fouled several times in the penalty box. Only one of the decisions had gone his way, and he'd scored from the spot in the sixty-second minute. It had been the only goal in an ugly game played to an unceasing cacophony of whistles and derisive air horns. He'd returned to the marina penthouse in a dour mood. Desmerelda had smelled alcohol on his breath. She'd not been at the Estadio Nacional; the baby is heavy in her now, and sitting in one position for long periods is difficult. More to the point, she no longer wants to be engulfed by those battering waves of sound, the dreadful human roars. Illogically or not, she imagines them penetrating her womb, instilling their savagery in her unborn boy. She had started to watch the game on television, but had fallen asleep after only ten minutes or so. When she'd carelessly admitted this, he'd grunted that she hadn't missed anything. In fact, he'd felt hurt, felt she had taken another step away from him.

During the night the baby had been restless, pressing Desmerelda's bladder. She'd pictured him struggling against his cramped anchorage inside her body. Her sleeplessness had driven Otello, once again, to one of the guest bedrooms.

Now, in the morning, he is out of sorts. His bruises have flowered. He is anxious about his sore Achilles tendon. He wants to make an appointment with the Rialto physical therapist. Now. He doesn't want to do the midday event at Beckers. Apart from anything else, he ought not to be putting weight on the foot.

"We've *got* to do it," Desmerelda says. "It's been set up for weeks. The people at Beckers have spent most of the night filling a whole floor with *Paff!* stuff. The posters are up, the website went live at six this morning, and we've got all the magazines coming. This is a really big day for us. For me."

"Yeah, well."

"What's that supposed to mean, 'Yeah, well'?"

"Look, Dezi, this whole thing, it's . . . well, you're central to it. You and Dario and what's-her-name . . ."

"I take it you mean Harumi."

"Yeah. And I haven't had a great deal to do with it, have I? It's you that everybody will want to talk to."

"Oh, no. No, no. If you think that I'm doing this without you, forget it. What, stand there in front of everybody, seven months' pregnant with your baby, surrounded by these fantastic shirts with your face all over them, and you're not *there*? How's that going to look? How's that going to make *me* look? Does the word *stupid* come to mind, by any chance?"

"Look—"

"No, *you* look. If you're not there today, it's going to suggest very strongly that you're not committed. And that is going to be very bad news for our product."

She's right, of course. So he says nothing.

"Do you happen to know how much money is invested in *Paff!*?"

"Well—"

"No, you don't. I do. It's a lot. So, Capitano, if I can lug Raúl down to Beckers, you can manage it with a sore heel."

Raúl. That's one thing they have agreed on at least. The baby's name.

Detective Sergeant Martín Torres swiveled away from the monitor and said, "It's her. I'd bet my pension on it." He tapped a finger on the magazines that Navarro had gone out and bought. "These are her too. But it's crazy."

"Yes," Nemiso said. "There's also this."

He dropped a small brown envelope onto the desk. The self-adhesive label on the front was printed with his name and rank and the address of the CCB. Inside, there was a postcard, the kind you can buy in any number, anywhere—plain, the space for the address marked out in lines, the space for the stamp an empty rectangle. A picture of the soccer star Otello, cut from a magazine, had been glued to one side. Glued to the other, a three-word newspaper clipping:

OTELLO LOVES CHILDREN

Below it, in penciled capitals:

AND PICTURES OF THEM. ONE DAY HE'LL GO TOO FAR.

It had been delivered three weeks ago. He'd sent it to forensics, out of habit. There had been no prints, no DNA traces, nothing. At the time, busy with other matters, he'd given it no further thought. There had been no reason for him to connect it with the Bianca case.

Torres studied it before passing it to Navarro. "It's something and nothing," he said.

"True," Nemiso said. "But let's stay with the something. Because we've got nothing else. Until now, this case was as cold as the girl."

Torres nodded. He thought, but didn't say, that it was the kind of case that would go cold. Another dead street kid. But for some reason his boss had a hornet in his shorts about this one. Which meant trouble.

Nemiso said, "I believe Otello and his wife live at the marina complex. Ever wanted to see how the other half lives, Martín?"

5.2

DIEGO WAS WIRED. It was all he could do to contain himself. He kept going over everything. It was like watching the ball bouncing along the roulette wheel, knowing that it would settle where you wanted it to, all the bets were in, it would drop where you knew it would drop. Thrilling, actually. Unbearably thrilling. But it was in slow motion.

"Patience," he told himself daily.

"Patience," he told the ever-patient Emilia.

DIEGO *is dressing for the Beckers event when his phone rings. It is 10:21 a.m.*

DIEGO: Hi, Capitano.

OTELLO: Listen, Diego. We have a problem.

DIEGO: It's not Dezi, is it?

OTELLO: No. The police are here.

DIEGO: The police? What do they want?

OTELLO: They want me to go downtown with them. Now, if you can believe that.

DIEGO: I don't understand.

OTELLO: Me neither. They're also taking my computer away. I don't even know if they can do that. Can they do that?

DIEGO: Uh . . .

OTELLO: Wait. Hang on.

[*It seems that* OTELLO *has turned away from the phone to talk to somebody.* DIEGO *waits, in an agony of exultation.*]

OTELLO: Diego? Listen, that lawyer we used to sort out that business with Michael. Perlman, was it? You got her number?

DIEGO: I can find it, yeah. But—

OTELLO: Call her. Now. Tell her to get down to... Wait a minute.

[*Again* DIEGO *strains to hear what the poor fool is saying to someone else.*]

OTELLO: Yeah. The Central Criminal Bureau— Special Investigations Unit. Ask—no, don't ask—*insist* on speaking to a Captain Nemiso.

DIEGO [*indulging himself*]: How do you spell that? No, never mind. Capitano, what the hell is all this about? Haven't you explained that you and Dezi have to—

OTELLO: Diego, I gotta go. Get Perlman, okay? Right now. I'll call you back soon as I can.

◆ ◆ ◆

Diego slides open the glass doors to the balcony that runs the length of his apartment. The sky is an unsullied blue. He inhales, deeply, the light breeze. When his nerves have settled, he goes to his CD rack and selects a recording of waltzes by Richard Strauss. He cranks up the volume and, when the lush and jaunty music swells, goes out onto the balcony and dances. He is wearing a shirt the color of the sky, a silvery tie, and black socks. Trouserless, gazing with rapt attention into the eyes of his invisible partner, he dances.

When the waltz is over, he goes back inside, stabs the music off, and calls Consuela Perlman's office. He gets her secretary and leaves a message. Then he puts on his second-best suit.

10:56 a.m. The offices of El Sol. *Mateo Campos is grubbing through the pages of a celebrity magazine called* Rich *when his phone rings.*

"Yeah."

Eleven seconds later he says, "Yeah?"

Then he says, "I don' suppose you wanna give me your name? I didn' think so. This is bullshit, right?"

But the line has gone dead. Campos thumbs the recall buttons.

10:57 a.m. A phone booth in the lobby of TFN, the city center train terminal. Diego is pleased when the phone rings, but

347

ignores it. He has a small notebook in his hand. When the ringing stops, he puts another fifty-cent coin in the slot and dials a second number.

Mano Valdano of *El Correo* reacts to the call in pretty much the same manner as Mateo Campos. However, because the caller's voice was sober and articulate despite its coarse northern accent, Valdano summons a junior reporter and a photographer and sends them over to the CCB. Just in case.

10:59 a.m. Mateo Campos uses the little finger of his right hand to dig for earwax, which is something he does only when he is thinking, so there's usually plenty in there. Then he gets up and ambles over to the desk of his colleague Estevan Ponte. He leans down closer to Ponte than Ponte would like.

"Listen, Stevie—I just got a call from someone saying that the cops have hauled Otello down to Central."

"What?"

"Yeah."

"What for?"

"The guy didn't say. But he did say they took sonny boy's computer away as well."

"Wow."

"Yeah. You got any way of checkin' this out? Nine chances out of ten it's some idiot making a prank call, but I don' wanna sit here wipin' egg offa my face if it turns out to be true."

"Okay. Give me five minutes."

348

Ponte is an amiable and cultured man whose specialty is lurid coverage of murders and kidnappings. He has nurtured social and financial relationships with a number of police officers and civilian police employees. He takes his cell phone out into the corridor and calls an admin supervisor at the CCB.

11:03 a.m. Diego is walking back to his car when his phone rings. He checks the caller ID. Desmerelda again. He doesn't answer this time, either.

11:04 a.m. El Sol. Ponte walks as casually as he can manage to Campos's desk. Taps Campos on the shoulder.

"It's true. Come outside."

Back in the corridor, Ponte says, "Yeah. They brought Otello in just over twenty minutes ago."

"Christ on a bike."

"My contact doesn't know what's going on, but she says he was logged in by Captain Nemiso. Know the name?"

Campos shakes his head. "Should I?"

"He's a serious dude. Heads the Special Investigations Unit. So we're not talking traffic offenses here."

"What about the computer thing?"

"That's true too, apparently. And the two usual reasons for confiscating computers are financial naughtiness or—"

"Kiddie porn. Oh, dear God, do we dare hope?"

"Hope, Mateo, is something you do sitting on your

349

backside. I've already called up the cameras. Let's get over there."

11:10 a.m. The train terminal parking lot. DIEGO'S *Maserati.*

DIEGO: Dezi, I'm so sorry. I've been making calls. Have you heard from him?

DESMERELDA: No. Where are you?

DIEGO: On my way over to you. Is that right? Is that what you want me to do? Is Michael there yet?

DESMERELDA: Yes. The police are asking *him* questions now. Diego—

DIEGO: Dezi, what on earth is going on? I feel completely in the dark here.

DESMERELDA: Did you call that lawyer, what's-her-name?

DIEGO: Yes. Dezi, *please*. Tell me what this is all about.

DESMERELDA: I've got just about as much idea as you have.

DIEGO: So what actually happened?

DESMERELDA: What happened is, three cops came here this morning and started asking about this girl. One of the kids we used in the *Paff!* shoot. Bianca something or other. Turns out she was murdered the same night. The same night as the shoot.

DIEGO: *What?*

DESMERELDA: Yeah. Awful. I can't believe it. She's on the *posters*, Diego. She's in the spread in *Moda*. She's everywhere.

DIEGO: Oh, my God.

DESMERELDA: Yeah. Unbelievable, isn't it?

DIEGO: I mean, how come nobody told us about this?

DESMERELDA: I dunno. I guess, well, I dunno. Nobody made the connection. I dunno.

DIEGO: Okay. So listen, Dezi, why did they take Capitano downtown?

DESMERELDA: I don't *know*. It's crazy. One of the cops, this woman, went to the study wanting to look at our computers, look at the pictures of this girl on the *Paff!* disks, you know? Then she comes back and suddenly everything goes weird. I mean, do you think he . . . Oh, God, Diego. I don't know what to do. I don't know what to think. I mean, they took his laptop *away*. . . .

[DIEGO *sorts through his CDs while he listens to her fighting back tears. David Bowie? Bartók?*]

DESMERELDA: Sorry. I —

DIEGO [*soothingly*]: It's okay. Look, Dezi. This is some kind of misunderstanding. Or setup. I'm sure it'll be sorted out in no time. I'll be with you in fifteen minutes or so. Right now, let's try and focus on the Beckers thing.

DESMERELDA: Oh, God, I don't know if I can face it. I must look terrible.

DIEGO: I'm sure you don't. That's quite impossible.

11:27 a.m. The young reporter from El Correo *and his photographer are escorted, without undue politeness, from the CCB building. They are rearranging themselves at the foot of the steps up to the building when Consuela Perlman and a colleague emerge from their chauffeur-driven car. Inside the building, Perlman marches up to the duty officer's desk, presents her card, and demands to speak to Nemiso.*

11:28 a.m. A large SUV pulls up, illegally, in front of the CCB building. It disgorges Mateo Campos, Estevan Ponte, a photographer, and a two-man video and sound team.

Campos and Ponte bustle up the steps. Their photographer knows the *Correo* photographer.

"What you doin' here, man?"

"Ah, you know. Routine stuff."

"Bullshit. Otello?"

"Yeah."

"Damn!"

Campos and Ponte, full of false indignation, are ejected from the building and descend the steps.

Campos lights a cigarette and looks the kid from *El Correo* up and down. "Your parents know you're down at the police station?" he asks.

The kid has the sense to get his phone out and call the *Correo* office for reinforcements.

Passersby who have nothing better to do — but who have a nose for anything out of the ordinary — start to gather. Because cameras mean that something is happening, and if you're in the right place, you might have a chance to be in a background shot on the TV news and wave.

11:34 a.m. Inside the CCB building.

Torres takes the stairs down to the lobby. At the head of the last flight he surveys the comings and goings and identifies Consuela Perlman and the sharply dressed man with her. They are a dark and sober little island in a sea of purposeful motion. He descends toward them unhurriedly.

"Señora Perlman? Sergeant Torres of the Special Investigations Unit."

She does not introduce her colleague. She says, "I believe you have a client of mine, Otello, in custody."

"No, señora. Señor Otello is not in custody. He is here voluntarily to help us with our inquiries relating to a murder investigation."

She blinks, like someone who cannot believe a fly has had the audacity to land on her lunch. She looks him up and down: the haircut, the mustache, the brown leather jacket, the jeans, the Italian shoes.

"Don't you dare play games with me, Sergeant," she says. "My client has not killed anybody, and you know it. So if he is being questioned, I'd better be there. Unless you want to be sued until your eyes bleed. Shall we go up?"

12:04 p.m. The third floor of Beckers department store.

No one expects the illustrious couple to appear exactly on time, so there is eager anticipation, and a certain amount of jostling for camera positions, but no real anxiety. The *Paff!* team members smile at everybody as they check details for the last time. Dario and Harumi are being interviewed by the fashion editor of *La Nación.* Four young boys and three young girls—a rainbow of Otello shirts—warm up their freestyle ball routines. A couple of other kids—sons of Beckers's marketing director, as it happens—stand, self-conscious in their *Paff!* baggy sweats and baseball caps, clutching brand-new skateboards. Sales staff, and several security men and women disguised as sales staff, patrol among the mannequins and clothes racks.

The podium that Desmerelda and Otello will stand on is bathed in light.

12:27 p.m. Desmerelda's car. Michael Cass is driving. Diego is in the back with Desmerelda. Her phone rings.

"Where *are* you? What? But why? Don't you know what time . . . Yes, *yes!* We're almost there. Oh, God, Otello. You've *got* to come. What? I can't hear you. Please. *Please.* This is a *disaster!* I can't . . ."

Then she lets out a little scream. Otello has ended the

354

conversation with a harsh obscenity and the line has gone dead. She turns to Diego with tears in her eyes.

"What, Dezi? What did he say?"

"Two blocks to Beckers," Michael Cass says, glancing at her over his shoulder. "You okay?"

"No! Stop the car. Stop the damn car, Michael."

Otello's expletive is not, in fact, directed at his wife. It is merely an expression of shock. He and his lawyers have been ambushed as they leave the CCB building. From out of nowhere, a number of people with cameras and microphones are in his face, shouting questions at him. Some of the questions contain the word *computer*. He stumbles back, almost falling. Consuela Perlman also swears, surprisingly vividly. Her colleague reacts swiftest; using his briefcase rather like a gladiator's shield, he repels the attackers while Otello and Perlman retreat up the steps and back through the heavy glass doors.

12:31 p.m. Beckers.

By now, there is considerable agitation and impatience. Once again, the store's managing director sends a minion down to the main atrium, through which a carpeted pathway to the escalators is fenced off from the throng by chrome posts and rope railings.

Then, at twenty minutes to one, the head of security, stationed at the top of the escalators, touches the phone plugged into his ear and raises his thumb in the direction of the MD, mouthing silently, "They're here."

The stills photographers jostle like players positioning themselves for a corner kick. The freestyling kids go into action, balancing their soccer balls on their foreheads and insteps. The hot TV lights come on. The soothing Muzak switches to the bass-driven pulse of Desmerelda's three-year-old number-one hit "If Looks Could Kill."

And she rises up into it all. Into the applause. She's wearing an outfit designed and made for her by Dario and Harumi. ("We will reinvent maternity wear," Harumi had promised.) The *Paff!* signature colors are worked into a pearl-white dress and long jacket that make no attempt to disguise the pleasingly bell-shaped protuberance that juts in front of her. It's an outfit that boasts of her condition; it's an outfit that would make anyone die to be pregnant. Cass looms behind her, resplendent in a loose charcoal-gray suit and pale yellow shirt, heading an escort of Beckers staff. Flash light plays on her face.

"What's up with her?" a photographer murmurs, keeping his finger on the drive button.

"I dunno. She looks wiped out. Where's Otello?"

Where's Otello? Where's Otello? *Where the hell is Otello?*

Desmerelda stalls; she does not know where to go. *Camera flash flash.* A woman in a suit shakes her hand and speaks. *Camera flash.* Then it's Harumi. Her lean arms around her.

"Dezi? What's wrong? Where is Otello?"

A man on a sort of stage is speaking her name. He looks

down at her, holding out his hand. She thinks, *I can do this,* and steps up. Hands help her. As always, no one, no face, is visible outside the vibrating sphere of light. She hears her own multi-tracked voice singing, "Don't look at me that way, unless you mean it, mean it." There are microphones close to her face. A line of kids wearing *Paff!* appears, level with her knees, dancing to the music. One of them looks up at her, grinning. A pretty dark-skinned girl with wild hair.

The music fades; other voices become audible. She holds on to the mic stand. Oh, God, she needs to pee. No, she doesn't. *Camera flash.*

"Hi, everybody. Thank you for being here today. This is so *cool*, isn't it? Listen, I can't talk for long, for obvious reasons." She puts her hands on her hips, pulling the pearly jacket back, displaying the famous protrusion. There is applause, a few faint whoops.

"I just wanna say that for Otello and me, this is a great day."

She should not have said that. She doesn't know why she said that.

"The culmination of—"

A voice, two, or maybe three voices from beyond the glare: "Where *is* Otello, Dezi?"

"Where's the man, Dezi?"

He's at a police station. They're asking him questions. There's a dead girl. There must be porn or something on the computer he says he never uses. Everything is breaking loose.

357

She says, "We're proud . . . *Paff!* is . . ."

"Dezi!"

"*Dezi!*"

Camera flash *flash* *flash*.

Why is the stage tipping? She clings to the mic stand with both hands. She's losing her balance; her body is too heavy for her legs. She's going to fall. She mustn't. God, this is going to look awful. Where's Michael?

Michael!

5.3

PHOTOGRAPHS OF DESMERELDA'S tearful swoon into the arms of Michael Cass feature prominently in the evening papers, and there is extended coverage on the television news. The fact that the drama is inexplicable does not prevent reporters from explaining it. Experts are wheeled in to testify that women in the later stages of pregnancy are prone to attacks of uncontrollable emotion. The word *stress* is used repeatedly. Concern for the baby is piously expressed. Otello's absence from the promotional event attracts comment. WHERE WAS OTELLO WHEN DEZI NEEDED HIM? asks *La Estrella*, typically.

A good question. Now he is where he thinks he's needed: in the well-appointed waiting room in the private wing of Santa Theresa Hospital. Pacing up and down with his phone in his hand waiting for Diego to call him back. Michael Cass sits staring at a nice reproduction of Van Gogh's *Starry Night*, or whatever it's called.

The senior nursing sister comes through the blond wood doors and says that Desmerelda is comfortable. That there is no danger of miscarriage.

"I want to see her."

"I don't think that's wise, señor. She is sleeping. We have given her a light sedative."

Cass detects the discomfort in the woman's voice. Dezi has told her she doesn't want to see her husband, he thinks. He glances at Otello: has he had the same thought?

It seems not, because he says, "Can she come home?"

"We would rather she stayed here overnight. The doctors would like to examine her again in the morning. Then if all is well, she should be able to leave."

Otello stares at the nurse. He looks baffled, hurt, diminished. His left hand closes into a fist, opens, clenches again.

Cass gets up and puts his arm around Otello's shoulders. Gently he says, "Better she stays here, *compadre*. Why take risks, huh? C'mon, let's get you home. It's been a rough day."

Otello falls asleep in the back of the car. At the marina, shouts and bangs and camera flashes wake him.

"Michael? What's going on? What are these people doing here?"

"Feeding," Cass says, and powers the car through the gates.

◆ ◆ ◆

360

The following morning, both *El Sol* and *El Correo* have EXCLUSIVE banners across their front pages. *El Sol*'s front page is divided in half vertically. On one side the distraught Desmerelda; on the other, Otello leaving the headquarters of the Central Criminal Bureau in the company of his "elegant female lawyer." Beneath the pictures is the headline WE KNOW WHY DEZI WEPT. *El Correo* is slightly more restrained, even though it has very similar photographs on its front page. Both papers make much of the taking away of computers. They sail very close to the legal wind, mentioning recent child pornography cases.

By midday, the marina complex is besieged. The company in charge of its security (already trying to deal with inquiries from the Special Investigations Unit) drafts in extra staff, including two more dog handlers. The wealthy inhabitants are greatly inconvenienced. They do not like being photographed in their cars as they come and go. They are the kind of people who do not want the common herd to know where they live.

The jostling journalists do not really know why they have gathered. They are like whale hunters in fog; there's a ripely rancid smell in the air, but they do not know where it's coming from. The only bright spot in their day comes when Michael Cass brings Desmerelda home in the Hummer. They jump in the air, trying to get pictures of her shrinking into the backseat of the huge machine.

◆ ◆ ◆

361

Next day, the gates of Hades open wide. Somehow the Bianca connection makes the front pages of both *El Sol* and *El Correo*. Reporters from all over the country hasten to catch flights to the capital.

Nemiso, on his way to work, bought multiple copies of the newspapers, and as he walked down the corridor to his office, he pushed doors open and threw them in, saying, "Which one of you whores leaked this for the price of a couple of drinks?" His startled juniors studied the photos of a simpering, beautiful child under headlines declaring that this was the DEAD GIRL at the center of the SHOCK OTELLO INVESTIGATION.

Nemiso's phone was ringing when he closed his door, and he ignored it. He went to the window and gazed unseeingly down at the parking lot until he had steadied himself.

His team had been marking time for thirty-six hours, and he was immensely frustrated. Interviews with just about everybody connected with the *Paff!* label had failed to explain how Bianca Diaz made the transition from a hovel in the Triangle to the pages of fashion magazines. The children who had modeled the clothes were "amateurs." They were "just kids off the street." No one seemed to know how they'd found their way to a basketball court in the eastern suburbs. The name that kept coming up was Marco Duarte, David Bilbao's assistant. But Duarte—along with Bilbao and, no doubt, a twittering circus of hairdressers, makeup artists, and bulimic models—was on location "somewhere in Arizona." Where their telephones didn't work, apparently. Nemiso's calls and e-mails to the state police headquarters in Phoenix had met with little interest and had resulted in no cooperation. So he and his team would have to cool their heels until Bilbao and his coterie returned from the United States in—Nemiso checked his watch—a little under thirty hours. In the meantime, the Otello business was degenerating into the dangerous farce that he, Nemiso, should have predicted. And perhaps might have avoided.

He exhaled a deep breath and went to his desk. There were several e-mails; the second was from the office of the minister of internal security and had a red exclamation mark alongside it. Nemiso would need a strong coffee before he opened it. He stuck his head through the doorway into the squad room and summoned Maria Navarro.

By sunset, the siege of the marina complex has become very lively indeed. Already the occupants of two apartments that have a good view of Otello's penthouse have found it convenient to take unscheduled holidays. Rival newspapers have offered them quite ridiculous sums of money to rent their homes, so why not? (Soon other residents will succumb to similar offers. As will owners of boats moored in the marina. Balconies and decks will be manned by unsuitable people toting cameras and binoculars. On their return, the owners will find that their fridges have been looted, their carpets ruined by cigarette ash, their rooms and cabins filled with takeout food litter. But never mind. The insurance will cover it.)

Faustino had been detained at work by an editorial "summit meeting" about the Otello-Bianca Affair. He had not been alone in arguing that no such thing existed. The fact that Mateo Campos and *El Sol* claimed that it did more or less proved that it didn't. Nonetheless, he had come under considerable pressure from Carmen d'Andrade to use his "personal connection" with Otello and Desmerelda to secure *La Nación* an inside story. To get Carmen off his back, he'd agreed to try, while having not the least intention of doing so. Before the meeting, in a hasty and furtive conference in her office, he and Nola had agreed to say nothing about their personal knowledge of Bianca, in order to protect Bush and Felicia. They both knew that it would be a difficult and dangerous secret to keep. If their colleagues—if Carmen—found out . . . well, there'd be hell to pay, and then some. And Faustino couldn't be certain that nobody else working in the *Nación* building knew that the wild-haired kid who hustled errands right outside was the brother of the "slain child model" at the center of "the Otello mystery." What about Rubén, for instance?

More pressing, more sickening, was the question that Faustino needed and feared the answer to: did the boy himself know yet? If he did, or when he did, would he keep quiet?

And what in God's name was wrong with the elevators

tonight? He jabbed his thumb against the down button again.

One thing was certain. Bush would have to stay away from *La Nación*. For everybody's sake. At least until this Otello nonsense had blown over.

The elevator pinged its arrival, and by the time it had descended to the lobby, Faustino had made up his mind. He'd go over to the Triangle tonight. Talk to the boy, persuade him—pay him, if necessary—to stay there, lie low. He checked his watch. Ten past seven. The kid should be back there by now.

He wasn't. He was sitting halfway down the patio steps in lamplight.

"Bush?"

The boy turned his head and looked up at him. He was holding a copy of *El Sol* that he'd gotten from somewhere. The kiosk, maybe, or a trash can. His sister's picture, and Otello's, on the front page. Bush's face was full of mute yet dreadful questions, and Faustino's heart stumbled.

"Wha's this mean, Maestro?"

"Nothing," Faustino said.

Bush stared at him. He held the paper up. "It's Bianca," he said. "How come they got pictures of her?"

Voices descended from above and behind them. Faustino grabbed the paper from the boy and took his arm. "Come with me, Bush. Come on."

Faustino half led, half dragged the boy to the ramp into the parking garage.

365

"It's Bianca," the boy repeated. "I don' unnerstan'."

Faustino unlocked the car and opened the passenger door. "Get in."

Bush gaped at him.

"Christ, Bush. Get in. I'm taking you home."

It was all being recorded by the CCTV cameras. Paul Faustino bundling a boy into his car. Leaning across him, apparently fumbling with the seat belt.

He parked on the street where the car could be seen from the yard through the doorway of the ruined house. The door of the shed scraped open as he and Bush approached it; he could not see Felicia's face but heard her murmur, "Bush?"

"Yeah," Faustino said quietly. "And me, Felicia. Paul. Let us in, please."

She had not lit a candle. It was intensely dark inside.

"Wha's happenin'? Bush, wha's up?"

"Bianca," the boy said, and then some other words that were muffled. The two kids might have embraced; Faustino couldn't tell.

"Listen," he said. "I'll be back in a couple of minutes, okay?"

He headed blindly for the back door of the bar, then thought better of it and went out onto the street. Voices, laughter, and elderly rock music spilled out of La Prensa's open door. There were ten or so customers inside, none of them the kind of person Faustino would have cared to get into an argument with. They looked him up and down as he entered, then went back to their drinks and conversations. Fidel stared at him, paused in the act of pouring rum into a couple of shot glasses. On a shelf behind the counter there was a TV set with the sound off. To Faustino's horror, it showed Bianca's face. As he watched, the camera pulled back to reveal that it was a photo in a magazine held by a reporter. Faustino glanced around the room. As far as he could tell, no one was paying any attention to the *Eight O'Clock News*.

Fidel said, "Evening, señor. You'll be wanting the restroom, huh? It's out the back."

"Right," Faustino said.

"Come, I'll show you. Nina? You wanna look after the bar a second?"

Out in the dark, they spoke in low voices.

"Jesus, Fidel."

"Yeah."

"You saw the papers?"

"A guy came in lunchtime with that *El Sol* rag. I damn near had a heart attack when I saw the front page. I can't get my head around this Otello thing."

"Don't bother trying. Look who's running the story."

"Yeah. But he had her picture on his computer, is that right?"

Faustino shrugged. "So they say. I dunno. But right

now I'm more concerned with Bush and Felicia. I brought him back just now. He's in shock, I guess. I tried to explain things to him, but I don't think he took it in."

"For some reason that don't surprise me."

"No. But what worries me most is that he'll get identified. Tracked down by *El Sol* or some other dog pack. I tried to tell him he needs to stay off the street. Lie low for a while. I don't know if he got the message. Look, Fidel, could you and Nina . . ."

Fidel had turned his head away. "That your car outside?"

"Uh . . . yes."

"Nice. I wouldn't leave it there too long, if I was you."

Faustino ground his cigarette out with his foot. He felt sorrowful rather than angry. "Okay, Fidel. Okay."

"Listen, man," Fidel said, relenting. "I appreciate your concern. You're trying to help. But you're out of your depth. You see all this as a *problem*."

"Well, isn't it, for Chrissake?"

"No. A problem is a thing that can be solved. A thing with a solution. There are no solutions for kids like Bush. For them, solutions are undreamed-of luxuries."

"I don't understand what that means."

"No. Of course you don't. Okay. I told you this before, but I'll tell you again. Nina and me, we gave shelter to three kids. Now we got two. One down, two to go. This was never a place of safety. Shelter, maybe, but not safety. Kids like these, they're *never* safe. That's not a *problem,* man; it's the goddamn *reality*. And there's no solution to reality."

Fidel detected a slight rise in volume from the bar and tipped his head toward it.

"Bianca was a face, you understand? Probably, by now, a lot of street kids will've seen her on the front of the papers, posters, whatever. Older people too. Some of them might know, or have some idea, where she lived. They'll know Felicia. They'll know Bush. And for an amount of money you'd no doubt consider pathetic, they'll say anything to anyone who asks. Now, what was it you wanted me and Nina to do?"

"Nothing," Faustino said. "I'm sorry."

"Forget it," Fidel said. "You're okay, Faustino. But I gotta go."

Faustino stood in the darkness for a lonely minute. Then he went over to the shed and tapped on the door.

"Felicia? It's me."

She let him in.

"I can't see anything," he said.

A match flared. It lit up the shed for a ghastly second and then became the tiny flame of a candle that reflected in the eyes of the children and, he presumed, his own.

"Bush, Felicia. Listen, do you trust me?"

After a slight hesitation that disappointed him, Felicia said, "Yes."

"Good. Okay, then. I want you to get in my car and come

with me. Now. Is there anything you need to bring with you?"

Felicia said, "Where you wanna take us to, Señor Paul?"

"Somewhere safe. Where no one will know where you are."

Their eyes guttered at him.

"We're going to my place," Faustino said disbelievingly.

5.4

THE CURTAINS OF the penthouse remain drawn. It is now almost a day and a half since Desmerelda and Otello have seen daylight. They do not watch television. They eat snacks from the refrigerator.

They have started to find it convenient not to be near each other. When Desmerelda takes or makes calls on her cell phone, she goes into another room. She seeks refuge in sleep a lot of the time, her hands cupped protectively over her baby. She showers frequently. Despite the coolness of the air-conditioning, she often feels hot and unclean. Once or twice she has had to suppress a mad desire to go out onto the balcony and display her swollen womb to the pitiless cameras.

Otello is beginning to feel that physical heaviness, the lethargy, that tends to overcome him when he doesn't train. His Achilles is still slightly swollen and sore. When he sits for any length of time, he rests it on a bag filled with ice cubes. Tresor has texted—*texted!*—him to say that because of the injury *and 4 other obvios resons* he will not be playing on Wednesday against Gimnasia. He has, in fact, played his last game for Rialto, although he does not know this yet. He is full of sullen rage because his wife does not believe what he says about the file hidden on his computer. Because there is no way she *can* believe him. The situation is insane; it's driving him crazy. It's like coming home and finding your living room occupied by a vast boulder or something. It doesn't make sense. And because it doesn't make sense, you can't do anything about it. He'd searched desperately for an explanation. Any explanation, other than the only one.

"Okay," he'd said, going into the bedroom this morning. Or last night or whenever it was. "That party we had here, what was it, three weeks ago? Remember? There were people here I hardly knew. One of them coulda done it. Like for a joke, maybe."

"Joke," she'd said flatly, then looked at him. "You think anybody hates you that much?"

He'd slumped against the door frame. Wanting so much to lie down with her.

"Dezi. It's got to be something like that. Got to be. I mean, who else? Michael? Diego?"

"Don't be ridiculous."

"So who, then?"

She'd shrugged. As if she'd lost interest. It had nearly killed him, that shrug. She'd done it several times since.

So he has given up pleading his case. He is alone with her, and with her he is alone. His marriage, he thinks, is in the early stages of eclipse; the shadow has already taken its first bite. He drinks Coke, topping it up with white rum, hoping to kill the worm eating him from the inside.

Diego calls frequently. He tells them, reluctantly, what the papers and TV are saying.

> OTELLO: What about Shakespeare?
> DIEGO: Well . . .
> OTELLO: What?
> DIEGO: Isabel is calling a strategy meeting tomorrow, apparently. I haven't been able to actually talk to her. Hey, I have to tell you this. Tell Dezi too. The sales of *Paff!* have gone through the roof. Like the man said, there's no such thing as bad publicity, eh, Capitano?

Indeed, there is not. "Bianca" outfits, fitted with tiny yellow commemorative ribbons, are really hot. It's a struggle to keep up with demand. Thus, fashion becomes an extra ingredient in the spicy stew of celebrity and politics and crime that feeds the sharks.

Faustino had shown Bush and Felicia around his apartment. It was ridiculous, the number of times he'd apologized for things.

"There's just the one spare bedroom. Is that okay with you guys? Or maybe you could sleep on the couch in the living room, Bush?"

"That's okay, Señor Paul," Felicia'd said, and he hadn't known what she'd meant.

They'd been so numb yet at the same time jittery, staring at the framed photos on the walls, the books, the stuff left lying around unhidden so anybody could steal it. He'd shown them the bathroom, the fridge, how to work the stove, the electric kettle, the remote for the TV, and they'd gazed at it all like it was life after death. He'd demonstrated the shower for them, getting the sleeve of his shirt soaked in the process.

Now he took chicken fajitas from the freezer and heated them in the microwave, showing them how to do it. But they watched his face, not what he was doing. They ate cautiously at first, then ravenously. It made him heartsick to watch them. He slid the food from his own plate onto theirs, got a beer from the fridge, and sat smoking and drinking until they had finished.

Later he said, "Look, tomorrow, I've got to go to work. I want you to stay right here, okay? I haven't got a spare key, so if you go out you won't be able to get back in again. Understand? So stay here. Use anything you want. Don't answer the phone. I'll try not to be back late."

Sometime in the night Faustino awoke from a familiar dream in which he entered a room empty of anything other than menace and, when he tried to leave, discovered that the door had shrunk to the size of a cat door. His mouth felt like it had been gagged with a tramp's sock.

He headed for the kitchen. The lamp he'd left burning in the passageway showed him that Bush had gone from the living-room couch. Alarmed, Faustino went to the spare bedroom. The door was wide open, and there was enough light for him to see that Bush was huddled on the bed with Felicia, his arms clasping her. The girl's eyes were open, but she didn't speak.

In the kitchen Faustino gazed at his reflection in the window. "What are you doing?" he asked it. "What in God's name do you think you're doing?"

5.5

IN AN IMMIGRATION interview room at the airport, it took Nemiso less than two minutes to get Juicy Montoya's name out of a sunburned and very frightened Marco Duarte.

The CCB computer coughed up a good deal of information about, and several unflattering photographs of, José Maria "Juicy" Montoya. He'd last appeared before the Third District Court eighteen months previously, when he'd been acquitted of extortion because the prosecution witnesses had failed to appear. The court record included his place of residence, which turned out to be three rooms in a building that might have been posh once but had forgotten when. The apartment showed all the signs of a sorry life and a hasty departure. At the bottom of an otherwise empty wardrobe there lay a soiled and crumpled shirt. Torres found a business card in its breast pocket.

"'J. M. Montoya,'" he read out. "'Swift Financial Reclamation Services. 9 Castana.'"

Nemiso put down the plaster model of Christ the Redeemer that had stood on top of the TV set. The words GENUINE SOUVENIR OF RIO were hand-painted on the base. "Where's that?"

"The Triangle."

"Ah," Nemiso said. "Call Navarro and tell her to meet us there. And to bring some uniformed men."

The doors were locked and the steel roller blind lowered when they got there. Two officers used a battering ram to open the place up. The top drawer of Montoya's desk had been pulled out and emptied. The newspaper in the waste bin was the previous day's edition of *El Correo*. An old-fashioned safe, olive green, stood against one wall. Nemiso tugged experimentally at its door, and it swung open to reveal a half-empty bottle of rum and two cans of beer. At the back of the bottom shelf, a single ten-dollar bill.

Torres said, "I'd say our guy made a spur-of-the-moment decision to go on vacation. Probably just after he saw this morning's papers."

"Yes," Nemiso said wearily. "Okay, you know what to do. Airports, train stations, bus stations. Find out if Montoya owns a car. Whether he does or not, check rental car places. Start with the budget ones."

He tried to inject some briskness, some urgency, into it; but he had the very strong feeling that he had been misdirected. That he'd been piloted into a tributary that would dwindle to nothing in the middle of nowhere.

Down at the marina, a group of freelance paparazzi decide that the cruiser they've rented isn't in prime position. One of them knows boats. He jump-starts the engine and backs away from the floating jetty. Others see what he's doing and with varying degrees of success try to do likewise. The resulting jockeying for position incurs damages that will total three million dollars.

Two streets from the subway at Independencia, there's an Italian-style café bar frequented, late afternoon, by commuters. It's a place where you can take the edge off the day before making the homeward trek to the suburbs. The kind of place where two well-dressed men drinking coffee at a corner table will not attract unwelcome attention.

"Otello and Desmerelda Brabanta were in entirely legitimate possession of CD images of the children modeling their clothes," Nemiso said. "Bilbao's office sent them two complimentary copies of the disk. Detective Navarro saw them almost as soon as she went into the study. My problem is that Otello had apparently installed an edited version of that disk onto his hard drive, and labeled it in a misleading way. Forty-four out of the fifty images in that file are of the murdered child Bianca Diaz. In most of them she's modeling bikinis."

"Right," Faustino said.

"And when our technical people went through Otello's laptop, they discovered that he'd apparently visited a number of porn sites."

Faustino dawdled his spoon in his coffee and said, "Child porn?"

"No."

"So, our national hero has feet of clay. He does the sad normal thing that millions of other men do. Disappointing, perhaps, but not, as far as I'm aware, illegal."

"How well do you know him, Paul?"

"I've interviewed him a few times. Met him and Desmerelda socially once or twice. More to the point, I've watched him play. Lots of times. There's an honesty in him. Maybe that will sound strange to you. Or possibly pretentious. But the idea that he could kill a child is absurd."

Nemiso said, "Ten years ago, I convicted a man who'd sexually abused, then murdered, several elderly women. He was one of the most charming and articulate men I've ever met. And very honest. It took me a long time to believe what I knew about him."

"You know as well as I do that Otello didn't kill Bianca Diaz," Faustino said.

Nemiso turned to watch an animated discussion at the bar. Without looking at Faustino, he said, "On the night she was murdered, Otello had played an away game against Esparta. He flew back later that night. CCTV cameras at the airport confirm that Michael Cass met him. Otello claims he booked that flight because his wife had been taken to the hospital and he wanted to visit her first thing in the morning. Cass dropped him off at the marina apartment just before midnight. Bianca was probably killed sometime between ten o'clock and four the following morning. Otello has no alibi for much of that time. The security cameras at the marina are wiped every three weeks, so we cannot establish that Otello didn't go out."

Faustino signaled for two more coffees. "Okay," he said. "There was opportunity. What about motive?"

"Yes, well," Nemiso said. "My cynical sergeant, Torres, suggests blackmail. That Bianca knew Otello, had had relations with him."

"You believe that?"

"No. Nor does Torres, really. But he's a Metropoli supporter."

The coffees came.

"It's not just ridiculous, Hilario. It's a setup."

"Who would want to damage such a man?"

"Loads of people. Nutcases. Envious people. People who want to bring down heroes. But maybe it's not about him at all. Maybe it's about a different kind of captain altogether."

Nemiso lowered his cup silently onto its saucer and leaned back in his seat.

Faustino dropped sugar lumps into his espresso. While watching his fingers do it, he said, "I hope you'll forgive me, Hilario, but I've done a bit of research on you. And I've talked to Nola. It seems to me that there are certain people, certain politicians in particular, who'd be more than happy to see you embarrassing yourself. To see you getting involved in a scandal and coming out covered in stink rather than glory."

He looked up into Nemiso's disconcerting gaze. "But then I am, as anyone will tell you, a dyed-in-the-wool cynic."

Nemiso smiled, eventually. "Yes, I've heard that said about you. I've also heard that you have taken Bush and Felicia into, let's say, protective custody."

"Is that illegal?"

Nemiso shrugged. "Probably not. But is it wise?"

As soon as he'd opened the door and put the lights on, he smelled them. They were where he'd left them, on the bed in the spare room, their knees up against their chests, their feet in the folds of the rucked-up sheet.

He said, "You had anything to eat?"

"We're fine, Maestro."

Faustino nodded and sighed at the same time. He went through to the kitchen and checked the fridge, which was exactly as he had left it. He went back to them. "Are you hungry?"

Felicia looked up at him and said, "A bit. But we don' know what to do."

"Right," Faustino said, and went through to the living room and called his usual takeout place. Then, needing a pee, he went to the bathroom. There was a turd resting at the bottom of the toilet bowl. "Dear God," he murmured, and pushed the chrome button on the toilet. The face in the mirror said, *They can't stay here. You know that.*

After washing his hands thoroughly, he went back to the kitchen and poured two glasses of orange juice. He sat on the end of the bed while the kids drank greedily.

"Right, team, listen up," he said. "Here's what we're going to do. Felicia, you're going to come out with me. I've ordered some food for us all, and right next to where we pick it up, there's a store that sells clothes and stuff. We're going to do a little shopping, okay?"

She gazed at him silently.

"Then, when we get back, you guys are going to take a shower and put on some clean clothes. Then we'll eat. Maybe see if there's a half-decent movie on TV. How's that sound to you?"

He recognized and despised the jocular, no-nonsense tone of his own voice. It was exactly the tone his father had used when proposing some manly expedition to his disappointing son.

Bush said, "I'm not comin' too?"

"No. I think it's best you stay here."

The kids exchanged glances.

"Okay," Bush said. "You're in charge, Maestro."

5.6

OTELLO WAKES UP on the couch with a mouth that tastes of rats' bedding. His watch tells him that it's just before ten. It takes him a while to work out whether it's day or night. Day. He gets to his feet, wincing slightly at the fiery little twinge that runs up the back of his ankle, and limps to the small window at the far end of the L-shaped living room. He eases the curtain open a little, just enough for a one-eyed view over the young trees to the security fence. The daylight sticks a dagger into his hangover. The mob is still there, of course. Smaller than before, perhaps? Maybe not.

He treks to the master bedroom. There's a travel bag on the bed. Desmerelda is in the bathroom, taking toiletries from the cabinet and dropping them into a cosmetics case. She has to stand on tiptoe to reach the top shelf; her big belly rests on the basin. Otello finds this both slightly grotesque and very poignant. Her stretched calves are lovely.

"What are you doing?"

Without looking at him, and calmly, she says, "I've had enough. I thought this would be over by now." She straightens, one hand supporting the baby. "But there doesn't seem to be any end to it, does there? I'm sorry, d'you want to use the bathroom?"

She goes through to the bedroom. Otello empties his bladder and brushes his teeth. The buzz of the electric toothbrush vibrates to the top of his skull.

She is applying her makeup. Carefully and slowly, as if getting ready to face the cameras. He leans against the door frame, looking at her reflection.

"What are you doing?" (Didn't he just say that?)

She jiggles the mascara brush in its tube. "I'm going down to the villa."

"You can't."

She does the upper lashes of her left eye.

"Dezi."

"Yes, I can. I have to. I feel poisoned. I want to be outdoors. In daylight. In the garden." She says this one lash at a time.

"It'll be the same there—you know that. They'll be there as well."

"Farther away. A mile away. Outside the gates. They won't be able to get to me."

He presses his fingers into his forehead. There seem to be thousands of tiny knots beneath the skin.

"Dezi, the baby is due in eight weeks."

"Seven."

"Okay, seven. You told me you weren't supposed to fly."

"Michael's driving me down."

"*What?* Dezi, it's *nine hours* by car. You can't do that. And, and, what, you think Michael can just come and collect you, like it's a normal day? They're still all out there, you know."

"Michael's bringing the Hummer. He says if they don't get out of the way, he'll run them over."

She turns her attention to her right eye.

"Dezi, this is stupid. Crazy. I'm going to call Michael, tell him to forget it."

She lowers her hands and looks at him in the mirror. "No," she says. "You're not going to do that."

The expression on her face hasn't changed, but somehow everything else has. It's like the very air is full of cracks that he can see another picture through.

He sits on the edge of the bed, not looking at her.

"All right," he says after a while. She has moved on to lipstick. "I'll come with you."

She kisses her lips together, checks them, and laboriously, hefting the baby, turns to face him.

"No."

"What?"

"I'm going without you. That's the whole point. I need to be away from all this. And *this*"—she makes a loose gesture toward the world waiting outside—"is all about *you.* I've done nothing. I haven't hidden pictures of girls on my computer. I haven't been dragged off by the police to answer questions about the murder of a child. I'm *having* a child. I refuse, I absolutely refuse, to be a victim anymore. I've been humiliated for the first time in my life because of you. Made to look a fool because of you. *Imprisoned* for the first time in my life because of you. So what I need to do, what I'm going to do, is go to the one place where I feel, where I can . . . not be part of all this. Understand? I need time to get ready for Raúl. If you come with me, you'll bring all of this shit with you and I won't be able to do it."

He gapes at her. His mouth is actually slack. He looks like a baffled boy on the verge of rage or tears.

She says, "I need some space, Otello. And I need you to stay here, to protect me, to put an end to all this. Can you do that?"

"I dunno. I don't understand what's going on. I need you, Dezi. Don't leave me."

She says, "Do you love me?"

It's tears.

"Yes," he says. "You know I do."

"Then let me go. Just for a while."

He nods, eventually. "I didn't do anything," he says.

She stands and walks around the huge distance of the bed and holds her hands out to him. "Yes, you did. You made me happy. You got me pregnant. Come on. Get up."

He does, somehow, and she leads him out to the huge swathes of curtain that separate them from the world, and before he can stop her, she presses the switch that opens them. They draw apart and the gray day outside is instantly spangled with flashes of light from walkways and balconies and boat decks. She slides the glass doors open and steps out onto the balcony, pulling him after her. Voices call, yell, their names. Cameras flash like a restless constellation of stars. At the rail she stops and turns to face him.

"Kiss me," she says, reaching her right arm over his shoulder and pulling his face down to hers. "Come on, kiss me."

He does. It is awkward-looking because of Raúl being between them. He has to stoop over and down to her. Their lips, their mouths, meet. Howls and whoops rise from below. The daylight is obliterated by camera light. A million front pages are born at that instant. They will show Otello and Dezi's parting kiss. They will show Desmerelda looking normally fabulous and her husband wearing a creased white T-shirt and pale gray boxer shorts. They will show her perfectly manicured left hand giving the world the finger.

After she and Michael have gone, Otello sits for a while. His thoughts are like a child pursued down an alleyway, seeking escape but finding only walls, barriers. The conclusion he comes to in the end is that he is hungry, so he goes to the freezer and takes out a pizza and puts it into the microwave. The oven pings while he is sitting at the breakfast table, startling him. He cuts half the pizza into neat wedges and eats two of them. Then he goes to the fridge and takes out a bottle of white wine. After three glasses he loses interest in the pizza and idly picks bits from the top of it. Shrimp. Artichoke. He finishes the wine.

Later, he wakes up on their bed. His phone is going off. Then it stops. He stares at the ceiling for a while, then swings his legs off the bed and walks a little unsteadily into the dressing room. He pulls open a drawer and scoops up handfuls of her underwear and spills the silky garments over his face like water.

He calls her. Her phone is off.

When Michael Cass plowed through the storm of light and noise outside the security gates, he left a good deal of confusion in his wake. Despite the smoked glass of the vehicle's windows, it was possible to make out that there was only one passenger in the back, and that it was Desmerelda Brabanta. Or was it?

"Maybe it's a decoy, man."

"Nah."

"Could be."

"Otello was down on the floor between the seats. I bet ya."

The paparazzi army divides. Several cars and half a dozen motorcycles set off in pursuit of the huge and sinister vehicle.

Cass makes a dummy run north through the suburbs rather than east toward the coast. He drives steadily, mindful of Desmerelda's condition, and soon his pursuers are clustered close behind him. He chooses busy single-lane streets, minimizing the opportunities for the paparazzi to come alongside.

Otello pours another shot of rum into his Coke and calls Diego's home number, then his cell. He gets the answering service on both. He can't think of a message, so he hangs up.

Desmerelda pulls herself upright. "Michael?"

"Yeah," Cass says. "I know."

They're on Buendía now, still heading north. He has been changing lanes randomly and varying his speed, but he cannot prevent the hunt from drawing level from time to time. Now, again, he catches camera flash in the corner of his eye.

Desmerelda's voice is slightly high-pitched, but not panicky. "Can we go any faster?"

"I don't think that's gonna help. You might want to consider lying across the seats."

"I can't do that. I'm the wrong shape."

"Yeah, I s'pose you are. Bear with me, Dezi. I'm gonna pull off the road in a bit and see if I can reason with these guys."

He sees the place he has been looking for: a cheap and cheerful café popular with long-distance drivers, its front-age hung with a string of blue and red lightbulbs. There are a few cars and pickups out front, but Cass eases the Hummer down the wide, potholed track to where the big trucks park. The paparazzi follow, hanging back, uncertain. Cass drives at walking speed until he finds a space between two huge trailers and pulls into it and stops. He turns the engine off and reaches across to take something out of the glove compartment.

"This shouldn't take a minute," he says.

He gets out and locks the doors. The pursuers have halted in a ragged formation behind the row of trucks, their motors idling. Cass strolls toward them between the towering trailers. He holds the ice pick up behind his right forearm, out of sight. The nearest car is a green Honda with two men in it. He stoops as if to speak to the driver. Then he displays the ice pick briefly before driving it into the wall of the Honda's front tire. When he pulls it out, there is a very satisfactory hiss. The driver starts to open his door, yelling, "You son of—"

Cass steps back and slams the door shut with the sole of his foot. Then he stabs the rear tire and proceeds to the next car, a Ford. The fat man behind the wheel gets a good look at the ice pick, fumbles the car into reverse, and hurriedly backs off. He slams into a motorbike, toppling it. The motorbike driver starts to yell something about his leg and his camera but Cass can't quite make out what it is because the man is wearing one of those helmets that cover the whole head. Cass gives the front wheel of the Ford the ice pick treatment and straightens up.

The remaining car and the bikes are attempting to maneuver themselves away from him in the space between the lines of trucks. They're not doing very well because they are watching him rather than each other. Cass strolls closer to them and puts his left fist on his hip, holding his jacket open so that the gun in his shoulder holster is clearly visible. He stays where he is until they have sorted themselves out and sped away.

Ten minutes later Cass takes the next exit off Buendía, crosses the bridge over it, and returns onto the southbound lane. At the Carrer Circular he gets onto the East Coast Highway. The low sky has taken on a threatening purplish intensity, but far ahead of them the cloud ends in an almost perfectly straight line above a realm of golden light.

Cass grins happily. "Well, it looks like we're heading in the right direction."

Desmerelda doesn't answer. He glances over his shoulder and sees that she is asleep.

5.7

LATE IN THE afternoon, the concierge is having a sneaky beer with his brother-in-law, Sal, who is in maintenance, when the phone buzzes. The light on the switchboard tells him the call is from the penthouse.

"Hey," he says, pointing a finger upward. "It's him." He picks up the handset. "Señor."

He listens, frowning. "Which ones, señor? Okay, sure. Ten, maybe fifteen minutes?"

He hangs up. "Guess what? The man wants the newspapers. All of them."

Sal pulls his mouth down at the corners. "I wouldn't, if it was me."

"Nor me," the concierge says. "No way." He takes his car keys out of the desk drawer and holds them out. "You wanna go? He tips well, usually."

◆ ◆ ◆

The man's hair is dripping onto the collar of his overalls and the edges of the newspapers are wet, so Otello supposes it must be raining. He hands over a twenty-dollar bill and takes the bundle awkwardly because he forgot to put his rum and Coke down before answering the door.

When he has spread the papers out on the floor, scores of Otellos look up at him. He does not recognize them all. He backs away, refills his glass, takes a long swig from it to steady himself. Then he gets onto his hands and knees and crawls among the newspaper pages, examining them.

Here he is on a flight of steps, his hand raised as if to deflect something thrown at his head.

Here he is with Dezi. He has never seen this picture before. She looks somber. She's wearing dark glasses and a big hat. Dezi is elsewhere on the floor, too. Pregnant in most of the pictures. Dezi again. And again.

Here he is with his arms around Bianca Diaz and another young girl. What? No, it's not her. She's over there, and over there, and here. This is another girl. Years ago, an orphanage in Espirito, was it? Maybe.

Here he is laughing with someone . . . My God, it's Nestor Brabanta.

But in most of the pictures he looks insane. Wild, ferocious, eyes wide or tight shut, teeth exposed, howling, his clenched fists in front of his face. Primitive. Murderous. In close-up.

Otello is so mesmerized, so appalled, by these images that it takes him several seconds to understand that he is

393

looking at himself celebrating goals. For some reason he finds this funny, and giggles. His giggling swells into full-blown laughter, and soon his eyes and nasal passages are wet. Tears fall onto the newsprint, blurring it. When the fit passes, he wipes his face on the hem of his T-shirt and tips more rum into his glass, spilling a little when he hiccups.

He returns to the papers and tries to read.

What's the story? His eyes slide from page to page. Nothing joins up; nothing makes sense. It's just people saying stuff, making stuff up.

There *is* no story. Of course there isn't! He could have told them that! He told *her* that. But she wouldn't listen.

BIANCA A NATURAL, SAYS HER PHOTOGRAPHER

Bianca Diaz, the murdered teenager linked to Otello, could have gone on to be a supermodel, according to top fashion lensman David Bilbao.

"It's a tragedy," he said. "She was one of those faces that the camera loves. I was so shocked when

OTELLO HAS DAMAGED RIALTO'S REPUTATION, SAYS

Says who? The headline runs onto the next page. But he cannot find the next page. He swivels around on his knees, looking for it among the scattered and crumpled sheets of paper. He is distracted by the photograph of his wife in Michael's arms.

How far will they have gotten? He looks at his watch, but it's not there.

OTELLO MYSTERY BOOSTS SALES OF PAFF!

SHAKESPEARE TIGHT-LIPPED ON THE OTELLO AFFAIR

CHILD PORN A BILLION-DOLLAR BIZ

Picture of the Duke, da Venecia, in *La Nación*. What's he got to say, then?

> The Rialto chairman, Umberto da Venecia, yesterday yielded to mounting pressure and made his first public comment on the increasingly wild speculation surrounding the club's star player, Otello. On Monday the international striker was questioned by police investigating the murder of a teenage girl, triggering massive media interest.
>
> "I will not comment on the case itself," da Venecia said, "except to point out that Otello has not been charged with any crime, and therefore there is no question of his having been suspended from the team, despite such allegations in the press. Otello continues to have our full support."

Blah blah . . .

On the subject of their top goalscorer being dropped for their next game, da Venecia said, "Otello is injured. It is as simple as that. If he were fit, he would be playing."

Otello reads these words twice, squinting. They were slithery, coming and going in and out of focus. Some were clearer than others. *Murder. Crime. Suspended. Support.*

He gets upright on his knees. Yesterday, an hour ago, he couldn't have. Not without hurting, the hot wire burning up to his calf.

Yes! A drink. *Salud!*

He wants to tell her that it doesn't hurt anymore. That none of it does. That he's read it all, that it's nothing, that it's full of absolutely nothing. Some sort of joke. We took it too seriously.

That's it, exactly: *we took it all too seriously.*

It strikes him as a major insight. *We took it all too seriously.* So important. Terrible that he hadn't thought of it earlier. She wouldn't have gone.

He uses the arm of the sofa to lever himself to his feet. Where's the phone? He pictures her, answering. Him speaking the words that are as bright as neon. Her listening, then saying, "Michael, I was wrong. It's all okay. Turn the car around. Take me home."

At the third attempt he clicks on her number. Gets her lovely voice saying, "Hi. Sorry, but I can't take your call at the moment. Leave me a message."

5.8

NO ONE KNEW what Hernán Gallego did with his money. He'd been in politics for almost fifty years: nearly half a century with his claws in the public purse. Common sense insisted that he must have salted away millions, but he lived as quietly as a spider in a monastery outhouse. His colleagues amused themselves with rumors that he'd built a fabulous domain in the far South and populated it with fabulous prostitutes. Male prostitutes, possibly. (He'd never married.)

In fact, he never left the capital unless it was on government business, and then reluctantly. He lived where he worked. The new and expanded Ministry of Internal Security occupied a glittering crescent of glass-and-steel offices in a floodlit emptiness. Within this crescent, embraced by it, was a garden: an expanse of ruthlessly maintained lawns and geometric flower beds. And at the end of this garden, just within the security walls, was the old, original ministry: a three-story building with a classical Spanish facade disguising drab and functional offices. One quarter of the top floor was an apartment intended for officials to overnight in at times of crisis.

Gallego had occupied these rooms for eleven years and had never troubled to refurbish them. He had, however, installed in one of the smaller rooms a big plasma-screen digital television with surround sound, and a pair of huge leather armchairs that resembled crouching pachyderms.

On this evening of premature darkness he occupies one of these chairs and Nestor Brabanta the other. Brabanta is drinking the cognac that he has had the foresight to bring with him. Gallego is, as usual, drinking Pepsi. He has a four-pack, uncooled, close to his feet. They are watching the extended early news.

"Ha!" Gallego exclaims. And again, like a darting crow: "Ha!"

The screen shows the press conference that Hilario Nemiso has been pressured into giving. It is an unruly affair, and the NTV cameraman is having to shift position to get an unobstructed view of the proceedings. Nemiso himself sits at the center of a table along which microphones are ranged. To his left, three other police officers: a stout young dark-haired woman named Navarro and two men from the CCB's legal department. To his right, but at some distance, sits a severely handsome woman who gazes out at the melee with barely disguised disdain. Camera flash flickers like sheet lightning over all five faces.

"Who's she?" Gallego says.

"Consuela Perlman. My daughter's lawyer. And mine, now and again."

Gallego gleams at his friend. "Excellent. Can't do any harm to have an uppity Jew getting in on the act, eh?"

On screen, Nemiso manages to impose something like silence on his impatient congregation.

"I repeat, I shall take a limited number of questions *after* I have read a statement."

"By God," Gallego croaks happily, "that poker-faced prig is really rattled, isn't he?"

Nemiso reads from a typescript. He is noisily interrupted several times, and when this happens he stares unspeaking and expressionless into the middle distance until he can once again make himself heard.

"I have called this press conference in order to correct inaccurate, irresponsible, and misleading reports in the press and other media relating to the investigation into the murder of Bianca Diaz. I hope — indeed, I expect — that this statement will forestall the appearance of further stories of this kind. They are extremely unhelpful to us, the police. They are also deeply injurious to the reputation of Otello." Here he glances at Perlman.

"Pompous fool," Gallego mutters over the sounds of protest, and some jeering, that come from the TV set.

It takes Nemiso fifteen minutes to get through a speech that should have taken him five.

"To conclude, and to ensure that there is no misunderstanding: Otello was not arrested. He was not taken into custody. He is not, and never was, a suspect in this case."

"Shit will stick, though, eh, Nestor?"

"Otello has cooperated fully and willingly with the Special Investigations Unit. In fact, he and Señora Brabanta provided us with information that has proved very useful, and we are grateful to them. Our search for the killer of Bianca Diaz continues."

Babble erupts. Nemiso points into the mob, leaning forward and cupping his ear. He has to ask for the question to be repeated. Brabanta and Gallego manage to hear only part of it.

". . . take Otello's computer away for examination?"

"It is perfectly normal police procedure in cases like these," Nemiso says, and turns his eyes away from the questioner. But there is uproar among which only isolated words and phrases can be made out.

". . . three days?"

". . . you mean, cases like these?"

"Captain, Captain . . ."

". . . child pornography . . ."

Nemiso sits out the hubbub. He is clearly struggling to mask his anger and contempt. He looks like a furious Buddha.

"I thought . . . I am deeply disappointed that individuals in this room are raising the subject of child pornography. I thought I had made it perfectly clear that child pornography has nothing whatsoever to do with this case."

Interruptions.

"I repeat: the pictures of Bianca Diaz on Otello's computer were entirely, ah, legitimate. They were not, any of them, in any way, pornographic. Otello and Desmerelda . . ."

Gallego says, "Do you know, I don't think I've ever enjoyed anything this much. Isn't it excellent? Because it doesn't matter what Nemiso says. It doesn't matter how many libel writs your Jewish woman throws around. Our gloriously scabby press is not going to let Otello off the hook. And Nemiso has made such a mess-up of the whole thing that I'll have every reason to transfer him to San Juan or some other godforsaken hole up North to take charge of the traffic department."

He takes a celebratory swig of Pepsi. "You know the only thing that riles me, Nestor?"

From the depths of his chair, Brabanta makes a sound — something like *"Gnuh"* — that encourages Gallego to continue.

"It's that *we* didn't organize this. I said, didn't I, before the election, that this is exactly the kind of thing we should do. Stitch the black so-and-so up, neuter him. Silence him. You remember that, Nestor? Eh?"

Brabanta does not reply. A few moments earlier he'd experienced a wave of tiredness so extreme that he'd had difficulty swallowing the cognac in his mouth. The television had lurched out of focus. He couldn't see anything clearly that was farther away than his shoes. He'd forced himself to sit more upright, but as he'd done so, he'd felt as though something was trickling down the front of his face. He could not imagine what it was. It was like blood trickling from his scalp. He'd tried to wipe it away, but his arm and hand refused to move. Then a darkness moved over his brain like the curtain at the end of a play. He could almost hear the swish of it, feel the stroke of its hem.

When he wakes up, Hernán is peering at him around the side of his chair, repeating the word *Nestor*.

Brabanta says, "It's all right. I'm just a bit drunk," but it's as if he is mumbling into a pillow on a bed that is a great distance away.

Gallego does not hear him. "Nestor? For God's sake, man. What's wrong with you? *Nestor!*"

Brabanta gazes up at him with a comical, lopsided leer on his face. His left eye winks. "Shnight. Shnunk. Wassarm?"

"Hell's teeth, Nestor," Gallego says. Then he sees the way Brabanta's right hand is cupped inward, connects that with the foolish droop on one side of the face and the mute pleading of the one good eye.

"Jesus," Gallego murmurs, and goes to the intercom. He hits the red button that will summon his men, two of whom are paramedics.

5.9

OTELLO IS TEMPORARILY baffled when Desmerelda doesn't answer her phone, but then he gets another idea. Another good one: *stop hiding*. God, if only he could think this well all the time. If only he weren't so . . . distracted. By stuff. *Stuff*. He drinks a toast to this insight.

He plays soccer — that's what he does. So he heads off down to what Dezi likes to call the Trophy Room Ha Ha. No, not *Ha Ha*, he tells her now. Should've told her before. Not many men have stuff like this, Desmerelda. Medals, all of that. *Respect*. Tokens of it, anyway.

It's the smallest of the guest bedrooms, but not much smaller than the yard of the house he grew up in. No bed in it now. A black leather swivel chair and a TV he watches recordings of games on. The shelves display trophies, some of them very ugly; also medals in Perspex cases; a pair of cleats once worn by Diego Maradona; signed photographs — Kaká, Beckham, El Gato, Henry. On the walls, more medals hanging from long gaudy ribbons, more photographs, pennants. Beside the door, hanging from a hook, a big net bag of soccer balls: souvenirs of internationals, cup victories, hat-tricks.

He takes the bag down, opens it. The balls tumble across the floor. Some are soft, disheartened-looking, but several are still match standard, more or less. With difficulty, he gathers these and puts them back in the bag, slings it over his shoulder, then remembers.

Can't run out looking like this, man.

He puts the bag down again, goes to the chest below the window and drags open the top drawer. Shirts, dozens of them, swapped for his own with other stars, other captains. He pulls them out one at a time. Red and white, River Plata. Blue, Italy. Yellow and green, Brazil. Some are signed. Here's a white England shirt signed by Jenny. No, Terry. Red and black, Flamengo. Is he looking for one in particular? He can't remember.

But no, of course! What was he thinking? He abandons the scattered shirts, picks up the bag of balls, dribbles a slightly flabby one out of the door and along the passage. He plays a more or less successful one-two against the wall, and aims a shot between the legs of the table in the hall. He gives it a little too much lift and it smashes the Tiffany glass lamp. Whoops. Like dead butterflies on the carpet. Sweep them up later. Watch your feet.

In the dressing room he struggles into a pair of sneakers

and out of the grubby T-shirt. He rifles through the closet until he finds his own unique *Paff!* shirt. Its color is an acidic yellow so bright that it is almost fluorescent. On the back his face smiles through the number 23 in black and lilac. He has forgotten what the English word on the front means. He puts the shirt on and admires himself in the mirror. There are one and a half Otellos: a ghostly twin stands behind him. He closes an eye and it disappears. Good. He lifts his left foot, pulling the toes up to test the Achilles tendon. He loses balance and staggers sideways into the closet, but this does not bother him because there is no pain in the ankle. No pain anywhere, now. Excellent.

On his way out, he spots the drink he'd lost track of earlier and pauses to drain the glass. He shudders as it goes down, then holds himself erect and inhales deeply, preparing himself. Focus. Eliminate everything else. Weakness. Doubt. Fear.

When the elevator indicator chimes, the concierge looks up. When the doors hiss apart and Otello himself emerges, he is so surprised that his mouth drops open to display the wad of gum stuck to his lower front teeth.

"Theñor?"

"Hi. How ya doin'?"

"Uh, good. You going out, Señor Otello?"

"Got to. Can't sit aroun' up there. Geddin' stale. Outta condition. Need to put some trainin' in."

Cautiously the concierge says, "It's raining out."

"S'all right. Good. Good for strikers, rain." He winks. "Puss a lil' wiss. Puts a lil' whip and hiss on the ball, you know? Keepers, no. Keepers hate rain."

He smiles.

"Yeah," the concierge says. "I guess they do."

The glass doors slide open for him, and Otello goes out. He is surprised, momentarily disconcerted, to discover that it is dark. Never mind. He doesn't mind floodlights. Likes them, actually; they shrink the world to the size of the field. Besides — and this thought pleases him — he has the right kind of shirt on for dark work. He goes down the steps and weaves along the illuminated walkway and through the line of low trees. The rain cools and cleanses him. There are several cars sweating jewels in the brightly lit parking area, but plenty of free space for him to work in. He does a few high lifts on the spot, the balls bouncing against his back.

He feels good; he castigates himself for not thinking of this sooner. Why had he sat up there, brooding, rotting, for so long? Letting all that *stuff* get to him, suffocate him? Then the happy thought strikes him that the steel mesh of the fence over there is like a goal net, and the uprights are more or less the right distance apart. Ideal. So, a bit of loosening up, then shooting practice.

The ranks of paparazzi have thinned. Several have been summoned to Nemiso's press conference. Others have simply given up, convinced that Otello was in the tank that drove out in the morning with that psycho Cass behind the wheel. The returning bike boys had been full of it.

"What a piece of work that Cass is! He wouldn't have pulled a stunt like that if Otello hadn't been in the car with La Brabanta. Because he's Otello's guy, right?"

"No, nah. He's *her* guy. Been having a thing with her for ages, man. Wouldn't be surprised if the baby . . ."

"Ah, c'mon. You believe that, you believe anything."

"Yeah? I have reliable sources, my friend."

"Sure you do. They'd be the same reliable sources told you the Diaz chick had an address book full of big names, right?"

And back and forth, keeping their spirits up while the rain came down.

Now the silent freelancer who's been keeping his camera dry inside the comical green parka gets it out and aims it through the fence, and if he weren't such a dork, he'd keep quiet. But he doesn't, and his excited little exclamation alerts the others. They turn as one, triggered like a shoal of fish.

"Who's that?"

"What?"

"Over there. See? Who's that?"

Eyes go to viewfinders; wet hands twist lenses.

"It's him. It's him!"

"It is. Christ, it is."

"What the hell's he doing?"

Motor drives whir.

"He's training, man. Look at him."

"What's this mean? Something's happened we don't know about."

Cell phones come out.

He does a number of slow runs—five, maybe, he loses count—combined with upper-body twists. His balance isn't good, after all that time banged up in the penthouse. That's why he stumbles; that's why the world tilts.

Then he lines up six of the balls about a yard apart, taking a long time to get them straight, and runs zigzag step-overs along the line. It is absolutely astonishing that he falls over, finds himself on his back on the tarmac with bright lines of rain arrowing into his face. He laughs at himself.

"You know what? I think he's smashed."

"Yeah, look at that. He's out of it."

The word has spread. Guys from other parts of the marina stakeout congregate behind the fence. The security men murmur into walkie-talkies. The one with the slobbery dog loops its leash twice around his fist and starts to walk back and forth, looking over his shoulder to where the bright yellow figure struggles to his feet.

He picks up another ball and studies it. In the wet glare he cannot make out the name scrawled on it. Ronaldo maybe, or Robinho. He bounces it, catches it on his instep, then takes it on a weaving run between the other balls. He gets to the fourth one before his control goes. His ball cannons into it, knocking the others out of line, and suddenly he can't tell which is which. They're rolling everywhere. He collects one with the underside of his shoe and for no reason drives it away into the rain-streaked darkness. The crowd roars.

"Otello! Otello! Over here! This way, man!"

His supporters are gathered behind the away goal beyond a barricade of twinkling stars. So yes, he will give them what they want. He shepherds the balls — each with its own ghost now, so it's difficult — in that direction. Then, without the least indication that it's what he'd planned, he takes the real ball, the one that matters, on a diagonal run toward the penalty area.

And you're being closed down. No support to your left, your overlapping right back is covered, so go for it. Don't signal the shot. Fake the pass out wide, shoulder the body-check aside, get into space. But the ball is too close to your feet and the fullback is coming across to block. You can't get the shot in. So you do that amazing thing you do: stop the ball dead, dummy a right turn, switch your weight to the left, turn all the way. The fullback slides past you with his left leg bent under him, his arm out, his mouth open, his hand reaching to clutch at your beautiful shirt. The keeper is already committed to a dive toward the near post. He knows what you have done but is powerless to do anything about it. His body turns but his legs

409

can't. You've swiveled and the goal is there in front of you as big as the world. Someone hammers into your back and you go down, but it's too late. You've already hit the ball and you know from the feel of it, the lovely fat square level heft of it on the front of your foot, that it's on its way home and you can rejoice, run past the goal toward all those people that you love and who love you, and fall on your knees in all humility and let them chorus your name:

Otello Otello Otello.

"This way, Otello!"

"Where's Dezi, Otello?"

". . . young girls, Otello?"

". . . kill her, Otello?"

". . . Bianca?"

What are they saying?

Electrical lightning and pouring rain.

". . . comment, Otello?"

". . . porno?"

"Porn, Otello?"

His fingers cling to the steel mesh. He is so tired suddenly. They are not fans, after all. Not people. He has made a terrible mistake. They have long eyes on white stalks, like insects. Predators. He must get up. But he is so tired. His legs have stopped working.

They take brilliant pictures, these lucky few. The fallen Otello, clutching the wires of his cage. Drunken, wild. His face gaping at the rain. Or, if you prefer, howling tears.

His sleek head lowered like a penitent. His saturated and ridiculous shirt clinging to his chest, with the cartoon map of Africa and the foreign word FAITH on it. Some of the greatest sports photos of all time. Works of art. Iconic. Worth millions, globally.

5.10

S IX MONTHS LATER, Paul Faustino was having lunch with a possible girlfriend at the Salamanca, where the food was almost as daring as its prices. She was speaking enthusiastically about hypnotism. In particular, she was being enthusiastic about the success of hypnotherapy in curing nicotine addiction. Faustino's attention had wandered, and so had his gaze.

"Paul? Paul, am I being tiresome?"

"No, not at all. I'm sorry. I was distracted by a couple of people over there. No, please don't look."

It was a strong point in her favor that she didn't.

He said, "Forgive me. I forgot that I was off duty." He lit a cigarette. "What were you saying?"

For the next forty minutes he tried very hard to divide his attention fairly between his companion and the table where Diego Mendosa was lunching with a burly American with hair like rippled zinc. Faustino knew who the American was. Knew that he was a close friend of the governor of California, that he was unnecessarily wealthy, and that he owned a soccer team called the San Francisco Goldbugs. But Faustino was less interested in him than in Diego Mendosa. The man had recently endured almost unimaginable embarrassment. His most famous client had been ruined. He was the intimate friend of a man whose reputation lay wrecked and dismembered like the statue of an overthrown tyrant. He was party to a calamity. But look at the shine on him, the smile!

Faustino lingered over coffee until he was sure that Mendosa and the Yank had left. He paid the bill without the slightest flicker of incredulity, then gallantly helped his date into a cab, deferring promises.

He walked the fifteen-minute distance back to *La Nación*. He hated agents, on principle. Bloated leeches swarming on the body of the game. He could remember a time when they didn't exist, when clubs had scouts who discovered great young players and . . .

He stopped himself. Scoffed at himself for harking back to a golden age that had never existed. When innocent genius boys were found in slums or in the outback. Nonsense. Soccer was a business like any other. Find a resource, use it, exploit it, charge the maximum you can get for it. It's just business; yesterday's trash and tomorrow is the next day's trading. Assuming a very modest ten percent agent's fee—it was almost certainly more than that—Diego Mendosa would've made five million out of Otello's transfer to Rialto. And another couple of million—U.S. dollars—out of his sale to San Francisco. Plus his percentage on whatever it'd cost Rialto to break Otello's five-year contract. So no wonder the man had looked pleased with himself. Something like nine, ten million for two years' work? Not bad at all. Still, like it or not, one had to admit that Mendosa was good at what he did. And a great deal more civilized than most of his kind. For him, at least, some benefit—some considerable benefit, in fact—had come from the death of poor little Bianca Diaz.

A dark thought unfurled in the baser part of Faustino's mind and brought him to a halt. *Mendosa?* Could he have . . . ? No. Absurd. Illogical. He shook his head like a man pestered by a fly and scuttled quickly through the gloomy pedestrian tunnel under San Cristóbal. Even in daylight the place gave him the jitters.

Diego tosses his jacket and tie onto the sofa on his way to the drinks cabinet. He pours a generous malt whiskey and proposes a little toast to himself. Then he carries his glass through to the main bedroom, making a soft *tcha-tcha-tcha* sound by clacking his tongue against the roof of his mouth.

"Well, my love, I would say that was a *most* satisfactory piece of business. Yes, indeed. Dreadful people one has to have dealings with, of course. Still, beggars can't be choosers." He laughs quietly and takes another sip. "And, I must say, a perfectly acceptable lunch."

414

He turns to Emilia. "Speaking of which, I suspect you might be hungry. Yes? Good. Excellent! I was a little worried that you might be off your food."

He sets his drink down on the bedside table and goes to the big glass tank that takes up most of the room's shorter wall. Set in its base there are three shallow drawers. From the first he takes a pair of long stainless steel tweezers. Then he opens the second drawer, lifts its ventilated plastic lid, and uses the tweezers to seize a locust. The insect is about two inches long. Diego is quick; he has the creature pincered before it can unsheathe its wings. He closes the drawer, lifts the lid of the glass tank, and drops the locust onto a broad leaf, where it crouches. Emilia hardly moves. She merely lowers her body very slightly, adjusting her grip on the branch. Her eyes swivel and blink in opposite directions. They always thrill Diego, her eyes. They are, he thinks, black pearls set in cones of golden beads.

But now, perhaps in response to the presence of the locust in her tank, she changes color almost imperceptibly. The beautiful turquoise green of her throat takes on a yellowish blush. She moves forward along the branch with exquisite delicacy, her divided feet hesitating before they grasp. The long tail hangs far below her, a tight dappled coil. Diego wills her on, hardly daring to breathe. She's such a big girl now: as long as his forearm. Her eyes are facing forward, locked on to her prey. The locust is a full yard away.

For an infinity of seconds she does nothing. Diego is in an agony of impatience. Then she unhinges her mouth.

It is almost the full length of her triangular head. The fat bulbous tip of her tongue appears between her lips. It is reddish purple and glistens stickily. Diego's own tongue emerges a little way; he cannot help himself. Emilia pauses, agape, teasing him, making him wait. Then she strikes. And, as always, Diego fails to stifle a cry, a small moan of shock, of pleasure. Emilia's improbable tongue hurtles out of her, a wet fleshy rope. Its gluey bulb envelops the locust. In the time it takes to blink, the insect is reeled into her mouth. A wing and a limb protrude from her jaws. She shrinks her eyes, crunches, gulps, crunches again. The wing and the limb are gone. The scaly wattles of her gullet pulse.

Diego straightens and sighs. *"Bon appétit,* darling," he murmurs.

He picks up his whiskey and goes out onto the balcony. As is usual on these occasions, he feels vaguely sad. It is the enviable simplicity of her needs, her appetites. An opportunity seized; a hunger appeased. None of this never-ending desire for more and more and more. He has done great and monstrous things. Yet there is the city below him still: unshaken, vertical, dumb. The dust has settled. The shock waves have dwindled into ripples. The prospect of having to begin all over again almost overwhelms him.

He drains the glass, puts fire into his belly. Checks his watch and goes inside. His call is answered on the fourth ring.

DIEGO: Luis? Hi. This is Diego Mendosa. Is this a good time to talk? Are you alone?

MONTANO: Uh, yeah, it's fine.

DIEGO: Good. Did you have a chance to consider my proposal?

MONTANO: Yeah. It seems sound. The thing is, like I said, it'll be difficult to get out of my present contract, you know? Things could get nasty.

DIEGO: That's not your problem. I handle all that. I can be pretty nasty myself, to be honest. When it's in my client's interests, of course.

MONTANO: So I hear.

[DIEGO *lets that pass.*]

MONTANO: So, how confident are you that you can get me back to Rialto?

DIEGO: Extremely confident. And I wouldn't say that if I didn't have good reason to.

[*A short pause.*]

MONTANO: Okay. But all hell will break loose up here if we do it.

[DIEGO *notes the use of "we."*]

DIEGO: Don't worry about that. I'm quite good at managing hell. I've been through it recently.

MONTANO: Yeah. Without getting burned, by all accounts.

DIEGO: Absolutely. Couldn't do this job unless I was fireproof. So . . .

MONTANO: So, okay. Let's go for it.

DIEGO: You accept?

MONTANO: Yeah. I do.

DIEGO: Excellent! It'll be an honor to represent you, Luis. We'll do great things together, I promise you.

Faustino sat at his cluttered desk and used scissors to cut a two-page article out of the previous day's edition of *La Nación*. The scissors were heavy and old-fashioned; he'd had them a long time. The article was one of his own.

A GIANT TOPPLED BY MIDGETS

On the eve of Otello's ignominious departure for the U.S., **Paul Faustino** *reflects on a modern tragedy*

He skimmed it again. In the three days it had taken him to write it, he had revised and reworked the piece several times, mostly toning it down. Yet it was still bitter, angry, accusatory. It lacked balance and gravity. It was almost unprofessionally sincere. Almost, God help us, *youthful*. Now, dulled by his rich lunch, he found himself wondering if all — or any — of this passion was genuine. And even if it was, was it . . . *appropriate*? Heroes come and go; sand castles are swept away by the tide: you might as well hurl your childish rage at the deep indifference of the sea. The only grown-up emotion is disappointment.

He folded the article and slid it into a clear plastic wallet. At the doorway into his library he paused and surveyed the windowless storeroom stuffed with files, scrapbooks, photo albums, yearbooks, and whatever else his life consisted of. Library. Archive. Museum. Mausoleum. Catacomb.

He opened a big box file labeled OTELLO and dropped the wallet in.

Epilogue

O N A CLEAR DAY, the deck of the Café Catalina in San
Francisco, California, provides an almost uninter-
rupted view of the Golden Gate Bridge. This afternoon,
however, a copper-colored haze has settled on the bay. In
it, the bridge looks insubstantial, the shadow of a fallen
sword or crucifix. As is usual in the lull between lunch and
cocktail hour, the Catalina is quiet. There is only one cus-
tomer in Renata Parry's section — a handsome, athletic-
looking black man who'd come for lunch with another
guy but had stayed on, alone. They'd both had the Chef's
Seafood Platter and shared two bottles of the very good
Chablis, although the black guy had seen off most of the
second one. After she'd cleared their places and gone to
fetch their coffee, the lighter-skinned man had produced
a nifty little voice recorder from his bag and set it on the
table. So it had been an interview situation, and Renata had

supposed therefore that the good-looking dude had to be Someone. They'd talked in Spanish—a language that Renata has inherited from her Mexican mother—but with an accent she hadn't recognized. Their conversation had lasted an hour, maybe more.

Renata had been on her way over to their table to see if they'd needed anything else, when they'd both gotten to their feet. They'd shaken hands, but then the black guy'd wrapped his arms around the other one in a big hungry hug, which the other guy had looked kind of awkward with.

When the journalist or whatever he was had gone, Handsome had ordered a rum and Coke. He'd gone through a few more since then. Too many, maybe. She'd watched him out of the corner of her eye while she'd busied about, setting up her tables for dinner, putting out the evening menus. Most of the time he'd just sat expressionless, watching the bridge fade. But now and again she'd seen him shake his head slightly and move his lips as though having a murmured conversation with an invisible companion.

Now he catches her looking at him, so she smiles and goes over.

"How're we doing, señor? Can I get you something else? Coffee, maybe?"

She speaks in Spanish, thinking he might be surprised. Pleased, even. But it's like he doesn't notice, or maybe just takes it for granted. For what must be the third time that afternoon he squints at the name badge on her tunic.

"Yeah, um, Renata. I'll have another one of these."

Tapping the nail of his forefinger on the glass, which isn't empty.

She hesitates very briefly, but he doesn't notice that either.

Kim, the barman, puts the drink on her tray. "Same guy?"

"Yeah."

Kim grimaces. "Watch him," he says.

Renata sets the glass down on Handsome's table and picks up the now empty one. "Shame about the weather," she says. "You get a great view from here on good days. You been in the city long?"

"Yeah. Quite a while now."

Then he looks up at her and smiles. It's a beautiful smile, Renata thinks.

"You don't know who I am, do you?"

"I'm sorry, señor," she says sincerely. "I'm afraid I don't."

He nods, and smiles again. He picks up his drink.

"Nor do I. *Salud.*"

The garden of NESTOR BRABANTA'S *house.* BRABANTA *is parked in the shade of a large umbrella.* DESMERELDA *sits in a deck chair watching* RAÚL, *who is clumsily but intently taking toys out of a brightly colored plastic tub and putting them back again. Her phone rings. She checks the caller ID and answers.*

DESMERELDA: Paul, hi. You're back?

FAUSTINO: Yes. I got in about an hour ago. I'm at home. I just picked up your messages.

DESMERELDA: How was he?

FAUSTINO: Well, okay, I guess.

DESMERELDA: Meaning what?

FAUSTINO: Meaning, he looks fine. I would say he has definitely not been bingeing on burgers slumped in front of the TV, snorting coke, any of that stuff. He looks and sounds pretty much like his old self, most of the time.

DESMERELDA: Drinking?

FAUSTINO: Oh, I dunno. Some, maybe. He's got a lot to deal with.

DESMERELDA: Yeah, tell me about it.

FAUSTINO: Sorry. But, for example, he knew, of course, that to the Yanks soccer is . . . well, that they don't quite get it. A world religion they don't belong to. But it still surprises him. He's the most expensive player San Francisco Goldbugs have ever bought, but he can still walk down the street and almost no one knows who he is.

DESMERELDA: That sounds kinda nice to me.

FAUSTINO: Yeah, I suppose it would. So, uh, are you still at the villa?

DESMERELDA: No, we came back last night. I'm at my father's house.

FAUSTINO: Ah.

DESMERELDA: Raúl likes it here. [*She sounds slightly defensive,* FAUSTINO *thinks.*] I'm selling the penthouse — did you know that?

FAUSTINO: Um, yeah. Otello said something about it. So, er, how were my kids?

DESMERELDA: "My kids." It cracks me up when you call them that.

FAUSTINO: I use the phrase merely to indicate my sense of responsibility for them.

DESMERELDA: Sure you do.

FAUSTINO: So, are they behaving themselves?

DESMERELDA: Paul, I keep telling you. They're great. I'm happy, knowing they're there. Give up on the idea that I'm doing you a favor, okay? You did me one. Bush is *crazily* conscientious. He knows how to look after the pool now. He does the gardens. The cars are *spotless*. Like, he never stops. And Felicia, well, she's a really lovely girl, isn't she?

FAUSTINO: Yeah, I think she is.

DESMERELDA: She's *fantastic* with Raúl, when we're down there. He loves her. He calls her Fisher. Hey, listen, he just heard me say her name. He's looking around for her. Isn't that *sweet*?

FAUSTINO: Yeah. My eyes are brimming with tears. [DESMERELDA *laughs.*]

Raúl makes one of those sudden and incomprehensible decisions that small children make. The bright squeaky toys are no longer interesting; the shape in the shade of the umbrella is. He gets up onto his feet, finds his balance. The fat plastic diaper makes him walk astraddle, like a duck. He reaches his grandfather's wheelchair and puts his plump brown hand on Brabanta's frozen claw. Brabanta turns his asymmetrical face toward the child and weeps.

"It is entirely normal," the stroke specialist had told Desmerelda, "for victims to respond to all kinds of emotional stimuli by crying. What we might call the brain's emotion circuits will have been damaged. Confused. Tears do not necessarily indicate unhappiness. They might equally be a sign of pleasure, say, or gratitude."

Felicia has long since lost her fear of the big white machines in the villa's utility room. The washing machine delights her now; she likes the way it pauses in its slosh and tumble, ticking, as though making up its mind what to do next. Sometimes she opens the door of the tall freezer just to feel its cold and misty breath on her face and throat. And sometimes she goes to stand on the terrace beyond the pool and closes her eyes. She counts to ten, as slowly as she can bear it, and when she opens her eyes again it is all still there, still real. Not a trick.

Her feelings about La Señora remain complicated. Raúl's mother, the Desmerelda Brabanta who now employs her, isn't the Desmerelda Brabanta that Bianca enviously worshiped. She's not the pretend whore-goddess whose pictures hung over Bianca's head like a dream. She has, now, the gentleness that sad people have. But, all the same, it *is* her. Felicia finds herself thinking this, watching La Señora play with the child, watching her chatting to Bush. It *is* her. It is *her*. She is to blame. And she has saved us.

Erroll, the gardener, has taken to the boy, which he thought he would not do. The city kid with the crazy hair who knew the names of nothing, who'd never held a pruning knife, never even used a goddamn hose, in his life. But Bush — he has the name for the job, at least — is solemn and watchful and careful, which Erroll likes, being that way himself. And the boy does the heavy work, which Erroll is starting to feel a bit too old for.

Erroll is also teaching the boy to read, which is a slow and faltering process because the truth is that the gardener is only semiliterate himself. They use the book Bush has gotten from God knows where. Stole it, maybe, sometime in his previous life. Sure couldn't have bought it, seeing as it cost more than a week's wages. *The Wonders Under the Sea*. Together they clamber across the long words that jag like reefs through the text.

When Desmerelda is there and Felicia is busy with Raúl, Bush keeps Michael Cass company on his patrols. Cass has given Bush a pair of binoculars, and they sit together at the head of the path that leads down to the beach, under the tilted and rustling palms, studying the boats that still, after all this time, come too close. They see other things, too.

"Hey, what're those? Dolphins, porpoises?"

"Porpoises," Bush says.

Bush and Felicia live in the previously unused staff rooms above the big four-car garage. They occupy this miraculous space carefully, almost religiously. They are, as Desmerelda tells Faustino, as good as gold, as quiet as mice. Except that they have a vice, a secret sin. Bush worries about it, but it gives Felicia such pleasure, she has such a need for it, that he cannot bring himself to refuse her. So, just now and again, on nights when they are alone at the villa, they steal into the main house and lie together on Desmerelda's white-sheeted bed, their limbs intertwined like the roots of adjacent trees.

Bush, despite himself, eventually falls asleep. Felicia, with her head on his shoulder, watches the ghosty shiftings of the curtains, grieves at the granting of her desires, and listens to the distant susurrations of the sea.

MAL PEET is the author of *Keeper*, winner of the Branford Boase Award and an American Library Association Best Book for Young Adults; *The Penalty*, a New York Public Library Book for the Teen Age; and *Tamar*, a Carnegie Medal winner. He lives in England.

AS PAUL FAUSTINO LISTENS, CELEBRATED GOALIE EL GATO TELLS HIS STORY — ABOUT THE JUNGLE, GHOSTS, BUT ABOVE ALL, ABOUT SOCCER.

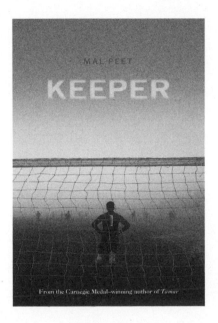

Keeper

★ "This stirring adventure . . . defies expectations. . . . Both lyrical and gripping." —*Kirkus Reviews* (starred review)

"Readers scrambling for soccer stories will be begging for this captivating tale."
—*Bulletin of the Center for Children's Books*

WHEN A FAMOUS SOCCER PLAYER IS KIDNAPPED, PAUL FAUSTINO FINDS HIMSELF UNRAVELING A DARK AND DANGEROUS MYSTERY.

The Penalty
Mal Peet

"The surface mystery will intrigue readers, but it's the deeper questions about religious belief, salvation, and how best to confront the past's shocking inhumanity that will linger." —*Booklist*

★ "Stunning, original, and compelling."
—*Kirkus Reviews* (starred review)

www.candlewick.com

WINNER OF THE CARNEGIE MEDAL

Tamar
Mal Peet

★ "A fifteen-year-old girl named Tamar receives a box from her grandfather who has committed suicide. In it are clues to her grandfather's past and her own identity, but she must go on a journey to make sense of the clues. . . . An elegant work that is both a historical novel and a reflection on history. . . . Simply superb." — *Kirkus Reviews* (starred review)

★ "Tension mounts incrementally in an intricate wrapping of wartime drama and secrecy. . . . This powerful story will grow richer with each reading." — *Booklist* (starred review)

www.candlewick.com